Milly Johnson was born, raised and still lives in Barnsley, South Yorkshire. A *Sunday Times* bestseller, she is one of the Top 10 Female Fiction authors in the UK, and with millions of copies of her books sold across the world, Milly's star continues to rise.

Milly writes from the heart about what and where she knows and highlights the importance of community spirit. Her books champion women, their strength and resilience, and celebrate love, friendship and the possibility of second chances. She is an exceptional writer who puts her heart and soul into every book she writes and every character she creates.

Find out more at www.millyjohnson.co.uk or follow her on X @millyjohnson or Instagram @themillyjohnson.

Milly Johnson

same time *next week*

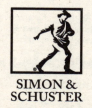

SIMON &
SCHUSTER

London · New York · Amsterdam/Antwerp · Sydney/Melbourne · Toronto · New Delhi

First published in Great Britain by Simon & Schuster UK Ltd, 2025
This paperback edition published 2025

Copyright © Millytheink Limited, 2025

The right of Milly Johnson to be identified as author of this work has been asserted
in accordance with the Copyright, Designs and Patents Act, 1988.

1 3 5 7 9 10 8 6 4 2

Simon & Schuster UK Ltd, 1st Floor,
222 Gray's Inn Road, London WC1X 8HB

Simon & Schuster Australia, Sydney
Simon & Schuster India, New Delhi

www.simonandschuster.co.uk
www.simonandschuster.com.au
www.simonandschuster.co.in

The authorised representative in the EEA is Simon & Schuster Netherlands BV,
Herculesplein 96, 3584 AA Utrecht, Netherlands. info@simonandschuster.nl

Simon & Schuster strongly believes in freedom of expression and stands against
censorship in all its forms. For more information, visit BooksBelong.com.

A CIP catalogue record for this book
is available from the British Library

Paperback ISBN: 978-1-3985-2361-6
eBook ISBN: 978-1-3985-2359-3
Audio ISBN: 978-1-3985-2360-9

This book is a work of fiction. Names, characters, places and incidents are either
a product of the author's imagination or are used fictitiously. Any resemblance
to actual people, living or dead, events or locales is entirely coincidental.

Typeset in Bembo by M Rules
Printed and Bound in the UK using 100% Renewable
Electricity at CPI Group (UK) Ltd

MIX
Paper | Supporting
responsible forestry
FSC® C013604

For my late mam and dad who I miss every day because I will never get used to not receiving a 'daughter' card again.

Thank you for the typewriter, the hash and pancakes, the 'how to pick up spaghetti' lessons, the sunny Spanish holidays, the budgie who was the world's crappiest flyer, the trips to Glasgow in an articulated lorry, the pink milk pan present, the pocket money, the old films and the music, the warmth, the fun, the laughter, the love, the looks on your faces when you first saw my babies. The best jigsaw pieces of our lives together; special, irreplaceable, unforgettable. Thank you for so many glorious memories.

Nothing in life is beyond repair. Strong and beautiful things can be made from the most broken of pieces.

LINDA FLOWERS

Chapter 1

The café had been open two full weeks before Amanda Brundell managed to check it out. She didn't know how that was, because she had been champing at the bit to go since she heard the refurb had been completed and it was once again ready to open its doors. Maybe, she reasoned, as she pulled up in the empty car park, it was something to do with her loyalty to Bettina Boot, who'd been the previous owner. Maybe she was frightened that walking in might make all her old memories of how it used to be disintegrate, because it had been such a beloved place and she wanted to keep them intact. More than beloved even: a little sub-planet where she could just *be* for a sacred forty-minute visit, away from everything else. Every*one* else. She felt Bettina's coffees and cakes work on her frazzled nerves like a masseur might smooth the knots out of a crunchy back.

Bettina had died on the job; just keeled over while cutting into a coffee and walnut sponge. People said that it was 'what she would have wanted' and though a ludicrous statement really, Amanda knew what they meant. Bettina had slowed down but was resisting retirement, which she wouldn't have taken to well. The café was her life, and as beloved to her clientele as it was to Bettina herself. Amanda had discovered it five years ago, after a flood on the road had diverted her route home and she'd called in for an urgent wee stop. She'd bought a coffee for the privilege of using the facilities and had only intended to throw it down her neck and go, but there had been something about the place that made her want to linger. She ordered another coffee with a slice of Victoria sponge and sat, enjoying the gentle background music – tunes of yesteryear – and the soothing ambience. The décor was faded-Victorian drawing room, with pristine starched white tablecloths and a surfeit of doilies. It was the oddest little place, a genteel oasis of chat, sipping from bone china cups, eating cake with delicate forks. Since that introduction, Amanda had quite often made a pit stop at it between the drive from work and to her mother's so she could decompress in the company of pensioners and a slice of the 'special cake of the day'. It had fortified her, just as surely as if someone had recharged her internal batteries. She had been gutted to roll up one day and find the place closed and a notice in the window written by Bettina's daughter to say that an era had ended.

Now it had opened with a new identity and had become 'Ray's Diner'. The door had been painted in red stripes and white stars on a blue background. It wouldn't have the mis-matched crockery and the homemade gateaux under glass domes on the counter, with buttercream that tasted as if it had been made by the angels. And it wouldn't have Bettina, who was as old as the Pennines and treated every customer like a prodigal child. But she was curious enough to try it.

Amanda hated change. She even hated the word 'change'. There were too many of those around at the moment:

changes in the local road system, changes in the manage-
rial set up at work, with rumbles of redundancies and the
changes happening in her own body that signified the end
of her child-bearing days. Not that she'd ever gone down
that road; she'd actively avoided it. The only thing she'd ever
tried to breed were her two guinea pigs when she herself
was a kid and she couldn't even manage that – and who'd
ever heard of guinea pigs who didn't want to bonk each
other? She owned the only male and female guinea pigs on
the planet that preferred to cuddle up platonically and hold
a squeaky conversation about the price of curtains. Basil was
definitely asexual and Rosemary must have been electively
celibate. Still, they had an incredibly long life together and
when Rosemary died, Basil didn't last much longer without
her. Must have been nice to find someone so devoted to
you that life without you just wasn't worth chutting about.
Amanda's life was just work and duty, work and duty on
a grim continual loop, her old dreams and ambitions long
consigned to the bin and sealed with ashes of regret. And
now there wasn't even a Bettina Boot slice of cake to look
forward to and she needed one after the day she'd had. Oh,
it really had been a classic first of April and she'd been the
first-class fool entertainment.

She pushed open the door: she hadn't realised it used
to creak until she realised it hadn't creaked just now.
Everything was different. There were upholstered benches
where the round tables had stood, a black-and-white cheq-
uered floor in place of the soft, old brown carpet and there
was a long counter with white and silver bar stools instead of
the much shorter old wooden one with the enormous retro
silver till sitting on it.

The main difference was that the place was totally empty,

except for a man behind the flash, new counter cleaning the glass door of a chiller cabinet. Amanda had never seen this place devoid of customers before and that only added to her sadness. This place wasn't meant to be empty.

The man turned round and Amanda blinked, because just for a moment there he could have been someone from her past, someone who could never have reached this age, but it was as if he were the man of the boy she'd once known: Seth Mason, tall, wide shoulders, blue eyes that always held the promise of a smile. *Just for a moment.* She gave her head a rattle. As if she wasn't going barmy enough without imagining reincarnations in blurred timelines. Seth was long gone, and seeing echoes of him in random strangers was not going to help her shake off her present sadness.

'Well hi there,' he said, and the spell was blown. This man had an obvious American accent even with just those three words; a *drawl*. Seth would have said a shy, 'All right,' his voice broken, but still hovering in the boy-range, still in the process of sinking down the octaves.

'Are you open?' asked Amanda, checking just in case the lack of customers was down to something she'd missed: a neon sign on the door saying 'CLOSED FOR STAFF TRAINING'. The way her brain was operating at the moment, this was entirely possible: ninety watts short of a hundred-watt lightbulb.

'Yep, I am,' said the man. 'Welcome to Ray's diner, my diner, for I am Ray.' His head dropped in a bow. 'Take a seat, I'll bring you a menu over.'

She sat in a booth and had just taken off her jacket when Ray of Ray's diner delivered the menu.

'Here you go, pie of the day is blueberry. Can I get you a drink while you decide?'

She only wanted a coffee really but now she felt obliged to have something more substantial to accompany it.

'Black americano, please.'

'Sure.'

He was straight over with a mug in one hand and a large glass pot of coffee in the other. Whenever she saw waitresses in American diners pouring these out in films, she always thought the coffee would taste extra delicious. She was delighted to find, from the first sip, that it matched her expectation. She asked him for a slice of blueberry pie when he came back to take her order. It seemed to be a speciality of the diner.

As Ray was bringing over the plate with the pie on it, the door opened and the first of two people walked in. Amanda recognised them as old patrons of Bettina's. The diner owner had just flashed his most welcoming smile when they reversed their steps and left. They obviously didn't like what they saw. Amanda watched Ray's smile wither, and his shoulders rise and fall as he sighed.

He put the plate on the table in front of her. It was a generous cut, with both a blob of clotted cream and ice cream on the side.

'On the house,' he said. 'As my first ever customer.'

Amanda blinked in confusion. 'I thought you'd been open a couple of weeks.'

'Yuuup,' came the reply. 'Although I've nearly had a few. They tend to do that open-the-door, look inside, disappear *thang* you've just seen. I did advertise in one of the local newspapers. "Open midday, Ray's famous pies and coffee for everyone." They printed *midnight*. I'm still not sure if anyone turned up. Probably not. Even for free treats.'

'The *Daily Trumpet*?' asked Amanda, without needing to ask really.

'That's the one.'

She winced inwardly.

Ray drifted off to let her eat in peace, and then turned back. 'Do you mind if I ask, did you ever come here when it was Mrs Boot's café?'

'All the time,' Amanda replied.

'It was always busy, that's right isn't it?'

'Yes, it was. She had a very loyal clientele. I'm sure they'll come back, eventually.' There was plenty of choice on the menu that would appeal to them if they'd embrace the new. 'It only takes one or two to spread the word.'

'Thank you.'

Ray went back behind the counter and Amanda picked up a fork and plunged it into the pie. It was fat and bursting with blueberries, just on the right side of tart. It would easily have passed muster with the old crowd. And they would have enjoyed the chirpy swing music. Doris Day was singing 'Perhaps, Perhaps, Perhaps', and sounding as if she was commenting on what Amanda had just said.

She ate her pie and drank her coffee and felt really sorry for him, cleaning an already immaculate servery in preparation for the many who might not come. She knew she was over-sensitive to people's feelings, something inherited from her dad because her mother certainly wasn't like that. It had got stronger over the last couple of years, probably a by-product of menopausal anxiety. Yep, the bloody thing had stripped away her ability to finish most sentences she started, to sleep properly, to remember the simplest of words; it had turned her into a water sprinkler and made her heart thump like Red Rum's at Aintree and in exchange it had gifted her with the ability to take on everyone else's emotions. She could feel Ray of Ray's diner's despair as clearly as if she was absorbing it through her skin and she had no idea why it should affect her. He was a random American bloke running a café. She should have insisted she pay for the pie and coffee, then thank him and go but instead she lingered and opened up a conversation.

'I work in marketing. I have a few ideas I could suggest that might help.' She waved her palms defensively at him. 'Please tell me to butt out if that comes across as patronising.'

'No, it really doesn't. Do you mind if I sit with you?'

'No, not at all,' said Amanda.

Ray grabbed the jug of coffee and slotted himself across from her, replenishing her mug.

'Getting Bettina's customers back would be your first port of call. Have an OAP discount; they can't resist a cut-price cake. If you haven't complained to the *Daily Trumpet*, then you must and insist they give you a free replacement ad – a big one. They always do. And Bettina used to have a noticeboard where people could advertise stuff: gardening services, pet taxis, special deals, that sort of thing. It was quite famous, daft as it sounds. All her regulars made a beeline for it and read everything on it. I'd be tempted to put it back.'

Amanda could have suggested more but she didn't want to come across as a know-it-all. Giving him an insight into the local community was a good place to start and from the look on Ray's face, he seemed receptive to her suggestions.

'I did think about having some sort of supper club or something. I'm open to that, if you know of anyone who might want to use this as a meeting place to talk and break bread. A discussion group maybe, a book club, new moms' get-together.'

'I can certainly put the word out for you,' said Amanda,

although, personally, she'd had enough of discussion groups to last her flaming ages. But one of her mother's neighbours had been a regular here and no one had a bigger mouth than Dolly Shepherd.

'That is really helpful,' said Ray, smiling over the table at her and once again, Amanda thought how he could so easily have been Seth Mason plus thirty-odd years. She'd never forgotten him; his memory still shone as bright and beautiful as the boy himself had been.

'Thank you . . . ' He left a space for her to insert her name.

'A . . . Amanda.'

Ray held out his hand for her to shake.

'If I hadn't given you the pie and coffee gratis already, I'd be giving you the pie and coffee gratis,' he said, all the while holding on to her. He had a nice meaty hand with a strong grip. She liked that sort of hand. Small hands on men, soft doll fingers, revolted her.

'So what do you do in marketing?' asked Ray, finally letting her go.

'I work for Mon Enfant. It's a firm that specialises in baby equipment, but I've worked for supermarkets and food outlets in the past. I've done a lot of consumer research in my time.' She took a sip of coffee; it really was very good. 'What's your history?'

'English mom, came out to Dripping Springs in Texas on holiday with a friend, met my dad and fell head over heels. Couldn't live without each other, so she went back and they got married. He worked in a kitchen but always wanted his own place and mom was like, "We're gonna make this happen" and together they did. When my daddy died, my mom wanted to come home to England again and I moved back with her. My marriage had broken down and I felt like I needed a total scene change.' He laughed. 'Sorry, I'm telling you way too much detail here. In short, I always loved Yorkshire when we came to visit, I felt very much at home in this small corner of it, and so I knew that one day I'd live here.'

'Is your mum still around?'

'No, she died. They had me kinda late so she had a good long life. I had my own restaurant in Austin, I thought I could bring it over here but ... I'm starting to think that I've made a grave error. So you reckon I should ring the *Daily Trumpet*?'

'That's your next job, yes. I think most people get their pensions on Thursdays so they're feeling flush. You could have a Thursday "Meet Ray" morning event to bring them in. Once they're over the threshold, you'll have them in the palm of your hand.'

Ray smiled and Amanda thought what a good-looking man he was. A little craggy; sun-ray crinkles at the corners of those blue, blue eyes telling her he was no stranger to laughter. Trimmed dark hair, artfully peppered with grey; a pretty boy goatee that perfectly suited the shape of his face. He looked like a man who took care of himself, without being the type to stand in front of the mirror staring into his reflection like a modern-day Narcissus – she'd been out with one of those once. She wondered if Ray had found a new wife. If he hadn't, he'd soon find one around here. Women would be queueing up if they knew someone like this was in town and he made his own desserts.

'I like that a lot. "Meet Ray Morning". That's gonna happen.'

His eyes were looking skyward, blinking with the activity going on behind them.

Amanda drank the last of her coffee. It was time to leave. Her inner alarm clock had just rung and she needed to go and sort out her mum. Her little interlude was at an end for today, but there was a bright spot in that Bettina Boot had a worthy successor. *The queen is dead, long live the king.*

Amanda reached to her side for her jacket and her bag.

'Well, thank you, Ray,' she said. 'It was so nice to meet you.'

'I think I should be the one saying thank you, Amanda.' His voice seemed to caress her name, it came out as *Amenda,* slow and savoured, which was a change from how she usually heard it, barked at her with the vowels short.

He saw her to the door. 'I look forward to seeing you again.'

'And me too you.' Which didn't make any sense and was about par for the course these days.

As she headed off to her car, she couldn't remember the last time a man had said he was looking forward to seeing her again; it made her feel a bit fluttery. Her foot slipped off the accelerator because she wasn't concentrating enough to place it on properly and she chuckled to herself. One month's worth of HRT patches and was this her libido coming back? What a wasteland it was going to find itself in if it was.

Chapter 2

'Do you think you will be able to do anything with him?' the woman asked Sky, her voice, her eyes, her whole expression full of hope. The teddy bear in Sky Urban's hands had been savaged by a puppy who had found its way into an upstairs room and taken the teddy from the bed. It had been her son's, she explained. A soldier, killed on active service in Afghanistan. Everything she had of his had multiplied in emotional value since that terrible day in 2010. She had kept his room as a shrine, because she couldn't bear to move anything and she knew it was daft but sometimes when she went in there, she could – even for a blessed moment – believe that he was at college, studying for his A-levels and in a few hours he'd come bouncing in to raid the fridge before his tea.

'I'm sure I can make him as good as new. I'll use the torn pieces as stuffing so nothing will be thrown away. He'll be intact,' said Sky. She could match the fur, no problem and the eye, because it wasn't one of the really old teddies. These ones had been widely available and in monetary terms were worth very little, but to Mrs Pettifer, the teddy was priceless.

'If you could, it would mean everything. It was his

favourite. It went everywhere with him once upon a time,' said the woman, her throat constricted with emotion and her eyes shiny with gathering tears. Sky imagined there was a bottomless pit of them shed and waiting to be shed over her boy. The woman sniffed, embarrassed at getting all upset about a toy, but Sky understood. Her only child's essence was pressed into it, his boyhood sleeps, his kisses and breath. She'd be giving her back so much more than a mended bear.

'You trust him with me,' she said. 'I'll give you a ring when he's done.'

'Thank you.' The woman's hand stretched out, squeezed Sky's, a gesture that was weighted with gratitude. She turned, walked towards the door, and as she went through it, another customer came in before it had shut. Sky recognised her, of course; not a customer after all. Assured and glamorous: Erin, the repair shop owner's wife. Mrs van der Meer was always polite and nice to Sky, but there was something about her that put Sky on edge. Maybe it was the fact that Sky was secretly in love with her husband and as such, found it hard to look her in the eye.

'Hello, Sky, is he about?' Erin smiled at her, dark pink lipstick perfectly applied. Today she had a beautiful pea green coat on, obviously expensive. She always dressed so brightly, so confidently.

'He's in the office, shall I get—'

'No, it's okay, I'll find him.'

Erin headed for the office. She didn't wear a wedding ring; neither of them did. And whenever Erin came into the shop, which was rarely, Bon greeted her as if she were an old friend he hadn't seen for ages, rather than the wife he'd be going home to later. It was most odd.

*

'Only me,' said Erin, pushing open the office door.

Hearing whose voice it was, Bon van der Meer turned around, stood up from his desk and embraced her. 'Well hello there. Nice of you to drop by. Coffee?'

'No thanks. I'm all coffee-ed out today. Oh, go on then.'

Bon smiled. 'Your arm never did take much twisting. Caramel or vanilla? I've got a new machine I want to show off.' He opened up a drawer where there was a stack of coffee pods and waited for her response.

'Just give me an espresso if your fancy gadget can manage it,' said Erin. She watched him choose a pod, open the machine then load it in carefully. Everything that Bon's hands touched was treated with care: *everything*. The machine began to make a series of strange noises.

'The downside is that it sounds as if it's being strangled,' said Bon, waiting for it to perform. It delivered and he handed the mug of dark liquid over. 'There you go.'

'Thank you. I gather you didn't get your post before you came to work today.'

Bon shook his head. 'Nothing arrived, why?'

Erin reached into her handbag and pulled out an envelope. 'Decree Absolute. We are officially no longer married.'

Bon froze for so long that Erin hooted.

'God, Bon, you actually looked disappointed for a moment there.'

'I . . . I knew it was coming but . . . I'd put it to the back of my mind. Oh my days.' Bon gave his head a shake as if to shoo away the shock. 'I don't know what to say. Come here.'

He cleared the distance between them in two strides and put his arms around her again. Erin let herself savour his hold. He was such a strong man, physically and mentally, a wonderful human being. *Why couldn't we choose who to love*, she thought for the hundredth time at least.

'You'll be able to find yourself a good woman now,' said Erin, when he had released her. 'One who doesn't leave you for another woman.' She cocked her head towards the outside of the office in the general direction of young Sky's station.

'If you mean what I think you mean, don't be silly.'

Erin did mean exactly that because she knew him, probably better than he knew himself. But then wasn't that always the case, she thought, that others could see in us what we couldn't see in ourselves? She hadn't a clue who she was any more.

'She's gorgeous,' said Erin in a low voice.

'She's also half my age.'

'You don't look fifty-two.'

'I'm forty-nine – just. As you know, so don't be cheeky.'

They both grinned at each other.

'You must find yourself someone too,' said Bon, perching on the edge of his desk.

Erin took a sip of coffee before replying to him.

'I want a long rest from all that relationship stuff, Bon.'

'I meant in time; you don't need to rush anything. Don't risk making a mistake because you're mixed up or lonely,' he said.

She didn't say that she was a walking mistake and that's why she intended to keep her distance from anyone who might knock on the door of her heart. It hadn't been a mistake to leave Bon, because she'd married him for the wrong reasons. She liked everything about him; he ticked every box on her sheet apart from the one that weighed more than all the others. She loved him – as a friend, a brother even, but

she had never been *in love* with him and she had really tried
to be. She'd known from the off that there was no one better
to have your back than Bon van der Meer and she had hoped
that in time, she would have felt what she should have felt
for him, but she couldn't. But she regretted the way she had
left him — and for whom. She'd hurt him and she would do
anything to heal the damage she had done him.

'Seriously, are you doing all right?' asked Bon.

She wished she could tell him the truth, but she shouldn't.
She'd promised herself that she'd lie in the bed she'd made
and not burden anyone else with the fallout. Bon, above
anyone, didn't need to know.

'Honestly'— *ha* — 'I'm fine.'

'Should we go out and . . . celebrate? Is that what people
in our position do?' asked Bon.

'No, we absolutely shouldn't celebrate the end of the mess
I caused.'

'Oh, shush now,' said Bon, spotting the faint tremor in
her voice, not so expertly disguised.

'I'm only glad we managed to do it without arguing over
the air-fryer and the toilet brush,' Erin joked.

Bon affected an affronted look. 'Oh I don't know, I'm
still bitter that you took the toilet brush.' He was kidding,
of course. They'd both taken nothing from their marriage
that they hadn't brought to it.

'It feels like the end of something, doesn't it?' said Erin.
Even though we ended a long time ago.

'Or maybe it feels like the beginning of something else,
something better. Change is always scary,' said Bon. 'And
you know I will be the first to wish that you find the happiness you should have. You've been through the mill a bit,
haven't you, *bokkie*?'

Erin smiled at the name he'd always called her, a South African endearment, but it brought a rush of tears to her eyes as well because she didn't deserve his sympathy, his kindness. She took another drink of coffee to stop her letting everything out because Bon hadn't a clue how much she'd been through and she didn't ever want him to. Bon, he was well-named; a good person. She wished that he would meet someone who fitted him like his missing other half, before she would wish herself the same. Sometimes Bon's innate goodness was so painful to be around, it burned her like light from a pure sun.

'Have you told Sky about us?'

'No. Why should I?' said Bon.

'Does she still think we're *married* married?'

'I don't know. I haven't discussed it. Why would I?'

'Oh, Bon. Really?'

'Yes, really.'

She didn't ask why, she knew what he was like. He wouldn't have wanted to tell anyone his marriage was over until it was signed and stamped absolute. He was a man of order, of straight lines, unlike her: she was chaos person-ified. But she did wonder if there was a little part of him that suspected Sky had a crush on him, and clinging to his married status was an added layer of protection against her because he would see her as young and fragile and he wasn't a man to put his own needs before anyone else's. Yes, there were twenty-two and a bit years between them, but there had been six years more of an age difference between her own mother and father and they'd been very happy all their long married life.

'Well now you can tell whoever you like,' Erin said to him.

'In my own time. I'm not one for spreading my business to people who have no need of it,' he answered her.

Erin knew that Sky tensed whenever she visited; it wasn't her imagination and she knew why that was: her intuition was strong and to be trusted. It had been screaming at her for over two years and she'd chosen to ignore it and look where that had got her.

'You work quite closely together with the people here. I thought it might have cropped up in a conversation.'

Bon replied to that with nothing more than a shrug, just as the clock on the wall chimed the three-quarters of the hour.

'Okay, gotta go. I'll see you soon ... ex-husband.'

She said it as a joke, but the words hung in the air as discordant bells. 'Ex-husband' sounded as if they were now put further at a distance. She felt a rise of tears within her and she and turned and left before they fell.

In the shop, Sky was talking to a woman with long, salon-perfect ash-blonde hair; or rather, she was being talked at. There was a brunette with her who was less glossy; a grateful sidekick, Erin guessed. Her spidey senses kicked in, so she didn't leave immediately. She could hang around another five minutes to find out why the blonde woman was smiling and squawking like a seagull who had just found a discarded portion of still-warm chips, but Sky wasn't reciprocating any joy. She browsed one of the shelves full of the teddy bears that Sky had made. She picked one up and pressed it; it really was lovely, just the right amount of squash factor and its face was so adorable.

'I was just passing and I thought I'd bring in my friend Helen to see this place,' the blonde was saying. 'We've just had a lovely afternoon tea in the teashop over there and I said, you must go in and see the repair shop and Sky and her bears.'

'I didn't know this Spring Square ... thing existed till Angel said. So it's a repair shop then, is it? Like on the TV?' Brunette Helen looked around, taking it all in: the work benches down both sides busy with projects in progress, the grand hand-carved counter by the door and Sky's unit with the sign she'd painted bearing her company name: 'Sky Bears'.

'What do they mend?'

'They restore anything if they can: furniture, toys—'

'Oooh, sorry, *restore*,' brunette Helen cut in, duly corrected and gave her own hand a small slap.

Bitch, thought Erin. She knew her type.

'And aren't these amazing,' blonde Angel was saying. She had the sort of voice that made Erin want to cover her ears to save them from being perforated. Sky's bears *were* amazing but the blonde still managed to inject a syringe full of something derisory into the compliment.

'Sky and I were *friends* at school,' the blonde was explaining to her counterpart and Erin noticed the odd weight she laid on the word 'friends'. She also noticed there was no affirmation of that from Sky, who was standing stock still, tolerating what looked like major discomfort. There was a flush blooming on her cheeks, showing easily on her pale skin.

'Yes, I remember you telling me *all* about her,' said Helen, turning her attention fully to Sky.

'We grew up in a very odd time, didn't we, Sky? Under the shadow of the Pennine Prowler. Some more under it than others.' Angel smiled sweetly.

'Your dad made toy bears as well, I heard. How lovely that you're following in his footsteps.' Helen smiled sweetly.

There was something off about this conversation, Erin was sure of it. Something sly and secretive floating under the words like a multi-toothed predator hiding just below the surface of the water. She'd seen and heard enough now, because she had no idea what was going on here but she would bet the blonde had never been a 'friend' of Sky's. More than likely one of those awful class bitches you hoped you'd never bump into again. Every schoolgirl had one of those. She stepped briskly forwards with the teddy bear still in her hand and put it on the counter, forcing sidekick Helen to step back.

'Excuse me, but I'm in rather a hurry. I wonder if I could buy this,' Erin said, her tone deliberately clipped as if annoyed at being kept waiting. They got the message.

'Oh, we'll . . . er . . . go. Nice to see you again, Sky. You take good care.'

'And you,' returned Sky, the words forcibly pushed out of her by an automated politeness reflex.

Erin waited until the women had gone before she spoke again. She saw the tension drop out of Sky's shoulders when the door shut behind them.

'I'm gathering that was the sort of *friend* you could live without,' Erin said, hunting in her bag for her purse.

'You could say that.' Sky gave a little smile, wary and wobbly. 'Thank you for butting in.' She picked up the teddy to put back on the shelf.

'No, no, I really want it,' said Erin.

'Really? You sure?'

'You look shocked to have made a sale.' *Or did she just look shocked to have made a sale to me,* Erin thought.

'I'm always shocked, to be honest. There's so much work in them, I can't charge any less than I do.'

'Nor should you. You don't have to explain that to me; I can tell.' It wasn't a line.

'This is one of my favourites.' Sky held up the bear, smiling at it as if saying a silent goodbye. Then she took some tissue paper out of the drawer. 'He's called Peter.'

'Yes, I saw the embroidered name tag. He's lovely.'

Peter had lining in his waistcoat and a tiny pencil sitting inside a top pocket with a red silk handkerchief. The amount of detail was nuts.

Sky folded the tissue carefully around the bear.

Erin produced her bank card.

'Has that woman been in before?'

'Yup. I try and swerve her if I can. I just wasn't quick enough today.'

'If you have a problem with anyone, you just go and find Bon and he'll see them off for you,' said Erin, in earnest. She couldn't imagine Sky being the sort of person to tell someone to do one. Erin had always been able to do that, at least in this kind of scenario. She was a human Dalek: dalekanium outer shell; a jellified, blobby, pathetic mess within.

'Thank you, Mrs van der Meer.'

Erin didn't know whether to tell her or not, that she wasn't really Mrs van de Meer, despite that still being her official name, but something stopped her. It had been Bon's decision not to say, for his own reasons, and she should respect that. Maybe that's what she had done to him, made him more guarded about what he gave away of himself.

It had been a big bone of contention with Carona that Erin still used her married name. It was one of many bones of contention, actually. She had insisted that when they were married, Erin *had* to take her name, even though Erin had decided when she was finally divorced, she would go back to her maiden name of Flaxton and stay a Flaxton. She had never told Carona, but she'd felt more protected being Mrs van der Meer, as if some of Bon's strength was embedded in the name, like a shield to hide behind.

Erin forced Carona out of her head and her attention back to Sky.

'Well, thank you for Peter. He will be treasured. I have the ideal person in mind to give him to.' Erin hoped the sale and her rescue mission had helped at least a little to break down whatever wall stood between them. There had never been a reason for it to exist.

'I hope they like it.' Sky said.

'I know they will.' *Because it's for me.*

Erin walked out of the shop with her purchase. What a strange, unsettling day, she thought. Too many changes to get used to in too short a time. She should be feeling some peace now, some solid ground beneath her feet, but today's news had set her back. She knew what she needed to do to start regrouping, but it wasn't so easy to turn over and expose your soft underbelly, when all your self-protective instincts were screaming at you to do quite the opposite.

Chapter 3

Amanda put the plate down in front of her mother and watched her lip curl up like a child about to be force-fed spinach.

'I wasn't really in the mood for salmon,' said Ingrid Worsnip.

'It's good for you,' said Amanda, who did try and make sure her mother ate healthily, which was more than could be said for her half-brother, golden bollocks Bradley, who shoved something in the microwave and sat hovering over their mother, waiting for her to finish so he could shoot off home. He did it every single time he was on mother duty and then he'd lie and tell Amanda that he stayed a good two hours with her. She knew he was lying because she could clearly see him on one of the concealed cameras she'd set up in her mum's house a couple of months ago, after she'd noticed a downturn in her mum's mobility. There was one in the kitchen that covered all of the dining area as well, one in the lounge and another at the bottom of the stairs. She respected her mum's privacy, the cameras weren't there to spy on her, she just checked in occasionally to make sure everything was all right and her mum wasn't lying there helpless, having had a fall.

But she would confess that she'd started spying on Bradley when he turned up to do his duty. He'd come in, give his mother a kiss and then slam something he'd brought with him in the microwave, which he'd take the money for from her change jar. Then he'd sit with her at the table as she ate, and either read her newspaper or fanny about on his phone, making the odd grunt of engagement when she tried to converse. On a couple of recent occasions, though, Amanda had tracked him going upstairs and into their mother's bedroom and she wondered what he might be looking for because he seemed to be in there quite a while.

Amanda didn't really like Bradley that much. There was too much of his father in him, a man whom Amanda had detested.

Her own father, Fred Brundell, had died on her eighth birthday and she'd adored him. He'd been a cobbler with his own shop but he loved a bit of wheeler-dealering, chasing the buck, buying bargains at second-hand markets and selling them for a profit; he was gifted at it. He'd left his wife financially comfortable, enough for her not to have to work, so she could carry on being a stay-at-home mum for their daughter. But within two years she'd coupled up with Arnold Worsnip, who worked in the local ironmonger's and couldn't have been more unlike her first husband if he'd tried.

He and Ingrid were married without much preamble. It seemed as if one minute he'd turned up to take her out and the next his feet were firmly under the table. He'd seemed quiet and amiable before the wedding but then he moved in and turned into a dictator. Ingrid let him be the disciplinarian, which involved him taking every half-viable opportunity to drag young Amanda over his knee, to pull up her skirt and spank her bottom. At first, Amanda thought he was just a nasty bastard. It was only later on she realised he was a perverted one. They'd had a talk at school about people touching you in a way that made you feel uncomfortable and it had struck a loud chord. So the next time he'd tried to do it, she'd been ready to spin and land a perfectly aimed knee in his goolies and with it the threat that she'd go to the police. He'd left not long after, though her mother had never gone into the nitty-gritty of why he moved out.

Arnold went to live in the flat above the ironmonger's, eventually buying not only the business but the whole building. Amanda suspected the money her dad had left to provide for her had ended up providing for him instead. He and Bradley weren't at all close but Ingrid made sure he stumped up for his son. He never married again, because he'd been lucky even to get married once, the creepy shit. Creepy shit with little soft doll hands that delivered a surprisingly stinging slap.

Ingrid doted on Bradley, spoiling him rotten in a way she'd never spoilt her daughter and she really hadn't done him any favours. He'd been a spoilt, entitled little boy who'd grown up into a spoilt, entitled little man, one of those people who turned selfishness into an art form. When Ingrid's health started to decline, the plan was to split the care of their mother equally between the siblings; yet Amanda seemed to have copped for three-quarters of it at least. He'd married a woman who for some reason looked at him as adoringly as if he was Richard Gere; as if his ego hadn't been inflated enough over the years by a mother for whom he could do no wrong. Dolly Shepherd, who lived next door to Ingrid, once said about him, 'He'd have eaten himself if he could,' and Amanda couldn't have put it any better.

Ingrid reluctantly lifted up her fork and prodded at the fish.

'It's undercooked. It's pink.'

'That's what colour salmon is, Mum. It's perfectly cooked.'

'I don't fancy it. I think I'll just have a bun.'

'Not until you've eaten your dinner,' insisted Amanda, before it slammed into her from left field, that upset of world order, that she was having another of those moments where she was becoming her parent's parent.

Ingrid cut a piece off and stuck it into her mouth, chewing it like an actor from *Grease* might chew gum, but with a recalcitrant grimace. It couldn't have been too bad, though, because she went in for another forkful. And another. And when she had finished she said, 'That was torture.'

Just for a second, Amanda felt like a bully, before her thoughts were replaced by sensible, kinder ones to herself that said, *Mum really doesn't do anything that she doesn't want to.*

Amanda took her plate away and brought in the sweet treat she'd picked up from the little Tesco around the corner. A strawberry tart, Ingrid's favourite. She dived into it as if she hadn't been fed for a month, cream and glaze sticking to her face.

'Our Bradley and Kerry are having a marvellous time in Turkey,' she said, spitting pastry crumbs. 'They're in the middle of a heatwave.'

'How lovely.' Amanda hadn't meant it to sound sarcastic but that's how it came out.

'His hotel is four star, did I tell you?'

Just a few hundred times, Amanda didn't say. And that he'd decided to extend the fortnight by another week and just expected her to pick up the slack, without even asking if that would be okay.

'Did he ring you, Mum?'

'Well, how else would I have known they were having a heatwave?'

Amanda ignored the snap. 'What else did he say?'

'He didn't say anything else. He just rang and said it was a very quick call to tell me they were having a marvellous time and how hot it was and he hoped I was well. And that he loved me lots and couldn't wait to see me again.'

Then Ingrid sighed in the way she usually sighed where soppy thoughts of her baby boy were involved.

Amanda could imagine him saying that. He was very good at flannel, was Bradley and he knew that a 'love you, Mother' was all that was needed to convince her she was still the centre of his universe, when she was anything but. It wasn't Amanda's job to dismantle that belief, though, if it kept her mum happy. But she wished that she had the same effect on Ingrid, since her mother really *was* the centre of her universe. Ingrid's health, her medical appointments, her quality of life dominated Amanda's life and there was nothing she could do about it other than carry on carrying on.

'What's up with you? You look tired,' said Ingrid, licking her fingers while staring at her daughter.

'I'm not sleeping well,' replied Amanda. She hadn't slept well for over two years. And sometimes when she did fall asleep and had a chance of a good kip, the sensation of waking up in a bed so damp she thought she'd wet herself put paid to that.

'Why's that then?'

'It's the menopause, Mum.'

'Well, we've all had to go through it,' said Ingrid, as if Amanda was a weaker being for even mentioning it. She'd been lucky, flew through it as if she'd been on a greased sledge, give or take some joint pains and a little bone-crumbling. 'My auntie Hilda had to go into the nuthouse with it.'

'I know how she felt,' Amanda muttered to herself.

'She forgot how to talk. Came out with all the wrong words. They thought she was brain-damaged.'

Amanda also knew that feeling and she'd been so perturbed by it that it had driven her to the docs. The doctor wouldn't give her HRT because she'd had her last period over five years ago, even though she'd broken down in the consulting room. She'd been palmed off with some antidepressants that would make her sleepy at night and a leaflet about mindfulness and yoga. She couldn't even get into the recovery position, never mind the lotus, with her unbendy limbs.

She'd thought that her only option was to put up and shut up, until she'd been in the hairdressers and overheard the woman in the next chair waxing lyrical to the stylist about her HRT. She'd had to go private, she said: the Hathor clinic. She'd had an adverse change of life with the menopause, she went on, and she could feel it was changing back again just for slapping a patch on her arse twice a week.

Amanda remembered the name from school when they'd done a project on Egypt. Hathor, the goddess of love and femininity, protector of women. She'd looked up the clinic when she got home and booked an online appointment. She'd had a consultation with a doctor who said that HRT might be very beneficial for her symptoms and Amanda could have sobbed with gratitude. The patches hadn't kicked in yet, though, because today she'd been in the middle of a presentation to the new head honcho at work and she completely lost her thread, called the annual budget an animal budgie and her immediate boss, Philip, had had to step in and rescue the situation.

'I'm on HRT now,' said Amanda.

'HRT?' Ingrid scoffed. 'Judith from two doors down went on that and died not long after.'

'Judith who got run over?'

'Yeah, her.'

Amanda shook her head. 'Well you can't blame HRT for that, Mum.'

'I never said I did.' Then Ingrid gave a small gasp, remembering something to gossip about. 'Ey, do you know who's died? Brian Unwin. I got the shock of my life.'

Amanda's face registered complete bafflement, which annoyed her mum.

'Brian. He used to knock about with your father. I'm glad I got some sympathy cards in the sale. Buy two get two free, I knew they'd come in handy. They're having the wake at the Hoppleton Arms.' She pulled an impressed face. 'That would be a dream come true for me, to have a wake at the Hoppleton Arms.'

'Lord, Mum,' Amanda exclaimed. She didn't even want to think about that sort of thing. Anyway, she didn't have to because she knew her mum had written a will years ago and detailed all her demands in it, including her own funeral arrangements. She was very on the ball with her paperwork and refused to delegate the managing of it to Amanda because it was 'my private business and mine alone'.

Ingrid had always been sharp mentally as well as physically able. She kept an immaculate house and wouldn't let anyone else do her cleaning, even though Bradley had volunteered Kerry's services – for a price, of course. She wrote longhand letters to people and toddled off to the post office to send them before she went to the local coffee shop in the mornings to meet up with her crew. She was still fiercely independent and Amanda liked that she was, but recently she'd noticed her mum slowing down and some moments where she wasn't as lucid as she used to be; and the slipping of standards scared Amanda, because she knew they signalled the first steps towards the edge of an abyss.

She watched her mum get up from her chair after three failed attempts and rub her hip when she was standing. She had an eighty-year-old body and the stresses were starting to tell; and Amanda was aware of how quickly things could change at this age, they weren't going to be given a year's notice that Ingrid's legs had given up. She moved around fine on the flat but she'd started to struggle with stairs and that was a worry, because there was no downstairs toilet in this house and her mother would cut off her head before she'd use a commode.

'Mum, wouldn't you prefer to sell this place and get a little bungalow?' Amanda asked, not for the first time. She'd always been rudely rebuffed before, accused of insinuating Ingrid was infirm, and she was sure part of the reason for that was Bradley putting her off the idea of a move because he wouldn't want to be roped into helping. He couldn't even be bothered to boil some vegetables from fresh for his mum's tea, so having to give up time to box up their mother's life was something he'd avoid at all costs, even if it was in her best interests. This house was in a prestigious area and stood on a large plot; those that were put up for sale were snapped up as soon as they went on the market.

'Bradley said if I did that, I'd not find one as good as here.'

Amanda growled inwardly; she was right then.

'Of course you would.'

'It might be nice, though.'

Amanda's head jerked. Had she really just heard that? Her very first possible *yes*.

'Darlene from the coffee shop has just gone into a council house bungalow up by the park. It's got one of those bathrooms where you sit on a chair to have a shower and don't need to have a curtain. She says she wishes she'd done it years ago.'

Amanda leapt on it. 'Shall I start looking?'

Ingrid's tone changed.

'Oh, I don't know what Bradley would say to that.'

Sod Bradley, Amanda said in her head.

'Well, it's not up to him, it's up to you, Mum. Just think, in a couple of months you could be in a little bungalow all of your own.'

There was a bungalow-rich estate just five minutes away. They were a bit pricey but the sale of this house to downsize would easily cover one. The move would be laborious, but it was entirely doable. Their mother wasn't a hoarder and what she had would easily fit into a much smaller property. Bradley would just have to get his arse in gear and help.

The further along things were before Bradley returned from his holiday in Turkey, the more chance there was of him not being able to change her mind back.

Ingrid thought about it for a few seconds and then said, 'Well, you can have a look around, I suppose.' She smiled at her daughter, and the sad part about that was that Amanda couldn't remember the last time her mother had smiled like that without having said the word 'Bradley'.

Chapter 4

Underneath their shining veneer of smiling, suburban re-spectability, Valerie and Dennis Hutchinson were the worst kind of tuppence-ha'penny snobs. A couple who would have described themselves as philanthropic, because they gave ten pounds every Christmas to the Marie Curie charity; Christian, because they went to church every now and then and were on first name terms with the vicar; worldly – and cosmopolitan – because they had a German cleaner who had undergone gender reassignment. They were virtue signallers of the highest order.

They didn't really need a cleaner, but it was prestigious to brag they had one. Their 'town villa' (terraced house with high ceilings) never collected much dust because the Hutchinsons were too tight to part with any skin cells. They paid Astrid for three hours one afternoon every week and she vacuumed carpets, cleaned the windows inside and pol-ished the wood; though she had to search hard for anything to do because, in between the Wednesday stints, Valerie was on top of any mote that dared to be seen on her radar. Astrid was allowed to stop halfway through her shift for a coffee, a bargain brand the Hutchinsons had bought to give to trades-people and which Valerie kept in a different cupboard from her Waitrose Gold Roast; but she rarely bothered because it was *scheußlich* – awful.

Occasionally Dennis would interrupt her duties with a thoughtful tap on his lip and say, 'Can I just ask you ...' and question her about her old life. Astrid never tried to pretend that her previous self hadn't existed because it made her appreciate this one all the more: the contented butterfly that had grown from the unhappy caterpillar who had once upon a time played rugby for Frankfurt. She appreciated that Dennis might be nosey, because people were and, as such, she always answered questions politely, even his increasingly intrusive ones. But tolerant as she was, she found that her patience levels were wearing thin. Not just with him, but with everything. Something was changing within her, she could feel it happening and she didn't know to what it was attributable.

She had come to terms with being a widow, so it wasn't that. Her marriage to antiques dealer 'Cutthroat Kev' had been sweet and way too short but she'd felt blessed to have had him for any length of time. Kev had been a huge man in personality and stature and he had made her feel both protected and cherished, the way she had always tried to make other people feel. It had been wonderful to be on the receiving end of it and she would be forever grateful for that. It was more that she felt as if life were a big orange and she hadn't squeezed enough juice out of it, and the clock was ticking. Some of the oldies she'd cleaned for over the years had had such little lives and she wanted more from hers, although she hadn't a clue what form that fulfilment could take.

After a year and a half of working for the Hutchinsons,

she knew that if Dennis Hutchinson asked her one more gratuitously invasive question dressed up as innocent curiosity she was likely to swing for him and she didn't want to feel like that because Astrid was a gentle person. Battling on a rugby pitch had once been her way of battling everything that felt wrong with her life: her frustrations and fear, her sense of futility and desperation at being incompatible with her own body, and she didn't have that outlet any more.

Kev had left her more than well provided for. She had a beautiful house; she didn't need to clean for anyone, but she chose to because she liked to do it. Or at least she had until recently. The Hutchinson house was her easiest, but the one she was always most glad to have finished. Valerie and Dennis presumed because Astrid was a cleaner that she was broke and she was lucky to have them pay her for her services. After all, they would have said, who would choose such a 'lowly profession' if they didn't have to.

Luckily Astrid had always been revered by her other clients, to whom she brought joy – and cake, because she loved baking. Her 'oldies' had looked forward to her weekly visits when she'd make their houses sparkle, change their beds, wash their laundry and more importantly put the kettle on and sit with them after her shift, but sadly there was just one of them left now. She also cleaned at Bon Repair twice a week, after closing time. She did a lot of thinking when she was mopping and dusting around in there and recently she'd had too much thinking time. Plus two days a week she worked for The Crackers Yard where she would sit around a table enjoying the craic, and constructing Christmas crackers with an ensemble crew. She could fill up her days but it was at night when she felt Kev's loss most of all. She missed having someone to cook for – and with, because together they replicated everything the Hairy Bikers had ever made. She missed discovering a new box set with him and sharing a bottle of wine and holing up in front of a log fire and having cheese on toast suppers. Kev was the best of people, someone whom the Hutchinsons wouldn't have entertained even as a virtue-signalling exercise, because they would have considered him uncouth. He made no apologies for preferring darts to lawn tennis and couldn't tell a Châteauneuf-du-Pape from a cherry Coke. And they wouldn't have considered him a businessman because he'd earned his money trading barbers' shops memorabilia at antiques shops and fairs and didn't wear a shirt and tie and sit at a desk. Kev was worth a whole parkful of Hutchinsons and more. And today, she missed him more than ever because he'd have been up through the night making a cake so he could serve it up as breakfast in bed for her with a rose in a vase and a glass of champagne.

As Astrid was packing up to go, Dennis handed her the envelope with her wage in it, but he snatched it back at the last second and she knew another of his questions was coming because this manoeuvre was his *modus operandi*.

'Astrid, can I just ask . . .' She was right then. '. . . What was your name before you changed?'

Astrid put on her best smile and answered him sweetly.

'Verpiss Dich.' She made 'piss off' in her native language sound like a hyphened name, such as Michael-Paul or Andrew-Mark,

'Verpiss Dich,' Dennis repeated thoughtfully. That's quite a mouthful. You *krauty* people do like your long, complicated names though, don't you.'

'Ja, we do, dun't we?' she replied in her hybrid Brandenburg/broad Barnsley accent.

She held out her hand for her wage and, now satisfied, he let her have it. As she was putting it in her handbag, Valerie Hutchinson appeared at the door. Invariably she always checked around after Astrid to make sure she had completed her tasks and always found something to criticise. Today was no exception.

'I don't think you did the skirting boards in our bedroom, Astrid, but it doesn't matter, you can do them next week.'

'There was no time, as you vanted me to refold up all the towels in the airing cupboard,' Astrid answered. Had this been any of her other clients' houses, Astrid would have squeezed the job in gladly, but the Hutchinsons didn't give an inch with her and so she didn't give an inch with them.

'Have you told her, Dennis?' urged Valerie, giving her husband a nudge.

'Er, no.' He coughed then, as if making a major announcement. 'Well, as it's your birthday this week, we've rounded up your money to the nearest ten.'

Oh wow, a whole two pounds.

'Danke,' said Astrid, trying not to get it wrong and say *wanker*.

'And we've bought you a present.' Valerie grinned and from behind her back she produced a plain, white carrier bag. Well, this was a first, thought Astrid. She hadn't ever had a gift before – for birthday or Christmas – just the usual rounding up of her wage so she could go mad and blow the bonus on a newspaper.

'You can open it now,' said Valerie, anticipation of a big reveal lighting up her expression.

Astrid parted the handles and pulled out the contents: a BOGOF pair of replacement mop heads.

'We thought you were due.' Valerie was beaming. It

wasn't a joke. She and Dennis really did think this was a viable present.

'Well, I don't know what to say.' That was true, Astrid really didn't. 'Maybe I'll leave them here.'

'Oh yes, of course, that was the whole idea,' said Valerie, as if it could be in dispute.

'We wouldn't want you using them for someone else,' said Dennis with a chortle and a cautionary wag of his finger.

Astrid put on her own version of a chortle before saying, 'In Germany we have a custom. When someone gi's us a gift, we give 'em one back.'

'Oh,' said Valerie, her pencilled-on teak-brown eyebrows rising in surprise.

Astrid reached into her pinny pocket. 'I have it in here somewhere.' She pulled out her hand, the middle finger raised.

'Here you go,' she said. Then she picked up her cleaning box, marched a path through the Hutchinsons like Moses through the Red Sea and resisted the urge to slam the door behind her enough to shake it off its hinges. She really was getting too old to hang on to her patience in the face of such *scheisse*.

Chapter 5

Well, it was a day later in coming than she'd expected, thought Amanda, as she switched on her Mac and the first email she saw was one from Linus's PA, asking if she would pop up to the directorate at eleven. She knew what it was about, of course; her disastrous presentation to him on Monday, when she'd done a modern-day equivalent of the Morecambe and Wise/Andre Previn sketch: *I'm saying all the right words, but not necessarily in the right order.*

Philip, the head of her department, had really wanted the team to dazzle in that meeting and she'd let him down. He'd stood up and taken over, manipulating her off to the side as if she wasn't embarrassed enough, standing there stuttering, her dark brown hair lank, face shiny because her sweat glands had chosen this time of all times to crank up and pump out every bit of moisture inside her that they could find. She had been convinced ever since that people were laughing about her, discussing her: *Did you see that walking fountain and how can we get her out of the company?*

So at five to eleven, Amanda set off from marketing like a condemned prisoner, upstairs to the top offices with the newly fitted bouncy blue carpet that denoted she was now in 'director zone'. She took a tissue out of her pocket and dabbed at her temples before knocking on the door of Linus's PA. She was twenty-five, assured, smart and had no idea that one day this could be her: damp enough to grow mould, tired yet unable to sleep, brain fog so thick it could have appeared in a James Herbert novel; ready for the knacker's yard.

The young, slim, dry, coherent woman showed her through to Linus's office.

Linus Hastings Crowther, aged twelve.

Slight exaggeration. Linus had his fortieth birthday on the same day that Amanda had her fifty-fourth. He'd been in situ for three months. Amanda wasn't the type to think a boss necessarily had to be older to be efficient, because Linus was *very* efficient and he'd gone through the business like a dose of salts, making it pull up its britches. He was one of the famous industry 'superpowers', whizz kids who had turned into whizz men who flitted from company to company working their magic, applying a seasoned axe with the skill of Uhtred son of Uhtred to the dead wood and one did not get into those lofty positions by being Mr Nice-Guy. Many of these behemoths were on the psychopathic scale with their charming veneers and ability to sleep like a baby after separating a family man from his salary when good business sense dictated it. Anyway, her neck was so damp that if he intended to apply an axe to it, the blade would slide to one side. Maybe that's what happened in Mary Queen of Scots' case, because she remembered from history that it had taken a couple of attempts at least to separate her head from the rest of her. Was Mary having her last hot flash? As if her execution wasn't enough horse-crap on her day.

'Ah, Amanda, do come in and take a seat', said Linus with a smile. It looked genuine enough, but how could it be? He wasn't here to offer her a promotion because he thought she'd handled herself with aplomb in the boardroom, and it was too much to hope he was looking for a new court jester. Philip, no doubt, had been distancing himself from the debacle, dripping his poison into Linus's ear about her. Linus gestured towards the chair at the other side of his enormous desk. Mon Enfant spent a lot on their office furniture. At least for the executives, who had throne-like leather swivel chairs, and the best drawers and cupboards that South American mahogany trees could make.

As Amanda sat, Linus got up, as if he were on the other end of a see-saw.

'Coffee? Tea? Water?'

Unexpected. 'I'm fine, thank you.' She'd better deny herself the opportunity of spilling it all over herself. It wouldn't be a great look, covered in coffee as well as perspiration pouring out of her forehead as if there was a dodgy tap behind it.

'Sure? I'm having one.'

'Not for me, but thank you.'

Linus walked to one corner of his office where there was a water cooler. He took a glass and held it up to the dispensing nozzle. Amanda studied him from the back, noting how snow white his shirt was. He always wore white and all his shirts looked fresh out of the packet. And all his suits were tailored to fit his long slim build but surprisingly wide shoulders. He couldn't have got that shape off a peg.

Linus returned to the desk and sat on his chair. He took a sip and Amanda waited for the shitstorm to begin. The sooner it did so, the sooner it would stop.

'Well, it's nice to finally have a one-to-one with you, Amanda. We've only really said hello in passing so far more or less, haven't we?'

'Yes,' Amanda tried to smile and failed dismally. The tension in the air was thickening by the microsecond.

'So . . .'

Here we go.

'I've invited you in because of . . .' He paused, and Amanda filled in the rest of the sentence for him in her head: *. . . of some concerns about you being in charge of an annual budget you can't even pronounce.*

Amanda swallowed, felt her cheeks begin to glow with an uncomfortable warmth. Looking for a new job at her age was going to be a laugh.

She was wrong though. Linus started his sentence again.

'Can I be frank? I want to talk to you . . . because you're a woman.'

That was also unexpected.

'Not quite with you, Linus,' Amanda said slowly, in case she was missing something that was glaringly obvious.

'There aren't a lot of women in this company, are there? Which is odd for a firm that specialises in baby equipment. Why do you think that is?'

No, there weren't, that was true. It didn't help that the head of HR was a closeted misogynist and only set on men, where he had a choice. Also there had been three other women in the marketing department until Philip became its manager and he'd managed to drive them all out with his rigid, ungiving leadership style. He seemed to think they were an alien race out to make his life difficult when they needed to leave early for a school emergency or to take an elderly parent to an appointment or had rung in sick with crippling period pains. She'd seen the way he'd looked at her when she'd had to stand by an open window just to cool down for five minutes or disappear off to the loo mid-meeting because her bladder now gave her ten seconds notice to get there. But could she say all this to Linus or should she just rattle her head and play dumb. That would have been the safer course, but too often these days the brake on her better judgement just didn't operate like it should.

She'd expected to come into his room and be given a warning for being incompetent, maybe a push towards the exit door, that's what the climate of this company had in-stilled in her to presume but it hadn't happened. What did she have to lose by saying to him what she'd tried to say to HR on three separate occasions? She hadn't even tried to sit Philip down because he'd have run off with his fingers in his ears singing 'la la la'.

'This is not a woman-friendly organisation, Linus. It's scared them all off.'

There, it was out, the words hanging in the air in twenty-foot, flashing neon, unmissable letters. Words that acted like a slap on Linus's face, from the look of it.

'You're going to have to explain that statement,' he re-plied eventually.

In for a penny . . .

Her tongue darted out of her mouth, wetted her lips in preparation to give him the big reveal. She realised that whatever she said couldn't be taken back, there was no rewind button and so she'd better get it right.

'A little understanding of women's health circumstances would go a long way in this industry. I don't know why it's taking so long for management to realise this. We lost a wonderful young graduate last year because she was going through terrible monthly pains with her periods and needed time off when they struck her, even though she didn't want the time off because she was fully committed to her post. She was prepared to work from home on such days but she wasn't allowed to. In the end it was suggested to her that she might be better off finding a job more flexible to her condition, even though it was totally within our remit to be that flexible, so she did and she's thriving at Tesco – our loss was very much their gain,' Amanda began. It had greatly angered her when she found out about it. She just hoped that Linus was ready for more matters female and gynaecological because her gun was loaded with them.

'We lost Mo from Marketing because she had a parent who was terminally ill and Philip wouldn't give her any time off, nothing, not even to use up her holiday days, so she had no choice but to hand in her notice. Sandra, dreadful depression thanks to the menopause. She'd been a solid worker for fifteen years and yet she was made to feel like an inconvenience, a drain on the company, so she left. And take myself. The menopause has hit me like a sledgehammer, Linus. I forget things, I say "animal budgie" when I mean "annual budget" in meetings' – she thought she'd get that in – 'I sweat, I get panic attacks sometimes, I can't sleep at night so I arrive at work with eyes swollen and bloodshot and sometimes I find myself forced to take a cat-nap at my desk in the afternoon, leading to some sneering – from Philip, again – as if I'm some sort of mid-week party girl. I have to pause meetings to go to the loo, and I *know* how I'm being talked about behind my back for all this and trust me, that does nothing for my already hormonally-induced elevated anxiety levels. I've been here for over twenty years, never even took a sick day. I know my job inside out, I've even won awards but this past couple of years, all I can think of is getting to the earliest retirement date I can reach and then handing in my notice, because I don't like what I'm seeing regarding how women are treated here, how *I'm* being treated here. Yes, there are always going to be those who ride the system, but there are plenty of women who have been loyal and hard-working and are going through changes over which they have little control, and you'll lose the ones you haven't already if this firm doesn't alter its ways.'

She was well aware she was giving him a monologue worthy of Shakespeare, but she had his ear and she wasn't going to waste the opportunity.

'Yes, our mothers put up and shut up about the menopause but we shouldn't have to, Linus, because it's not myth or made up; these changes happening within us are real and they tend to clobber us when we've got elderly parents and children to get through their own difficult stages. It can impact on our whole lives and it needs to be talked about more, not less; it isn't a dirty secret and it shouldn't be treated as such. Have you any idea how many things it affects: our mental health as well as our physical, our bones, our joints, our sleep, our bladders, our self-worth, our hair, our skin, our heart rates ... and don't even get me started on the *rage*, Linus.

'I don't know what vitamins to take and do I take them with black pepper, turmeric, ashwagandha, apple cider vinegar? I don't know what sort of collagen; bovine, marine, or even if any of them do any good – powders, capsules, gummies? I don't know why I've apparently got a folic acid deficiency, because who knew women of my age were supposed to take it. Magnesium helps for sleep – or does it, and if so what sort? And then you've got size zero celebs on the TV pratting about, not a bead of sweat on their heads after a two-hour session with their personal trainers, sponsored by companies, telling us we'll all have superpowers if we take their stupidly expensive supplements ... and how we want to believe them, so we stump up. If men went through the menopause, there would have been definitive programmes and information and help in place for years.'

She let loose a long breath by way of a full stop and allowed that to sink in. If Linus's expression was anything to go by, it would take some time. He looked buried under the avalanche of her words. She dabbed at her face with a fresh tissue because the effort of saying all that had made her start sweating again. Who even knew that top lips could drip as much? She was a living, breathing example of what she'd just been describing. But then her dad had always told her to tell the truth. Her mother left any disciplining to him so he'd take her out for an ice cream and they'd sit on a wall, or in a café, and he'd give her the gentlest pep talks which sank in far more than a slap or shouting would have. *Always tell the truth and be true to yourself.* And she had, give or take the odd little white lies that she'd told to spare the feelings of others.

'Well, thank you for being so candid,' said Linus, nodding slowly, thoughtfully. His brain was clearly chewing on her words, as if they were one of her bloody useless collagen gummies. 'This ... this has totally bypassed me.' He gave a small laugh, rooted in a mix of confusion and embarrassment.

'I've tried to raise this with Carl in in HR on numerous occasions. No point with Philip.' Sod it, they needed dobbing in, Amanda decided.

Linus pressed his hands together, tapped them against his mouth as if setting his thoughts to a rhythm.

'So what do we do?' he asked eventually. 'How can I help change things? Make them better?'

Amanda gulped. 'Really?'

'Well yes of course. I don't want to add to the list of men who are ignoring this in the workplace. How do we approach it sensibly and sensitively? How do we march forward? I'd like your assistance if you could.'

This really wasn't turning out for either of them as they expected when she walked in through Linus's office door.

'I was hoping to beat Carl into submission by trying to pin him down again. I had some fresh ideas, I can collect more. I don't mean forty extra days holiday per year sort of ideas, let's be clear,' said Amanda. 'Constructive, workable suggestions that will improve things for women at certain stages of their lives while causing the minimum disruption to the company. There's a meeting place in the middle. You'll always get the odd person who wants to milk the complications of their sex, but for all women to be judged on that basis is unfair.'

'I totally agree, Amanda. This is very exciting.' Linus was talking and thinking at the same time; she could virtually see the cogs turning in his skull. 'This could really send wide ripples throughout every workplace in the country,' he went on. 'We could *lead*.'

Amanda nodded. 'Yes we could.' Initially it would need someone at Linus's level to make changes with HR because Carl had all the bending capabilities of tungsten. He and Philip were a pair in that, which was probably why they got on like a house on fire – each recognising a fellow twat in the other, was the general consensus.

'May I ask what your personal circumstances are – at

home, your set-up, as background?' asked Linus. 'Do you have a family to care for, for instance?'

She found his curiosity touching and she trusted its face value so she answered honestly.

'I'm single, I have no children. I have a mother in her eighties to care for and I see her almost every day after work and at weekends. I've had to use most of my holiday entitlement up to take her here, there and everywhere.'

'My own mother cared for both her elderly parents as well as holding down a full-time job and bringing me up. My childless uncle, who could have done much more, didn't,' Linus traded with her.

'I have a brother too and it's more or less the same scenario.'

Linus gave her an understanding smile before he spoke again.

'Amanda, can you compile a report for me of what you were going to take to HR? I mean I could, I suppose, look things up on the internet but it would carry more weight if someone like yourself, going through what you are, could show me first-hand what might be useful.'

'I did intend to hold focus groups, talk to women outside Mon Enfant . . .' Discussion groups within the company so far had proved useless. No one wanted to talk in case it was held against them, plus they didn't trust that anything would be done anyway, so it was pointless.

'Then please still do that. I can give you a small budget for whatever you need. And I'll make sure that Philip gives you some leeway if you have to arrange anything in office hours.'

'Well, that's very kind of you,' said Amanda. The seed of an idea popped into her brain that would stretch to benefitting someone else, too.

'It would be good to stop women who work for me bending so much they snap.' Then he looked at Amanda as if he
might be talking about her and she swallowed.

Linus glanced at his watch.

'If I may be so bold . . . you look totally shattered. Go
home, recharge, and we'll see you back in the office on
Monday.'

'Go . . . go home?' she repeated to clarify.

'Yes, Amanda, go home.' He smiled. 'I'll let you tell
Philip.'

At home, Amanda sat at the table with a sandwich from
the bakery around the corner, a pot of tea and her address
book. She flicked to the 'B' page and typed a number into
her phone. It connected after two rings and a husky, friendly
voice poured from it into her ear.

'Hello, stranger. How lovely to hear from you.'

'You know how it is, Barb, weeks turn into months.'

'. . . And into years. Trust me, this I know. What have you
got for me? Is it a sex-scandal scoop?'

Amanda laughed. 'No, it's pie with ice cream scoop.
Blueberry pie, genuine American blueberry pie.'

'Tell me more,' said Barb with a purr.

'New diner opened up on Spring Hill just outside
Penistone. Absolutely gorgeous gen-u-ine Texan bought it
and he's having a bit of difficulty luring customers in, which
is a bummer because it's fab. Just needs a magic wand waved
by a hot reporter.'

'Oh yeah?'

'Do you know any?'

Barb hooted. She had a laugh like a female Sid James.

'Seriously. It would make a great feature and if he offers

to ply you with pie, say yes immediately. And you'd go to heaven obviously for doing someone a good turn.'

'I'm on it. What's it called?'

'Ray's Diner.'

'I'll get it in this weekend.'

Chapter 6

'Do you think a tie would be over the top?' Steve asked, looking at himself in the mirror.

'I would have said so,' replied Mel, standing behind him. The white shirt open at the neck and jeans ensemble was perfect. Sexy, actually. A tie would alter the vibe totally. But then again, she had as much experience of school reunions as he did. Was there a dress code? She imagined anyone who was a bit of a knob back in the day and wanted to show off that they were now in charge of Coca Cola UK would have put a suit and tie on. Steve wasn't that man, he didn't need to prove anything to anyone.

He pulled a face. 'I don't even want to go. It'll be crap.'

'Oh, give up. You'll enjoy it,' Mel admonished him because he always moaned about going out and eight times out of ten he grudgingly enjoyed himself. 'You said you were looking forward to it up to this morning.'

'I don't know what to expect.'

'You won't be on your own.' Mel smiled. 'But you'll have aged better than most, so you have that on your side.'

'Cheers.' He hadn't taken that as a compliment.

'I mean it, I'm not being sarky.' She slapped him playfully. Steve *had* aged well. His mid-brown hair was thinning a bit so he went with it and kept it cropped short and it suited him better anyway, unlike his younger brother Dave who had grown his long to swirl over the bald bits. Steve had good style, he watched what he ate and his physical job kept him fitter than a lot of men at fifty-two. Everyone thought Dave was the elder by five years, when the reverse was true.

'Do you think your old flame might be there, what was her name again?' asked Mel, even though she knew full well what her name was. *The girl that got away* as Steve had jokingly referred to her a few times over the years. Their year's 'it' girl, because every school year had one and an 'it' boy, an unattainable whom everyone fancied.

'Saran,' said Steve. 'Saran Sykes. She'll be about forty stone with a moustache now.' He jiggled his hardly-existent stomach. 'Says me, Twiggy.'

Mel chuckled. 'Just go and have a good time. It'll be great to catch up with old pals and have a look around the school again.'

'Some memories within those walls, Mel,' said Steve with a sigh. Batty Street senior school would be demolished next month and someone had had the great idea of having a school reunion before the wrecking ball did its damage, and had gone ahead and arranged it.

'I don't even know if anyone from my class will turn up,' said Steve, seemingly intent on talking himself out of it now. Mel wouldn't let him though; she knew he'd regret it if he didn't go.

'Well, you'll find out when you get there.' Mel picked up the car keys. She would be driving him to Batty Street but he was getting a taxi back. The organisers had put a bar and food on. 'Just don't get drunk and deck a teacher.'

'They'll all be dead.'

'Don't be daft. Some teachers I had at school were fresh out of college, and only about seven years older than me when I was sixteen. Don't forget to take loads of pics.' She knew he'd have a good time; people usually did when they weren't really looking forward to something, it was nearly always better than expected. It would be interesting, if nothing else, she'd bet.

'I don't know why I said yes to this. I won't be late home.'

'Oh shut up, will you. Be as late as you like. I'm going to have a long bath with a good book and a massive glass of Baileys.' Mel grabbed his chin and squeezed it. 'For good-ness' sake, cheer up. You look as if you're off to be hanged. It'll be fun.'

'No, it won't. It'll be full of knobs who head up ICI and earn millions lording it over everyone. And there's me, just a painter and decorator.' Steve half-chuntered under his breath.

'Oy. Don't undersell yourself. You aren't *just* a painter and decorator. You're a businessman with your own company and two lads, a van with your name on it and with your books full for god knows how long in advance. Anyway, it's far too early for this,' said Mel, shaking her head.

'Too early for what?'

'You, you bloody grinch. We've just had spring, you aren't due for another eight months. Come on, let's get off.'

Steve sighed. 'If I must.'

Mel pushed him through the door with a laugh. She would replay that moment so many times over the next few weeks, wondering where they would have been if only she'd

said, 'If you really don't fancy it, don't go.' But she would
never know, because she didn't say it.

★

Erin headed slowly towards the teashop in the corner of
Spring Hill Square. It was closed now for normal business
but open to host a club, Molly's Club, as it had become
known. A place where bereaved people gathered and
talked in the hope of healing together, when they were
ready to share, to start to rebuild. Erin wasn't sure if she
ever could, she wasn't even sure she deserved to, but she
needed to try.

No one knew she was here, not even Bon. Then again,
she wasn't *there* yet because she'd trod these exact same steps
last week, parked in the far corner so her car wouldn't be
spotted, walked across the square at the pace of a man ap-
proaching the gallows.

A tall, smart man wearing a Crombie and carrying a
briefcase-type bag also coming from the car park overtook
her, headed to the teashop, walked straight in without hes-
itation, as she should have done. She imagined following
him, sitting in a circle, the heat of eyes on her, feeling the
pressure to tell her story: why she was there, what she had
caused, all that hurt and pain and for what? She imagined
people wearing fixed sympathetic smiles while very different thoughts about her were racing around their brains in
response to the words stuttering out of her mouth.

She couldn't do it.

Erin spun on her heel and groped for the car keys in her
pocket. No, she couldn't go in. Not tonight. Again. This
was not a good idea, whatever had made her think it was.

★

Mel had just dragged out the ironing board when the landline rang. Hardly anyone called on that these days and she picked it up, expecting it to be someone trying to sell her something. They might fool more people if they didn't sound as dodgy as hell. She'd strung one along for nearly five minutes last month out of sheer devilment.

'Mel, is this you?'

A female voice she didn't recognise.

'Yes,' she answered tentatively.

'It's Joss. Joss Binchley.'

Flaming hell. That name was a blast from the past.

Joss must have taken her momentary silence for loss of memory.

'We were at school together—' The creep of embarrassment entering her words.

'Oh for goodness sake, Joss, of course I remember you.' *Blimey*, thought Mel, *was it national school reunion day?*

'I got your number from your Zoe. Well, our Traz did, they're still in touch. Do you remember Traz? She said to say hello.'

Another memory dragged out of the bag. Joss's sister Traz was wonderful. They were close in a way that she and Zoe weren't. Best mates as well as sisters.

'Right, right.' Jeez, she didn't know what to say now the initial flurry of 'hellos' was out of the way but rather than there being any awkward silence, Joss hopped straight back in.

'I'm calling because I've moved back up north and I'd love to see you. I mean, I know we haven't seen each other since my first wedding anniversary and probably a million things have happened to us in between. God, that party seems like it belonged to another lifetime.' She laughed.

The memory of it flooded Mel's brain. She hadn't realised it was still saved in her head. She was forgetting valuable things at a rate of knots these days and yet her brain clung on to useless images and info – like peristalsis from an old biology lesson. A picture of Jamie Fenton entered her head in glorious technicolour. He'd looked like Martin Kemp only even yummier. All the girls fancied him and all the boys fancied Joss so it was nailed on they'd gravitate to each other and lock on. They'd had a huge party in Joss's parents' house for their first anniversary. Her dad sold cars and was loaded.

'Dear lord, yes. How many years have you clocked up now?'

'I've been divorced for twenty-two months and three weeks exactly, not that I'm counting.'

'Oh, I'm sorry to hear that,' said Mel.

'I'm not. The wanker,' Joss growled. 'Anyway, look, I've not rung you to talk about him. How did we fall off each other's Christmas cards lists, Mel?'

Mel allowed herself a smile at that because she'd just had the same thought. 'I have no idea either. It's what happens I suppose, time passes and then you wonder what sort of reception you'd get if you tried to pick up where you left off again, so you don't try.'

'Look, rather than natter on the phone, are you free at the weekend? I'd love to talk face to face. Maltstone Garden Centre? My treat.' Joss sounded so keen to meet up. So it seemed a mini school reunion was on the cards for Mel too.

'Sure. What time?' she said. 'I'd love to see you.'

★

Sky walked into the house and the lovely smell of Italian food greeted her. Her housemate, Katy, waved to her.

'I hope you haven't eaten,' she said. 'I've made us some tea.'

'No, I haven't.'

'Well, it's nearly ready. I'll stick some garlic bread in and we can eat in ten minutes precisely, so do what you have to do first.'

What a nice surprise, thought Sky, and it would offset seeing Angel again on Monday. There was something about Angel Sutton that soured the whole week she appeared in. And if ever there was a misnomer . . .

'Shall I nip to the shop and get a bottle of wine?'

'I've got one. No need.'

Sky chuckled. 'Have I missed my own birthday?'

'No, now go, and hurry up.'

Katy was a good housemate to have. There had been three of them sharing the ground floor of 8, Barclay Road, until last month when Jordan had moved out. They'd all been respectful of each other's space and divvied up the cleaning jobs fairly and they hoped that when the new person moved in, it would all still work as smoothly. Jordan had finally got enough money together to embark on his first mortgage and they both wished him well but missed him. He'd been great and they'd felt better for having a fit – in both senses of the word – male on the property.

Katy was dishing up when Sky arrived at the table. A red wine had been poured for her and slices of garlic bread with bubbling cheese on the top sat on a plate between them.

'Okay, this looks great. So let's cut to the quick, what do you want?' said Sky, pulling the chair out.

'Your life savings,' replied Katy.

'What on earth would you need three pounds twenty that desperately for?'

'Ha.'

Katy sat down opposite, picked up her fork and then put it straight back down. The mood changed in a click of fingers.

'It's an apology, Sky,' she said, looking suddenly serious.

The journey of the garlic bread to Sky's mouth halted.

'What for?' Because she couldn't imagine what Katy would have to apologise for, other than nicking a Jaffa Cake out of her supplies, but they'd all nicked the odd biscuit occasionally.

'Sky . . . Ozzy's asked me to move in with him, and my tenancy agreement is up in less than a month, so I'm leaving. No point in asking Wilton for any refund, because I won't get it, so I'm not giving him the satisfaction of turning me down.'

That was true; their landlord, Wilton Dearne was as tight as they came. Sky tried not to look gutted but she didn't make a very good job of it.

'When?' she asked.

'Tomorrow.'

'Tomorrow?' Sky gasped. 'No, that's way too soon.'

'Most of my stuff is at Ozzy's anyway. I know after Jordan going this is the last news you need. I feel shit, if it helps.' Her lip looked distinctly wobbly. Sky left her chair and went to the other side of the table to give her a squeezy hug.

'Don't be daft, Katy, this was always going to be a temporary arrangement for us until we got on our feet. None of us really wanted to be here forever, did we? Someone was bound to be last out.'

'I know,' said Katy, wiping her eyes with her fingertips because Sky's hug had pierced something inside her that was now leaking. 'I hadn't a clue he was going to ask me, even though I've been hinting and last night he said, *let's do it*. It's been good fun, hasn't it? But I know you've just signed for another six months and you might end up sharing with some right horrors.'

'They can't be worse than you two,' said Sky, putting her own feelings aside to try and make Katy feel better.

Katy sniffed, and more tears fell.

'I feel terrible. I'll tell Ozzy I'll leave it a bit.'

'Give up, now, come on,' Sky lifted up her glass. 'Let's make this meal a celebratory one, not commiseratory. This is great news, there's no point in hanging around this dump any longer than you have to.'

'Sky, I thought you'd hate me,' said Katy.

'As if,' replied Sky, holding up the act.

'We'll stay in touch, won't we?'

'Of course we will. Anyway, you never know, in two weeks I might have met the man of my dreams and be telling Wilton that I'm off and he can keep his money too.'

'I hope you do, that would be the best news,' said Katy.

There was a fat chance of that happening, thought Sky as she loaded up her fork while keeping her smile firmly fixed for her friend's benefit. One: she couldn't afford to lose that amount of rent money, plus the bond Wilton would keep. And two: she'd already met her dream man, and he was off limits.

Chapter 7

'Crackers, that's what this business is,' cackled Iris Caswell as her old but deft fingers rolled up the casing of a Christmas cracker.

'Oh god, not that line again,' said Venus, the new girl, who had fitted in with the crew from the moment she'd stepped over the threshold with her purple hair and dry wit. The Pandoros, who owned the small but successful factory called The Crackers Yard, wouldn't have employed anyone who looked down on corny jokes, didn't pull their weight, didn't mind sticking on the kettle even if it wasn't their turn, and who didn't pass the Iris test. As Iris always said, 'I haven't got to my nineties without knowing a thing or two about people'.

'She'll do,' was her verdict when Annie Pandoro asked if Iris thought the pouty teenager passed muster. And she had done. She reminded the crew of young Palma Collins when she first turned up at the factory with her pink hair, one of their favourite people to have walked through the doors, now married to a British champion boxer, and a mother of three.

Joe and Annie Pandoro had bought the company off the peg when it had more or less run aground and, with the help of a wisely picked workforce, had made it into the success it was today. It was situated on an industrial estate between the villages of Maltstone and Higher Hoppleton, easy to get to with plenty of parking. The order books were full, profits rose year on year and the staff loved coming to work.

'Long before you arrived, there was a woman called Gill Johnson who sat right where you're sitting, Venus, and she said that every single day: *Crackers, that's what this business is,*' Iris told her.

'How the hours must have flown by,' said Venus with a click of her tongue. Iris chuckled at her cheek but she was on her own. There was something up with both Annie, holed up in the office like an agoraphobic mole, and Astrid, who was beavering away with her brow lowered as if she was in a faraway place.

'Summat on your mind, Astrid?' Iris called down to the bottom of the long table. She had to repeat it.

'What?'

'Earth calling Astrid. You've had a stick up your bum all morning, what's up with you?'

Astrid snipped the ribbon on her cracker and sighed heavily.

'On Tuesday, I gave the finger to Mr and Mrs Hutchinson.'

Venus pulled a shocked face. 'You?' Astrid might have been six foot four and built like an Amazon warrior queen, but she was probably the politest person Venus had ever come across in her young life and the least likely ever to give pensioners a rude digit.

'Ja, me,' replied Astrid.

'They must have done something bad for you to do that,'

said Iris, equally as shocked. 'Whose turn is it to put the kettle on? We need a cuppa and a birthday cake break to digest this revelation.'

'I'm sure it's my turn,' said Venus, getting up. 'I mean I've only made twenty today.'

Venus got some plates and cut wedges of the birthday cake that Annie had brought in for Astrid that morning. Her husband, Joe, had made it and their little boy, Massimo, had stuck the chocolate buttons on the top. Iris didn't want the grisly details to start until the coffees had been dished out, and kept shushing Astrid until then. Annie joined them from the office when Iris waved her in through the window.

'What's up?' she asked.

'Astrid's told the Hutchinsons to do one,' said Iris, almost with pride in her voice. 'About time. I never liked them. They show their faces in church every so often just to get some brownie points with *Him*.' She pointed upwards. 'But He's got their number. And it's six hundred and sixty six.'

'They bought me a mop head for me birthday,' said Astrid, correcting herself immediately. 'Two actually, as they were in a buy one, get one free pack. Although I was expected to leave it with them so I didn't use it for any of me other clients.'

Iris's jaw dropped open and she nearly lost her forkful of cake.

'The cheeky bleeders. That was the straw that broke the camel's back then, was it, because I know you haven't been happy there for a while.'

'Yes, that is right,' said Astrid, feeling better already at having let it out, because she'd been visited by the guilty fairy and wondered if she'd gone over the top with her reaction.

'That Dennis is a creepy beggar. He once felt my bum in a jumble sale. He said it was an accident,' said Iris. 'If he'd got any closer to me, I'd have ended up in the maternity unit nine months later.'

Astrid smiled. It had been the first time she'd smiled since being here last week.

'He asked you one too many questions about your bits for my liking,' said Iris, who wasn't renowned for her political correctness or up-to-date terminology, though her good intentions were never in doubt. 'It's not what decent people do, though Dennis and Valerie Hutchinson consider themselves holier than the Virgin Mary.'

'Yes. He was too interested in my anatomy. I think he would have liked me to strip off so he could do a full examination and nothing short of it would stop the questions.'

'It's none of his business, is it?' said Venus. 'Did you ask him what shape his willy was or how low his balls hung?'

Astrid threw back her head and laughed. 'No, Venus, but I wish I had now.'

'Well, good for you,' said Iris. 'It's not as if you need the pittance they paid you anyway, is it?'

'Ah, but they gave me two pounds extra for a birthday treat.'

'What did you buy with it, another house?' asked Venus.

'The mop head wasn't even Vileda. I don't think it would have fitted the stick.'

'Kevin left you well set up, didn't he?' said Iris. 'I don't know why you're still cleaning if you don't have to.'

'I like cleaning, Iris. But not so much the Hutchinsons really.'

'You're too bloody soft,' was Iris's verdict on that.

'I only do two clients now and they are lovely. I am

proper happy just having them and working here. So if you ever vant me to do an extra day, Annie, just shout up.' She beamed at Annie, who didn't mirror the smile but instead stopped eating her cake and dropped a long, heartfelt sigh at the same time.'

'Annie, love, what's up?' said Iris, immediately concerned because like Astrid, Annie was usually walking sunshine and yet here she was looking more like a storm cloud.

'I haven't known how to tell you,' said Annie, rubbing her forehead. 'Joe and I . . . we're moving to the coast. We're retiring early.'

Silence met the news but Iris, Venus and Astrid all guessed at the words that would follow and they were right.

'I'm sorry, but we're selling the factory.'

Chapter 8

'Careful, careful, you watch.' Edek Urbaniak dipped a gloved hand into the bowl and scooped up the bubbles from the soap. He then gently worked it into the fur of the teddy bear in his other hand.

'Only on the surface,' he explained to his daughter. 'Inside this bear, is very old wood wool and we must not get it wet or it will be very bad for him.'

His fingers were huge but gentle and that was the quality that Sky most associated with him, his gentleness.

He'd let her make the bear's new ears. He'd shown her how to make a pattern from the old ravaged ones and choose the fabric which best matched the much-beloved centenarian toy. Then, when she'd finished them, he'd fastened them on with the tiniest of stitches.

'When you mend a bear, you often mend a person too so you take the best care to get it right,' said Edek, smoothing the lather onto the teddy's fur, then wiping it away along with the residue of dirt.

It had looked an impossible task when the man had brought 'Wellington' in with his tattered ears, split paws and belly, grubby fur and half the stuffing escaped and yet here he was, rejuvenated and having a final rubdown, before being returned to the grateful hands of his original owner's grandson.

'There, look at him, Sky.' Edek held up the bear, who appeared to be smiling just a little bit more than he had when she first saw him, even though that was impossible because the stitching at his mouth was one of the few things they hadn't needed to touch. 'He's perfect. His ears are the best bit of all.'

Sky smiled because she knew they weren't really, but her dad wanted her to feel that they were, because he was like that, a person who always considered the feelings of others before his own, before he'd descended into the spiral that dragged him down to the point of no resurfacing.

It was funny to see a man cry over a toy when he came to pick up the restored Wellington. She had seen the same reaction many times since but that first time always stuck in her mind. Like her father said, when you mend a bear, you often mend a person. But no one could mend him, not even her with all the skills he had taught her. She had never managed to make him whole again.

'Penny for them,' Bon said to Sky, pulling her out of her reverie.

'You looked in another world there.' He smiled at her and it brought a warmth to her chest that always arose whenever he addressed her or looked in her direction or breathed near her.

'I was just thinking about something,' she said, making light of it. But it wasn't light stuff at all. Angel Sutton had the ability to do that, make her thoughts return to the past where even the best of her recollections were stained at the edges. She couldn't think of her dad without thinking of the knotweed that had wrapped itself around him with an unrelenting hold and eventually killed him.

Angel should have been nothing to her now they were grown up, but childhood memories ran like deep cuts that refused to heal.

Angel had been *the* rich kid at school who'd had extravagant parties and so other girls sucked up to her. Her wealthy, entitled family had brought her up to think she was something above everyone anyway, but the fact that Sky Urbaniak remained resistant to her was a thorn in her side. Angel and her group of cronies would make fun of her because her school skirts came from the market and not from the proper uniform shop. And they thought she had a stupid foreign name. And she had really stupid pale skin and 'see-through' hair. It all calmed down a little when Sky's mum died and she was given a temporary break; then it revved up again when old rumours were poked awake about the possibility of there being a second Pennine Prowler who was never caught. When Sky left school at sixteen and went to a different sixth-form college from that lot, she'd hoped she would never see any of them again. Every time she saw Angel, it reopened old wounds enough to feel fresh pain again and unsettled her for days.

'There's a birthday cake in my office,' said Bon. 'Tony's wife sneaked it in, so in about ten minutes, I'm going to gather us all together.'

'Aw, that's nice,' said Sky.

She could have listened to him speaking all day; she adored his accent. He'd been brought up in South Africa: the slight rolls of his 'r's, the hard consonants, especially at the ends of words, the distorted vowels; hardly any of it had been ironed out by years of living in England. Everything about Bon van der Meer was perfect: his gull-grey eyes, his lovely mouth, his shoulders, his dress sense, his thick steel-coloured hair that had just started to wave at the cut point and that he pushed back from his face with his strong, clever hands. Not conventionally handsome by pretty-boy standards maybe, but undeniably masculine. She loved him, she loved everything about him and she knew it was love, not a crush, not a pash, because there was no mistaking it.

'Everything all right?' he asked, because whatever she'd been thinking about when he'd broken into her thoughts had downturned her mouth and made her eyebrows crunch.

'Yes, fine.'

'Bon, Bon. I'm just nipping out for five, don't start without me.' Peter came racing past them, whispering too loudly to be anything like discreet and tapping the side of his nose. Peter Cushing was their upholsterer, who traded under the name of Peter's Cushions. He always said he had two choices with a name like that: to follow his dad into the upholstery trade, or become a vampire-slayer, but there wasn't a college course for the latter.

Sky was fond of all the people she worked alongside in Bon's repair shop. The last place she'd worked in wasn't half as nice or friendly, run by an old curmudgeon who hated kids, which wasn't a great personality to have when you ran a toy emporium. Bon Repair was split into units and each paid him a weekly rent for their space. He was more than fair with what he charged and they all had a generous portion of working area. There was Peter, and Ricky 'Tick Tock', who restored old clocks and watches; Mildred 'Picture Perfect', who cleaned and touched up old paintings and photographs; Chippy 'Chips Away,' who mended ceramics; 'Jock of All Trades' who cut keys, mended shoes and sharpened tools; 'Adam Amp' who was a wonder with anything electrical that needed refurbishment; Willy Woodentop, who restored wooden furniture; and today's birthday boy himself, Tony 'Toy' Cropper who repaired old toys, except for teddy bears – he and Sky had an understanding about that. Sometimes, when Tony was overrun with work, he'd ask Sky to help him mend any dolls because it wasn't his favourite job and it was extra revenue for her.

They were a cache of kind people, it was a good mix. Bon had his own space across the bottom of the unit, where he built bespoke desks. He was a master of his trade; his creations were amazing, each one his own design. He liked to bury secret compartments in the belly of the structure that only he and his buyer would know about. Sometimes Sky would watch him working on his latest piece, lost in everything but the task in hand, and she could see the devotion and care he poured into what he made and she wished he could pour the same into her, touch her as tenderly as he smoothed his hand over wood. She was jealous of that wood.

'You're making a good job of that repair,' said Bon to her, looking at the soldier's teddy bear on her work bench.

'It isn't a hard job, but it's an important one,' she replied.

'I've paid for an advert in *Up North* about us,' said Bon, adding when he read on her face that the name didn't mean much, 'you know, the monthly magazine.'

It dawned on her then. 'Oh yes, the thick expensive one.'

'That's right. So you might get a flurry of orders, with any luck.'

'Hope so,' said Sky. She'd have to dip into her meagre savings if she didn't sell some more bears soon.

'So don't forget, cake in ten minutes. Synchronise your watch,' said Bon with a wink, stepping away to chat to one of the others. Though he could have stayed chatting to Sky for much longer, and that's why he didn't.

★

It was a good job that Steve didn't have any work on that day because he still wasn't up at ten o'clock, and that was unheard of for him since he was usually awake with the cockerels. Mel had been asleep when he got in from his school reunion. She'd waited up until eleven and then she'd lain in bed reading for a while, so he couldn't have got home before midnight.

She'd been up early because she'd taken the week off to declutter the house. Steve never threw anything away and the garage, the loft and cupboards were too full of junk, so she'd put her foot down and ordered a skip. She was enjoying herself, too; it was very cathartic. *Don't be throwing anything valuable away,* he'd warned her. *A 1980s game of Cluedo with half the pieces missing is not going to be valuable, Steve,* she'd thrown back at him. There were no Ming vases in the skip, just rubbish that had no place in their house any more.

She cocked her ear because she could hear shufflings upstairs, and so she abandoned the task of emptying the drawer full of a big stack of his trade magazines, going back years, and went into the kitchen to put the kettle on. When Steve came down there was a builder's mug of milky tea waiting for him; he walked over to the kitchen table, squinting as if the light streaming through the big window was an assault on his eyes.

'Oh dear,' said Mel and reached into the medicine cabinet for a couple of ibuprofen. She dropped them beside the mug and sat down on the chair next to him.

'So I'm figuring it was a good night, then.'

'Better than expected,' he said, having a slurp of tea. 'It was nice to see everybody.'

'And was Saran there?'

'Aye, she was. We had a little chat.'

'And was she forty stone with a moustache?'

'Nope.'

Mel tilted her head at him and that small action seemed to ignite his impatience.

'What are you looking at me like that for?'

'I'm just waiting for the details.'

'What details? I had a good time and I'll probably meet up with a couple of the lads again. I was wrong to think I wouldn't fit back in with them, but what's the point in me giving you a list of who's doing what when you don't know any of them?'

'Well, no, but—'

'I'm glad I went. There's not really much else to say.'

'So I did the right thing pushing you to go, then?' Mel tried not to look too smug. 'I do get some things right, don't I?'

'Some things,' he relented, which was as much of an admission as she'd ever get from him because Steve wasn't really one for gushing.

He tossed the tablets down his neck and took another drink of tea, then put the mug back down on the table, pushing it away from him.

'Sorry, I can't drink that. I might have to go back to bed for a bit.'

'Get yourself upstairs, then,' said Mel. 'I could come up with you if you like.' She winked playfully.

'I can't think of anything worse at this moment in time,' said Steve, getting up. And Mel laughed, because she knew what he meant really, but still it stung a bit.

Chapter 9

Amanda had a good sleep for once, a full seven hours, apart from the wee break somewhere in the middle. Was that the HRT starting to work? Oh, she did hope so. She had a coffee and then rang Baker's the estate agency, to make an initial enquiry. As soon as she said she might be interested in selling a house on Winter Place, she could tell they were keen. Great big fat commission on a house there, an easy sell.

The weather wasn't conducive for a long walk, it was typical April, blinding sunlight one minute, heavens opening the next. She found herself ringing up her mum to ask if she would like to go out for lunch.

'I could do, I suppose,' said Ingrid in her all-too-familiar grudging tone and Amanda once again wished that they had the sort of mother/daughter relationship others had, where they were more like friends who enjoyed each other's company, and who looked forward to sharing some quality time together. Just for a change it would have been nice to hear the words, 'Ooh, that would be lovely', instead of feeling that she was forcing her mother to put herself out. She wouldn't have been like that if Bradley had suggested it; she'd have had her coat and shoes on and be waiting by the door as soon as the call had ended.

As she was pulling up outside her mum's house, Dolly Shepherd from next door was just nudging her old Jaguar into her drive. They passed the time of day and Amanda told her that she'd been to check out Bettina Boot's old place and it was wonderful, and that the new owner was giving pensioners discounts. She knew from learned experience that one should never underestimate the reach of a geriatric PR machine which was more powerful than something even Steve Jobs could design. Dolly Shepherd made the spreading abilities of wildfire look incompetent.

Amanda had bought another camera for her mum's bedroom. She'd dispense with its services when she found out what Bradley was hunting around for in there. It was very unobtrusive and would sit happily with all the knick-knacks on the large antique whatnot. She should have been able to trust her brother but she didn't wholly, and there was no point in being direct and asking him why he was poking around because he'd only deny it or lie, so it was best to do her investigations undercover. He'd always been fox-cunning and she could guarantee that whatever he was up to, it wasn't for their mother's benefit and that's what was concerning her enough to turn into a temporary Sherlock Holmes.

She knocked on Ingrid's front door to alert her before unlocking it and walking in.

'Only me.'

Ingrid was in the lounge, patting some powder onto her cheeks.

'You look nice, Mum.' She was a smart woman, even if everything she owned was either black or navy.

'I've not had this on for years. I'm surprised it fits.'

'I don't know why it shouldn't, you've been the same size for as long as I can remember.'

'I've always been lucky with my weight,' said Ingrid, nodding agreement. 'Have you put some on? You're looking a bit fuller in the face.'

'No, I've lost a bit recently actually,' replied Amanda, thinking, *great*. She wondered if their mother ever said as much to Bradley, who had a pot belly the size of a kettle-drum these days. It wasn't healthy for him, not that he'd take advice from her on the subject.

'I'm just going to the loo.' Amanda nipped up the stairs and quickly into her mum's bedroom. She positioned the camera in between her Staffordshire flatback pot dogs on the shelf, pulling away a skein of cobwebs that had settled on them. It looked as if they hadn't been dusted behind in a while which was odd and sad, because it wasn't like her mum to have dust anywhere around. She remembered as a child, moaning when she was all comfortable and her mum wanted to shift the sofa or chair she was sitting on to clean under it because her mum wasn't one for missing out the unseen places. She'd obviously got to the stage where she needed a bit of help now, that was clear and the realisation brought some pain with it.

Ingrid was standing by the window and huffing at the weather when she went back down.

'Don't worry, you've no walking to do,' Amanda assured her. 'Just into the car and out of it at the other end.'

'If you say so.'

Amanda noticed she'd put too much powder on and it was too dark a shade for her skin and looked like a mask.

'Here, Mum, let me just adjust your make-up a bit.'

She smoothed a tissue over her skin, she had lovely skin her mum. Amanda was gentle but her mother twisted and turned her head like a toddler.

'That's better. Now, you'll do.'

'I've had to miss my morning coffee for this,' said Ingrid, dragging her coat off the back of the chair.

★

Erin finished the last of her tea and put the mug into the dishwasher, aware that her feet were dragging across the kitchen floor. She was in conflict, half of her wanting to get on with the thing to be done, the other half of her dreading it but she had to because she had taken time away from her job in order to force her hand. It was her firm, a graphic design company; she didn't need to ask permission, but she rarely took days off because she would rather have been in her office than in this space.

Most of the furniture had been sold or donated to charity months ago, the things Carona had brought with her to the apartment, the things they had bought together: all too painful to keep. The bed they shared, large and ridiculously expensive, had been the first thing to go. What was left now were Carona's clothes, her books, the minutiae of her life. Erin had put them all in the spare room out of sight, where they sat absorbing her energy through the walls.

She'd given Carona's sister — her only attending relative — her jewellery at the funeral. She'd taken it reluctantly and said, 'I hope she treated you better than she treated us.' It was a small service, no wake. Carona had always said that if anything happened to her she didn't want people gathering afterwards and talking about her when they hardly knew her. Maybe, though, she was frightened no one would turn up.

It had been a full six months now since Carona had died and Erin still thought of her every day. The two and a half years they were together had felt like much longer, maybe because of the roller-coaster ride, those initial highs promising much more than the lows that followed. She didn't know if what she was going through was grief, because that road had a beginning and an eventual end. Whatever this was, she was stuck on it, great mounds of complications hindering any potential forward movement. She sometimes woke up in the middle of the night, feeling the press of their weight on her chest like boulders.

Erin steeled herself and opened up the door, ripping off the first of the black bags on the roll. She loaded the first with Carona's underwear for the clothes bank at the dump, even though some of it still had the tags on. The books filled two huge boxes: Kafka, Nin, Pasternak, Proust, books meant to sit on shelves and impress, not to be read, and yet she'd pooh-pooh Erin's book choices, the contemporary romances she'd lose herself in to grab at some respite and comfort. Reading was a waste of time when they could be doing something together, she'd say. As if she was jealous even of the books in Erin's hands, their presence in her consciousness.

She bagged up Carona's clothes next; she had always been so beautifully dressed. Erin could have sold these: the Vivienne Westwood skirt, the Jimmy Choo sandals, the Ralph Lauren blazer, but there was a local animal charity that had a shop where the choice stuff went. She didn't break for lunch, she powered through and when it was done she rang them to arrange a pick-up time. They said they'd take the books too. Would tomorrow afternoon be okay? *The sooner the better,* she'd answered.

Tomorrow morning she had an estate agent booked to photograph the rooms and tell her what price she needed to pitch it at for a quick sale. The apartment was all hers. They'd written mirror wills and had life insurance on the mortgage that paid out extra in case of an accident. That's what Carona's death had been declared, but Erin knew different.

There were no photos in Carona's 'treasure box' of her past: she'd burned them all; no family, no past loves, they were dead to her. There were only ones of her and Erin, the cards Erin had sent her, pressed flowers from bunches Erin had bought her, serviettes from places they'd eaten at, tickets from places they'd been to. And diaries, filled with her long, looping handwriting eating up all the white spaces.

Erin picked up the first her fingers fell on, opened up a random page, saw the childish doodles of hearts and flowers and the shouty capitals. She could hear the accompanying audio in Carona's voice, reading the entries out with all the accompanying histrionic emotions and so she closed it and put it, with the others, in the bag destined for the incinerator in the garden.

★

'Yes, you can take those away,' said Ingrid to the waitress, flicking her finger at the plates.

'Was everything all right for you?'

Ingrid squeezed her lips together. 'I've had better. Much better.'

'It was great,' Amanda said to counterbalance the

criticism, because the poor waitress didn't know whether this was a complaint that needed to go to the kitchen with the plates, which were clear of everything but a couple of shreds of lettuce. 'Thank you. We enjoyed it.'

Of course it was adjudged to be substandard because Ingrid always enjoyed a meal more when she had something to moan about. Only Marks and Spencer's scampi would have scored the full ten marks. Or anything that Bradley cooked, the Marco Pierre White of the microwave.

'Would you like to see the dessert menu?' asked the waitress, returning with them.

'We can have a look, I suppose,' said Ingrid, holding out her hand for one.

She'd glance at it, then sigh and say she didn't fancy anything really but might have a little ice cream. It happened every time.

'While Bradley's in Turkey he's having his teeth out and a new kitchen put in,' said Ingrid as she scanned the menu.

'Blimey, how big's his mouth,' replied Amanda, although it was a rhetorical question because she knew the answer to that one: not as big as his ego. The joke flew over her mother's head, though.

'He's having white gloss.'

'Are we talking teeth or kitchen?'

'Don't be stupid, Amanda. Kitchen, of course.'

Amanda's brain rewound a few frames. 'What did you say he was having done with his teeth?'

'He's having venereals. In Turkey. Him and Kerry.'

The corner of Amanda's lip twitched. 'Veneers', presumably. That wouldn't be cheap and Bradley wasn't one for splashing the cash. 'Has he come up on the lottery?'

'Arnold died.'

She was *not* expecting that nugget of information.

'Arnold? His dad? That Arnold?'

'Well, of course I mean that Arnold. What other Arnold would I mean?'

Amanda was genuinely gobsmacked. 'When?'

'Last month.'

'Why didn't you tell me?'

'I just have.'

'I mean sooner, when it happened.'

'Because it's not really any of your business, is it? What was he to you?'

'Mum, stop snapping at me,' said Amanda; her patience would only stretch so far. They couldn't have a conversation like normal mothers and daughters. Eighty per cent of everything Ingrid said to her was barked. She didn't talk that way to Bradley; her voice softened, her words travelled to his ears like warm syrup, not barbed wire.

Duly reprimanded, Ingrid huffed and rolled her eyes.

'Arnold left him a few bob. He was still working in that ironmonger's because he was too tight to employ someone. And he never lived with anyone else after me so Bradley'll cop for the lot.'

Amanda shuddered at the thought of Arnold Worsnip. She hadn't seen him since she was a little girl but still his image, his voice, his dyed black block of hair, his stinging slap on her buttocks were all branded indelibly on her brain.

'You should never have let him smack me,' she said, many many years too late but the words had been sitting inside her to say and she never had before, so lord knows why they picked that moment to come out.

'It's a father's job to do the disciplining.'

'He wasn't my father, he was a dirty old man.' Words ground out between her teeth.

Ingrid jiggled her head as if she wanted to disagree but couldn't be bothered.

'Anyway, Bradley's got a good job so he's plenty of his own money. That's why he's getting his whole house done up.'

'Yeah, it's so good he's still sat in the same chair he was in at eighteen.'

'He's an accountant.'

'He's an accounts clerk,' said Amanda, putting her right because she felt like it. 'He failed his maths GCSE twice. It was me that got him through it the third time.'

It had been the one spot in their relationship where they got on all right, but later on she'd worked out it was only because Bradley needed her help. He could be awfully charming, even as a teenager, when he was on the scrounge.

'Anyway, Kerry's given up her chef job and she's going to stay at home and be a housewife.'

It was darkly funny how she elevated Bradley to being an accountant and Kerry, who worked in Ketherwood Fried Chicken, to having fourteen Michelin stars to her name, and yet she'd downgrade Amanda with a dismissive 'she sells prams' if anyone asked about them.

'She burnt herself on the frier and is getting some compensation,' Ingrid went on.

'Money's just flying at them then, isn't it?' Amanda replied. She had to say what else was on her mind because it had been festering there for decades.

'Mum, you used my dad's money to help buy Arnold that ironmonger's, didn't you?'

Ingrid didn't directly answer the question. From the

look in her eyes she had drifted off somewhere, to an old memory. 'Fred always told me to buy gold. "Gold is worth more than gold" he used to say and he was right. He used to buy it cheap off people and watch the price, sell some when it went high and then keep hold of it when it dipped. Lord, he was canny. He stored it like a squirrel for a rainy day. I've still got it in that same tin but I can't remember—'

She snapped out of the reverie. 'I'm sure I'm going funny. I don't know what I'm talking about.'

She put the menu down on the table.

'I don't fancy anything. I might just have an ice cream if they've got a plain one.'

Chapter 10

Mel pulled the clothes out of the washbasket and pushed them into the machine and caught a strong whiff of alien scent, which she traced to the shirt Steve had on last night. *Chloe*, she could tell it a mile off because her sister wore it. Or rather it wore her sister because a bottle lasted her about a week; she sprayed it on her skin with the same ferocity she'd use with a fire extinguisher. It was to be expected, though, even with Steve who wasn't a kissy-kissy sort of person. They'll have all been so pleased to see each other last night, there would have been transfers of perfumes and aftershaves and lipstick marks going on all over the place. And that was totally fine.

She'd never been a jealous type because she'd had no cause to be jealous and she didn't envy anyone who had that complication in their lives. She was just joshing when she was teasing him about Saran Sykes. People had pasts and those people were bricks on the path to where they were now, *who* they were now, even if they were unrequited loves like Saran. She had the male 'brick' equivalent in her own life in David McAvity, whom she'd fancied for over a year and then when he finally asked her out, he never showed up, totally ghosted her. She was smarting from that when she met Steve in a bar. His first night on the job being a part-time barman, her twenty-second birthday. He'd asked her what she wanted and she'd said, 'You' because she'd been pissed on Diamond White and black. She couldn't remember giving him her number so it was a proper shock the next day, when her mother woke her calling up the stairs:

'Melinda, there's someone called Steve on the line for you.'

She couldn't remember what he looked like either.

Still, she took a chance and went out with him and liked it so much she went out a second time, and a third. Her first real boyfriend, his first real girlfriend. They married when he'd finished his apprenticeship and she was in her third year working at a local bank. It wasn't what she wanted to do, she wanted to be a rock star but everyone laughed when she said that: her sister Zoe thought that was especially hilarious. To her mum and dad it was just a daft phase, but they didn't have a bohemian bone in their bodies and wanted her to be settled and stable in a good 'proper' job. So she got a job in the South Riding bank and instead strummed away on her Fender in the back bedroom. And when she and Steve got together, he'd laughed at her once-lofty ambitions too. He said that he'd always wanted to be an astronaut, and he had more chance of being one of them than she had of lighting up Glastonbury. But, at least, he did give his approval to her teaching a few kids how to play for some pin money.

She swallowed her dream and watched someone else live out theirs because she'd taught young Ron Chopra who was rhythm guitarist in The Metrodomes. She'd followed their rise over the past seven years from doing the local clubs to appearing on posters supporting much bigger groups at festivals and last year at Reading. She'd never expected Ron to give her a public shout out, which was lucky because to her knowledge he never had or she might have had a rush of hopeful pupils to her door, but she was quietly proud of her achievement via him, that she'd made someone catch their star. That she'd showed it was possible, even if not for her.

'Ah, but he's a lad, it's different for lads,' Steve said when she'd showed him an article in the *Yorkshire Standard*. Female rock bands weren't that thick on the ground, were they?

'Heart, Suzi Quatro, The Bangles?' she'd thrown back at him and he'd made that face that said, *give over, they weren't in the same league as Quo.*

It would have been nice to teach her own child the guitar, but they'd never been lucky like that. It hadn't worked naturally and two rounds of IVF had only brought her heartbreak. Steve said that enough was enough, he didn't want to adopt and he wouldn't be talked round from that, so they'd accepted a childless life and it had been a comfortable one. Steve had an excellent reputation and always had as much work on as he wanted and her job was steady in the bank; and the cheap mortgage had allowed them to pay it off early on their nice semi and extend it at the back. They were financially secure, they both had nice cars. They went out for nice meals, they had a nice fortnight's holiday in the sun every summer and a nice week's holiday in the sun every autumn.

Everything was nice, no worries. So why was Mel constantly having to ignore that big gaping well of unfulfillment that sat inside her?

★

When they got back to Ingrid's, Amanda put the kettle on and then noticed the crumbs around the toaster as she was waiting for it to boil. When she nudged it a motherlode fell out of the crumb tray. Amanda moved it to scoop them all up and saw the build-up of grime on the tiles behind it. She felt ashamed of herself that she hadn't spotted it before: that her mother must be struggling to keep up with her house-work and was too proud or stubborn to admit it and had just been cleaning up the areas that showed.

She settled her mother with a coffee and put the TV on and nipped upstairs on the pretext of going to use the loo. She checked around, saw the build-up of dust on the skirt-ing boards, the bits on the carpet. Then she wondered how long it had been since her mum had changed the bedsheets, because if she couldn't flick a bit of dust away, she was hardly going to be able to wrestle with a double duvet cover. Maybe she should have a word with Bradley when he came back and let Kerry come in and clean the house 'for a price'. Her mother liked Kerry, as an extension of beloved Bradley, and it would be company for her while she was here.

Amanda walked back down the stairs she had walked up and down for decades and yet now, they felt a sharper angle than her stairs at home. This house had served her mother well for many years, but it was no longer the most ideal one for an old lady to be in, especially one that lived alone.

Her mum was nodding off in the armchair, her drink untouched. Studying her face, she looked older somehow than she had even a little while ago. Old and tired, like an antique clock winding down. She hadn't thought of her mum as particularly vulnerable until recently; she was a constant, someone who would always be there, just getting a tad stiffer and slower every year, but never to the point where she'd 'stop'. It hit Amanda like a slap that that there would be a day when she was gone and there was no way of telling if it would be a long or short journey to that end. Ingrid was showing the odd sign of getting muddled, like in the pub when her mind wandered off to her long-dead husband hiding gold inside a tin; she was taking longer to get out of a chair, struggling more on steps and that's why Amanda made sure she stayed a little longer every visit, took her mum out more often, checked on her bowel movements, told Bradley he needed to up his ante because Amanda knew that one visit from him equalled twenty from her. It had always been the case, she had lived with it, but still occasionally it was a wasp sting in a sweet spot.

She lifted up her coat and her bag to go home.

'Mum, I'm off. I'll see you tomorrow.'

'I'm going to have a little sleep. That fresh air has knocked me out.'

'Okay.' Amanda kissed her on her still-powdery cheek.

But at the door, the thought of the grime in the kitchen and the dust upstairs pulled her backwards. She took off her coat again, rolled up her sleeves, bent down to the undersink cupboard and reached for the Mr Muscle and a cloth.

Chapter 11

On Saturday morning, Sky was awoken by the sound of the front door opening. It was only seven a.m. when she rolled over to look at the clock. Katy had moved out, she should have been alone in the house. She sat bolt upright and listened; someone was definitely shuffling about in the hallway. She threw herself out of bed and slipped on her dressing gown. She opened her bedroom door and peeped around it to see the front door wide open and a suitcase and some boxes on the mat. A few seconds later the landlord, Wilton Dearne appeared, carrying another one. He shut the door with his heel and waddled towards the kitchen.

'Morning,' he said, as he passed her.

'Morning,' she replied automatically; there was certainly no warmth in the greeting. She knew he couldn't just turn up and enter like that because he'd done it once before and Jordan had thrown a fit about it, citing tenants' rights. But Jordan wasn't here any more and she knew any threat from her about her rights was likely to fall on stony ground.

Luckily, they'd needed to have only minimal dealings

with their landlord in person, because he gave Katy and her the willies – not literally, although they suspected he would have, given the chance. Wilton Dearne was an odd character, with his greasy floppy hair and raspy chest. He dragged his feet over any maintenance that needed to be done and when the gas fire started popping, Jordan had to threaten him with court action before he did anything about it. He occasionally gave them an obligatory twenty-four hours notice to enter and 'check things were in working order' which probably meant to confirm there was no evidence of drug-fuelled orgies and the place was kept clean and tidy, as per the strict tenancy agreement.

Sky heard him rattling about in the kitchen and when she went to investigate, found him putting some things in the fridge.

'Can I help you, Mr Dearne?' she asked.

He carried on without stopping as he replied, 'No, thank you.'

He must have known she would be wondering what he was up to and he was making her work for information.

'Can I ask what you're doing?' she said.

'I'm putting some food in this fridge,' he answered her, with a huff of annoyance at having to explain himself.

'Whose food?' she asked, pressing him for details that were essential.

'Mine,' he responded, pausing momentarily to pull up his joggers. They were stained and fraying at the bottoms. He didn't look like someone who owned four rental properties outright. She and Katy had wondered if the other three were as shabby as theirs was.

He closed the fridge door and picked up the empty cardboard box.

'I'm having some work done on my house,' he said. 'So, while that's happening I'm going to be staying here. No point in having two rooms going begging when I could be using one.'

He smiled at her as he passed and she caught a whiff of his scent which seemed to be a nasty mix of smoke and stale sweat, nothing like the Vibrant Leather fresh scent of Jordan or the sweetshop perfume of Katy.

'Besides, it'll be good for you having a male on the premises,' said Wilton, throwing the words over his shoulder. 'A bit of company for you.'

★

Amanda picked up a copy of the *Yorkshire Standard* when she was in the shop buying some milk. It was a daily paper and on Saturday there was a culinary supplement focusing in on one of the restaurants of Yorkshire. She knew that her friend Barb had been good as her word because on the front page, advertising what was inside, there were the words. 'Meet Ray Morning: Texas comes to Barnsley.'

She couldn't leave it until she got home so she took out the supplement to read in the car. The whole front cover was a full-colour photo of Ray standing behind his shiny counter. And she was amused to discover that Ray's surname was in fact 'Morning' so the 'Meet Ray Morning' tag had a double meaning and made him sound extra sunny.

> The pie is magnificent, bursting with blueberries and it comes with a quenelle of clotted cream and home-made ice cream that scores a solid twelve out of ten on the delicious scale . . .

'Oh, god bless you, Barb,' said Amanda aloud. She'd given him some real generous lineage and the photo was fabulous; there were more pics inside of a towering burger and Ray holding a plate of pie, laughing. Lord, he was hot. If this didn't get all the eligible women in the area running up to Spring Hill, nothing would. Amanda was salivating reading the descriptions of some of the dishes, Barb really had a talent for food reviewing. He hadn't got too extensive a menu, he explained, because he didn't want to drive himself or his kitchen team into an early grave. There would be a change of menu on the first of every month, but the most popular favourites would remain a constant, when he knew what they were.

Amanda found herself smiling. She'd planned to go shopping in Meadowhall this morning but it could wait. She thought she'd call up to Ray's and take a copy of this article with her, hoping that she wouldn't find him alone, drumming bored fingers on the counter. Plus there was that other thing she wanted to ask him about, which might or might not be a rubbish idea.

When she reached Spring Hill, she was delighted to see there were cars parked up. She walked in to see six booths filled up with people and a familiar face acting as serving staff: Jean had been Bettina's waitress and was in her mid-seventies. A masterstroke.

When Ray looked up and saw her, his face was split in two by a grin. He came rushing at her from behind the counter. She prepared herself for a hug, but he just took her shoulders in his hands and squeezed her. *Damn.*

'I owe you. Breakfast is on me, whatever you want.' He pushed her to an unoccupied booth and slid into the other side.

'No, no,' she protested, 'I just came to see how you were doing and to bring you one of these.' She handed him the newspaper. 'They've given you a great write-up.'

Ray took it from her. She'd already folded it to the page so he could read about himself and he gobbled up the words quickly.

'And you have Jean working here, I see?'

'She walked on in and asked for a job. I can't say I needed a waitress with no customers to serve but I found myself saying yeah, why not, I had a weird hunch. This' – he tapped the newspaper with his finger – 'is amazing. And, er . . . you must have been doing PR for me because I've had some of the place's old customers come up saying they'd heard about pensioner discounts.'

She winced slightly. 'I hope that was okay. I shouldn't really have said it, in case you didn't want to go with that suggestion.'

'Oh my goodness, yes, that was absolutely fine to say . . . And the reporter really ran with your "Meet Ray Morning" tag. I might use that on my free *Daily Trumpet* advert. You were right, they did offer me one and I said I'd come back to them with what I wanted them to print.'

'That's good news. Ray, I'd like to see if I can start a group for women and I need a venue. I have a small budget that would cover some teas and coffees and biscuits. I don't really know where to start, other than to find some place to hold it and—'

'There's a room in the back,' Ray interrupted her. 'There are chairs and a table. Wanna see?'

Well, that was rather convenient, thought Amanda. 'I'd love to.'

'Come on.' He led the way, past the loos to an adjacent door.

'I'm just using it as a storage room at present. I didn't really know what to do with it. Jean said that the previous owner used it as a smoking room in bygone days.

There was a sturdy, square table shoved against the wall and some wooden folding chairs resting in a stack beside them. The room had been painted recently, as the walls were a clean, pale grey.

'I pulled the old linoleum up and found these floorboards underneath, aren't they great?' said Ray. They were indeed, far too nice to have been covered up, though a sanding and polish would see them restored to all their former glory.

'It's a work in progress, but any good for you?'

'It's perfect,' said Amanda with a smile. She pictured herself with a group of women all sitting around the table, talking, chatting, just letting off steam about what they were going through in life, sharing things they'd learned that might be useful to others. And maybe out of those sessions suggestions might emerge about improving things in the workplace for women. She wouldn't advertise it as a focus group, though; a friendship group would be more attractive.

'What day would be best for you?'

'Take your pick,' said Ray, 'though maybe avoid Fridays and Saturdays.'

'Oh, absolutely. I was thinking of Tuesday, maybe?'

'Just tell me what you need me to do. You can have it gladly, no charge for any of it,' said Ray, opening his arms wide as if welcoming in the idea.

★

Mrs Pettifer turned up at eleven to pick up the teddy bear that Sky had mended for her. She was crying before she'd even seen it, the mere prospect of having it returned to her was enough. The finished product nearly finished her.

'It's beautiful,' she said. 'Just like it was when I bought it for him.'

'I used the pieces I had to cut off as stuffing, so not a bit has been thrown away,' said Sky.

Mrs Pettifer held the bear out at arm's length to inspect it and then pulled it to her chest, held it as she must once have held her boy. Sky could imagine the thoughts running through her mind, memories both sweet and sad vying with each other for dominance.

'I don't know how to thank you,' Mrs Pettifer said, her voice a whisper riding on a crest of tears.

'Oh, I'm just happy to help,' said Sky. 'Here, let me wrap him for you.'

Mrs Pettifer watched as Sky wrapped the bear up in white tissue paper, as she had once wrapped up her baby boy in a soft white blanket. *They are not ours to own, they are merely on loan from God above,* the priest had said at his funeral and those words had brought a modicum of comfort where there was little comfort to be had at all. She'd had to scratch for scraps of it over the years.

Her hand was shaking as she held her bank card against the machine to make payment. She put the receipt in her handbag and turned to leave with a nod and a smile, quickly, before she made even more of a fool of herself. If only she knew how many times in the repair shop they'd seen simi-lar, thought Sky: a grown man in floods of tears after Tony had mended his father's bagatelle board; the old fella who'd broken down on switching on the bakelite radio Adam had restored, which his late wife had bought him as a wedding present, and hearing, by sheer coincidence, their first dance song at their reception playing. He was convinced it was a message from her to say she was with him, and no one was going to argue with that. Things that could be mended often took the place of loved ones who couldn't, and assumed their importance. Emotions settled in possessions, wove invisible threads around them that attached themselves to people. But one day Mrs Pettifer would be gone and the teddy she treasured would be someone else's rubbish. The here and now was a treasure in itself, because it was all that was important, all they could be certain of; that much Sky knew for sure.

She wrote down the sale in her accounting book and picked up the bear she was working on now: a special bear for someone she knew just a little but liked a lot.

Her father had taught her everything she knew about her art. She'd been holding a needle since before she could read. He'd been like a bear himself, huge, mightily built, cuddly and kind, not a mean bone in his body. He was an apprentice trained upholsterer originally, who somewhere along the line had encountered the joy of toy restoring, and that became his profession. People called him 'the teddy bear man' which was sweet in the beginning, before it turned out to be his curse. How anyone could have thought he could be a killer was beyond those who knew him, but gossip got inflated by lies and people were quick to accuse, because it was human nature to need someone to blame.

This year it would be twenty years since Wayne Craven, the Pennine Prowler, had been arrested and convicted. Sky knew it would all be dragged up again and it would keep getting dragged up until the mystery of the second man was solved, even though there were too many people who remained convinced it already had been.

★

Erin typed the words 'Pennine Prowler' into her laptop. She'd meant to look him up after she last went up to Bon's shop but it slipped her mind with all the house stuff she had to do. She vaguely remembered seeing the case on *Crimewatch* and the newspaper headlines asking, '*Is This the Lancashire Ripper?*', but she was a twenty-something living her best life in London at the time, and both then and now, had no fascination with crime unlike some. She didn't want to read disturbing details, didn't want to read about people with warped personalities. Her interest, though, had been piqued by the scene between Sky and those dreadful women last Monday because it was an odd thing to insert into a conversation, those comments about growing up in the shadow of a killer, unless they had significant meaning. There was plenty of information on the case: she read a selection of stories covered by everyone from the *Daily Mail* to the *Daily Trumpet*. Give or take a few details, she got the gist of what it was all about.

The Pennine Prowler, Wayne Craven, fitted the profile of a serial killer as if he'd been moulded especially for it. He came from a dysfunctional family and was picked on and bullied at school for his small size, his pale skin, ginger hair, his light, high-pitched voice and low intellectual ability. As a grown-up, he wasn't attractive to women and how he treated them reflected the anger he felt at constantly being rejected by them, although none of them ever reported him to the police. Had they done so, and had there been a record of his DNA in the database, lives might have been saved; which caused a lot of extra heartache for these abused women in the form of survivor's guilt. He could also be glib, a smooth-talker when it suited and eventually charmed a much older woman into marrying him after a courtship too brief for her to uncover the rot in his soul. He was arrested only two months after the wedding and she never believed he was guilty, despite the damning DNA evidence and his eventual confession.

There had been a single survivor – Gillian Smith – from one of the earliest attacks, before he had refined his methods to leave no victims alive. She was found by an early morning dog walker in Skelshill, Lancashire, blue-lighted to hospital and there put into a medically induced coma to help her chances of recovery. It was nothing short of a miracle that she lived and had some, albeit sketchy and very fragmented, recall of what had happened to her on that night. She was adamant there were two men: one spoke a lot, the second remained silent and spectral, but he had been much bigger and more brutal than the other. But essential DNA evidence from that attack had been tragically lost by a young SOCO which might have confirmed the Pennine Prowler was actually a *folie à deux* , plus the police at that stage were reluctant to believe Miss Smith, given the battering she'd taken. Much later, recovered DNA from subsequent attacks suggested there was one perpetrator only and the samples obtained pulled up no matches on any database.

It also didn't help that the police were concentrating on the Lancashire side of the Pennines, where all the incidents took place. They were convinced it was a local man who knew the area inside out. They were, unbeknown to them, not too far off the mark with that as Craven had been born in one of the gritstone villages bordering Saddleworth, and moved over to Penistone with his mother when his father ran off with another woman. She returned to visit her family there often, taking young Wayne with her.

Years passed. Then Gillian Smith, by chance, happened to be in a pub in Millspring, Yorkshire where Craven was drinking and she recognised his voice. It had been unmistakable. She rang the police from the toilets. Craven was taken in for questioning and his DNA matched the saved samples. Every attack made was linked by similarities, trademarks, but there was a certain chaotic element to some of them that lent a marked difference. By now, the police experts had begun to suspect Craven might have committed *those* attacks alone but that the others had been carried out with someone else more organised and meticulous. A second man, as Gillian Smith had insisted all along.

The police had done their best since then to make Craven give this other person up. They'd leaned on him: *Why would you be happy with him out there while you are taking the rap for both of you*, they'd said, but he had stuck to his story that he'd always acted alone. That in itself had indicated that this must be someone Craven felt extremely loyal to. He was an odd personality, dysfunctional and complex, and yet he could be fiercely loyal in exchange for the smallest kindnesses: that much had been clear in prison, and conflicted with the psychiatric assessment that he was a true psychopath.

Then, five years into his sentence, he was diagnosed with an inoperable brain tumour and turned to the Church for comfort – or insurance. The police found a crack to squeeze into when Craven said he was finally ready to tell them the truth: that there *was* someone else, but he toyed with them, manipulative to the last. Maybe he really had intended to disclose the name with his dying breath, but he went downhill too rapidly to keep control of the narrative when a stroke left him unable to speak. The police interviewed him again in hospital, reeled off names of people he knew, had worked with, had worked for, was related to; people who had protected him at school, lent money to him to bury his mother, were kind to his wife when he went inside. He didn't give up the name, and slipped from them in too easy a death.

Erin found a sensationalist headline from five years ago: **WAYNE CRAVEN TOOK HIS SECRETS TO THE GRAVE ... OR DID HE?** A retired policeman had been interviewed about the cases he'd been involved with. He'd been the one at Craven's deathbed, reading out the names. He let slip a curious detail: that the only name the dying Craven responded to in any way was that of his lifelong friend: Edek Urbaniak, known locally as 'The Teddy Bear Man' because he was a restorer of toys.

'Wow,' said Erin aloud. It couldn't be a coincidence: Sky Urban, Edek Urbaniak and the bear connection. Was this her father? Is that what the blonde had meant about living under the shadow of the Pennine Prowler – *some more under it than others*?

There was a scathing article about some DNA which was lost by human error and could possibly have led to the killer or killers much earlier and saved seven women's lives. That was some cross to carry for the person who was responsible, thought Erin.

She typed in 'teddy bear man, Wayne Craven' and skimmed through the entries. She found a death notice from six years ago:

**Edek 'Eddie' Urbaniak, known affectionately as
'The Teddy Bear Man'. Penistone, died peacefully
in Juniper Hospice.**

And in the comments someone had written:

'Rot in peace, you murdering bastard.'

Chapter 12

Mel rolled up to Maltstone Garden Centre at the allotted hour, parking next to a very smart Porsche with a personalised number plate that unmistakeably belonged to Joss. She'd always been one of the golden girls who was destined to float through life on an equally golden slide, but she was too nice for anyone to begrudge her that.

She'd thought quite a bit about Joss since the phone call, pulled some old memories out of boxes. She really hoped that Joss hadn't changed too much from the fun person she'd been. Her family were minted, but she'd never lorded it over the other girls and had cringed when her dad picked her up from school in his Rolls Royce. She used to tell him to park around the corner if he was going to do that, so as not to show her up. She had a brilliant singing voice too, a strong vibrato, terrific range and she could hold a note forever. Mel was sure the music teacher, Miss East, was jealous of Joss because she never gave her solos in the choir, which was criminal. Her best mate, Sue Fletcher, had been a drummer and she'd got into the school band, but Miss East had criticised her so much that she left. Mel had applied to join it too but Miss East said there were no places for guitars in her precious band. Joss and Sue wrote songs together and were going to start up their own group and asked Mel if she fancied it; then Sue got pregnant at seventeen and that kind of brought things to a halt.

Mel walked into the café and looked around. A woman stood up and waved and Mel recognised her immediately: the adult version of the spirited schoolgirl she used to be. She looked fabulous, Her hair was all choppy and rock-chicky, fairer than Mel remembered it, but she'd aged like a fine wine – compared to Mel, who sometimes felt she was ageing like an old cheese, complete with veins and crumbling edges.

Joss opened up her arms and then closed them around Mel, who breathed in the scent of Flower by Kenzo; Mel recognised it because she'd once had it bought for her as a present but it didn't smell right on her. It did on Joss though. Mel felt as if she were being embraced by a magnificent bouquet.

'Now, it's on me, no arguments,' said Joss, sitting down and putting a menu in Mel's hands. 'Pick first and then we can talk.'

They both chose the same: quiche and salad and chips to share, a glass of white wine.

'I wish I weren't driving,' said Joss when the waitress had gone. 'I could just stay here and talk and get pissed with you. We'll have to do that another day and I don't mean waiting another thirty-odd years. Mel, it is so good to see you, you look great. How are you?'

'I'm okay, apart from an old fart memory and a dodgy knee. I daren't go to the docs because he'll just tell me to lose weight and I can't bear the shame.'

'Mel, you just look the same to me as you did at school.'

'Plus five chins.'

'Stop. There's enough people out there to put us down, we shouldn't do it to ourselves. Don't say no to HRT. Honestly, it is fabulous. I can't have it any more, alas, as I've had . . . well, you don't want to know. I'm okay now though.' She touched the wooden table with a flat palm. Mel could guess what she meant and her face creased in sympathy. Maybe she hadn't had quite the smooth ride then that Mel had imagined for her.

'Well, you look really amazing, Joss,' Mel said, because she did.

'All bought and paid for,' said Joss, poking herself in the forehead. 'If I hadn't had a bit of help I'd have had jowls down to my knees. And hair extensions. My hair's gone so thin since I went into the menopause. Yours hasn't, look at it . . .' She reached over the table and cupped a handful of it. 'It's like a fire.'

It was too; Mel was very proud of her red hair, which hadn't always been the case at school where gingers weren't *de rigueur.*

They caught up on some history and Mel was quite astounded to hear how much Joss had gone through in her life. On the upside, she'd built up a fabulously successful toiletries business and had all the trappings of wealth. On the downside, she regretted working too hard to have children, and a dysfunctional, controlling relationship had driven her to the edge of a nervous breakdown, and that had made her mind up for her that it was time to change things before it got any later. Mel's own story felt very banal alongside all that drama.

'Do you remember when Sue Fletcher and I were going to start up a band?' said Joss, laughing as she ate a chip.

'I do, then she got pregnant and left school.'

Joss's smile closed down a little, like a cloud passing over the face of the sun.

'She loved that boy. He died young and her life went into a tailspin. She's had it rough. I've been seeing quite a lot of her over the past few months.'

'I'm so sorry to hear that,' said Mel. She couldn't imagine having the gift of a child only for it to be taken away from her. Was it worse than never being able to have one? She didn't even want to think about it.

'Mum and Dad aren't getting any younger, so I thought sod it, I'll just move all my operations up here. Traz is in Australia and one of us needed to be around, though they're pretty independent, in fact it's been them looking after me over the past couple of years, if I'm honest. I'm staying with them for a while. It's so weird being back in the childhood home.'

'But at least it's *that* home. You've plenty of space. I could never imagine having to go back to my mam and dad's. There wasn't enough room to swing a mouse, never mind a cat.' She sipped her wine; it was only house wine but it tasted sweeter for the company.

'Mel . . . ' Joss took a meaningful pause before carrying on. 'Sue and I are finally putting that band together. We have a bass guitarist, a vocalist – me – Sue on drums and we'd like you to join us.'

Mel waited for Joss to crack the joke but she just sat there with her two perfect arches of eyebrows raised, waiting for a response.

'For real?' Mel answered eventually.

'Yes. Call it a mid-life crisis, call it whatever you want to call it but it is finally going to happen. We can rehearse in my parents' barn. It's just a bit of fun and I don't know if you've let your skills slide but if Status Quo can get away with three major triad chords and the occasional seventh, then so can we. It's just a bit of jamming, see where we go. Not sure we'd end up on *Top of the Pops* if they ever revived it, but who cares. What do you think?'

I think you're barmy, Mel didn't say.

'I never let them slide. I do some teaching,' she did say. Also, 'Aren't we a bit old for that?'

Joss hooted. 'Old for what? Getting together and playing some tunes. I need to get it out of my system. Jamie stripped all my self-confidence away. I feel so angry with myself that I wasted so many years being unhappy. I thought my depression and anxiety was down to being perimenopausal, probably because he used to tell me my hormones were sending me loopy, but they weren't – it was down to me being married to a control freak. So I feel as if I have been let out of a cage and yes, it might be mad but I really want to do this. Sue needs it, and can you remember Gina Adamczyk – Titch? She was the year below us at school and Miss East couldn't stand her either and wouldn't let her in the school band. She wouldn't let anyone in unless they were good on a sodding recorder. What a bloody awful sound they made. Like nails down a blackboard.'

Mel did remember Titch Adamczyk, a fellow guitar player, and the violin as well if her memory served her correctly.

'There's no pressure, but you were the first person I thought of when I decided to do this, even before I thought of asking Sue. I know you really wanted it back then. My dad's been waiting for this moment for well over thirty years. As soon as I told him he rushed off and started clearing the barn out ready. Promise me you'll think about it.'

And Mel said she would think about it, even if she wouldn't because she could just imagine what Steve would say if she announced she was off to band practice. But what she would think about more was having people around her who thought that dreams should be lived, and not shelved. That's what she would have encouraged in her child, if ever she'd been lucky enough to have one.

Chapter 13

As soon as the words came out of her mouth, Mel wished she could have caught them in the air and pushed them back down her throat. She'd had such a lovely, giddy lunch with Joss that it was spilling over, especially now her tongue was oiled with a second big glass of wine.

'Who wants you to what?' asked Steve, his loaded fork hanging by his lip, the peppercorn sauce dripping from it onto his plate.

Mel tried to underplay it then. 'Just playing music together. Like we used to when we were kids.'

'That's not what you said, though, you said you were joining a band with a load of fifty-plus women,' said Steve.

'Well, it is, sort of, but we aren't going to be doing gigs and things. Forget I said anything.'

Steve put the meat into his mouth and chewed and Mel knew that he had forgotten it already because she was not the type to go and seriously join a band. She worked in a bank, she was steady-away, not some mad impulsive creature. She wished they were both a bit more impulsive, but everything was so regimented. Like this meal: every

Saturday night she made peppercorn steak – although occasionally she'd break ranks and do a Diane sauce. Upset of world order. Then they'd watch a film or a couple of episodes of a box set and go to bed for the Saturday night conjugals. Creatures of habit. Mel would have liked it if they were more adventurous under the sheets, but they'd fallen into complacency and maybe it was too late to do anything about it now. She knew she had her part to play, putting up with the status quo, being a husband-pleaser because if he was content, she was content. She hadn't pushed to revolt against the monotony much because she knew he worked long hours and just wanted to relax at home rather than go and see a band or a film or a play. He would go if she was keen, but if his heart wasn't in it like hers was, that would sour it.

'A band, ha,' said Steve, after clearing his mouth; he'd obviously not forgotten it after all. Then he added, 'At your age.'

Mel's eyebrows crunched. 'What do you mean, "at your age"?'

'Mel, love, come on, you're fifty bloody three years old. Do you think I'd want you to make a fool of yourself?'

'If you'd said to me that you'd been accepted on an astronaut's programme, I'd have asked you all about it, and said *go for it* if that's what you really wanted to do,' said Mel, cutting into her steak with increased ferocity.

'No, you wouldn't, you'd have rung an ambulance and told them to bring a straitjacket because I'd gone bonkers. I'd certify myself!'

'No, I really wouldn't—'

'Mel, I'm glad that you've met your friend and had a nice little trip down memory lane, but face it, love . . .'

He didn't finish his sentence but he didn't have to. He meant she'd never be the next Taylor Swift and she didn't have the heart to argue with him, to tell him that's not what she wanted to be. He was only being kind, she told herself; he didn't want to see her set up for a fall.

'I told her no anyway,' said Mel.

'Thank god for that.'

Mel felt stupidly tearful all of a sudden. It wouldn't have hurt him to say, 'You should join the band, you just never know where it might lead', even if he was sure it would lead to nowhere. But he was hardly likely to do that at this age when he'd laughed about such a thing when they'd been in their early twenties.

She changed the subject. 'So you're working again tomorrow, you say?'

'I have to if I want to get this job finished. It really needed two of us on it but . . . too late for that.'

'Where is it again?'

'Over Doncaster way.' Steve flapped his hand in the vague direction of further south.

'What are you doing?' she asked, trying to sound interested, as a spouse should do.

'Taking off layers of old paper that's fused to the wall. It's a bugger to get off.'

'Whereabouts in Doncaster?'

'What is this, twenty questions?' said Steve with a laugh, but also an underlying snap in his voice which brought her up sharp. He never usually minded her asking about his job and what he was doing. He usually liked to talk about the houses he visited and the quirky things he found in them – and the quirky people – and she liked to listen to him.

'Sorry,' he said, recognising how he'd just come

across. 'I'm tired. I shouldn't have committed to working tomorrow.'

'No, you shouldn't,' agreed Mel, her voice warm with sympathy. 'You need *some* downtime after a hard week. I can't remember the last time you worked on a Sunday.'

'Needs must. I'm going to get a bath and go to bed early tonight.'

'I'll come up with you.'

'No, stay down and watch a film or something,' said Steve. 'The dragon isn't going to be tempted out of his cave tonight.'

'I didn't mean I was coming up for *that*,' Mel said, with some indignation. She wasn't some sex maniac who'd pounce on him when he was tired; what did he take her for?

He gathered up the plates when they'd finished eating, put them in the dishwasher and planted a kiss on the top of her head.

'That was lovely, that. See you when I get back tomorrow. I might be late, so don't bother having any tea ready, I'll pick something up on the road.'

He had disappeared into the hallway by the time she'd turned to reply to him. He never went to bed at this hour, even when he was working early. It all added to the weirdness of the day, because it had shifted too much silt from the seabed of her life and she wasn't sure if that was a good thing or a bad.

★

What decent landlord in his fifties thought that moving in with a twenty-six-year-old female tenant was acceptable, thought Sky as she passed by the lounge to go to her room.

It looked as if Wilton would be stationed there for the night, which put it out of bounds for her. He'd been in residence just under twelve hours and the house felt totally different already. It smelt differently, too: fustier, and when she went into the kitchen it stunk of cigarettes and she didn't want to sit in there and breathe it in, it wasn't good for her. Ordinarily she'd have enjoyed Saturday in front of the TV with her housemates, or alone if they were out. She was fine with that, because her bedroom wasn't really big enough to double up as a personal sitting room, and the sofa might have been old but it was huge and squashy and perfect for sprawling out on.

When she went up to the loo it was to find that Wilton hadn't flushed it properly after he'd used it. That was the last straw. She picked up her coat and her car keys. Adam the electrician at the repair shop had been talking about the new diner place that had opened up on Spring Hill and there had been a really intriguing piece about it in the *Yorkshire Standard*. She always bought it on a Saturday because it had a section about all the big houses for sale in Yorkshire, the dream mansions with their acres of land and many bedrooms. Even a small home of her own seemed a dream too far away with no prospect of a change on the horizon. She'd eat out rather than spend her Saturday night confined to barracks stressing, because stressing wasn't great for her health either.

She wasn't shy about taking herself off out to the cinema or for a meal. She might never have gone out at all if she were. She'd lived by herself since she was twenty, when her dad died and the lease had expired on the house they shared and the owner wouldn't renew it as he wanted to sell, so she'd had to leave it. She hadn't had any real close friends in her life, she'd mostly kept herself to herself. Her dad always said that looking back, he'd probably made a mistake not moving to another town; but then, he didn't want anyone thinking he was running away when he had nothing to run from. They'd carried on living in their little half-isolated cottage on the road out of Penistone, where, conveniently many said, no one could see any comings and goings. But there was not a scrap of evidence to support him being Wayne Craven's accomplice, although people could always manufacture it if they were keen enough, and they had.

The criminal profiler had said that Craven's accomplice was bound to be someone like him: bullied, indolent, glib, flitting from job to job with a wasteground of broken relationships behind him. That alone should have set her father completely out of the frame for no one could have been more solid in every way, loving and faithful to his family than big Eddie Urbaniak. He'd spent everything he had on consultations and treatments to make his wife well again, and when he couldn't, his focus became on bettering the quality of her remaining life. Then he'd had to bring up his daughter single-handedly when his wife died way too young.

So what that he'd gone to school with Wayne Craven and stood up for him as a boy because he couldn't stand up for himself and was kind to him as an adult? He had been kind to everyone. So what that when his name was mentioned to Wayne Craven on his deathbed, Craven had smiled? All that meant was that Craven remembered that Eddie had been consistently good to him, the only person who ever had. But every time the story was revived in the press, the whole flimsy rumour machine started up again. Some people, Sky knew, *wanted* the second man to be a big, gentle

Polish-born bloke who made and mended teddy bears for a living, because that would make an entertaining story. And one of them, for sure, was Angel Sutton.

The diner looked inviting, and a really nice man, who introduced himself as Ray, showed her to one of the booths in a quiet corner. There were a couple of flyers tucked between the salt and pepper pots on the table. One said: **LADIES OF ALL AGES: MAKE NEW FRIENDS. TUESDAY FRIENDSHIP CLUB 6 P.M.** and she didn't consciously commit that to memory, but it happened all the same.

She chose a burger and a moon-pie-flavoured milk shake and tried not to think about creepy Wilton Dearne who was waiting for her back home.

★

Mel clicked on her laptop. She was fed up and Saturday night TV was rubbish. She'd flicked through Netflix, Paramount Plus and Prime, and despite all the offerings, there was none that took her fancy.

She felt a bit sly really going onto Facebook, but she was just curious for a reason she couldn't name. She found social media a bore at best, couldn't see the point of taking a picture of your dinner and posting it online to entertain folk, but the devil made work for idle hands, as they said. She wanted to see if there were any photos of Steve's school reunion. She wanted to see if there were any photos of Saran Sykes.

She was easy enough to find because, even though her status was married, she was still using her maiden name. Her profile picture showed her wearing a pink tunic in a beauty salon but the header was a group shot of what was obviously the party at the school. She was bang in the centre with Steve at one side of her, his arm draped around her shoulder. She looked glam, perfectly blonde, tanned, a cracking figure; great arms that she was happy to show off in a glittery top with no sleeves; boobs that worked against gravity; big snoggy lips. Her wall showed loads of photos of the night. There she was dancing, chinking glasses with other women, laughing, having a great time. On another, someone else was in main focus larking around, but she was in the background with Steve. Her back was to the wall and she was smiling up at him as if he'd said something amusing, or sweet. Steve looked good in the photos: handsome, happy. There he was again with her, and they were talking animatedly by the look of it, behind them was a row of three blokes doing the can-can. It was odd seeing him with another woman so close, looking like a couple. Mel felt the stirrings of something alien in her gut, a silly, acid jealousy that was pathetic, but she felt it all the same.

Chapter 14

Astrid unlocked the door of the repair shop and waited for the beep of the alarm to start up that would give her a count of ten to key in the code, but it didn't, which was odd.

She walked in cautiously, sensing she wasn't alone.

'Hello?' she called and nearly jumped out of her skin when she saw a figure jerk to a sitting position from a supine one on a velvet chaise longue that Peter was re-covering for a client. Astrid shrieked and so did the figure. Astrid dived for the light switch.

'Who the hell are you? Come out und show theesen,' she barked.

'Astrid, it's me,' said a familiar voice.

'Sky?' Astrid patted her chest in relief. 'What are you doing here in the dark?'

'I was finishing something and I thought I'd take five minutes. I must have nodded off,' Sky stretched the cricks out of her back. The chaise wasn't the most comfortable thing to lie on, but she'd needed a solid sleep she couldn't get at home – although it didn't even feel like home any more. Wilton had been living there for just over a week now and rather than it being the temporary stay she'd hoped, he had brought more of his things over and set up a load of gaming stuff in the lounge.

'My goodness, what could be so important that you were working at this blumming time?' asked Astrid.

'Do you want to see?' said Sky. She went over to her work bench. She reached into the drawer and pulled something out that was wrapped in blue tissue. She handed it to Astrid.

'I wanted to finish it because it's late. I was hoping to have it done for your birthday but I got held up on another job and I didn't want to rush it.'

Astrid's hands reached over tentatively; she hadn't expected anything. She didn't know Sky well enough to be on present-exchanging footing, even if, from what she knew of her, she did think the young woman was a treasure.

'I heard you talking one day,' said Sky. 'I knew this birthday was going to be hard for you, with it being the first one without Kev.'

Astrid took a teddy bear out of the tissue paper. He was dressed just as Kev used to dress in jeans with a shirt, sleeves rolled up, waistcoat and a Peaky Blinders tweed cap. There was a gold bracelet around his wrist, a replica of the one that Astrid now wore around hers. There were even tiny business cards, miniatures of the ones Kev had, with 'Cutthroat Kevin, Barber's Shop Memorabilia' printed on them and tucked into the back pocket of his jeans; plus a leather wallet with a tiny photo of Astrid in it, which Sky had drawn.

Astrid had to sit down before her legs gave way.

'I asked around,' said Sky. 'Bon told me that Kev always carried a picture in his wallet of you. I asked in the Pot of Gold if any of the antiques dealers had photos that I could borrow so I could get the details right.'

Astrid stroked the bear's mutton-chops beard, darkest brown with the merest peppering of grey. Sky had even stitched in the little mole under his eye. The bear's brown eyes shone, she'd even got the lopsided smile that Astrid would always remember. She broke down.

Sky was horrified.

'Oh god, Astrid, I didn't want to do this to you. I'm so sorry, I thought it would cheer you up.'

'*Ach!* You have no idea, I am so happy,' said Astrid, tears flooding out of her, looking as if she had sprung a leak. She was hugging the bear close to her chest, sniffling, smiling, crying, a mess of emotion. She pushed the bear out to arm's length to study him again.

'Kev, you are the most beautiful bear I have ever seen,' she said. 'I will treasure you for ever.' She cuddled the bear again before wrapping him carefully back into the tissue, then she picked up her bag of equipment. 'I have to clean now and then I will take little Kev home. I don't think I will ever be able to thank you enough, Sky. I know how much work goes into your Sky Bears. You must let me pay you—'

'Oh no, no, no,' Sky protested. 'It was something done in my spare time, and it's a gift and you must always accept a gift because if you block the flow of receiving, the energy gets all clogged up. That was what my dad always said. It's bad luck, bad karma.'

'Well, thank you, then I will,' said Astrid, quietly, choked. 'You must go home now and to a proper bed.'

'Yes, I will,' replied Sky, though the prospect filled her with dread. She felt like a spare part in the house and she wondered if Wilton's design was to have her pack up and leave because he couldn't have been so naturally gross, he had to have been putting extra effort in. The wording in the tenancy agreement was very clear that the house should be respected and no smoking inside it, and yet he puffed away like an addicted chimney and left a trail wherever he went. She didn't want to breathe it in, it was bad for her and she had to look after herself. She couldn't even leave any towels or toiletries in the bathroom because she knew he'd use them. She didn't want to engage in small talk with him in the kitchen; they had nothing in common. No, she didn't want to go for a drink with him, thank you. No, she didn't want to watch a film with him in the lounge, she had work to do. The house rattled with the sound of his snoring and only a thin, hollow, plasterboard wall separated his bed from hers.

She wished that Astrid hadn't turned up because her extended nap on the chaise was the best sleep she'd had since Katy left. She could feel the stress of the situation impacting on her and it couldn't be allowed to. But what else could she do but put up and shut up?

When she got home, she went straight into her bedroom and pushed her chair up against the handle before getting undressed. It was now an issue not having a lock on her door, because she was sure that Wilton was poking around in her things when she was out. She'd left a trap for him before she went to work on Saturday, a pair of black pants at an angle to a pair of pink ones in her drawer, and they'd been moved.

She slid in between her sheets and pressed her head against the pillow. She closed her eyes, but a faint familiar smell of smoke poked at the back of her nose. She pushed her face deeper into the pillow and it was even stronger.

She flicked on the bedside light and examined her pillow

and there she found two long hairs the colour of Wilton Dearne's. He'd not only been snooping in her room, but lying in her bed. Disgusted, she got up, ripped off the sheets and spread a fresh one over the mattress. She was too weary to tuck it in, so pulled the undressed duvet over her body just as it was.

Enough, was her last thought of the day. *Enough*.

Chapter 15

On the day of Amanda's first friendship club at Ray's, Linus caught up with her on the Mon Enfant corridors of power to ask how things were going. He said he'd collated loads of information and ideas from the internet, but he'd like to run it past her to see what was viable. He'd heard about a company initiative where employees were given menopause gift bags. They included a paperclip, to keep everything together; a pencil, to write down things before they were forgotten; and jelly babies, in case the women wanted to bite someone's head off. He didn't say any more because the cringe showing in Amanda's expression adequately answered the question, *was this a good idea?*

She wouldn't have taken offence at such a present, she said, because it was all about the intention, which sounded well-meaning, if clumsy; but some might. And there were more practical and less jokey things that a gift bag might contain: cooling mist, for instance, a fan, a sachet of superblend tea. She'd put her thinking cap on.

Philip was on holiday that week so the office had a much lighter vibe and that was contributing to her good mood.

She'd woken up to the sound of her alarm, and realised that she had slept a full seven hours and hadn't had to get up to use the loo or wring out a cold cloth to put on her face. It was a blessed relief. The HRT was starting to work, she knew it, and she wondered why she'd been so bloody stupid in not seeking help before, but soldiering on. 'I thought it was just all natural,' she'd told the doctor on the Zoom call. 'It is, but you don't have to put up with it,' had been her answer.

She liked her job, it was the best one she'd ever had and she'd had a few over the years. She'd got used to the half-hour commute to the near side of Huddersfield which was easy enough, and the people were, on the whole, a good bunch. She was paid well, but then she had worked her way steadily up the ranks; there were plenty of perks; she knew the industry inside out and she was respected by everyone, apart from Philip who she suspected was jealous that she was by far the better person for the job of running the department. She had been offered the position but had had to turn it down, because at the time, her mother had a health blip and Amanda just didn't want to take on extra responsibility.

She might have liked her job ... but sitting at a desk wasn't what she had ever planned to do with her life. From an early age, she'd wanted to be a chef, to work in a kitchen, wear whites, create; a pastry chef, more than any other department. Her mother had said she was daft for thinking of making buns as a career and should get a proper job. She'd had a place at catering college lined up, but her mother wouldn't help her out with the finance she needed. She said she wouldn't throw good money away on silly ideas – and cooking for a living was a silly idea.

So Amanda had got a job to earn some money to pay

for her course. It would be expensive in London but where better to go, she thought. But she'd never gone. Her mother had had an operation and needed her to stay around to help her look after Bradley. So she put off going for another year and that year became two . . .

Then she met someone and the relationship wouldn't have survived if she'd moved south. It didn't survive anyway. She didn't blame anyone for her giving up her dream, because she could have said *sod it* to them all and gone, but no one had ever instilled any confidence in her, any faith in herself, and when she eventually got some, it was too late to go to London because she'd have been the oldest student in town.

Years passed and her mother became more and more reliant on her always being around 'in case', because, as Ingrid said, 'it's a daughter's duty to look after her mother'. Which was rich, seeing as she didn't talk to her own, and had stuffed her into a nursing home rather than care for her. Amanda caved in to the pressures of duty, living a second-best life, always hoping that one day her mum would just tell her she loved her and mean it. Pathetic, she knew it was, for a daughter to crave the same validity as a son.

Amanda knew everything about the products of Mon Enfant and their competitors: the best cots, the newest toys, the most comfortable nursing chairs and yet she'd never had that maternal pull. That's what she'd told people anyway; the truth of it was that she'd fought it with every fibre of her being, because she couldn't bear the thought of bringing a child into the world whom she found unable to love, as her own mother had.

★

Astrid sat in Ray's diner having a coffee and a pastrami-on-rye sandwich, which was delicious. She'd gone up there on the pretext of asking if the owner needed a cleaner, but he'd taken on Bettina Boot's old one. She was feeling quite low because she'd been up to clean the house of her last remaining oldie, Mr John, and his daughter had been there. They'd decided to move him down to Cambridge with them. They'd been asking him for a long time; they had a big pile in the country and he'd have his own space but he'd always refused 'until the day came', he'd said. And it had now, because his only remaining friend had just died. Another loss to get used to, another change.

The diner was lovely, Astrid thought. Bright and cheery, the opposite of how she felt, because she felt dark inside, lonely and sad. A webbing had grown over the raw grief but too often it broke and she felt cut apart all over again. She plastered a smile on her face because she never wanted to bring anyone else down, be a *joy sponge,* but sometimes that smile needed too much scaffolding to hold up.

The owner – Ray – reminded her of Kev in a way, with lips that defaulted naturally to a smile, though Ray was a lot more handsome than Kev who had had, in his own words, the face of a bashed crab. Ray's features together worked in wonderful facial harmony. So had Kev's, but in a less conventional way.

And Kev had been much bigger of course. Both Kev and Astrid seemed to have been made by a god who had been working to an augmented scale, and they liked that they were different together. Kev looked like someone you wouldn't want to meet up a dark alley if you didn't know who he was – but if you did know him, then he was exactly the sort of man you'd want to meet up a dark alley, because there was none better to safely escort you home. He had the kindest eyes. Texan Ray had the same sort of eyes, sparkly and genial.

She missed Kev as fiercely as she had loved him when he was alive, and she still couldn't get her head around the fact that someone so big, so strong, so *vital* could be felled by some fucking tiny bacteria. There was quite a renowned grief club that took place every Wednesday in the teashop in Spring Hill Square and she'd considered going, but she could hear Kev's voice in her head: *'Never mind sitting around talking about me and crying, I want you to go out, Astrid, and enjoy yourself'*, because he was a life-is-for-living kind of guy. He wouldn't be happy looking down and seeing her so lost, so unfulfilled.

She idly picked up one of the flyers slotted between the condiments on the table and saw that it was advertising a friendship club for women of all ages on Tuesdays at 6 p.m. *'No need to book, just turn up.'*

She felt a small poke in between her shoulder blades, a nerve twitch as if someone had tapped her. And in her imagination she heard Kev's voice saying, *'Something like that is exactly what you need, love.'*

★

That afternoon, Amanda had eavesdropped on a conversation that two of her colleagues were having by the coffee machine. One was house-hunting and telling the other about a service called Scopesearch. It cost a tenner to register and allowed you to search on prospective properties: mortgage providers, subsidence, flood damage, Radon gas, disputes with neighbours, previous house sale information, up-to-date valuation. 'It's brilliant. It's what solicitors use and far more detailed than Zoopla,' they were saying.

As Amanda walked back to her department, she repeated the name over and over so she wouldn't forget it, which was a distinct possibility, and then wrote it down as soon as she got to her desk. She wondered if the HRT would ever start to work so well that she'd retain information for as long as she used to, in the days when she could follow even the lengthiest questions on *University Challenge*.

★

That dreaded voice again.

'Sky, I'd hoped you'd be here.'

And no Mrs van der Meer around to save her this time. She could have done without this today because Sky had a headache prodding at her temple, thanks to a night of broken sleep. She was on edge all the time in that house now; it was awful living with Wilton Dearne and his odours.

Angel was by herself on this occasion, so she had no one to play up to.

'Do you restore tools in this shop, do you know? My grandfather is seventy in September and no one knows what to buy for him, but after leaving here last time I suddenly had a mad idea.'

Sky didn't ask her what the mad idea was, she wasn't at all interested in any of the Suttons. They saw themselves as big fish in a small pond, all of them. Angel's grandfather Archie had started off as a tradesman but had wisely bought up a lot of the cheap property around Barnsley with his profits. His son now ran 'the empire', as the Suttons called it and both of them were considered arrogant tossers to deal with.

They didn't care; wealth was the only measure of worth they needed and they even revelled in their rather imperious reputation.

'Yes, you need to see Jock of All Trades,' said Sky, pointing down to the far end of the shop.

'What are you working on?' asked Angel. 'I mean, I know it's a bear. Is it a new one or a mend?'

'It's new,' replied Sky. A stock piece. She was just stitching the growler into his tummy. It had to be positioned correctly, her dad had taught her: *the holes always facing the back seam, so when he is picked up for a cuddle he makes a noise of contentment.*

Angel gasped as a fresh idea hit her. 'Oh my, what if you were to make grandy a bear. I'd pay you, obviously.'

Obviously.

'The waiting list is over a year,' said Sky, thinking quickly. She didn't want one of her precious Sky Bears looking anything like Archie Sutton. He'd stoked the fire about her dad being the associate of Craven the Prowler, saying that they'd been at school together and 'the Pole' had protected Craven from bullies. And that he'd let him visit his house while his young daughter was there. *Now didn't that just tell you how close they were?* Sutton had given Craven plenty of casual work, so his name had also been on the list of 'persons of interest', something that he'd found highly amusing. Everyone else found it risible, too, to think that he could have had any involvement: but somehow, an amiable man who mended toys and had never crossed swords with anyone was higher up on the list of suspects than someone most people found to be grandiose at best and intimidating, even threatening, at worst.

'Couldn't you squeeze it in?'

'Not a chance, sorry.'

'Please, please, please?'

'Honestly, I can't.'

'Really? Not even for me?'

Especially not for you. 'I'm already behind on orders, I'm afraid.'

Angel sighed impatiently. 'Oh well, that's a shame. I would have paid extra too,' She flicked her hair over her shoulder. It was expertly dyed blonde, the same shade as Sky's own natural colour. Angel had always made fun of Sky's hair at school, said it was transparent because Sky bleached it with Domestos. And yet here she was, doubtless spending a fortune on trying to get the identical tone, and then interspersing it with extensions sold from their heads by impoverished Eastern European women.

'Well, I'd better get on, where do I go?' asked Angel, flashing her ultra-white perfect smile. She was very pretty, but then her mother had been a model apparently. It helped that she could afford the nails, the most expensive make-up, the beauty therapy; the T-shirt with Chanel emblazoned across the front and double-C diamond earrings – they'd be the real thing. A glossy, sparkly, smooth veneer concealing a rotten core, because Sky didn't believe for one second that Angel Sutton had changed an iota in the ten years since they'd last been at school together.

Ten years wasn't enough by half to forget what misery she'd caused Sky at school. Only once had Sky turned, when Angel and her gang were following Sky home and one of them had said, 'Do you think he killed her mother as well?' And Sky had turned and swung her loaded satchel, which had knocked big Bronty Konig flying. It hadn't stopped anything then. And Angel smiling at her and being polite and wheedling for a favour didn't soften any of Sky's feelings for her now.

'Like I said, you want Jock of All Trades, under the blue sign,' said Sky.

'Excellent. Well, see you again.' She sounded so well-mannered, so butter-wouldn't-melt.

Sky felt the tension drop from her shoulders as soon as Angel Sutton turned and made her way down to Jock. She switched her attention back to the bear, trying to stem the flood of unbidden memories that came to her every time that dreadful woman was in her orbit, when Bon's voice broke in and scattered them for her.

'Who was that?' He put a coffee down on her work surface. 'I made you one. You haven't taken a break all day.'

'Thank you,' said Sky, feeling heat rising in her cheeks. She always felt warmer in his presence, as if he were a sun and she a small, insignificant planet.

'So . . . friend or foe?' He asked. 'I overheard you saying you couldn't make her a bear. I don't think I've ever known you turn a job down before.'

He'd been listening to her, then.

'The office door was open, I wasn't snooping,' he said, as if he somehow knew what she was thinking.

'Foe,' said Sky in a low voice. 'One of the Sutton family, you're bound to have come across them. They think they own this area.'

'Yes, I know them,' said Bon, with a slow nod. He knew that Shaun McCarthy, the developer and owner of Spring Hill Square had had a couple of run-ins with the patriarch of the Sutton family, when he'd refused to sell him some adjoining land. No one forced Shaun to do what he didn't want to do and it hadn't gone down well with the Suttons.

Maybe it was a family trait that they couldn't accept things not going their way.

'I try and avoid her, but she caught me today. And a couple of weeks ago, when your wife kind of chased her off for me by buying a bear.'

Your wife. Bon felt now that he couldn't ignore the fact that she wasn't any more. It would have been weird not to say so: actively lying, rather than just not declaring it.

He wet his lips in preparation for letting the truth out of them.

'Mrs van der Meer is . . . no longer my wife.' The words, once spoken, sounded odd, deceitful. And from the look on Sky's face, he'd confused her in his attempt to bring transparency.

'We actually split up three years ago, but it was entirely amicable. Our divorce finally came through recently.'

'Oh,' was all Sky said, belying the maelstrom of thoughts in her head. *Three years?* Did that mean he must have wanted Erin back, not to have said anything, carrying on the pretence of them still being a couple, hoping that he'd never have to admit to it, hoping they'd mend whatever was broken between them? She should have been overjoyed to learn that he was unattached, but somehow the discovery had the opposite effect. Maybe he suspected what she felt about him, and had held up his marriage as a shield to fend her off. She had no right to be taken into his confidence but still, she felt insulted, hurt; there was no relief.

And Bon saw her eyes flickering and blinking, an indication of the activity that must be happening behind them.

'It's nice you're still good friends,' said Sky then, gathering every scrap of self-preserving strength inside her. 'Thank you for the coffee.'

It sounded like the dismissal it was. She needed distance from him, to think about what it all meant, because it did mean something, she was sure of it.

'Your turn to make them next time,' he said, in a bid to end their interchange on a friendly note. He hadn't expected to feel as he did for revealing such a small truth, but the clarity had brought with it a complication that he didn't really understand.

Chapter 16

As Mel sat in the doctor's surgery waiting for the nurse to take a blood sample and check out her vitamin levels, she picked the least tatty offering from the magazines on the middle table. She chose the glossy mag supplement from the *Yorkshire Standard*, which had a picture on the front of a bloke in the middle of an American diner. She knew where it was, because she'd been there, but just the once because it hadn't been her cup of tea – a pensioner's café, dark and a bit grotty, she remembered. It couldn't be more different from that now. She thought it would be worth a try, a treat for Steve – and herself, somewhere new. They sometimes went out for a curry or a Chinese with his brother Dave and whichever girlfriend he happened to have at the time. They all looked the same, petite, much younger than him and pretty, and it wasn't worth getting to know them because they'd change so often. His wife had been lovely and she and Mel had become friends, but when their marriage had ended so acrimoniously, she'd buried the whole family in the metaphorical grave with him and that was that. Steve and Dave's mother declared her the devil incarnate because no one had ever been good enough for her immaculate conceptions: Mel included.

She decided to be spontaneous and book them a table at the diner for tonight. He'd probably protest and say he was tired, and to that she'd say that she was as well but couldn't be bothered cooking, so someone else was going to do it. He'd grumble a bit but he'd go along with her. It looked great from the photos and there was steak and eggs on the menu and Steve would find it very hard to grumble with his gob full of that.

Her name flashed up on the moving sign above reception. *Melinda English, go to Nurse Beckett's room.* She got up and walked down the corridor, hoping that Nurse Beckett would find out what her system was lacking that was causing the odd underlying anxiety that she couldn't shake, like staring at a picture where everything looked right but you knew something was wrong and couldn't find what. Maybe it was a new symptom of the menopause, another one to add to the list, but it was interfering with her sleep and she wanted to nip it in the bud.

She didn't have it bad compared to some, she knew. Her memory was a bit crappier than it used to be, though she never forgot a note of music, and she got a few twinges in her joints that she knew might lessen if she dropped a stone. She wasn't exactly ready for growing a trunk, but her BMI was in the orange sector of the chart. Then again, she hadn't been what it said she should weigh since she was fifteen and mere skin and bone. She'd never get back to that, she'd look poorly. One of the girls at work said she was 'comely', like a sexy milkmaid which was sweet. And a little extra timber certainly hadn't interfered with her love life. Her libido was still working fine, though it was a shame she was so reliant on someone else pulling it out of the cupboard when it was required. They hadn't had sex again on Saturday. Whatever she did to try and rev him up, Steve remained as floppy as a dead snake, and when she'd said that she was going to the doctors next week and should she ask for some advice for him while she was there he'd blown a gasket. *There's nothing wrong wi' me*, he'd said, then he'd rolled rudely over and gone straight to sleep and she'd lain in bed worrying about that as well. She hoped all it would take to send her back to un-anxiety land was a zinc, a magnesium or a strong Vit C once a day.

★

Bradley was back from Turkey. Amanda's mother greeted her at the door with the good news when she called in to make her tea. 'Ooh and he's brought me the most beautiful tray thing for bits and pieces,' she cooed, showing it off. Tourist tat that was actually an ashtray, as the grooves around the edge indicated. It had 'Antalya' painted in the middle and a scene of sea and sand. To her mother it was better than a Fabergé egg.

'Very nice,' replied Amanda, admiring it for her mother's sake. She needed to see Bradley and tell him what was happening with their mother's house; the time for asking him was over. Also she wanted to see his cosmetic dentistry. He'd developed a way of talking over the previous years to keep his teeth hidden because the results of his poor dental hygiene left much to be desired, so it would be funny to see him showing off a fine set of expensive gnashers. And if that meant she was evil, then so be it. She'd go round soon and try and catch him in after work. She might even be invited in to see the new gloss white kitchen.

'I can't stay long, Mum,' said Amanda, serving up a baked potato, cheese and beans. 'I'm opening up a new club for women tonight. It's the first one. It's in the café that Bettina Boot used to have. It's an American diner now.'

'Bettina Boot didn't know one end of a kettle from the other,' said Ingrid with a huff.

'Nooo. You're getting her mixed up with someone else.'

'She broke up my marriage to Arnold, that trollop.'

The words rang out as if they had been sounded by a bell. 'What?'

'It was her fault he left me. They're still living together.' Ingrid plunged her fork into her baked potato. 'It's her son that inherited his money when he died.'

That made no sense and Amanda realised straightaway that Ingrid was talking rubbish, even if a stranger would have found her statements totally convincing because it wasn't the delivery of them but the content. She opened up her mouth to put her mother right but she went with it instead, to try and find out what was going on in her mum's head.

'I think they split up a long time ago. That's what I heard.'

'Who?' asked Ingrid.

'Bettina Boot and Arnold.'

Ingrid pulled a face. 'What are you talking about, *Bettina Boot and Arnold*? Have you gone daft?'

Amanda shivered. She really did need to speak to her brother about their mum. There was an acceleration at work here she didn't like at all.

★

Sky sold ten of her bears that afternoon. A woman who had seen the article about the repair shop in the magazine

Up North had journeyed down from Harrogate to check it out, specifically the Sky Bears. She had a shop called Plush in the centre of town and was always on the lookout for craftspeople's wares. She had customers all over the world who would be interested in commissioning bears, she said. It sounded very exciting, except Sky just couldn't whip up the joy today. A long bath and then a takeaway pizza shared with Katy would have sorted her out, but those days were gone.

They texted each other occasionally to check in. Katy was beyond glad she'd moved out but said she missed her, and they must get together soon but she and Ozzy were off to Canada to stay with his brother in a couple of weeks, so after that. She was horrified about Wilton moving in.

'Sky, he can't do that, surely?'

'Well, I think he can really, he's his own tenant.'

'You have to get out of there, Sky. This is no good for you at all.'

Katy and Jordan were the only people in whom she'd fully confided about her health problems, because they'd been living here together when Sky had to go into hospital for her hysterectomy. The two of them had looked after her, helped her recover, made her meals, forbade her from lifting anything for weeks. But she'd had to give Katy the full picture of her complicated health history, over and above the need for an early hysterectomy, because when Katy had witnessed Sky having an attack of angina one time, she'd been ready for ringing an ambulance. She'd cried watching her friend spray under her tongue, bringing herself out of it. Thank god the attacks didn't happen too often; but stress had the power to change that.

'Sky, really,' Katy was firm. 'I worry about you. Promise me you'll get out.'

'I promise,' returned Sky; she just didn't say when that would be. It wasn't so easy simply to cut and leave. She was hoping the five months left on her tenancy agreement would go quickly; she had no choice but to wait it out or lose her money and her bond and she just couldn't afford to do that. When she'd pored over the details of her tenancy agreement, it was clear that she only had exclusive rights to her room and no say in who else lived in the house. Even if she had a case for Wilton trying to rebrand their 'relationship' as owner-lodger, rather than landlord-tenant, reporting him to the private housing team on the council would all take time and stir up all manner of crap for her if she dared.

Wilton was boiling kidneys in the kitchen and the smell had permeated the whole house, slipping under the gap of Sky's door and stinking out her room. She squirted some perfume around but it wasn't strong enough to prevail in the battle of the odours, and she felt the first pricks of the familiar tightening in her chest. She sat down on the bed: breathing deeply, hoping the attack would pass before she needed her spray. *The perfect end to a perfect day.*

She'd felt flat and confused earlier when Bon had told her that Mrs van de Meer wasn't really Mrs van de Meer. He hadn't taken her into his confidence, because she was nothing to him but someone who paid him a fee for space in his shop. Yes, he might be polite to her and make her the odd coffee, but that was all it was, and she'd be fooling herself if she imagined there might be any more. She'd stolen off home when she'd seen that Bon was on a call in his office. Usually she'd shout goodnight, but today she'd let him read into her silence what he would.

She remembered that there was a friendship club up at the new diner tonight, and though going to something like that wasn't really what she would ordinarily have done, who knew, maybe she would meet some friends? And if she didn't, then she could kill a couple of hours rather than spend it in the company of a yeasty, vile landlord and that smell of boiling offal.

Chapter 17

Amanda was stupidly nervous as she sat on a table nearest the counter in the diner. She checked her watch. No one had come in yet, but then again it was only just a quarter to six.

'Relax,' said Ray. 'If they come, they come. If they don't, then you and I have a lot of cookies to eat between us.'

He smiled at her, winked, and Amanda tried not to feel as gooey inside as one of his cookies. He'd baked a batch for her, and they were sitting in the back room on the table with the coffee and tea dispensers and jug of juice. He refused to give her an invoice, because of all she'd done for him in starting the ball rolling, even though she'd said it was the company's money and not her own. 'Next time I will,' he'd replied. 'This time, it's on me.'

He tapped her hand because, though she didn't normally bite her fingernails, her teeth were playing with them.

'You're going to be a wreck by six,' said Ray. 'I can see myself having to perform the kiss of life on you by quarter past.'

Oh god, if only, she thought and then had a micro panic

because the voice in her head was so loud she worried she might actually have said that aloud.

'Excuse me, we have a booking,' said a red-haired woman who had just walked up to the counter. She had a man in tow behind her who was looking around, taking it all in. The diner was three-quarters full tonight, which was great. Both Ray and the kitchen were buzzing. As Ray was showing them to a table, a lone woman walked in and approached Amanda.

'Excuse me, do you work here? Is this where the women's group is?'

That's one, said Amanda inwardly, with an imaginary fist-pump. 'Yes, just go down there to your left, there's a sign on the door. Help yourself to refreshments.'

She didn't need telling twice, Amanda thought, watching her march down to the meeting room.

Another woman came in; young, pale, pretty, unsure.

'You here for the friendship group?' asked Amanda.

'Yes, that's right.'

Two then; thank you, God, she said to herself. It was better to be Billy-few-mates than Billy-no-mates.

★

Mel noticed the events flyer on the table when she picked up the drinks menu. They had a women's friendship club here on Tuesday nights. That might have been a nice thing to attend had she not been here with Steve. She would have liked to have joined something like that. She'd seen a couple of adverts in the local paper for start-up groups but they tended to be for knitters or stitchers or pensioners and she wasn't a fit for any of those. She'd joined a book group once and it had been dominated by a married couple who wrote stories together and considered themselves the definitive voices of all things literary. It had been enough to put her off reading for life.

'Are you having a starter?' she asked Steve, who had a face like a slapped arse. He'd just wanted to have a shower and eat the pie that was in the fridge, sit and watch the TV, not get togged up and go out, he'd moaned. She'd answered that there was nothing on the TV worth seeing on Tuesdays and putting a pair of jeans on and a polo shirt was hardly getting done up like a dog's dinner. They were only going out for a bite and she wanted a night off cooking. He'd relented, of course, but hardly with leaps of joy.

The menu looked lovely and as a waitress walked past with a burger, the smell of it drifted up Mel's nose and made her stomach growl with hunger.

'There's a pie on the menu if you still fancy one,' she commented.

'I can read, Mel.'

She bit her lip. It seemed that whatever she said at the moment, he was short with her. Her blood test results that she'd had back super-quick that afternoon showed that she had no vitamin nor mineral deficiencies, so her niggling anxiety wasn't down to a chemical imbalance. She'd come to the conclusion that the problem wasn't her; it was him. Something was off with him and she was absorbing it, but she'd learned over the years that the more she pushed him to talk about things he was uncomfortable with, the more he retreated into a shell or a cave or whatever it was that men from Mars hid in. That bloody book gave the male species a legitimate 'I can't do anything about it, it's in my nature' excuse to act like knobheads, in her opinion. But it wasn't half annoying when she was here trying to give him a treat and he seemed hell bent on bringing her down.

'The burger for me, please,' she announced when the waitress came to take their order. 'Extra cheese and the sticky sauce.'

'Steak and eggs then. Medium rare,' said Steve, as if someone had put their hand down his throat and forcibly pulled the choice from him.

They sat in silence, Mel wondering how long it would take for him to spark up some conversation. She'd love to have known what was going on in his head, because something was; he was somewhere else, not here with her where he should have been.

'How's the job in Donny going?' asked Mel eventually, wearing her best tolerant smile. She was determined to make him enjoy this evening. 'You must have nearly finished by now.'

'It's going,' said Steve. 'Slowly. I've got an overnight tomorrow.'

'Another one?' He usually hated overnights and did everything he could to avoid them because, he said, he liked his own bed too much. 'That's a shame.'

He shrugged. 'It is what it is.'

'. . . Until it isn't,' she finished off the saying with a trill of laughter. It was something his dad always said, and that Steve had adopted without even being aware of it. 'I bet you'll be glad to see the back of it.' It had been hanging around his neck for too long and maybe that's why he was raggy-tempered and couldn't get it up in bed on Saturday night. She really shouldn't have said anything about asking for medical advice on his behalf; she'd felt bad about that ever since.

'Nice in here, isn't it?' said Mel, watching the woman

with the dark-brown hair who'd been sitting by the counter when they walked in direct a couple of ladies around the corner, and she wondered if that was where the women's club was being held.

'It's a bit . . . "café" for me,' replied Steve, casting his eyes around. From the expression on his face, Mel guessed he wasn't as impressed as she was. Although, the mood he was in recently, even Versailles would have come up short.

'Look at the puddings they do,' said Mel, picking up the menu again and pointing to the back page.

'I'm not having a pudding,' said Steve. 'I need to lose some weight.'

You need to lose the black cloud more, thought Mel. A slice of Mississippi Mud Pie might have cheered him up. He almost always had a dessert when they ate out.

'Is everything okay?' she asked softly. She knew she shouldn't really, but her caring nature insisted she pose the question.

Steve twitched. 'Yeah. Why would you ask that?' Then he added pointedly, 'Again.'

'I don't know, you just seem . . . not like yourself.'

'I wish you'd stop asking me if I'm okay. I won't be if you keep on.'

'I worry about you. I don't want work getting on top of you.'

'I've been a painter and decorator since I was sixteen years old, Mel. It doesn't get on top of me.' He took a long sip of lager as if it was a full stop on the conversation.

'It's just that we're not getting any younger. I bet you don't race up the ladders like you used to,' she said, knowing that his back sometimes gave him gyp. It was another wrong thing to say.

'What's that supposed to mean?'

'I'm just saying that ... well, jobs where you're up and down ladders, physical jobs, stretching ... they'll take a toll on you, maybe earlier ... than if you sat at a desk ... '

She hadn't really meant to go that deeply into it, it was just a throwaway line.

'It's you going to the doctors to work out what's wrong with you, worrying that a spot is the start of a tumour, so don't go projecting your health issues onto me.'

That stung. She wasn't that worried that the little lump on her head was anything nasty, but it was best to check with a nurse while she'd been in the surgery getting her blood test. It wasn't her being a hypochondriac, just sensible, and she resented him saying otherwise. She wouldn't have scoffed at him had he been the one with something different concerning his body that he wanted reassurance about. Things invariably went wrong when you got older and so you kept on top of them; you didn't run away from them hoping they'd bugger off.

'Anyway, it's harmless. I thought it would be,' said Mel. She didn't tell him that the doctor had popped in to take a look at it and said it was a senile wart, because she could guess what sarcastic remark that might unleash.

'I could have told you that.'

She drowned the retort that she must have missed the part where he got his Doctor of Medicine degree with a mouthful of lager.

'It's really nice in here, I think.'

'You said that already.'

Oh, she'd just about had enough now.

'Why are you being so crappy with me, Steve?'

He pulled a comical face of disbelief. 'Are you trying to pick a fight?'

'No,' said Mel, 'I'm trying to have a nice evening. I thought this would be lovely, you and me and a place we haven't been to before.' A wobble was creeping into her voice. 'I thought, we should do more of this, once a week, going somewhere and making an effort to get out of the rut we're in. Don't you get fed up of it being the same routine all the time?'

The smiling waitress crashed into their exchange by her arrival with their meals.

'Here we go,' she said and put them down. 'Any extra sauces?'

'No, thank you,' they both said in unison.

'Looks nice,' said Steve, nodding appreciatively at the pile of food on his plate. And Mel hoped that was him finally making an effort to reset the evening, but it had been spoilt now and she wished she'd just cooked the bloody pie at home instead.

★

The first arrival – Janine – had hoovered up three of the giant cookies by the time that Amanda closed the door, accepting this was the only intake of women she was going to get tonight.

There were six of them there, including herself. The young blonde lady; Janine; two other women who had come together and didn't want a biscuit or a coffee, and someone else who got her knitting and a pattern out.

'I've never really done one of these clubs before,' said Amanda with an embarrassed chortle. 'I know it's the first and I'm hoping that news travels so we get some more to swell the ranks. Allow me to introduce myself.' And she

did, and she told them that she worked at Mon Enfant who
made baby equipment and that while she was collecting
information to help reform things in the workplace for
women who might be uncatered for at certain stages of
their lives, she'd thought of launching a friendship group so
ladies could come together and give some support to each
other, even if it was only in the form of a weekly natter in
a safe space. If anything constructive came of it, she'd use
that for her research, but it wasn't the main purpose of the
meetings.

'Well, I can help you there,' said Janine, taking another
biscuit. 'I had a terrible menopause. Terrible. I've told them
at my place, that when I'm off it's for genuine reasons and I
shouldn't be expected to fill in any sickness forms. It should
be the law that they have a women's specialist on site—'

'Well, that depends on how big the firm is, surely,' interrupted the knitter, not looking up from her creation. 'Small
businesses can't afford stuff like that. It'd cripple them.'

'Then they should make me redundant and give me dis-
ability money . . .'

And on Janine droned, about all the things in life she
should be entitled to and Amanda wondered what the hell
she'd been thinking of to instigate such an initiative.

The knitting woman left after half an hour; she just packed
up her stuff and walked out at the point when Amanda felt
her ears were going to bleed and she wished she could follow
her. Janine, though, had found a captive audience and dominated the entire evening. The two women who had come
together, and didn't eat or drink anything had stayed silent
throughout. They'd probably have gone sooner had they
been brave enough to move, Amanda thought, and when

they said their goodbyes she knew that was the last she'd seen of them. What a total disaster.

'Same time next week then,' said Janine as a parting shot and Amanda said, 'Goodbye' and was already dreading it.

'I'll help you clear up,' said the young blonde. Her name was Sky. That's about as much as Amanda knew of her because she hadn't been able to get a word in for gobby Janine.

'Oh, bless you but there's not that much to do.' Amanda sighed, defeated.

'The cookies were amazing.'

'Take some back with you. Please. I'll get you a bag.'

'I'll have one now if I could,' said Sky. 'Can I get another coffee, please?'

She was in no rush to go home.

'Of course you can. And I'll have one too with you,' said Amanda. Sky pumped them out of the containers into two fresh mugs and retook a seat at the table.

'I didn't really know what to expect,' Amanda said. 'I'd hoped it would be better than this car crash.'

To her surprise Sky chuckled. 'It was certainly good entertainment.'

Amanda dropped her head into her hands but joined her in laughing.

'It was the longest two hours of my life.'

'Still, I've learned a lot about vaginal dryness and why you should have automatic time off work for it.'

Amanda snorted. The laughter was well needed.

'Where do you work?' she asked Sky.

'Just over there,' she pointed in the direction of Spring Hill Square. 'At Bon Repair, the repair shop. I make and mend teddy bears.'

'Really? Is it a thing? Do people still want them mending?'

'Oh yes, you'd be surprised. And I occasionally help the toy man who is a bit busier. I think he gives me jobs out of the kindness of his heart.'

'Goodness, a kind man. Janine would dispute such an entity exists,' said Amanda, not really caring if she sounded bitchy to a relative stranger. The woman had wrecked her club single-handedly. She was like the inverse of Philip, with her man-hating diatribes. 'How did you get into that then?'

'My dad. He had a toy shop and doll's hospital. I worked with him ever since I was small.'

'Is he still . . . around?'

'No, he died six years ago. I'm an orphan. I've never really got used to calling myself that.'

'I've still got my mum,' said Amanda, 'but she's getting frail.' She thought again about that strange thing she'd said about Bettina Boot running off with Arnold. Bettina wouldn't have stooped so low.

'I'm sorry this was such a disaster.' Amanda sighed. 'I had hoped that when women came together with the same aim in mind, something good might come of it.'

'I enjoyed myself,' said Sky with a nod. 'Maybe for all the wrong reasons.' She gave a cheeky smirk and Amanda knew exactly what she meant by that.

'I'm going through the menopause myself,' Sky admitted to her. 'I was getting ready to tell Janine that if the situation arose. I was waiting for her to say that I couldn't possibly know what it was all about because of my age.'

'Really? How old are you?' She was either in her mid-twenties or she had some great face cream.

'I'm twenty-six. I had a hysterectomy fifteen months ago.'

Amanda winced at her revelation. 'That's very early to

go through such a big op.'

'Trust me, I'd take it over the pain of endometriosis any day. Yep. I was pretty unlucky in the gynaecological stakes,' Sky said with a small shrug of her shoulders. 'Quite an extreme measure, but on balance, well, I couldn't have kids anyway because I have a heart condition, a gift from the family gene pool. It's a bit like angina . . . but my mother's health never really recovered after she gave birth to me, so the docs advised me it would be the safest course of action. It happened, no point in bleating about it.'

Sky read Amanda's expression and felt an immediate rush of embarrassment.

'Sorry, I didn't mean to overshare all that. I don't talk about it normally. I manage it very well, so no one needs to know who doesn't know already. Did you lace the biscuits with a truth drug?'

She was making light of it, thought Amanda. What a lot of shit to be dealt to someone so young.

'Sometimes it's easier to talk to strangers,' she said. 'I think my whole street knows I'm on HRT.' It was a lie but she just wanted to make Sky feel as if she wasn't alone in opening her mouth before better judgement could shut it.

Sky nodded. 'I'm on it too and even though it's a low dose, I know it's helping.' Her insomnia had cranked up again recently, but she thought that could be attributed more to Wilton Dearne than to changes in her body.

'I'm going to get you a bag so you can take some of those cookies home. They'll only go to waste, so they might as well go to your waist instead,' said Amanda and bobbed out of the room.

Sky sat in the silence and sipped at her coffee. Tonight might not have gone as Amanda had planned, but Sky had been grateful for having her thoughts wrested from Bon, and Mr Creep at home. Maybe more women would come whom she might gel with. She had really liked Amanda and it was clear that she wanted her club to be a success. She'd stick one of the flyers on the noticeboard at work for her in the hope that some customers might see it. And she'd definitely come back the same time next week for Amanda's company, even if mouthy Janine did too.

Women needed friends and if they didn't have them, then they needed a way of connecting with like-minded females who might become their friends. Maybe if she'd had just one pal at school who cared more about her than getting an invite to Angel Sutton's parties, her life might have turned out completely differently.

Chapter 18

Mel and Steve bickered in the car on the way home. They never really argued, they always managed to sort things out before they got to that stage, but still, by their marital standards, this was as close to a proper row as they'd ever come.

'I didn't really want to go out, that's why I'm *off* as you keep saying,' he'd thrown at her. 'I'm knackered.'

'I thought it would be nice.'

'You said that already.'

'And you said *that* already.'

'What do you want me to say? Okay, it was all right tonight. Fantastic steak, amazing chips, magnificent eggs.'

'Then you should have told your face.' *You sarcastic arse,* she didn't add.

'Oh please, Mel, let's not ... I've got stuff on my mind, okay?'

She turned her head to look at him. 'Like what? Tell me, then.'

'Just stuff I need to sort out for myself.'

She slid from being annoyed with him back to worrying, but she forced herself to keep a rein on it because fussing would drive him underground. They had no money worries, he had plenty of work on; she really hoped it wasn't something to do with his health, but she'd just have to wait it out until he was ready to tell her. And worry herself stupid in the meantime. She slipped into fifth gear and they cruised home in silence.

In bed, he kissed her goodnight as usual and turned over. She was just trying to close off her thoughts when he said, without the heated sarcasm of earlier, 'It was a nice place tonight. Nice meal.' And she knew he'd been thinking about what a crank he'd been and this was his way of apologising without actually saying the words.

'Good. I'm glad you enjoyed it, Steve. We'll have to go back again and try something else on the menu.'

He didn't say that they would or wouldn't, but she felt better for him making the effort to end the evening on a conciliatory note and it allowed her brain to shut down and she slept.

In the morning, she was half-asleep when he left at six and she stirred when he kissed her on the cheek and said, 'Goodbye, Mel.' And just before she fell back into her deeper sleep, she thought that he never usually did that when he had an early.

★

Sky had taken to always having a chair lodged up against her bedroom door handle. Every little noise and creak would lift her from sleep, and there were plenty of those since Wilton had moved in. He had the tread of a dinosaur on the floorboards and put the telly on too loud and she was sure it was to provoke a reaction, so she didn't rise to the bait.

He was a very strange character. He'd once hinted to Katy that if she ever needed some extra money, he knew of a way and she hadn't asked him for details but had extricated herself quickly from his company. They'd both joked that he probably still lived with his mother and dressed up in her clothes. Sky couldn't imagine that if it had been she and Katy who had both left and it was Jordan who now lived here alone, he would have moved in then. But until her remaining five months were up or she won the Lottery, she was stuck without a way out. The sale of those ten bears was a welcome injection of cash into her bank account but it wasn't enough to allow her to walk out and write off all that rent she'd paid Wilton and the bond he owed her. Maybe she'd have to get a different job, something banal, nine to five that paid more and just do the bears in her spare time. It was a beyond sobering thought.

Chapter 19

No sooner had the estate agent put Erin's flat on the market than there was interest. Was she available that afternoon to show someone round? There would be interest at that knockdown price of course, but she just wanted out of it. It felt like a toxic space and she wished she'd never let her old house go so quickly. Carona had pressured her to sell it, rather than carry on renting it out. Now she wondered if that was because she didn't want to risk her having somewhere to jump to if things went wrong. She'd nagged Erin to buy something together with her – a love nest. Erin had never really liked the apartment that much, but in that period she'd been blinded. Or hoodwinked, she couldn't work out which it was.

She was working from home that day and had polished off what she needed to do pretty early on, so she could give the house a bit of a spruce and open up the Jo Malone reed diffuser she'd bought so the scent could wander and make the place smell extra-classy. This apartment was one of the more expensive ones in the block, with an upstairs and a balcony. She'd do anything to get this property off her hands and start again somewhere else. She didn't think she had a chance of beginning to repair herself until that happened.

She was definitely going to walk through the door of Molly's grief club tonight and not chicken out at the last minute, even if it was guilt more than grief that she needed to get to grips with.

★

Mel was stuck in traffic on the way home from work and young Jason Jepson was already at her house, sitting on the bench outside with his guitar in his case, waiting for her.

'I'm sorry I'm late, Jason,' she said, guilt-tripped at him trembling in the April chill. Even more guilt-tripped when he said, 'It's okay, Mrs English, it's not your fault. I was early.' He had such a good nature, as well as being a talented young lad on his instrument. She'd given him that guitar because the one he'd turned up with on his first lesson had been bought in a junk shop and the wood was warped, affecting the sound and it was sending her OCD levels sky-ward. She hadn't made a big deal about the gift so as not to embarrass him, had told him it was an old one he was welcome to and would save her taking it to a charity shop, but she could still see his face now, the way it lit up, still hear the hitch in his voice as he said, 'Really?'

His mum had rung up a few months in, throat clogged with tears and said that she couldn't afford the lessons for a while but when that changed, could Jason come back. And Mel, though she hadn't told Steve this, had said that she'd do them for free, just for him. Jason was guitar-mad, he always bossed the homework she set him and she could see him taking off where she never had. He was far better than any other pupil she'd ever taught and she wanted the full glittery success story for him, the way people should have wanted it for her. She'd encourage him all the way and counter-balance any scoffers who'd tell him to shelve any plans he had of becoming a musician and 'get a proper job' instead. She'd tell him to go for it if that's what he had decided to do, otherwise he'd end up one day regretting that he hadn't given it his best shot. And thirty-odd years later, when one of his friends came a-calling to ask if he'd like to join a band before it was too late, he'd say no because even the voice in his own head was telling him that would be pathetic.

She'd cheered up from last night's meal debacle and Jason had helped because he always brought a smile to her face. If she'd had a son, she would have liked one just like Jason Jepson. She made him a cheese toastie and a cup of tea when she was giving him his homework assignment. She didn't do it for anyone else, just him and sometimes – silly as it was – she let herself believe this was what being a mum would be like.

She was going to make the best of her evening alone anyway, while Steve was on his overnight in Doncaster. She'd called in at the new M&S food hall and bought herself a chicken tikka masala and a chocolate trifle and she'd open a bottle of Jammy White Roo and watch one of the new films on their Fire Stick. As her curry was rotating in the microwave she thought of her poor husband, who would be holed up in a Premier Inn no doubt. He'd have a burger somewhere and take it back to his room in a paper bag. She wished he were here. She'd make him a chippy tea and let him watch the snooker on the TV, because the world championships were on and he loved that, and maybe some no-pressure fussing might make him open up to whatever was troubling him, because something was and it wasn't this job in Doncaster. He wasn't exactly the Laughing Policeman, but they did rub along well together and had a few nice times along the way. Life was simple, easy, if a bit bland and totally predictable, but better than many had it.

The doorbell rang just as the microwave pinged the half-way mark for her to add water to the rice and stir. She went to the door, opened it and her whole life changed.

Chapter 20

Erin felt her jaw tighten a little more with every step she took towards the teashop in Spring Hill Square, just across the way from Bon's repair shop. She had to go in this week, no question. Molly, who ran the sessions, knew sometimes it took a couple of false starts to walk in and join them, but she wouldn't keep the space open for her for much longer; besides, it was unfair if someone else could be using it, so she had to stop being a wuss.

She felt her feet stall abruptly at the doorway and a microsecond later someone barged into her from behind. She turned to find a man there, dressed in a suit and carrying a briefcase as if he'd just come here directly from a top-level board meeting. Tall, dark-haired, dark-eyed. It was his eyes she noticed most of all.

'I am so sorry,' he said, voice deep and plummy, pure private education. 'I didn't expect you to brake so hard there, though it was my fault for being at your heels. Had we been cars, I would have been entirely at fault in an insurance claim.'

'It's perfectly fine,' Erin answered him.

'Allow me.' He opened the door and she walked forward. She was in.

'Welcome,' said Molly, who was standing there smiling in a way that told her, *I knew you'd get here eventually.* 'Come in, give Mr Singh your orders, he's waiting patiently for them.'

An elderly gentleman in a blue turban and a white apron with frilled edges was standing behind the counter, ready to dish up drinks and cut cakes by the look of the silver cake slice in his hand.

'I could only find this apron today. I look like Alice in Wonderland,' he said, chuckling. 'Now, what can I get for you both?'

Everyone else had cake, so Erin forced herself to choose something and join in. She hadn't been in this teashop before and she marvelled at the ambience because usually new-build properties hadn't the time to build up layers of sediment, essence from lives, but this café seemed to already have them in abundance. She wondered what had been deposited in her apartment for the next owners to inherit and hoped that someone would come along and overstamp it with better.

Erin took her seat and the man with the briefcase sat next to her, after asking her if she minded. He put down his coffee and plate of cake and held out his hand. She noted how square it was, how strong his grip was when he squeezed hers.

'Alex Forrester,' he said.

'Erin va . . . Flaxton,' she returned. It had been years since she had referred to herself by her maiden name and, weirdly, it was going to take some getting used to again.

'First time?'

'Yes. It shouldn't have been but I've chickened out before.'

'My first time was last month and it made me realise I wish I hadn't taken so long to pluck up the courage to join, if that is in any way helpful.'

'That's a good recommendation,' said Erin, while thinking this man really did have beautiful eyes. Soft and large with eyelashes some women would have killed for. She wondered what had brought him here and guessed it must have been the loss of a wife. Then she wondered if he was wondering about what had brought her here and she knew he would have got it totally wrong.

There was a fragile-looking man whose age was impossible to guess at, because he carried himself like a much older gent but his face was unlined, at least what she saw of it since he kept his head down, unwilling to seek eye contact, his long fringe obscuring his vision. He sat away from those who were already clustered in the circle: an old priest, all in black with a white collar and a tall, straight-backed elderly lady who occupied the chair next to him. She had a long face, long nose, loose neck and reminded Erin of Lady Rosemary on *The Herbs* that she used to watch many years ago. She imagined when she spoke, she'd have a voice like a duchess.

She was right. Her name was Dilys, she said, and she was there because she'd lost her twenty-year old cat and didn't feel as if she could tell anyone why she was so upset about for fear of them saying that it was 'just a cat' and there were far bigger problems in the world. The cat had been a constant in her life since her late husband had given him to her. He'd been a great comfort when her son emigrated to the other side of the world, taking her grandchildren with him, and when she lost her twin sister and then her husband. And Erin had listened and felt her pain because a pet had such ability to bring uncomplicated joy to a life, and a drench of sadness when it died. She'd had a dog when she was a girl and presumed they'd travel up life's road together until the end and it had been a wake-up call to find out that wasn't to be.

'But something rather remarkable happened last Friday,' said Dilys, crooking her finger and tapping it against her lip. 'I had my patio doors open and in walked a small scraggy stray. Obviously unwanted from the state of him. Very thin, full of fleas, with grass hanging out of his back end so I presume that's what he'd been trying to live on. Just strutted in, as if it owned the place. I loaded it into a carrier and took it to the vet. There was no microchip – not surprisingly – but they treated him, de-fleaed him and I picked him up the next day. I've asked around, but no one has claimed him. I have no idea where he came from, but he has stemmed something inside me that was leaking pain.'

She swallowed, overcome with emotion, sniffed and laughed at herself. 'Silly old woman, I know.'

'You aren't silly at all,' said Molly. 'Sometimes things are sent to us that we need and who knows who the postman is.'

'I wonder if it's Gerald. I wonder if he's up there thinking, "Dilys, do I have to send you another cat to sort you out? Well, here you go then."'

The priest nodded. 'I don't believe in coincidence. I don't believe that cat just turned up at your house when it could have turned up at any other house, but he was needed there most.'

'So far he's cost me two hundred pounds,' said Dilys with a smile. 'I said to Gerald, "I hope you're going to send me the money for this if it is you."'

'You look a different woman from how you looked last week,' said the priest. 'If I may say so.'

'You may indeed,' said Dilys. 'I feel it too. Just for a hungry scrap of fur. What magic, what sorcery. No wonder people used to think cats had powers.'

Erin had wanted a cat. Carona hadn't so they hadn't had one.

'Jesse, do you feel ready to talk?' Molly asked the man hiding behind his hair. Jesse's head gave the slightest of shakes. 'All in your own time,' said Molly, who knew that he would soon, because he was here and walking in through the door was the biggest step.

'How have you been, Father Paul?' asked Molly, addressing the priest.

'Good,' he said. 'I have a new housekeeper. She's nice, reverent, she brings a strong energy with her. And even stronger perfume.' He chortled.

'Well, that's a start,' said Molly. 'Alex?'

The man in the suit nodded. 'I don't think I've made any great strides this week but I've slept better and that helps. Without self-medication, I may add.'

'Erin? Would you like to tell us why you're here?' asked Molly softly.

Erin, feeling the heat of the attention, wanted to do a Jesse, shake her head and let them move on to other business. But something inside her knew better. She heard her own voice speaking:

'My name is Erin and I lost my partner, Carona, six months ago.'

★

Mel was glad she'd kept the chain on because she didn't know the person who was standing on her doorstep from Adam. A tall, lanky bloke with a Liam Gallagher mod haircut, heavy eyebrows and sideburns.

'Is this where Steve English lives?' said the man, in a strong Mancunian accent. He was taking the Oasis theme seriously.

'Yes,' said Mel, with a cautious smile.

'Can I have a word with him please?'

Who was he? thought Mel. People didn't tend to call up to the house wanting to speak to Steve about a job, but what else could it be?

'He's . . . ' Mel urged herself to be careful. It would be a bit stupid to tell him she was in the house alone. 'He's . . . in the bath.'

'Is that right?' said the man, who was quietly polite. Coldly polite. 'He's not away for the night by any chance, is he?'

'No,' said Mel, doing a really bad job of sounding convincing. 'Can I ask what you want him for?' She was primed for shutting the door and bolting it quickly if the man made any attempt to try to barge his way in, but he was keeping his distance so far, standing on the doorstep, feet together, hands by his sides.

'I want him to stop shagging my wife, that's what I want him for,' said the man. He stabbed his finger at Mel now. 'You tell him, when I see him he's fucking dead.'

A bucket of cold water appeared from somewhere and threw the contents in Mel's face. At least that's what it felt like. She was so shocked by the words she couldn't breathe.

'That bloody school reunion caused all this,' the man on the doorstep went on.

Mel could barely hear him for the blood pounding in her ears. She couldn't move.

'You tell him that from me,' said the man, his mouth now a tight moue of fury. He swaggered back down her path, shoulders thrown from side to side, got in his car and screeched off. And still Mel didn't move.

★

'I was married for five years,' said Erin, feeling the words leave her mouth, the first of a long ball-of-string of words. 'I was . . . content. He was a lovely man, wonderful, we're still good friends, though god knows how.' She took a sip from her teacup because her throat was already dry.

'I'd not had good relationships in my life until I met this fantastic person who ticked every box, I mean *every* box, except one. The "do you fancy this man enough to want to rip his clothes off" box.'

Erin eyes darted at the priest, hoping he wouldn't start crossing himself in disgust, but he listened in non-judgemental silence as others had listened to him when he'd braved his own story in Molly's safe space.

'I felt lonely' – she pressed at her heart – 'here. My marriage wasn't enough but it was also too comfortable to leave, and I know that makes me sound really callous and selfish, because I was. Then I met someone.' She swallowed. 'I'd never considered that I might be gay or even bisexual, I'd only ever dated and slept with men. But I went to a night-club after a work event and . . . there was Carona. She was like no one I'd ever met before: an artist, strong, flamboyant, confident, wild. I couldn't stop thinking about her, she impacted on my life like a freight train. I wasn't unfaithful, not physically anyway but emotionally I suppose you could say I was.'

Erin looked up, still expecting expressions of disapproval and seeing none.

'I'm ashamed of my own weakness, my recklessness. I knew the morning after meeting her that my marriage was over. A month later, I told my husband I was leaving him. He was more worried about me than himself, told me that I must do what I thought was right, but to be very careful. He knows nothing of what really happened after that. I've been too ashamed to tell him.'

Molly's benign expression told her she wasn't about to say anything new, that she'd heard it all before – and worse.

Erin didn't say that she was love-bombed because it sounded idiotic, but she knew she had been. She knew that Carona had moulded herself around her, pandered to her stupid ego, detected instinctively what was missing in her life and she had supplied it by the ton. Erin was drugged with desire, a fly staggering willingly into the spider's lair.

'She made me feel special and loved, the centre of her world; I was intoxicated and it was fantastic. I didn't take anything from my husband when I left, I wouldn't have, and he didn't take anything from me, we were both well set up before we married. I owned a house which I had rented out sometimes on short leases. I sold it, put the money into a top-of-the-range apartment with her. I was totally convinced this was a grand passion that only very few experienced. I have no idea what was going through my head. Something deep inside me must have been aware, though, because for whatever reason, I didn't press to rush through a divorce and Carona wasn't happy about that at all.

'Needless to say, it all started to go wrong, very, very wrong and we limped along because she made it extremely difficult for me to leave, and she died in a car crash after we'd had an argument. She'd stormed out. The last thing I ever heard from her lips was the c-word aimed at me. She had a very fast car; she drove it stupidly at the best of times, I hated being in it with her. I hated—' She pulled herself up short. She'd said enough for now.

'I felt very shocked, very sad that there was hardly anyone at her funeral, no family other than her sister who really didn't want to be there. There was no one who came to share memories of her, better memories than I had because all my happy ones of us had been stained, ruined, cancelled out by the awful ones. I've learned from her sister that her relationships followed a very similar pattern, except I hung in there much longer than most. If we hadn't argued that night she would have still been alive.'

'You don't know that. And the accident wasn't your fault. She was behind the wheel, not you,' said Molly.

'We had mirror wills. The life insurance paid off the apartment and I inherited everything of hers and I feel guilty about that because I was planning to leave her. I'd have felt much better if we'd split and sold up and just taken away what we brought to the relationship, as I did with my marriage. I think that guilt is what I feel most of all, not grief; guilt that I don't feel grief, and that's why it took me so long to come to your meetings, because I felt a fraud.'

'That's more common than you know,' said Molly, her voice like balm. 'And so is the impulse to spend the money in a way that benefits someone else other than yourself, to give it away, distance yourself from it. You need time to separate the money from the negative emotions that tie you to the relationship. It's just money. You can use it to better your life when you feel able.'

Erin sniffed and didn't realise she was crying until she felt a splash on her hand.

'That's exactly how I feel. I haven't touched a penny of it yet.'

'That's me too,' said Jesse suddenly, spurting it out. 'I didn't get on with my dad at all and I got all his pension money and his house when he died, and I don't know if that's because he had to give it to someone or deep down he loved me and so I don't know what that money means and I'll never get my answers now.' He started sniffling, pushing balled fists into his eyes like a child and Molly went to sit with him and Erin took in a breath and realised it was the first in a long time that her lungs had dared to fill to capacity.

★

Mel almost staggered back into the lounge after she had locked the door. She didn't know what to do first, she was totally disorientated. The man had asked for her husband by name, he hadn't just got the wrong house. It was rubbish, it had to be. She *knew* Steve. She'd known him for thirty-one years; she didn't know the Liam lookalike threatening and swearing like a yob on her doorstep. And she had no place believing what he said was true. *How dare he say those things?* She was angry at him, incandescent enough for the emotion to bring tears flying to her eyes.

She needed to talk to Steve urgently. She unplugged her phone from where it was charging up on the work surface and rang him. He always picked up. Even if he was busy, he'd pick up and tell her that he'd have to ring her back. He'd pick up and they'd talk and he'd tell her the bloke was a nutter and he'd no idea what he was on about.

He didn't pick up.

She rang again, let it ring for ages until it went to voice-mail. The message she left was all over the place.

'Steve, can you ring me. I've had a man at the door saying that you're . . . saying his wife and you . . . Just ring me, can you?'

He'd ring back straightaway. His phone never ran out of charge. It was always in his range. She texted him to ring her urgently.

Five minutes later she was still sitting at the dining table waiting, her foot tapping nervously on the floor, her fist tapping nervously on the table and the microwave beeped yet another reminder that something was sitting inside its belly that hadn't been taken out.

She went into the fridge and poured herself a large glass of wine, then gulped at it too fast and made herself cough. Then she went to the toilet upstairs instead of the one downstairs, *knowing* that as soon as she did that, the phone would ring and she'd have to run back down to answer it. It was sod's law.

It didn't ring.

She left another voicemail and a WhatsApp message as well as a text. And another. All unanswered. She felt con-sumed by panic and hadn't a clue where to put herself to stop the tumult inside her. He must have had an accident or something and be unconscious. Maybe his phone had been nicked. What had that man said about the school reunion?

She pulled up Facebook on her laptop: Saran Sykes's page, looked again at the photos, studied them forensically, scouring for clues. What was the conversation going on between them in that one where she had her back against the wall and was smiling at him? And to think she'd thought Steve's unrequited crush on her was a joke. Had they finally requited it? Had Saran realised what she could have had back then and gone for it now?

She turned her phone off and on again in case somehow he'd replied to her but a glitch meant all his messages were delayed.

Steve didn't shag other women. He didn't even flirt, he didn't eye up anyone, they'd had loads of disapproving conversations about his brother's shenanigans. He was *not* that guy. Her head started to drag substantiating evidence from anywhere it could, but rather than soothe, it did the opposite. *Is that why he didn't want to have sex with you on Saturday night? Is that why he couldn't get it up? Is that why he didn't want to go and eat at Ray's diner with you yesterday? Does this job in Doncaster even exist that is taking up so much time recently? Is that why his shirt stunk of Chloe when he came in from the reunion party, because it's what she wears?*

The questions fired at her like bullets and she had no armour to protect herself. She didn't know what to do except stare at her phone, cry, throw wine down her neck in a vain attempt to anaesthetise herself against the Catherine wheel of hissing sparks in her head that seemed to be saying *Saran Sykes* on a continuous sibilant loop.

★

'You okay?' asked Alex as he fell into step with Erin as they walked to the car park.

'I don't know,' she said.

'Let me guess, you're thinking *I've overshared, I need to beat myself up.*'

She smiled out of the corner of her mouth. 'Yep.'

'Don't go straight home,' he said, 'that will only continue and by the time you get to your front door you'll be looking for a leather strap with which to flagellate yourself. Last week, after I'd bared my own soul, I called in at a pub nearby and just sat and had a drink and . . . decompressed. I'm going there now if you want to follow me. The Spouting Tap in Little Kipping, appropriately enough. Out onto the main road, take a right, then a left and follow the road round the bend.'

And because Erin didn't want to go back to the flat she had inherited from her dead partner and wallow in the cesspool of emotions that had just been stirred up, she said that she'd meet him there.

Chapter 21

Alex was at the bar when Erin walked in; he'd just ordered a pint of cola and asked her what she would like. She had a half of the same. The pub was quite busy: quiz night, apparently. People were holding up pieces of paper and discussing answers from the snippets of conversation her ears gathered.

Alex sat down and again Erin thought what an attractive man he was, though the suit helped. She'd always thought men in dark suits and white shirts were hot. Bon had looked good in a suit. *Dearest Bon.* She wished he'd find someone to love. Or rather, she wished he'd let someone into his heart to love him. His portcullis was down but then he'd told her before, when they were taking things slowly at the beginning of their relationship, that he didn't want to make any more mistakes – and then she'd become his biggest.

Erin sat back against the cushions and realised immediately that this had been a good idea. She felt lighter somehow, as if offloading some of what had built up inside her had shed some physical weight. It had been stuck there, like a giant fatberg in a drain.

'I was interested to hear your story,' said Alex. He had a

voice that matched his attire, Erin thought: posh and sonorous. If he'd transformed into a bottle of wine, he'd have been a heavy red, a sagrantino.

'My "half a story",' Erin corrected him. 'I don't think anyone would be ready for the rest.'

'Oh?' Alex's features assumed a quizzical look.

'It would have been too much for one sitting. I'd have sent you all off home suicidal.'

'All of us in that group have tough stories,' said Alex, picking up his pint glass. His hands were large enough to make it look like a half-pint.

'What's yours? I should catch up really, shouldn't I?' said Erin, adding quickly, 'If you want to share.'

'I was in a same sex couple,' Alex began, which surprised her because her gaydar hadn't been triggered one bit. 'Although, I've had relationships with both men and women. I met Julian seven years ago at a Law Society dinner. He was a retired judge, much older than me; wonderful company, successful, cultured, intelligent, witty, dreadfully lost. He'd been a gay man all his life who never came out, just played the straight game for fear of being arrested or destroyed. He had two children and a loveless marriage. To cut a long story short, we fell in love and he tried everything to leave his marriage sensitively, respectfully but ... well, he was cast out like an unclean demon. His children cut him out of their lives, just as he had always feared might happen, as did his sister and brother, but his friends didn't and his reputation was a little dented maybe, but not demolished, however much his wife tried to bring that about. I wouldn't have let anyone take advantage of him; he would have given everything away but he didn't deserve to lose any more than he had.

'His family and he never did reconcile, and that broke his heart. I'd like to think I mended it as best I could because we had three fabulous, fantastic, wonderful years together once he was finally free of that straitjacket he'd laced himself into. Then he got ill. I was more or less his nurse when we married, more friends than partners by then, but I loved him dearly. He knew the vultures would gather and they did. We reached out to his son and his daughter before he died, a last-ditch attempt at making his passing easier, but they remained intransigent and I hated them for that.

'They, of course, made a ridiculous attempt to sue me for all manner of things when he'd gone, I dread to think how much money they threw on that stony ground. Near his end, Julian didn't want them to have anything more than they already had from him – he'd been very generous to them in the past. If he had changed his mind, I'd have honoured it, whatever his will said. He trusted me to do everything to the letter: the funeral, the disbursements, including the bank transfer of a penny each to his sister and brother by way of gratitude for how they treated him. He got great enjoyment from imagining that scene and it was, it has to be said, every bit of entertaining as he thought it might be.'

Alex smiled. 'I was holding his hand when he died; he just slipped away peacefully, he deserved nothing less than to depart with a calm, whispering breath. He left me a rich man. He said that he couldn't take it with him so he was hoping I'd spend it and enjoy it; and like you, I feel a lot of conflicted emotion about adhering to the strict terms of his will. I was the love of his life, you see, and he knew my love for him was genuine . . . but smaller.' He smiled fondly, his large brown eyes looking suddenly glassy.

'It sounds to me as though you loved him ... enough,' said Erin.

'I did love him, but I miss him as a friend more than anything. He was like a chandelier. He didn't just light up a room, he flooded it.'

'Carona was the opposite,' said Erin. 'She drained me, she sucked the light away and buried it in a black hole. What haunts me is that on the night she died, I had told her we were finished – again, but this time I meant it, I was at the end, the point of no return. She wanted me to go for a drive with her, to stop me packing my bags; to talk, she said, some place neutral. My instincts were screaming at me not to go. I wasn't about to get in a car with her when she was in such a heightened emotional state. She did everything to try and make me: cried, pushed, pleaded, swore, but I'd had enough, it was over. I heard her tyres squeal as she left; I should have stopped her. I've even wondered if I knew what would happen and that's why I didn't.'

'No,' said Alex, cutting in quickly, 'that's your mind playing tricks on you. More likely, surely, that you just wanted some respite from her pressuring you.'

'The police told me she was overtaking another car and drove into a bollard and do you know what – I believe, Alex, that if I'd been in the passenger seat, and there had been no car on the road to overtake, she'd have still driven into that bollard.'

A shiver rippled down her spine, like a eel wiggling in grease.

'I've never told anyone that before. She once said to me that we should die together because she couldn't live without me and she didn't want me to live without her. She was being romantic, I suppose, but it struck me at the time as being an odd thing to say; it scared me a little. It was too much; she was too much. It was recorded as an accident, but I know it wasn't. She planned to die that night with me or without me. I know how her mind worked. She wanted to haunt me for the rest of my life because that's the only way she'd keep herself in it.'

Alex nodded, absorbing her words. 'That's a heavy burden,' he said. 'I can understand your head being a complete cabbage.'

'Oh, it's the full veg shop,' said Erin with a humourless chip of laughter. Alex pointed to her empty glass. 'Let me get you another.'

'No, it's my round.' She stood and he held up an admonishing finger at her.

'I'm much bigger, I can barge my way through.'

She watched him walk towards the bar, head and shoulders above most of the people clustered around it. She saw how he smiled at the bar girl when he gave her his order, pressed back the change she tried to give him. He gave off a warm vibe that she would have liked to have trusted, but then the last three years had screwed with her internal compass. She'd have to start building up her instinct from scratch.

'Tell me about the priest,' said Erin when he was seated again. 'What was all that about a housekeeper?'

'Father Paul's is a very sad tale,' said Alex. 'He had a housekeeper for decades who he . . . liked.'

Erin raised her eyebrows. 'Liked or *liked*?'

'Oh, I think the inference is very much that he liked her as a man as well as a priest. And really he should have confessed to his bishop and created some distance, but he didn't. He would have left the priesthood for her but of course he never imagined that his feelings could have been reciprocated. She married, had a child, he was her source of comfort when that marriage ended. He never stopped loving her, he said. And when he was seventy-one last year and she was fifty-nine, she died. And on her deathbed, when he was attending her, giving her the last rites, her final confession was that she had always loved him and if he had given her one clue that he felt the same, she would have opened her arms to him.'

Erin was open-mouthed as she listened. 'Oh my god, I don't know if that's beautiful or terrible. How desperately sad.'

'If only one of them had made that leap to the other,' said Alex. 'Is it better for a love to keep burning on a low flame, or for it to blaze with the chance it might burn out?'

'I'm really not the right person to ask,' said Erin.

'I think the latter.' Alex nodded. 'Always the latter. I think of Julian and how happy his last years were for taking his chance.'

Erin, scarred, would have leant towards the former. But a picture flashed in her mind of Bon and Sky. Two people who really needed to take their chance and make that leap; she was sure of it.

Chapter 22

Mel awoke with a snort at the kitchen table. She'd slept face down on her arm which was now numb. There was an empty bottle of wine beside her which she couldn't remember drinking, at least not past the second glass which she had downed in one. Her throat was parched and her head was thumping. For one blessed moment, she believed that Steve was upstairs sleeping by himself in disgust at her passing out, before that illusion was shattered by the battering ram of the truth that he wasn't home and her spirits plunged downwards as if tied to The Big One in Blackpool on its descent.

How stupid to get pissed and in this state, she said to herself, the inner voice sounding as disapproving as Steve's mother's. What good had that done her? She pulled her phone towards her, let the lens try and identify the creased mess of her face to allow her permission to use it. No calls, no texts, no WhatsApps received.

She wasn't sure if it was the excess of alcohol or the no communication from Steve that made the contents of her stomach begin to slosh and rise and she only just made it to the downstairs loo in time.

Should she ring the hospitals in Doncaster? It was more likely he'd be there than in another woman's bed. This was *Steve*. Steve went up ladders and painted things, he didn't cock other women. *What about his parents?* No, she dismissed that immediately, she'd worry them daft if she told them she couldn't get hold of him.

She went back into the kitchen and filled a glass with very cold tap water which she pressed to the front of her head before she gulped at it and used the second half of the glass to wash down two ibuprofen. Then she sat back down at the table, picked up the phone again and groaned when her eyes registered the time. She was late for work. Sod it, she hadn't had a day off sick in years, she was overdue a virus. She rang her manager at the bank, sounding even more crap than she felt. Heather, her boss was only thirty-two but damned good at her job and kind. She told Mel to get back to bed and Mel felt so wretched she didn't even feel guilty about lying to her. Then again she really did feel crap, although not because she'd caught a bug but because her husband had gone AWOL and Saran Sykes's husband had turned up and said they were partners-in-bonk.

She sat with her head in her hands until the painkillers kicked in and gave her space to think. She wished she could have phoned a mate, but there was no one in her contacts on whom she could put all that. Her sister was the person she knew best but they weren't close. There was Joss – but she couldn't have a mini reunion with her after thirty-odd years and then just drop that in her lap.

Reunion.

The word gave her the first stepping stone to take on the path to sorting out whatever was going on. She needed to trace Saran Sykes and see what she had to say for herself, as her husband had traced Steve. She sent a prayer upwards, odd as it was, to ask that Steve might be lying in hospital with a light sort of concussion, his phone in a drawer beside him with a flat battery, and this had all been a terrible mix-up. She'd be laughing about it by tonight. A story to share over a dinner table with friends one day. *Please.*

★

Erin took a call from the estate agent first thing that morning. The couple who came around yesterday had put in an offer – the asking price. They wanted to move quickly because they were buying it for their daughter to rent from them, so there was no chain.

'You're joking,' said Erin. Mind you, looking at the flat yesterday through a prospective buyer's eyes, she shouldn't have been surprised. It was pristine, impressive and extra-spacious now that a lot of furniture had gone. Wherever she moved to, she'd buy new, start again from the beginning. She had the money to do it and, as Alex had said the previous night, no one could take it with them, so she should enjoy it, make up for some lost time and be kind to herself.

She could have sat there for much longer, drinking with him in the pub. He told her he was a barrister and she tried not to think about him in a cloak and a wig, being very dominant in a courtroom because she didn't want to spark into life any of those sorts of feelings. Anyway, she wasn't even a quarter-healed from what had happened to her and she wasn't so stupid that she didn't know a grief club was not the ideal place to hook up with someone. All those vulnerable souls. They all needed to mend first, put the work into themselves before they started looking outwards.

She'd done a lot of thinking since she got home last night and it had made her realise she had overdue things to say to Bon. And maybe she'd take the opportunity to administer a little push at his back, as maybe someone should have pushed Father Paul and the housekeeper.

★

Mel had a shower and washed her hair, then put on some make-up but there was nothing she could do about her eyes, the windows to her soul. They were dull, flat, dead, the colour of mould, devoid of the slightest sparkle they usually held, and no patting at the puffs underneath them would fix them. She looked like shit as well as felt like it.

She picked up her car keys. It hadn't taken long to work out where she could find Saran Sykes because she was a beautician with her own salon, Saran for Beauty: imaginative, as well as a tart. Mel had no idea if she'd be at her business or not today, but it was a starting point. If she wasn't then she'd go to her home, as Companies House had a registered address of 4, Swan Gardens, Whitebrooke. She knew the area; the old grounds of a former grammar school which had been turned into a sprawling, yet at the same time prestigious housing estate. She and Steve had gone to nosey at a property there in Drake Avenue last year. She tried to think back if that had been his idea. Had it been going on then? Did he want to be nearer to his lover?

The salon was in the middle of a row of shops not far away from where Mel supposed Saran lived. She pulled up outside it. She was shaking, because there was an easily recognisable Saran Sykes framed in the front window taking money from a customer at a counter. She looked like Ted

Lasso's blonde boss, with her Marilyn Monroe hair and big flash of smile.

Mel forced herself out of the car, feeling conscious of each step she took. She might have practised what she would say in the drive over but now the words crumbled to dust in her mouth as her hand touched the door, pushed it open.

Saran smiled at her, just as she'd been smiling when she was standing with Steve in the photo. Mel almost smiled back, it was just natural to reciprocate politely.

'Hello, can I help you?' Saran said. The cheek of her. Mel wondered why Saran hadn't recognised her. Surely she'd have looked her up to see whose back she was stabbing, whose husband she was fucking. Or maybe she was one of those people who didn't give a toss.

Here you go, deliver the line, Mel.

'I'm looking for my husband. I believe you know where he is.'

Perfectly done, Mrs English.

Mel expected a lowering of eyes, a blush, but the blatant cow was just standing there, her brow creasing as much as the Botox would allow.

'We . . . haven't got any men . . . in here,' Saran returned, sounding slightly confused, wary, as if she might suspect Mel was loop the frigging loop.

'Steve English. I believe you know him . . . ' – pause for effect – '. . . know him *well*.' She added a tail onto the 'l' so it sounded like a lick.

Yep, that worked. Saran's demeanour changed, the smile started closing up.

'I . . . know Steve from school.'

She was messing with Mel.

'Where is he then?' she demanded, her voice rising now.

Other customers and staff in pink tunics were looking over. Good. Let them all hear what a piece of trash Saran bloody Sykes was. Mel prepared to deliver her coup de grâce. 'Your husband turned up at my house last night to tell me you were screwing.'

Well, the lanky trollop wasn't expecting that from the way her eyes widened.

Saran came to the other side of the counter at speed. Mel thought she was going to either grab her arm and try and chuck her out or slap her but she did neither.

'Come in here,' she said and marched past the two women having their nails done at stations and opened a door.

Mel followed her in, ready to hear the sordid lot of what she had to say for herself.

★

Erin walked into the repair shop and smiled at Adam, who waved as he was walking about while chatting on the phone to someone, about electrics presumably. 'Do that and you'll blow your bloody head off,' he was saying.

Erin grinned to herself, they were such a good bunch here. And there, ahead, was the lovely Sky, who looked like a wisp of cloud: delicate and fair. Pale, actually; she didn't have a lot of colour in her skin at the best of times but she looked *wan* today.

'Hello, Sky,' Erin greeted her warmly.

'Hello, Mrs van—' she pulled up her words and Erin supposed that she'd heard, then.

'Erin,' she said. 'Please, after all this time you are very welcome to call me just Erin.'

'Okay,' said Sky with a nod.

'Is he in?' Erin pointed to the office.

'Yes.'

'Thank you.'

Erin knocked and entered. Bon was on the phone but waved her in.

'Next week is fine. I'll be around,' he was saying to someone, wrapping up a call. 'Yes Mrs Tan— okay . . . Gwyn . . . cash or bank transfer totally fine . . . yes . . . you can arrange your own courier or use ours . . . okay . . . we'll see you then . . . bye . . . bye . . . bye.'

He put the phone down.

'Mrs Tankersley's desk is almost ready for collection,' he explained.

'I think she wants you to call her Gwyn,' said Erin with a cheeky smirk.

'I find it odd, calling customers by their first names.' He came over, gave her a kiss. 'How are you?'

'I'm very good, actually. I've had an offer on the apartment.'

'Already?'

'Dream offer. Asking price, no chain.'

Bon raised his eyebrows. 'That's great. If you're ready to leave it. Don't rush anything, though, if you don't want to, *bokkie*.'

She needed to tell him the truth.

'Have you got time for a very early lunch?'

'For you, of course. There's a new diner five minutes away. Sky said it's good in there.'

'My treat,' she said. He pulled a face that said he disagreed, but they'd fight over that when they were there.

★

The room had a massage table in it and smelt of ylang ylang. As Mel moved into Saran's wake, she wasn't getting any whiff of Chloe. Appropriately enough, she was getting Poison, though.

'What's this all about?' asked Saran, when the door was closed. No smile on her fishy lips now.

'As if you don't know,' said Mel, trying to keep some sort of a lid on it. 'Your husband said it was all because of the school reunion. I saw the photos of you together on Facebook—'

Saran held up a hand, long, slim, with perfectly mani-cured talons.

'Can I just stop you there, sweetheart.'

Mel was struggling now. How bloody dare she. *Sweetheart.* The patronising cow. 'Don't you call—'

'My husband is currently on an oil rig about a hundred miles north-east of Aberdeen. He's not due home until next week, so whoever turned up last night at your house isn't anything to do with me.'

She was lying, thought Mel. That's why she'd brought her into this private room, to save her embarrassment. Saran pulled a pink phone out of her pocket and began scrolling with flat, splayed fingers and those stupid nails. She then turned it around and held it up to Mel's face.

'This is my husband. Is this the man you saw?' Saran's tone was confident it wasn't.

The man in the photo was bald with a grey clipped goatee, arms like bags of walnuts. He couldn't have been more different to the cuckolded husband if he'd tried.

Mel's jaw dropped. She scrabbled her thoughts back to the night before. Had the man actually said who he was? No, he hadn't, she'd just presumed . . . She felt sick. She sank down onto the chair behind her before she fell. Humiliation piled on top of everything else in her head.

'No, it's not him,' she said. 'Oh god, I don't know what I'm doing, I'm going mad. He said it was because of the school reunion.'

Saran pulled another chair up and sat on it and Mel felt warm hands close around one of hers.

'Look, love, that school reunion ... people had had a lot to drink.'

'He's not answering his phone,' said Mel. Saran's unexpected sympathy had burst a dam wall inside her. 'I don't know where he is.' Tears sprang to her eyes, she couldn't have stopped them if she'd tried and she didn't have the energy to try.

'Oh fuck,' said Saran with a sigh of resignation. She pulled a clutch of tissues from a box on a small table and pressed them into Mel's hand. 'Look, I don't know for definite, but ... I did hear something and I hope it's wrong. I've been where you are, sweetheart and I wish someone had told me, however much it hurt. The name you might want to follow up on is Chloe Cardinale. As was, I don't know what she is now.'

'Chloe?' *The perfume.*

'She was there that night. She was a couple of years below us at school so I don't know that much about her. But I saw them with each other ... '

The way Saran said that was telling.

'I'm so sorry,' said Mel, blowing her nose.

'Do you want to sit in here with a coffee for a bit?' said Saran. 'You're okay, we're all girls together in here. We've been through some shite between us.'

'No, I'll go,' said Mel. 'I've caused enough trouble.'

Saran saw her out. Mel kept her head down as she did the

walk of shame through the salon with Saran's arm warm around her shoulder.

'Good luck, love,' Saran said at the door.

Mel couldn't get away fast enough.

Chloe.

Chapter 23

'This is indeed good,' said Bon. It was full of pensioners, taking tea, eating big slabs of pie with cream on it. 'Also, it's not often I go somewhere where I'm the youngest in the room. Sky was right.'

'Wise as well as lovely. Don't close your heart off to her because of her age,' said Erin.

'Stop it,' warned Bon.

'The last time I was in the shop, there was a woman there who was making Sky quite uncomfortable. I stepped in, it cost me a bear,' said Erin, pausing conversation to choose something to drink as the waitress appeared at her side.

'Why was she making Sky uncomfortable?' said Bon, when they'd ordered.

'Apparently she was a bit of a bully at school,' replied Erin, noticing a flyer on the table advertising a women's friendship group on Tuesday nights. She took one, folded it and put it in her handbag to read later.

'She mentioned someone called the Pennine Prowler, have you ever heard of him?'

'Of course,' said Bon.

'I looked him up. Sky's father was under investigation for the murders.'

'I know,' said Bon.

'You did?' She was going to ask why he'd never said, but that was Bon all over, not spreading business that wasn't his to spread.

'We all know that in the shop. It's got nothing to do with Sky and no one I know believes it has anything to do with her father either, just idle gossip, people wanting to force jigsaw pieces into spaces where they don't belong. What did she look like, this woman?'

'Pretty, long blonde hair, expensive clothes, the same age as Sky but looks older.'

Friend or foe, the woman whom Sky wouldn't make the bear for. One of the Sutton clan.

'Is that why you brought me here?' he asked, confusion claiming his features as he put the menu down.

'No. Well, partly. You obviously told Sky about the divorce. She's stopped calling me Mrs van der Meer at long last. I didn't think it was fair she was deceived, Bon. Were you trying to put her off you by pretending you were out of bounds?'

'Don't talk rot,' he said, a sneer wrinkling up his lip. She knew him though, better than he thought she did and she wasn't talking rot, but she didn't press it.

'Anyway, I will be going back to my maiden name, so I don't step on the next Mrs van der Meer's toes.'

'I doubt there will be another Mrs van der Meer,' said Bon.

'You are much too wonderful to die sitting on the reborn batchelor shelf.'

'I didn't say that I intend to sit on a shelf, or that I have been sitting on a shelf.'

Erin's eyes widened.

'Bon van der Meer, are you saying what I think you're saying?' She hadn't expected that.

'Don't ask me to answer that question.'

'I wouldn't, even if I am dying to know, though, obviously.'

'Nothing lasted; that's as far as I'm prepared to go.' He held up his palm to signal that the subject was at an end. He certainly wouldn't have shared that no one made him feel inside like the young woman he saw every day; that was something he was trying to keep even from himself.

They gave their food orders to the waitress and as soon as she'd gone, Erin said, 'I went to Molly's club last night. At the teashop.'

'The grief club?' asked Bon, noticing that her tone was no longer playful but serious.

'Yes. I've had a couple of failed attempts at walking in but I did it – eventually.'

He tilted his head at her. 'You having trouble getting your head around things, *bokkie*?'

'You could say that,' replied Erin. 'I haven't been completely honest with you, Bon. Only because I didn't know where to start telling you what a car crash' – *ironic* – '. . . what a . . . a nightmare it was with Carona. If ever you wanted revenge for what I did, you got it.'

Bon's eyebrows lowered in annoyance.

'I don't want revenge,' he said. 'What happened to you?' His voice softened. 'Erin, are you going to tell me what you haven't told me?'

'I think, the night Carona died, she planned to take me with her,' seemed a suitable starting point.

★

Astrid delivered the coffees to the table.

'Bloody hell,' said Venus. 'A miracle. Someone else actually knows how to put the kettle on.'

'Oy, you, less of your cheek,' said Iris, chuckling quietly because Venus and her sarcasm amused her no end. She slipped a tiny bag of blue sweets and an even smaller blue teddy bear into a cracker and then tied up the open end with a bow of white ribbon.

'Gender reveal crackers. I've seen it all now. I thought baby showers were over the top. What next?' And she huffed a dry laugh.

'In America they have "conception day" anniversary parties,' said Venus, popping a blue combo into her cracker. 'Three months after the baby is born they have a do and they reveal where the baby was conceived the year before.'

Iris's breath hitched. 'You're joking.'

'I'm not, am I Astrid? They have balloons shaped like tadpoles and eggs.'

'They're not right in the head,' said Iris with a tut.

'And they have a cake in the shape of a womb.'

Her expression was deadpan but Astrid couldn't keep her face straight, and gave the game away.

'You little bugger,' said Iris. 'Mind you, there's many a true word spoken in jest.'

'Give us all the occasions we can handle, that's what I say,' put in Astrid, who was working on some St Andrew's Day crackers for November.

'I don't mind what daft things people celebrate if the cash is going into Joe and Annie's pockets,' said Iris. The trouble was, Joe and Annie were selling up and no one was sure if a new buyer would move the operation to the other end of the country. They'd been lucky having the Pandoros as bosses and it was likely new people would want to make their mark. They'd bring in their own new brooms to sweep clean; it would be the end of an era, and however much Annie and Joe said that they'd do their best to make sure they'd be looked after, they couldn't guarantee it. Someone was walking around the building with Joe at that very minute: a potential buyer.

'Have you thought any more about taking in a lodger?' Iris asked Astrid, because she needed to change the subject before they all got down from thinking about what was to become of them.

'Yes, I've shifted things around in the second bedroom. It's big and sunny and has a right nice ensuite.'

'Why would you want to have anyone move in? I thought Kevin left you plenty.'

'He did, of course, Iris, but the house is so big for one. It's expensive to heat and the council tax – *oof!*'

Astrid didn't have to let anyone share with her and she could afford the bills easily, but she didn't want to sound pathetic admitting she was lonely.

'I'm not telling you what to do,' began Iris, about to tell Astrid what to do, 'but do be careful who you let in to share with you, love. They might look decent but I'm sure Jack the Ripper had his charming side. And once they're in, you might not get them out again.'

'Look on the bright side, why don't you, Iris?' said Venus, wobbling her head.

'I don't want Astrid coming to work murdered.' Iris wagged a wise finger at the young woman. 'Yorkshire's had more than its fair share of serial—'

'Shh, I think they're here.' Venus sliced her hands in a 'kill the conversation' way. She could hear Joe talking to someone, working his way through the factory, his voice getting a little louder with every step.

Joe came into sight, behind him a man in a beige trench-coat with a man-bag slung across his body. He didn't smile when Joe introduced him to his 'terrific workforce'. Iris took against him on sight. She would say later that he looked like a miserable Columbo. And as for that bag . . . She couldn't get her head around the fact that men now had their own handbag ranges.

'Is this all your staff?' asked Manbag, his eyes dragging over the motley crew, who to his eyes appeared as an ancient crone, a child with too much attitude and an Amazon.

'Yes, this is everybody, apart from my wife Annie of course, who can't be here today. But in really busy times we have casual people we can call in to help or do the work from home. They're all very reliable.'

'Very reliable,' repeated Manbag, as if he didn't quite believe that.

'Very,' confirmed Iris, although she realised she shouldn't speak, but she didn't like Manbag's tone. Joe gave her a censuring side-eye.

'And that's all you need in-house to produce the quanti-ties you do?' Manbag circled the assembled crew with his finger.

'Yes,' said Joe. 'They are the best workers. You won't find better.'

'Hmm,' said Manbag, sounding like Alan Sugar just after one of the Apprentices had told him how great they were and should be saved. 'What are they working on?'

'Gender reveal crackers,' replied Joe. 'You have an

occasion, we can make crackers for it. The world is going crackers crazy. We're exporting more and more these days as well as catering to rising UK sales: Thanksgiving, Christmas, birthdays, engagements, weddings, gender reveals—'

'Conception anniversaries,' threw in Iris, her face straight. 'It's the new trend, apparently.'

Joe gave her the full evil eye.

'Ri-ght.' Manbag turned; he'd obviously seen enough. Joe followed, but not before he'd pointed at Iris and then sliced his hand across his throat.

All three women paused and winced at each other.

'I hope Manbag doesn't buy it,' said Iris. 'I don't think my heart could stand the excitement of working for him.'

'If he does, you two will be out. My job will probably be safe, though,' said Venus.

She was joking, but Astrid was inclined to believe her. He'd get rid of Iris, and from the way he'd looked at her . . . She'd seen that look too many times not to know what the significance of it was.

★

They ate and Erin talked and Bon listened to it all quietly, without question, until the end. She told him far more detail than she told Alex: Carona's unfounded jealousy and possessiveness; her manic mood swings, too many good times spoilt by them, until there weren't any to spoil any more. Only then did he comment.

'I can't believe all that was going on and you couldn't come to me,' he said. 'At the very least, I could have given you some perspective and helped you get out of it sooner. And no, I don't think you're mad for believing that you could easily have been in danger. It isn't unheard of for unbalanced people to think that if they can't have you, no one else can.'

'Don't.' Erin shivered. Hearing it from Bon made it too real.

'You can't allow her to live rent-free in your head, *bokkie*. You have to let her go, or she's won.'

'I'm trying, Bon.'

'Have you thought about where you want to live next?'

'I didn't want to start looking until I had a buyer. I like this area. Little Kipping would be ideal, though the houses don't come up that often, do they?'

'No, but there are some new houses just outside Maltstone being built, behind the church,' said Bon.

'Are there? Ooh, I'll check those out.'

'You can always lodge with me, if they want you out quickly and you need some time to look around.'

Erin raised her eyebrows. 'Back to the marital home?' It had been the most beautiful house she had ever lived in. Bon had an old rectory, with a slow-moving river at the bottom of the garden. Layers upon layers of happy dwellers over many years had made up the calm essence of that house. She hoped she hadn't lessened it for him.

'Yes, if it helps. Don't rush into buying something. I don't want you making more mistakes. But there is plenty of room, as you know.'

'That would set the gossip machine whirring.'

'You'd be in the guest quarters,' said Bon with a lop-sided grin.

And she knew he'd do that for her and it humbled her all over again. She felt her body deflate, as if his generosity had punctured her.

'I can't forgive myself for what I did to you, Bon. You are—'

'Erin—' He cut her off, then she cut him off.

'Let me finish, Bon. I want you to find someone who gives you the space to care for them. Unlike me; I always knew best. Except I didn't.'

'Erin—' He tried again, and failed.

'You are one of the best people I have ever met in my life. I don't know how we did it but I am so glad you remained my friend. I'm not sure I could have been as forgiving—'

'Erin, please shut up,' and the tone of his voice said he really meant it.

'Thank you,' he said, when there was finally silence. 'I never told you this because I thought it might . . . hurt, but maybe seeing as we are both in full disclosure mode then perhaps it's right I should say it now. I was glad when you said you'd met someone else, because I had been trying to find a way for a long time to tell you that I wanted to end our marriage. I hadn't found anyone else, for the record, but I wasn't happy. I liked you, but I didn't love you. Not in the way I should have as a husband. We were wrong for each other.'

He stopped speaking and let that sink in. Erin sat stock still, her mouth sliding open by degrees. In all this time she had never considered that might be a possibility.

'I wasn't even jealous. I was relieved that you felt the same as I did. I was happy you were happy, it wasn't an act.'

'Fuck. Me.' Erin's expression slowly segued into a smile loaded with her own relief. 'I wish I'd known that.'

Bon shrugged. 'Now you do.'

Erin felt whatever it was that had sat within her, jagged and scraping her insides raw, punishing herself on his behalf, suddenly lose its power to constantly remind her of its presence.

'I have never wanted you to find someone to love more than I do at this moment,' she said, beaming at him. 'I don't want you to be lonely.'

'I'm not lonely in the slightest. I don't mind my own company. Being alone and being lonely are quite different.'

That made Erin glad, that he was stable and content, but it would be a waste if he stayed alone, both for himself and for whoever the lucky woman might be who could share his life.

At the end of the meal, the waitress brought the bill and Bon snatched it up before Erin had the chance to. She scowled at him.

'When you've sold your apartment and have lots of money in your bank, *then* you can buy me a burger,' he said.

'I take back everything I said about you. You're a control freak.'

Bon reached across the table, took her hand and lifted the back of it to his lips.

'This has been one of the best lunches we have ever had. I was glad to pay for the privilege,' he said.

Chapter 24

Amanda had taken half a day off to take her mum to an MOT appointment with her GP, Dr Clitheroe. Ingrid put the doctor on an adjacent pedestal to Bradley. Just being in his presence had the power to heal any ailment she had, like Jesus. *Ooh yes, doctor, I'm feeling fine. Yes, fit as a flea. Yes, I'm managing to feed myself well and get about.* When they were leaving, Amanda did a sly turnabout, pretending she'd left her phone in the consulting room, and grabbed the doctor to tell him about her mum saying more and more strange things. He told her to keep her eye on it and if it got any worse, then to make an appointment where they'd have a chat with her, an informal test to see if it highlighted that she might need a referral to the memory clinic.

For the whole of the journey home, Amanda was subjected to the many attributes of Dr Clitheroe. Then somehow the subject slipped to Bradley, as it usually did, and how well he'd done for himself, and Amanda wondered if she ever talked to Bradley like this about her. *Oooh our Amanda's done brilliantly. She's got a really good job and a lovely little house that she's paid off.* She knew, of course, that it didn't happen.

She picked them up some sandwiches from the bakery and a cream doughnut for Ingrid and left her watching her afternoon soap while she started a deep clean on the house. She emptied the cupboards in the kitchen and scrubbed the fridge out, feeling ashamed that she hadn't noticed how bad things had got. There was some cheese tucked in a slot in the door that was covered in mould and tins in the cupboards that were well over a year past their sell-by dates. That her mother's cleanliness standards had slipped was a massive in-dicator of a decline; she'd always taken such pride in having a floor you could eat your dinner off.

Upstairs, Amanda moved the bed as far as she could to clean up the dust underneath. She noticed in her mum's wardrobe that some of the clothes in there had dribbles of food on them, as if they'd been hung up after wearing and not put in the washbasket, which was empty apart from some tights and pants. She took all the ornaments off the cabinet next to the window so she could shift it to get behind it. There must have been a rotting floorboard because as she was vacuuming, she found that the carpet sank in the corner. Maybe that's why her mum put the unit there, to cover it up. She thought no more about it as she put everything, now wiped down, back as it was, before moving on to tackle the bathroom. There was a smell in there that she associated with old people, of mustiness and wee, which she hadn't detected before. She traced the second to the bathmat and the former to the towels hanging over the radiator that she guessed hadn't been changed in a while.

Before she left, she asked her mum if there was anything else she could do for her. Did she want her bills checking?

'They're all on direct debit. There's nothing for anyone

to do,' said Ingrid. 'I'm not that infirm that I can't keep my house in order.'

It was heartening to hear. Maybe her recent confusion was a blip; Amanda hoped so. Just because she was physically weakening, it didn't mean she was losing her mental abilities at the same rate. She didn't want to think of her mother starting to slip away from her. A mother she'd never really had as much as she'd wanted to in the first place.

★

There was a Chloe Cardinale with a Facebook page but it was set to private, so Mel couldn't see what she looked like and she could hardly drive back to Saran Sykes's salon and ask. Even ringing her was out of the question, because she just wanted to bury the whole encounter and pretend they'd never met. *Chloe Cardinale.* She sounded as if she'd looked like Sophia Loren, with thick dark hair, eyes like cocoa beans and generous, kissable lips. She looked on Saran's page again at the reunion photos but couldn't see anyone that fitted that description. She couldn't find anything else, no Insta, no Twitter or whatever it was called these days, no LinkedIn. It probably wasn't even her name any more, if she was married. Or maybe she had blocked Mel in advance just in case she went snooping for her.

She rang Steve again, but it went through to voicemail. She'd seen enough lady-psycho films to realise that if she kept phoning she'd end up looking unhinged and give him all the ammunition he needed to stay away. So she texted; a reasonable message, she thought.

I know about Chloe Cardinale. I think we need to sit
down and talk.

She added:

You fucking cruel nasty twat bastard

Then she deleted that last line and pressed send. Should she
have put a kiss on the end? She wished she had. She always
put a kiss on; not having one was significant. Why was she
having to think this deeply? Would Steve be sitting there
thinking, *Should I answer my wife? What will be going through
her head if I don't? What does that lack of a 'x' mean on her
message?*

She thought about ringing Finn or Andy who worked for
him, but that wouldn't have been fair, putting them on the
spot. They may not even have known. There was *no one* she
could call. The team at work were great but they certainly
weren't close enough to talk to about this and besides, she
didn't want them to know in case it all blew over. They
talked about the weather and the odd awkward customer,
or how their teenage kids' heads were stuck in their phones;
they didn't talk about cheating lousy painter-and-decorator
husbands dipping their paintbrushes in other women's tins.

She picked up a book and tried to read to give her head a
break, but the words rebounded off her brain and wouldn't
be taken in. She made herself some scrambled eggs and toast
and ended up throwing them in the bin. She felt as raw as
if someone had ripped the top layer of her skin off and she
had to move around in air that was full of salt. Everything
hurt. She sat down at the kitchen table and sobbed. Great
gulping weighty tears, with streams of snot that she just let

run down her chin unchecked. She was just sitting there like a melted candle when the front door opened, closed and seconds later Steve strolled into the kitchen. He looked at her and then looked immediately away and Mel moved quickly to do a repair job on her face with her hands wiping and flicking wildly. Of all the states to catch her in!

She rose to her feet and then froze. 'Steve,' she said, unable to think of anything else because she had no idea what his appearance meant. He had his smart black jeans and a polo shirt on, so he hadn't been working. She hadn't seen that top before. It had the Armani logo on it; had he bought it to impress *her*? Who cares, he was back; nothing else mattered. A smile of hope flickered on her lips, to be quickly extinguished by his next words.

'Look, I'm not stopping,' he said, unable to meet her eyes. 'I know you . . . *know*. I think we both need some space.'

She didn't need any space. She'd had less than twenty-four hours of it and it had nearly killed her.

'I didn't know if you were alive or dead. I didn't know whether to ring the hospitals or if you'd been mugged or crashed . . .'

He rolled his eyes as if she was being dramatic for effect; he clearly hadn't thought about it from her point of view at all. He turned and left the room.

'Steve, what's going on?' She followed him up the stairs and into the bedroom where he took out a case from under the bed and starting loading underwear from his drawer into it.

'*Steve*,' she pleaded. 'Stop, just stop a minute. You have to tell me what's going on, I'm in pain.'

It sounded histrionic, manipulative even, though she hadn't planned to say it, it just came from the place that was whirling with confusion, like a tornado, ripping up her insides.

'I can't talk now,' he said, moving to the wardrobe and throwing tops and jeans, trousers, shoes into the case. She tried to stand in front of him to stop him and he puffed out his cheeks impatiently.

'I'll talk soon, but not now, okay. Just ...' He flapped his hands about in a 'back off' gesture.

'Steve, this isn't you. Please, just give me a couple of minutes ...'

He carried on scooping, pressing down on the clothes so he could get more in. Then he zipped up the case and heaved it off the bed.

'Don't leave me this way,' she said, sounding like a really shit version of the Motown hit. She had to go at half the pace he did down the stairs because her knee was throbbing: stress could cause a flare-up, she knew, and the last time she'd had stress this bad was when her mum died. By the time she'd hobbled to the bottom, he was opening the door. She threw her whole weight against it to shut it.

'No, you don't, not until you tell me what's going on,' she said, sounding deranged, even to herself. 'Whatever it is, we can sort it.'

'Please, Mel, just let me go.'

'Is it a mid-life crisis? Is it a daft fling and you don't know how to undo it, is that it?'

'I don't know,' he said. The hardness had left his voice. She thought he was softening.

'Steve, I love you.'

'Don't, Mel.'

He reached round her, pulled the handle and she was jerked away from the door as it opened.

'I'll be in touch, I promise,' he said, skirting past her. Then, just as the door closed, he said, 'I'm sorry.' She couldn't read what sort of sorry it was, even though she played it back over and over again in the hours that followed. Sometimes she imagined it was *I'm really sorry I'm doing this to you, forgive me.* Other times, *I'm sorry I pulled the door a bit hard there and sent you flying.* But mostly it was just something that had come out of his mouth that had no more content than a mere full stop.

Chapter 25

After leaving her mum's house, Amanda drove over to her brother's. She'd been trying, without success, to get hold of him on the phone since she'd heard he was back from his holidays, so she decided to spring a visit. She noticed immediately the brand new Audis on the drive, a big blue one for Bradley and a smaller red one for wifey. My, they were splashing the cash. Arnold must have left them quite the fortune, though she thought they'd gotten their hands on it early, because wouldn't his estate have taken longer to settle? Then again, maybe the wily old creep had got smaller amounts dotted around in banks which didn't require a grant of probate to access them. She pressed the doorbell and saw the nets twitch and then Bradley opened the door. He looked baked brown, tanned to within an inch of his life and so when he flashed his new smile it dazzled extra bright. Like the icing in an Oreo. His teeth looked too big for his face and too perfect, like piano notes. He must have been happy with them, though, because he wouldn't close his mouth and kept them out on display.

'Had a good holiday?' asked Amanda as she entered the sanctum of Bradberry Towers. They didn't do kisses.

'Can't you tell?' he said, showing off his arms. His voice had changed as well. Maybe his tongue needed some lessons in getting round his new teeth.

Kerry appeared in the doorway, looking as if she'd been to the Arctic rather than the Med but her new teeth were also from the Shergar range and were the same brightness as her husband's.

'Kerry can't take to the sun, so she stayed inside and played Candy Crush and then we met for lunch and the jacuzzi,' explained Bradley.

'Sounds idyllic. How's the new kitchen?' asked Amanda. 'Mum told me all about it.'

'Oh, er, it looks good,' said Bradley. 'I'll show you if you like.'

Amanda followed him through. The kitchen was like the furniture equivalent of their teeth: blinding and too much.

'Blimey, I need sunglasses,' said Amanda, shielding her eyes.

'We didn't skimp on price.'

'I can see that.' Top-of-the-range triple oven, she noted. Kerry was opening doors and showing off the new washing machine and dishwasher hiding behind them.

'I heard Arnold died,' said Amanda, coming straight out with it.

'Yes, I thought Mother might have told you.' Bradley always called her 'mother' when he was talking about her. Never Mum. Although he would sometimes call her Mum when he was with her.

'She only let it slip while you were away.'

Bradley shrugged. 'It wasn't a secret.'

'And this is a heat pump tumble dryer. Miele.' Kerry pronounced it, *my-elly*. She was still opening up doors and Amanda wanted to tell her to shut up.

'I thought *you* might have told me yourself,' said Amanda to her brother.

'Well, you had nothing to do with him, did you?' answered Bradley, his tone slightly clipped.

Amanda wanted to say that actually she did a bit, seeing it was probably her own father's money that had allowed him to buy his ironmonger's. But what good would it do? Bradley wouldn't have rushed to get his cheque book and recompense her. Plus she had bigger fish to fry.

'Anyway, I need your help with Mum,' she said, wondering if Kerry would show off her new kettle, switch it on and make her a cup of tea.

'Oh?' Bradley folded his arms and they sat high up on top of his stomach. If he shaved off those silly scraps of hair on his head, he'd look just like Buddha.

'She's not going to be able to get up and down those stairs soon. Her house would sell quickly, because they're snapped up in that area. I've contacted an estate agent and I'm going through the house, deep-cleaning it and getting it ready. I don't want you going against that, especially as she seems to listen to you more than me. So be on the same page as me, will you?'

Did she imagine that look that crossed his face, the one that just for a second looked like fear? She must have. Unless it was fear at actually having to do something that involved more work for their mum than sticking a cheap dinner in the microwave.

She waited for him to say that he agreed, but he didn't.

'I think Mum is fine where she is.'

'It's a lovely house and it's only going to go up in value,' said mousy Kerry, opening up something else to show off, but Amanda wasn't interested and she was miffed at Kerry sticking in her two-penn'orth. If the house wasn't sold and she and Bradley jointly inherited it, she couldn't imagine him telling her to hold off selling because it would be worth more in a few years' time; he'd want his bunce before the funeral flowers had drooped.

'It's a very nice house, but it's no longer suitable,' said Amanda, tightly. 'And an increasing value on it isn't going to do anything to stop Mum falling downstairs. She's up to the toilet god knows how many times—'

'Well that's good exercise for her legs,' Bradley said, cutting her off.

Amanda could feel herself colouring.

This was how every conversation between them went. Bradley would not listen to any counter-argument to his, because their mother had pumped him up full of his own importance until he was a fat balloon of pomposity.

'She told me that she would like a bungalow. So we are going to get her a bungalow,' Amanda said with quiet, but firm, determination.

'She has never said anything to me about wanting to move.' Bradley's left eye always twitched when he got annoyed. It was twitching like billy-o now.

'Well, I'm not being funny but you're hardly there, are you? For some reason she thinks you work ten hours per day more than I do,' parried Amanda. 'Did you know that she hasn't been cleaning her house for god knows how long? Maybe the bits on show, but behind the scenes, she isn't managing. And she will fall down those stairs and kill herself if we don't act. The house is too big and impractical now. In the meantime, maybe Kerry could clean for her if she's not working. *For a price*, as you once volunteered her services.'

Amanda gave her brother a pointed look.

'Kerry's actually hurt her back. We have a cleaner of our own.'

Kerry's back looked as agile as Olga Korbut's as she bent down and stretched up to show off the kitchen.

Amanda saw Bradley start to gnaw on his bottom lip with his bulky new teeth. He looked like a different person with those things, they both did. They'd certainly got their money's worth in materials.

'I will go and see Mother on Saturday and sit and talk with her,' Bradley said. He didn't like direct confrontation and was clearly uncomfortable at being put on the spot. He was more the sly sort. He'd stab someone from behind rather than in the front. 'I'll take her out for her tea.'

Amanda climbed down off her high horse then.

'Definitely?'

'Definitely.'

'That'll be nice,' she said. 'She has missed you while you were away. She's not getting any younger, Bradley, and she's been getting a little confused as well, and it's worrying me. You should be spending a bit more time with her.'

'I spend as much time with her as my busy life permits,' he said, pulling a stern face of indignation.

Amanda was done. This was as long as she could usually stand in her brother's company without wanting to nut him. He was selfish, with every letter in the word a capital one. All take and no give. He always had been and he always would be.

'Right then, I'll leave it with you to sort, because it will be happening, so I'd appreciate it if you made it easy and worked with me – for her. This is *all* for her, an old lady who needs our help and we are not going to get a lot of notice if things go very wrong.' She turned to Kerry. 'Don't put the kettle on on my account. Enjoy your new toys.' She smiled sweetly, feeling that smile stop at her cheeks and not extend into her eyes.

She tried not to stomp out of Bradberry bloody Towers or whatever pretentious twaddle they'd called it. She could feel the core of her bubbling, getting ready to blow. Whatever benefits her HRT patches were giving her to tone down any symptoms of rage, her brother had the ability to undo them all.

Chapter 26

That Friday night Sky came right out with it, because she couldn't stand it any longer. She had been in the bath and as there was no lock on the door, she'd had to take her chair in and wedge it up against the handle. There was a hole where an old lock had been which she'd stuffed with loo paper. Halfway through her bath, she'd seen that paper pop out as if pushed from the other side and there was a shift of light behind it, indicating movement.

She pulled the bath plug out angrily, dried herself off, dressed and struck while her internal iron was hot.

Wilton was in the kitchen getting some milk out of the fridge, fag a-dangle in his mouth. She didn't eat in here any more. There were bits all over the floor which she wasn't going to mop because she was hardly ever in there. The dining table had rings on it from cups and glasses and the work surface was covered in crumbs because he was incapable of clearing up after himself. There were plates in the sink from days ago and none of them hers.

'Mr Dearne, I've got a new job and I'm going to have to leave before my tenancy agreement runs out. Can you give me a refund on the rent I've paid in advance, please?'

To her surprise he didn't say an outright no, but instead said, 'When were you thinking of going?'

'I have to start in the next two weeks and it's too far to commute from here.'

Then he gave her an outright no.

'Sorry,' he added on the end, a weak squeak of a word.

'Well, how early could we end the agreement?' She stood firm. It had taken her a lot to get to this point and she couldn't allow herself to back down.

He laughed which set off a cough loaded with sputum that he swallowed before talking again.

'There's not much point in having an agreement and you signing it and then you saying you want out of it, now is there? Where's the logic in that?'

Sky was about as wound up as she could get.

'Were you looking at me in the bath just now?'

'Me?' he said. 'Absolutely not.' He had a stupid smile flickering on the corner of his lips.

'You've been lying on my bed when I've been out,' she said then. 'I found hair on my pillow and you've been in my drawers.'

'Chance would be a fine thing,' said Wilton with a burbling giggle that sounded weird coming from a middle-aged man. He wasn't taking her seriously at all. She'd had to keep washing her bedding, imagining him rolling around on it. Or foraging through her laundry basket.

Wilton picked up her carton of Greek yogurt.

'That's mine,' she said.

'I know, I know. I'm just checking the expiry date.' He rotated it in his chubby paw of a hand. 'Something in the fridge smells, I thought it might be this.'

'It's not even opened yet, so it can't be that.' *It's you, you're making everything stink.* 'You have no right to go into my room. If I pay rent on it, it's mine to keep private and I'd like to put a lock on it.'

Wilton swivelled his head around. 'I thought you were leaving?'

'I am. But while I'm here—'

'This, young lady, is my property. I own it. I admit I did go in to your room once when you were out to check your window locks because there was a draught coming from somewhere, and I felt faint so I sat on your bed and I must have dropped off for a minute. I have trouble with my blood sugar. I am pre-diabetic if you must know.'

For all sorts of reasons that was claptrap. Not the least of them being that there was a shelf in the pantry which was made up almost entirely of boxes of his Mr Kipling cakes and great big bars of whatever chocolate was on a special offer in the supermarket that week.

She was getting nowhere fast, but if she didn't give him everything she had now, she never would. This state of standing up for herself didn't come along very often but when it did, she needed to make use of its wind to power her sail.

'You have no business to enter a room for which I pay you rent, without any notice; I know my rights. I find your conduct intimidating and menacing. This is harassment and if you don't terminate my rental agreement and refund me I will have to take things further and force your hand.'

She was breathless and could feel her chest rising up and down more than usual. All Wilton did was tilt his head and say, 'Is that so?'

'Yes it is.'

'You're going to prove that exactly how?'

'I don't need to prove it. I could just go straight to the police.'

Wilton grinned and wafted his sausage-like fingers at her.

'Off you trot then. See how far you get telling them your landlord was checking your window locks for your own security. Also, you won't be getting any refund from me. Not. One. Penny.'

He peeled the silver foil from her yogurt and stuck his tongue in it, savoured the taste, rolled the foil back and placed it on the shelf again.

Sky turned away in disgust. She needed to get to her room right now, because she could feel the telltale pressure on her chest. He would never have given her what she asked for; she shouldn't have bothered, because now she'd made things so much worse.

Chapter 27

Mel didn't know where to put herself. Usually she loved the weekends, Saturday was her favourite day of all. She'd go up to the farm shop in the morning and buy two steaks for their tea, and treat herself to a slice of cake which she'd eat while reading the newspaper. A nice lazy day. But this Saturday was awful because she hadn't a clue where she was mentally – or where Steve was physically. She finally rang his brother, who obviously did know what was going on because she'd got no further than 'Hiya, Dave', only to be cut off with the words, 'Look, Mel, I know why you're ringing and it's none of my business. I've to keep out of it so I'm sorry. And please don't ring my mum or dad because it wouldn't be fair dragging them into it either.'

And with that the phone went down. She wouldn't have rung them anyway. She'd known Steve's father thirty-odd years and still found him impossible to converse with, and to his mother she had no value other than being attached to her precious elder son. But it sounded from that call as though Steve had already warned his brother she might be ringing and not to entertain her, which hurt her – if she could be hurt any more.

Nothing held her interest and she'd exhausted the internet trying to find something out about Chloe Cardinale. She put the TV on but she couldn't concentrate. She contemplated opening up the bottle of Jack Daniels she'd bought Steve for his birthday and throwing it down her neck until she found oblivion. A stupid, temporary thought, but she could understand why people did it.

She caught sight of herself in the mirror above the sink when she went to the loo and saw she looked a mess. Her eyes were flat and bloodshot through constant crying and she'd grown a cold sore overnight that was big enough to have its own nervous system – and no wonder. She hadn't washed her hair for days. Her mum used to say that ginger hair was the most special of all because it reflected what mood you were in. When you were happy, it shone and when you were sad, it looked dull and no other colour did that. She'd said that when a lad at school had decided to target her for her hair colour. Armed with the fact that she had 'superhuman hair' she'd refused to be a victim and he'd moved on to someone with a different vulnerability to be exploited. Today, however, her hair looked as shit as she felt. As shit as her whole life.

The doorbell went and her heart kicked. Though it was unlikely to be Steve, since he'd just walk in, like he had two days ago. Ordinarily she wouldn't have gone to the door with unbrushed hair, puffy eyes and a zit on her lip that astronauts in the International Space Station could have seen, had they looked down in a Barnsley direction, but right now she couldn't have given a toss.

She opened the door to a postman with a parcel that had to be signed for. She knew what it was: a silver money clip, with mother-of-pearl inlay, that she'd had engraved with

Steve's name for their upcoming anniversary. Just a small, daft thing. *Their thirty years anniversary.*

It took her a couple of seconds to realise who the postman was holding out his machine, even though he was in exactly the same place he'd been standing the last time they'd had an encounter: the foul-mouthed Mancunian with the Oasis head. The man she'd presumed was Saran Sykes's husband. She signed her name quickly and took the parcel from him, saying nothing because she couldn't think of a single thing to say. Then she shut the door and leaned her back against it and a million things zoomed into her brain of what she could and should have said to him. The bell rang again. The same postman was standing there.

'You all right?' he asked, quietly, not shouting now.

She didn't really know how to answer that, apart from 'I'm fucking fine, mate. Never better', and doing a bit of swearing of her own. But not even that would come out of her mouth.

'I presume he's not back,' he said.

She took immediate umbrage, she couldn't help it.

'What makes you think that?' She waited for him to respond with, *because you look as if you've just crawled out of a skip.*

'I'm so sorry,' said the postman, sounding as contrite as his twangy accent would allow. 'I shouldn't ov come round that night. I didn't really know what else to do. I was so angry. And I shouldn't ov sworn. It's not what I do in front o' women.'

She saw him swallow, watched his Adam's apple rise and fall.

'I'm just covering this round for a mate who's on holiday. I nearly knocked yesterday in case you were . . . but I was . . . wanting to say . . . I didn't know what to say.'

He still didn't from the sound of things.

'I'm Pat,' he then said and held out his hand. She looked at it as if it were a thing unrecognisable. Her own didn't even twitch up to meet it and his slid downwards as if weighted, then travelled at speed up to his forehead to scratch it. Then into his trouser pocket where it pulled out a folded sheet of paper.

'I've written my phone number on here in case you wanted to talk about *fings*. I don't know if you do.'

Her eyes focused in on it, then, she took it from him, an automatic response rather than a chosen one.

'I'll get on then,' said the postman. 'Busy day.'

She didn't know why he was hanging around her doorstep as if expecting her to say more. She had no words to give, she was scooped out of them, scooped out of everything.

She closed the door. It was only then she realised: *Postman Pat*. It was like a comedy without the humour.

★

The video doorbell alert on her mother's house went off and Amanda temporarily abandoned cooking her pasta to view who was calling on her phone. Even though she'd put a 'No cold callers, no canvassers, no salesmen' notice up, cold callers invariably thought they were an exception. Amanda always tried to see them off by talking through the speaker before her mother got to the door.

On this occasion, though, it was her brother. He was trying to use his key, but Ingrid must have dropped the latch. Eventually the door opened and she heard her mother's shriek of delight at finding him on her doorstep.

'I'm doing your tea tonight,' he said, giving her a kiss

and Amanda thought, *So much for taking her out for tea as you said you were.*

She saw Ingrid reach up and place her hands on his cheeks.

'It's lovely to see you. Did you have a nice time on holiday?'

'You've seen me since, I've told you all about it. Remember I brought you that dish for trinkets,' he replied.

Amanda opened up the camera app on her phone so she could see what was happening in the hallway.

Bradley was sniffing the air. 'Smells nice in here.'

'It's one of them things that you walk past and it squirts out scent,' said Ingrid. 'Our Amanda bought it. It's a bit strong for me.'

'Shall I switch it off? She'll never know,' said Bradley, conspiratorially.

Yes, she fucking will, said Amanda to her screen, watching Bradley fiddling with the back, taking out the batteries. Behind him, Ingrid giggled like a little boy hearing a fart joke.

'I've got a proper treat for your tea tonight. Kerry's plated you up some pie and peas. I'll just put it in the microwave. You finish watching your programme and I'll call you through.'

Amanda switched to the camera in the kitchen. As the pie was heating up, Bradley opened up the cupboard under the sink and poked around in it. Then the one next to it. What on earth was he always looking for? It wasn't Mr Muscle to give the place a wipe down, that was for sure.

'That's not long enough,' Amanda said, talking to the screen as Bradley took the plate out and set it on the table. Ingrid came to sit down and Bradley brewed some tea.

'Is it okay? She makes a good pie does our Kerry.'

'It's a bit cold, but it's nice,' replied Ingrid.

Had that been her, her mum have moaned to high heaven about it, Amanda thought. Bradley, lazy twat, didn't put it back in for another blast. And he poured the tea out from the teapot too soon, it would be as weak as witch pee. Rush, rush, rush to do what he had to so he could go back home.

'Now then, what's this I hear about you wanting to move,' he said, pouring himself a cuppa.

'My friend's got a lovely little bungalow. Our Amanda said I might be able to get one as well. I—'

'Mum, we talked about this,' said Bradley, cutting her off. 'This is your home for life. Do you really think you could settle anywhere else? Bungalows aren't easy to find and if you did want one, you might have to move right out to Great Houghton, Darfield, Ponty.'

What the hell are you saying, you manipulative cock? Amanda was furious. He was putting their mum off because a move would be too much trouble for him. Right, she was on her own here, obviously. But she'd win.

'Just going to the toilet while you're eating,' he said.

Amanda switched to the camera at the bottom of the stairs which captured the full moon of his arse going up them. He stumbled and she thought, *good*. Let his heart jump into his mouth and feel the fear of a potential fall. He didn't walk into the bathroom, though; he went left into the bedroom and started poking around again. She saw him open the drawer where her mother kept her pants and then the one below where all her tights were. Then he crossed to the bed and lifted the mattress up from the frame to inspect underneath. He was searching for something significant or valuable, but what? Her mother's jewellery box sat on top of the chest of drawers and he didn't go near that. If he had and she'd seen him take something, she'd have ripped out every one of those big ugly teeth with her bare hands.

He walked over to her whatnot and scanned his eyes across the knick-knacks quickly, at one point looking directly into the camera, but he hadn't spotted it. He left then and went downstairs. Amanda saw him whisk away his mother's plate before she'd swallowed the last mouthful and dump it in the sink without even washing it for her.

'I'm going now, Mum, it's just a quick one tonight. My pie's waiting for me. You're honoured, you got yours first.'

'Tell Kerry it was lovely.'

He picked up her hand and sandwiched it between his own.

'I hope you always trust me to know what's best for you, Mum.'

He called her 'mum' then, when he was talking fondly to her – or when he wanted something from her.

'Of course I do,' said Ingrid. 'You're my little boy. However old you get.'

Bradley smiled, leaned forward and kissed her on her cheek and Ingrid's arms came out to hold him, but he'd moved and they embraced only air.

Bradley took a choc ice out of the freezer and handed it to her.

'Here you go . . . I'll see you in the week. Kerry sends her best. Love you.'

'Love you.'

Then he left and the sight of her mum on the camera screen sitting there at the table eating that choc ice all alone twisted Amanda's gut into a dreadful knot of sadness.

Chapter 28

'Gorgeous that, Bon.'

Bon looked up to see Willy Woodentop standing with a coffee, admiring his handiwork: a restored oval partner's desk in burr walnut with eighteen drawers, including a hidden compartment in the knee hole. He'd bought it for a song at an auction, where it had been in a sorry state and needed some proper TLC to bring it back to its former impressive condition. One of their regular customers had come in, seen it when it was only half-finished and put a deposit on it. She knew what sort of craftmanship Bon van der Meer was capable of and she was prepared to wait for however long it took for him to finish the job, because he would never be rushed on anything like this. He put the time in, all the time it needed and no less.

'Not even I would have thought that was worth saving,' Woodentop added.

'I thought you were nuts when you brought it in,' called Adam, sitting at his bench and doing something with a radio. 'I mean there's restoring, and then there's what you've done with that.'

Bon had had to make ten of the drawers from new and replace the leather desktop. And the result was stunning. Bon was very good at sensing what could be salvaged, but also what couldn't be – however much effort he might put in. Like his marriage. He knew that whatever he did, it had been past the point of restoration and he'd had to let it go. There was a difference between keeping a relationship breathing and one living. But unlike furniture, he couldn't keep bits of it to use for future projects.

'Thank you, boys, I appreciate your compliments.'

'And girls,' Mildred called out, after taking the sable brush from between her teeth, 'I've watched that desk change from a piece of junk to something the President of the United States would be blessed to have in his big oval office.'

'Och, what do you know, woman,' Jock threw at her. 'Get back to daing yer wee pictures.'

'I've always thought it's better to be a master of one trade than a jack of a few,' Mildred countered. It was all playful banter between them and passed the days. They greatly respected each other and their skills.

'Mrs Tankersley's going to be verrrry grateful,' said Jock, rolling his 'r's like Private Frazer in *Dad's Army*.

'Make sure she's not too grateful, Bon,' added Mildred to that. 'I heard when she goes swimming in the sea, barracudas make themselves scarce.'

'Mildred!' exclaimed Woodentop, winking at Bon. 'Mrs Tankersley being a proper lady an' all.'

'Takes more than money in your bank to make you into a lady. Rough lot reinvented, came from nothing. I knew her mother, Thelma, when we were younger. She'd been cocked more times than Clint Eastwood's gun.'

Coming from the refined and genteel Mildred, that

sounded extra hilarious. Jock nearly spat his tea out. Peter, who was oiling the legs of the chaise that Astrid had found Sky asleep on, dropped his cloth in shock.

'All I'm saying is, you be careful, Bon,' Mildred went on. 'You've got a few bob and so has she. That, in her book, is enough of a firm basis for a great match. She wouldn't be looking at any of this lot' – she indicated towards her fellow craftsmen with a sweep of her brush – 'to hook up with. Mind you, I can't say as I blame her.'

Peter hooted and Jock shook his head, smiling. More banter ensued but Woodentop pulled Bon to one side.

'Can I have a quick word?'

'Course, Willy,' said Bon and they moved down the shop to a quieter place.

'Where's Sky?' asked Woodentop, looking around for her.

'Gone out for a sandwich.'

'Ah okay, good. Is, er . . . ' Woodentop looked around again, checking they were out of range of anyone else's hearing. 'Is she all right?'

'I think so, why?' asked Bon.

'I've been meaning to ask you, but I didn't know whether I should.' Woodentop's voice was low. 'I'm talking out of turn, so don't repeat owt. A few weeks ago, I took the missus up to the hospital and I saw her there – Sky. She didn't see us and I didn't want to embarrass her.'

Bon waited for Woodentop to go on and then prompted him when he didn't.

'What department?'

'The cardiac unit,' said Woodentop.

'Maybe she was visiting someone?' Bon suggested.

'Nope, she was sat in the appointments waiting room and she went in to see a doctor. I just thought I'd ask.'

Woodentop slurped from his *If you want a BIG WILLY, I'm your Man* mug that his wife had bought him. From the look on Bon's face though, he was as much in the dark.

'Ah, okay, I just thought you might have known.'

And off he went back to his station, leaving Bon pondering about Sky. As if she wasn't on his mind enough as it was.

Chapter 29

'Here you go,' said Ray, bringing a plate of gooey cookies through to the back room, still warm from the oven.

'Oh, Ray, you really didn't have to. I don't think there will be that many people coming anyway,' replied Amanda, hoping that her second friendship meeting didn't just consist of her and gobby Janine. If that happened, she'd close the fledgling club down and go back to square one. Or abandon it totally.

'Because of you, I have customers,' said Ray, then he tilted his head. 'What's going on with your neck there?'

'God knows,' she said. At least she knew it wasn't another present the menopause fairy had decided to chuck at her. It was simply tension she was carrying in her head and shoulders, tension caused by her shit of a brother who was doing everything to sabotage the plans she was trying to set in place to move their mum to safer accommodation. She'd rung him to ask how he'd got on with the conversation he'd promised to have with her. He'd told her that he'd had a think about it, and it would be too much: *'the stress would kill Mother'*, he'd decided. Amanda had told him that the stairs would kill her first and slammed down the phone on him. As she expected, her mum had gone over to Bradley's side and no longer wanted to talk about moving. No wonder her neck felt tight. She could hardly turn it. She'd had two lots of painkillers and it hadn't even taken the edge off it. And it wasn't doing much for her insomnia, either.

'Sit,' said Ray. He was insistent when she looked puzzled. 'Just do it.'

He pushed her down onto one of the chairs at the table and moved behind her. She turned to see what he was up to and he clicked his fingers and pointed forwards. She heard him rubbing his hands together. Then she felt those hands on her shoulders and totally stiffened.

'Oh, come on now,' he said, chiding her. 'You're kicking against me. I know what I'm doing. I learned how to do sports massage when I coached some football. I won't be as brutal as I should be but trust me, it will help.'

She gulped, had a sudden vision of herself lying on the table in front of her naked and covered in olive oil, being massaged by Ray wearing an American football kit. Those HRT patches certainly didn't stifle any wayward imagination.

'Turn to your right,' he commanded, gently manoeuvring her neck to where he wanted it positioned so he could smooth up and down it with his strong fingers.

'Ideally I'd have given you a good half hour on it. You need to go and book yourself in somewhere. You deskdwellers are prone to this, it's your weak spot,' said Ray.

At the moment she was made up entirely of weak spots, all of them wanting a massage.

'I need oil,' said Ray. 'You mind if I splash some on you?'

Was he joking? If he wasn't – yes. If he was – still yes.

He was joking, of course.

He kneaded, his thumbs circled, his fingers pressed; she wanted him never to stop. He was right though, she did need to book herself in somewhere. She failed to give herself the care she needed.

'OOoh.' She hadn't meant to make the noise but he got her in a sweet spot. It was directly connected to somewhere she shouldn't tell him about.

'That's it, good girl, you're softening,' he said.

He had no idea.

She heard Janine's voice outside talking to someone and she jumped up just before she walked in with Sky, the lovely silver-blonde young woman who made teddy bears.

'Thank you, Ray ... for the ... cookie ... things,' said Amanda, a bit at odds.

'Ooh, more of those gooey biccys,' Janine shrieked with delight, more or less leaping over the table to get to them. Had she been a racehorse, she'd have cleared Bechers Brook for them without even breaking into a sweat.

'Anytime,' said Ray, who had a habit of making things go gooey in the middle, it seemed.

Amanda checked her watch. It looked as if there would only be three people tonight, then. The knitter was a no-show and so were the other two silent women – no shock there. Then the door opened and in walked a woman with a glory of ginger hair, but very tired eyes.

'Hi, is this the women's friendship group?' Mel said. She couldn't quite believe she'd dragged herself to the shower, washed her hair, put on some clothes, tried to cover up the giant cold sore with artful dabs of make-up and made it out of the door. She just couldn't stand one more lonely night in the house. It would probably be a wasted effort but when you were desperate for some company and were actually thinking about contacting your horror of a sister – yes, things were that bad – then something had to be done about it.

Janine had brought with her a list of facts about the menopause. Not so much a list, as a ream. She had rattled off two pages of 'did you know' information about it – and she was by far from finished – when there was a knock at the door and it opened just a little for them to see a slice of person, statuesque with long blonde hair.

'Is this the friendship group?' asked the new arrival, shyly. She was well over six foot tall. 'Oh, hello.' Her lips curved into a smile when she spotted Sky.

'It is indeed, come on in,' said Amanda, eager to welcome a friendly face, though really she should do the woman a favour and tell her to run, run as fast as she could in the opposite direction.

'Sorry, it's for women only,' said Janine, just as Astrid was about to take a step inside.

Astrid's foot stalled.

'You come in right now,' said Amanda, furious that gobby Janine had the gall to police the door.

'Er . . . excuse me, but no.' Janine started making a series of jerky, affronted movements, her eyes raking up and down the newcomer. 'I thought this was a a friendship group for *women*. What are you?'

'She's an *Astrid*,' said Sky, leaping to her feet as if she was about to confess to being Spartacus.

'Well, I'm afraid, if *that*'s staying, I'm not.' Janine grabbed her copious notes, her bag and her coat. No one did anything to stop her. She marched out and shut the door rudely behind her, a statement of her outrage.

Astrid stood there not knowing what to do.

'Should I go?' she asked, eventually.

'You absolutely shouldn't,' said Amanda, cracking a smile. 'If only I had a guest-of-honour chair, it would be yours right now.'

It was strange how dynamics worked, thought Amanda a little later as she handed round more of Ray's delicious cookies. It was as if Janine's presence had dammed up a river that could now run freely. The atmosphere felt lighter by degrees. The coffee flowed. She'd never get to sleep with all this caffeine in her system, but sod it, this was more how she'd imagined her group would be. Preferably with a few more people, but this was a good start, easy company, though the redhead wasn't saying much.

Amanda had given her spiel again about where she worked and what she had tasked herself with doing, and that she hoped in the course of the weeks ahead she'd harvest some useful info about the menopause's impact on the workplace; but more than that, she hoped she could bring together some nice women to let off steam, share, support, chat, or moan in a safe, protected space. *Without some gobshite grabbing all the limelight*, she added to herself.

'I work for a bank,' said Mel, forcing herself to contribute because she was aware she'd been sitting there like an ornament. 'And a couple of years ago, head office asked anyone going through the menopause to do a survey. So a couple of us did; it came to nothing. We got a gift bag to say *thank you* which had a pen and three Tena Ladys in it. Oh, and some samples of Yorkshire Tea. Apparently the idea was that everything tastes better with a cup of tea. One of the women I worked with said she'd like to shove that effing tea bag down the CEO's throat. She was suffering with a bit of rage at the time. We kept her off the counter when we saw her turning red.' Mel smiled, for the first time in god knows how long.

Astrid threw back her head and laughed at that, along with the others.

'My mother-in-law didn't have a single symptom,' Mel went on. 'Some women don't know they're born.' *Mind you, Mother Nature probably thought she'd suffered enough having that personality*, Mel didn't add.

'I had an early menopause, thanks to a hysterectomy,' said Sky. 'I hope that's me done for a while on the change front.'

'I know why they used to call it the *change*,' said Astrid. 'I'm not going through the menopause but I have felt change inside me, unrest und anxiety. It's my age, I'm sure. And maybe my circumstances.' She gave a smile then that was right at the sad end of the spectrum. It was a smile that every one of the women in the room recognised.

'Well, you're among new friends if you want to talk about those circumstances,' said Amanda.

Astrid's expression morphed to that of someone mortified that she might have made herself the centre of attention.

'It's just life stuff of course,' she made light of it. 'Very small problems considering what some people have to put up with.'

Sky replied to that, 'Astrid, my dad used to say that we shouldn't try to bury problems because we think someone else might be going through worse. What you're feeling is valid and real and shouldn't be minimised.' She felt herself starting to blush in case she was coming across as a wannabe Confucius. 'For some context, my dad had a lot going on in his life and I didn't want to tell him that I'd battered a girl at school with my satchel and was worried about the repercussions.' Then Sky wished she hadn't given them that example because it didn't exactly cast her in a good light. But she spotted Amanda's eyes twinkling with some amusement.

'Sky,' said Astrid with a look askance at her, 'I can't imagine you hitting anyone with a school bag.'

'It was a big bag too. Full of loads of books and I didn't hit her hard enough, even though I knocked her flying off her feet,' Sky fessed up. 'She said something vile about my dad. I never did tell him what it was but . . .' Her voice trailed off because she didn't want to start unloading all that. She waved her words away. 'Anyway, sorry, I hijacked the conversation there. Would anyone like a fill-up of coffee?'

Everyone put up their hand.

'Okay, so what was it that brought us all here?' asked Amanda. 'What was it that made you think, *I need to go and mix with total strangers up at the new diner on the hill?* Because I'll confess, I might be mining for menopause info but I wanted the company of women and I wondered if there would be others like me. I used to have pals at school and somehow, when we grew up, we went our separate ways; they got kids, drifted into other friendships where there were other kids. I miss having a good mate. Someone to take me off the boil.' She was on the boil these days rather more than Stromboli.

'I am a widow,' said Astrid, taking advantage of a rare moment of bravery that happened to land with her. 'I met someone who loved me for who I am . . . now, and it was quite the shock for us both to find each other. I thought that people only found a love of their lives like that in books or in films, then I go and fall for a man and then he tells me he's fallen hook, line and zinker for me. And we married, we had a big wedding because he knew I always wanted to be a bridesmaid but I never was, so he made me a bride instead. And last year he died. He felt a bit poorly, he went to bed to sleep it off and suddenly he was getting worse. His body started attacking itself, trying to fight off the infection. He was six foot eight inches tall, he was bigger than a church door and he was felled by little, tiny germs.'

Her voice faltered; she coughed, sniffed. 'Sorry.'

Mel reached down into her handbag and pulled out a packet of tissues then whizzed it across the table to Astrid.

'Take the whole packet, I've got plenty,' she said. She was keeping the Kleenex company afloat single-handedly at present.

'I'm lonely,' Astrid admitted. 'That is why I am here. The place where I am most happy at work, they are selling. I have lost my man. My world is upside down. I don't need the money but I am hoping to rent a room out in my house just so that there is someone around to share the space with.'

'Be very careful then,' Sky warned her. 'If you get the wrong person, your home might not feel like your home any more. I live in a house and it used to be great, my house-mates were ace but now the creepy landlord has moved in and trust me, I would rather live alone any day than share with someone I couldn't stand.' She went on to tell them how bad things really were and how getting out wasn't as easy as it might appear.

Astrid blew her nose. 'You should come and rent my room, Sky,' she said.

'If it's still available in five months, I will.' Said aloud, 'five months' sounded even longer than the time it was.

'Just leave now, never mind about the money. I am sure we can sort out something.'

'Thank you, Astrid. I'll think about it.'

It was so kind of Astrid, but she wouldn't move in if she didn't have money to pay her rent. And she wasn't going to let Wilton get away with not giving her the bond back. She'd think of something and wouldn't say any more about it for now. Astrid was too generous and Sky wouldn't take advantage.

'What about you, Mel?' asked Amanda, because she looked like a woman who had been kicked to buggery, dropped and then picked up again for part two.

'Me?' began Mel, with a clip of brittle laughter. 'Up until three weeks ago if you'd asked me how things were going, I'd have said "I'm blessed". Lovely husband, no mortgage on the house, good job, secure. Then my husband went to a school reunion. He didn't want to go, I told him not to be so daft, he'd enjoy it. And it appears that he met someone that night and he's walked out on me to be with them. Just like that. He took the sandwiches I'd made for him, he went to work and he didn't come home. The man who I would have given a gold Olympic medal to for being constant couldn't even let me know he wasn't dead in hospital. I was going out of my head. He wouldn't answer my calls or my texts.'

Mel looked up and found a captive audience. She didn't think she would have been able to speak about it so objectively, as if this had all happened to another Mel in a parallel universe.

'The first I knew about what was going on was when *her* husband turned up on my doorstep to tell me his wife was shagging my husband. And if that wasn't bad enough, I got the wrong woman and went storming into her beauty salon to confront her and made a total arse of myself because her bloke was on an oil rig north of Aberdeen. Then the right woman's husband turned up again at my door on Saturday morning looking like a pound-shop Liam Gallagher, with the fucking personalised anniversary present I'd ordered for my husband — because he's only a postman ... and he's called Pat. And if that wasn't enough, I opened up the bloody present and they'd printed "SIEVE" on it instead of "STEVE".'

She breathed the full stop. There was silence and then the room erupted with laughter. All four of them, Mel most of all and she had no idea why she was laughing. And Astrid was trying not to and Amanda's eyes were squirting out tears, and Sky was apologising and trying to press the corners of her mouth inwards to stop. They were in fits and then it died to sighs of apology and smiles of sympathy.

'It's not funny, I'm so sorry,' said Amanda.

'Trust me, I needed to laugh,' said Mel. No, it wasn't funny — and it also was. Postman Pat who looked, sounded and even walked like Liam Gallagher. Lovely, kind Saran Sykes whom Mel had fantasised about punching; that sodding money clip with SIEVE engraved on it. You couldn't make it up. It was like being in a play written by someone who'd shuffled up a bag of tropes and pulled them out one by one to make a storyline from.

She told them then how Steve had come back to fetch his clothes and wouldn't engage with her, even though he must have seen how much she was hurting.

'It was just cruel,' she said. 'I was looking at someone I'd known for over thirty years and I didn't know him at all. I never thought he'd treat me like this.'

'Sounds to me like he's deflecting,' said Astrid, reaching for another cookie, 'shutting you out because your tears could make him feel guilty and a lesser man if he lets them in.'

'I have to agree there,' Amanda nodded slowly, sympathetically. 'He's creating some emotional distance, so he doesn't have to live with the shame of what he's doing to you.'

'I don't understand why, though,' said Mel, shaking her head. 'Maybe I might if he was highly sexed and I wasn't giving him what he wanted, but if anything it's the other way round. And thinking about it, because I've been analysing our relationship like a forensic scientist since it happened, it's always been me who suggested we go here and do this, putting the effort into us. If it was up to Steve, we'd sit in front of the TV every night apart from going out for a curry occasionally with his brother and whoever he happens to be with at the time. I can't get my head around any of it. What did I do or not do to make him into this man?'

She reached in her bag for a tissue. Trying to get into Steve's head from every angle had exhausted her. He'd turned into one of those puzzles with a treat in the middle that you couldn't get to because there was absolutely no way in. She blew her nose. If she could have sold snot, she'd have been able to buy herself a Porsche.

'Please don't start blaming yourself for his behaviour,' said Amanda gently. 'Just because you can't explain it, don't automatically presume it must be you who's at fault.'

Mel didn't say that she was already doing that. That she'd wondered if all this would have happened if she'd been a couple of stones lighter. Or had longer legs, or brown eyes instead of green and wore a more intoxicating perfume, or wasn't Mrs Boring works-in-a-bank.

'Postman Pat gave me his number in case I wanted to talk,' she sniffed.

'And do you?' asked Amanda.

'I could think of nothing worse at the time,' she replied. 'But I must admit, I am coming round to the idea. Should I?'

'I vould,' said Astrid. 'Information is power.'

'It's up to you, but yes, if it were me, I think I would too,' Amanda nodded.

'And me,' Sky added to them.

'Thank you,' said Mel. This was why she had braved coming here, to just *be* with other women who might have been around the block and had an inner compass that wasn't whirling in the dark. She was lost in her own life without a map and groping for a guide rope.

It was the time to bring the meeting to an end; the session had flown tonight without gobby Janine dragging them down, and Amanda knew that while she might not have collected any data about menopause in the workplace, the evening had been beyond valuable for them all.

'Same time next week, everyone?' she asked hopefully.

'Deffo,' said Mel, seemingly speaking for them all.

★

Sitting in her car, Mel pulled the piece of paper with the postman's number on it out of her purse and started off a text.

This is Mel English. I will chat to you if you like.

She hadn't even had chance to start up the car when a reply came back.

In person would be best. What about the Spouting
Tap in Little Kipping? It's out of the way. Tomorrow
at 7.30 pm suit?

She sent a thumbs up.

★

The diner was empty when Amanda came out of the back
room carrying the empties. Ray was wrapping up talking
to one of the chefs who was on his way home. This place
should be buzzing until at least ten. Ray didn't seem that
unhappy though, but then he was a glass-half-full kind of
guy, that was clear. She should ask him for some lessons.

'I heard you all laughing from in here,' Ray said to her,
smiling, taking one of the coffee pots from her. His hand
brushed against hers in the act of doing it. She thought about
his fingers smoothing down her neck earlier and her brain
fizzed like a shaken bottle of champers.

'They were a smashing bunch of women. I hope they
come back,' she answered him. 'Were you busy tonight?'

He rocked an open hand back and forth. 'Been better,
been worse. Not bad for midweek, I suppose. We have a
party of fourteen on Friday night and Saturday's more or
less full, so I'm good with that. How's the neck?'

Amanda tilted it quickly to the side. 'Terrible. Know
anything that could help?' An internal voice of disapproval
reprimanded her for flirting. She might as well have thrown
her knickers at him. She went for damage limitation. 'I'm
joking, obviously; it's eased up, whatever you did worked.
Thank you, I'm good now.'

'Go and book a long massage. Anyway, I've been

thinking, one night, I'm going to cook you dinner here,'
said Ray.

'Honestly, no thanks necessary. I—'

Ray shushed her. 'It's happening. Don't argue.'

She opened her mouth and that inner voice told her to
shut up and stop wrecking things for herself. She heeded it,
for once. So now she had something else to look forward
to, as well as the next Tuesday club, she thought as she said
a goodnight and headed out to the car.

She'd just zapped it open when the phone rang in her bag.
It was Bradley and Bradley rarely rang.

She answered it warily. 'Hi. Everything okay?' because
she suspected it wasn't.

'Mother's in hospital,' he said. 'Dolly next door called me.'

'What happened?' asked Amanda, feeling her heart
speeding in her chest.

A beat. 'Apparently . . . she fell down the stairs,' he said.

Chapter 30

Amanda raced to the hospital. Thank goodness at that time of night there were plenty of parking spaces, because during the day the whole area was always gridlocked with traffic. Bradley had said that Ingrid was in the acute medical unit, which was where they took people in the first instance, she knew that from previous visits with her mum. She caught the lift and then walked in and saw her brother and sister-in-law sitting on chairs outside a bay.

'How is she? What happened?' she asked, taking the third seat.

'Well, as I said on the phone, she fell, we believe.'

He had a really annoying way of talking, almost slow-mo, as if he was thinking about the position of every word before putting it down next to the one before it. 'Dolly, the neighbour, went round. She'd rung to tell her about a TV programme and Mother didn't answer so she decided to check on her and heard her calling for help. Luckily she has a key for emergencies, Mother said she'd missed her step and fallen. Dolly rang an ambulance and then Mother asked her to phone me. We came straight here because there was no point in going to the house, we'd have missed her if she was being blue-lighted.'

It wasn't the time nor the place but Amanda felt yet another a stab of hurt that their mum had asked for Bradley before her. It was the story of her life, to be put in second place and she should have been used to it, but still, it never failed to sting, this son superiority.

'And what have they said? Where is she?'

'She's having an X-ray; we've been told to wait here. She's hurt her head and side and legs and arm but she was talking fine, if a little disorientated.'

'I don't like hospitals,' put in Kerry. 'Everything always takes so long.'

'I will have to go and find a toilet,' said Bradley.

'There's one for visitors by the exit,' said Amanda. She was at the age where every jaunt out involved a recce for where the nearest loo might be.

Bradley stood up, hoisted up his trousers. These days they either sat above his mighty pot or well below it.

'We've got private health care. Platinum level,' said Kerry as they waited together.

'Lucky you,' said Amanda. Something else for them to brag about.

'Bradley had it through his job but we've carried it on. He got it free for long enough, so it all evens out now we've to pay for it.'

'Nice perk to have.' Out of sheer devilment, she was tempted to say that Mon Enfant had its own private hospital on site just to top her, but she couldn't be bothered.

Bradley returned. Amanda heard him before he came around the corner. He was half-man, half-battered accordion. It was a good job he already had private healthcare because they would never have taken him as a new customer.

Bradley sat down, sighed, looked at his watch. 'An hour and a half,' he said in a laboured whisper.

'That's hardly anything in an NHS hospital,' replied Amanda. 'I'm surprised she wasn't still in A and E on a trolley.'

They heard a trundle, the noise getting louder and then saw a bed nosing out from around the corner, heading towards them. Ingrid was lying on it. She had a dressing on the side of her head which was blanking one eye.

'Bradley?' she called.

'Yes, I'm here.'

'Is that you, Amanda?' Ingrid added as she was wheeled into the bay. The porter manoeuvred the bed into position. There were three other people in the bay, all elderly, all supine and sleeping.

'There you go, darling,' said the porter to Ingrid.

'Thank you,' Amanda said to him because no one else had acknowledged him.

A nurse appeared. Young, but with an undeniable air of efficiency.

'Hi, I'm Rashida. I'll be looking after Ingrid. Is she your mum?'

She looked at Amanda first.

'Yes, and this is my brother.'

'Have a seat. Can I take down some history from you?'

Bradley huffed tetchily. 'We've already done this once.'

'It's just a few extra details,' said Rashida, with more patience than Amanda would have shown him.

'Yes, you fire away,' she said, because she would have bet her bottom dollar that Bradley answered 'don't know' to most of those questions already asked. He wouldn't have had a clue about his mother's dosage of lacidipine and darifenacin for instance. Amanda sorted out all the tablets for the week and put them in a pill organiser for her.

Rashida took down the details she needed, including some things to write on the whiteboard above Ingrid's head, conversation starters for medical staff to engage her with. 'What does she like?' she asked, addressing Bradley.

'I don't really know,' he said. '*Coronation Street* maybe.'

'She hates *Coronation Street*,' said Amanda, butting in. 'She likes going to the coffee shop around the corner in the mornings with her friends. She does all her own paperwork and bills, she's always enjoyed doing that. She watches *Sunrise Town* every single day. It's a soap from Australia. Very far-fetched but she never misses it. And Chuck Norris in *Walker, Texas Ranger*. She fancies him rotten.'

Bradley had a dense look on his face as if all this was news to him, because it was.

Ingrid had gone to sleep and she looked settled. The nurse explained that she'd been given some painkillers and fluids because she was somewhat dehydrated. She asked if she kept up her fluids at home. Again Bradley gave a shrug of ignorance. Amanda answered, 'I've always made sure she has plenty of easy-access drinks in the fridge, she likes the little bottles of flavoured waters and I check the recycling bin for the empties to make sure she's having them.'

'When was the last time you saw her? She couldn't tell us how long she'd been lying there.'

Amanda looked to Bradley. He'd been on duty that teatime.

'Erm ... I didn't actually go today. I rang to make sure

she was fine about ... two—' although Kerry mistakenly dobbed him in by saying, 'eleven' at the same time.

'She was perfectly fine. I asked her.' Bradley's tone was abrupt and defensive because he could read the look of disgust on his sister's face. 'She was going to make herself some toast because she didn't think she'd feel very hungry ... later. She wouldn't have starved.'

As soon as the nurse had gone, Amanda turned on him.

'If you aren't going to go up, you should tell me.'

'She doesn't need someone to visit every day. You've made a rod for your own back, Amanda, going up when she has been perfectly capable of making herself something to eat. Some of us have lives.'

The implication was that she didn't. He was sort of right. And it was just bad luck that on the day when their mother didn't have company, she'd fallen. Amanda apologised to her brother for snapping at him and he accepted it, albeit with a huff of resignation.

'Well, if she's sleeping, we should let her,' said Bradley. 'She's in the best place, and needs rest.'

'I'll stay a bit longer,' said Amanda.

Bradley and Kerry both leaned in and gave Ingrid a kiss on her cheek which she would have liked, Amanda thought. She was surprised she hadn't woken up like Sleeping Beauty, but it was better she was out of it after what must have been a scary ordeal for her. She'd sign up to that Scopesearch site tomorrow and see what the up-to-date valuation on the house would be, because Bradley was unlikely to disagree with her now about selling up. How could he, when exactly what she had warned him would happen had.

She pulled up a chair and sat at the side of her mum, gathered Ingrid's hand into her own, bones covered in crepe paper, wormlike blue veins standing proud. Old hands. Her mother still wore her gold wedding band, the one that Arnold had put on her finger, because she had never stopped calling herself Mrs Worsnip. Amanda thought back to a time, before Bradley, when they'd go shopping and Ingrid would say, *Hold tight*. In the days when her hand always gravitated to her mother's like a magnet.

Ingrid's mouth was a long open O and she was snoring softly. It was hard to see the young woman she was once, the one whom her father adored, the woman he couldn't wait to get into bed on their wedding night. She couldn't remember her mother crying when he died. Maybe she did at the funeral that Amanda wasn't allowed to go to. She didn't even know it had happened until after it had, and that decision had been wrong, not to let her say that last goodbye to a father she loved. A funeral was not the place for children, Ingrid had said by way of an excuse much later. Not because of the gravitas and sadness, but in case they disrupted it by being children.

The woman in the bed diagonally across started shouting for a nurse to help her. She needed to wee. She was shouting enough to wake the other two women in the bay, but at least not Ingrid. Amanda put her chair back on the stack of others by the sink, placed her lips against her mother's warm cheek and whispered that she'd be back tomorrow. Then she crossed to the old lady who needed attention and pressed her buzzer for her.

At three a.m. in the morning, Amanda was nudged awake by a rogue thought.

What was it that Kerry had said about private health insurance? It was of significance but she couldn't for the life of her remember what it was or why her brain had felt the need to wake her up to ask about it. She went back to sleep and the thought crawled away into the corner of her head, for another time.

Chapter 31

It came with age, this ability to compartmentalise, thought Mel. She'd never considered she'd be capable of such a skill as to wear a dignified mask that said to the rest of the world: 'I am totally fine. There is nothing in my life you need to worry about. I am proficient at my job and can process your deposits and weigh your bags of change and hand over cash from your accounts with a smile on my face and you will never know what is going on inside my head, which is that I am a fucking wreck. I have had to force bananas down my neck to give me some energy, I've had to try and cover this ginormous cold sore on my lip so I don't frighten small children and nervous dogs and I haven't had more than two hours unbroken sleep all week.' Except that part was no longer true because last night, she'd woken up only the once and a decent chunk of shut-eye had really helped. She was sure that letting out her story in the back room of the diner was responsible for that. She'd felt listened to, she'd felt her feet standing on a sane oasis in a world that she couldn't make sense of any more and it had given her a place to re-charge, however temporary it turned out to be.

No one at work could have guessed anything was wrong and they saw her cold sore and maybe slightly tired look as evidence that she'd been poorly. But it took a monumental effort that day, even with her acquired skills of deportment, not to start screaming and thumping the cashpoint machine when it wouldn't give her any money out of their joint bank account because, as she was to discover after a furious phone call to customer services, she'd been locked out of it.

*

Amanda rang in to work to tell them she was taking a day off. A kinder boss might have said, *Absolutely, I hope everything is all right.* Philip was his usual unsympathetic self; it wouldn't have killed him to say he hoped her mother would be better soon. She knew he was more concerned that he'd now have to jiggle things around so he could keep to his original plans and sneak off for his golf date with the previous MD, an upset to his timetable that Amanda refused to feel guilty about.

She drove over to her mother's house to make sure everything was secure. Dolly from next door saw her car arrive and came over to ask how things were. Amanda told her she'd be heading up to the hospital shortly. She'd rung the ward that morning, but no one had answered so she'd presumed that no news was good news.

She let herself into the house and the smell hit her immediately. She traced it to the carpet at the bottom of the stairs. Her mum must have wet herself as she was lying there for god knows how long. Her older downstairs hidden cameras didn't have a record facility so she couldn't check, but it could have been many hours; no wonder she'd been dehydrated. She filled a bucket with water and some disinfectant and gave it a scrub with the doorstep brush that she found under the sink before she went upstairs to get some things her mum might need in hospital: a dressing gown, toothbrush and paste, nighties, slippers, a book, glasses because Bradley wouldn't have thought of it, he'd have rightly presumed that she'd automatically do it.

Now it was her turn to snoop because she wanted to get hold of her mum's paperwork so she could find out her financial situation. It may be that she could afford to buy a bungalow outright from savings which would speed things up. It wasn't without the realms of possibility because Ingrid was canny, a saver rather than a spender. And if her savings fell short, then she and Bradley would just have to step in and cough up and then claim back the money from the sale of this house. He was loaded if the cars on his drive, the white goods in his kitchen and the even whiter goods in his gob were anything to go by.

She tried to think like an elderly woman. It would need to be somewhere she thought was safe and not obvious at all to burglars. Her mother's generation often favoured putting things under floorboards and mattresses and she recalled spying on Bradley looking under the mattress and she wondered if that's what he'd been hunting around for.

Then she remembered when she was cleaning and the way the carpet gave in the corner behind the unit. It wasn't a heavy piece of furniture by any means to shift and well within the realms of possibility that an old lady might assume a burglar wouldn't think of moving a unit full of pot ornaments to see what was lying in the corner underneath it. Besides, thinking about it, her mother was more likely to have told her to get someone in to mend a faulty floor than to disguise it, being as houseproud as she always had been, at least until recently. There was a reason why she'd left that corner unfixed.

Amanda decided to check it out. She went upstairs, took all the ornaments off the unit, moved it out of the way, and pulled up the carpet to reveal a hole. The floorboard hadn't rotted: it had been smashed in with a hammer by the look of the splintered, shattered edges. And there was something sitting underneath it in the dark space. Amanda shone her phone torch on it and saw what appeared to be a large brown biscuit tin, the painted flowers that once embellished the top and side gnawed away at by rust. *Bingo.* She had to wrest it out because it weighed a ton and had been sat there for ages by the look of it, covered in dust and abandoned spider-weavings. It felt way too heavy for a few papers, though, so maybe this wasn't what she was looking for, but she was understandably intrigued.

It wasn't locked but it was hard to prise open and she buggered up a nail in the act of doing so. But the nuisance of that was eclipsed by the sight of the contents when the lid eventually gave, because she found herself staring into a pirate's chest, full of gold sovereigns, rings, chains, charms, bracelets – even spoons. She wouldn't have liked to have guessed the value of what she was holding in her hands, but she'd paid three hundred quid last year for a locket, the like of which was sitting on top of the hoard and looking almost lost among the bigger, weightier items. The shock of it dislodged the words her mother had said to her recently about her father buying up gold and storing it like a squirrel. *I've still got it in that same tin*, she'd said.

Amanda's heart was booming in her chest; it felt as if it were knocking against her ribcage in an attempt to make a bid for freedom. *Dear god.* Well, she couldn't leave this here in an empty house, could she? It was a possibility clued-up old-school burglars might call who'd make a beeline for under-Axminster treasures. With shaking, shocked hands, she tucked the carpet back into the corner, replaced the unit with all the knick-knacks and took the box of treasure with her for safekeeping.

★

Bon had noticed, when he was on the phone in his office, that Sky had been sewing with a smile playing on her lips, as if she was thinking about something who had amused her. Or someone.

He hoped it was someone, some handsome young man who would bring her some happiness. It seemed to him that she didn't have much of a life really. He knew that she rented a room in a house. He knew that she was alone in the world, that she'd lost her mother when she was a child and her father when she had just turned twenty. She'd cared for him in his last years, she'd missed out on going to university and having a wild time. He knew that she'd grown up under the long shadow of rumours cast about her father which must have impacted upon her. Woodentop and Jock had known Eddie, as they called him, and both said that Mildred the art restorer was more likely to have done what he'd been accused of. They were protective of Sky, they looked out for her because she was fragile, but especially because she was one of their own. And what Woodentop had said about her being up in the cardiac unit of the hospital as a possible outpatient had been playing on his mind.

His feelings for her were complicated and he was

frightened to look at them too closely, because what good would it do. When she first approached him to ask if she might rent a space in the shop, he'd been delighted, because Tony Cropper had been turning teddy bear work away for being too busy; but also teddies weren't something of a passion for Tony the way they were for Sky. So this sweet, refreshing young woman had been a welcome addition to the crew and fitted in with them like the last piece of a jigsaw. And she was very good at what she did, a true expert who had been taught by a true expert. What she didn't know about the history of bears, about the construction of bears, wasn't worth talking about.

She was always quietly cheerful, she made the most coffees out of all of them to distribute. He had no idea when he had started to think what her hair might feel like if he pushed his hand into it, what her lips might taste like against his own because it was something primal inside him that was responding to her. He had no control over it, but he did have control over what he did about it.

He had kept that all to himself because she was twenty-three years younger than him. And some would have argued that might be fine if he was a Rolling Stone but there was more than mere age separating them. Bon was life-experienced, Sky was an ingénue, an innocent. It was right and proper that she met someone her own age and they could grow and mature together. He knew she liked him. *Liked* him. And he would have been lying to himself if he said that he didn't like the warmth that bloomed in his heart at the thought that she might have a fraction of the feelings for him that he had for her.

When he was eighty, she'd be younger than sixty. He wouldn't want her to be saddled with an old man. He knew that the flame that had fanned into life for her would blow out eventually, starved of oxygen. He knew that the feelings she had for him would be diverted as soon as someone of her own generation wandered into her orbit and paid her all the attention she should have.

But yes, he thought of her far too much, and even though Erin had shared her deepest, darkest secrets with him, he would not share this with her because it would make it real, and it couldn't be.

He tried not to be drawn to Sky any more than he was to any of the others in the shop, but at the same time, he knew he took advantage of the flimsiest excuse to be near her when it presented itself to him. This morning was one such occasion, and though he hoped that the smile on her lips was because someone else had put it there, he also hoped that it wasn't.

'You look very chipper today,' he said to her.

'I am,' she replied.

She'd been thinking about the meeting at the diner the previous evening, how good it felt to talk, to listen to the women, to share. They were older, almost thirty-years in Amanda's case, and yet the age gap had been no barrier, it had been melted into oblivion by camaraderie. She'd laughed so many times revisiting the moment when mouth-on-legs Janine marched out after Astrid had walked in; and the collective relief of them all that she'd gone, which they'd celebrated with top-ups of drinks and squidgy cookies.

'Am I allowed to ask why?' enquired Bon, not sure if he wanted to know.

'Nothing really. I haven't won the lottery. I just had a nice evening.' She added, 'With friends,' because she felt as if they could be, and would be. This was the start of them, and she hoped the others felt it too and would be back at the same time next week.

And even better, when she went home, Wilton wasn't in and he'd stayed out all night so this morning she'd been able to have a peaceful coffee, even though she didn't like to think of his lips being on the same rim of the mug, but she'd given it a hard scrub first, as she did now with anything she used in the house, including the bath and the loo seat.

'Where was—'

They were interrupted by the front door opening and Gwyn Tankersley blasting in like a Siberian wind. Polished, preened, in heels and make-up, her hair an elegant caramel-gold twist secured by a single, glittery pin.

'Bon, where is it? I can't wait to see it,' she announced without preamble, lipsticked smile wide and glossy. Her eyes were only on him, they didn't even flicker in Sky's direction.

'Excuse me,' said Bon to Sky. He walked Gwyn Tankersley through the shop and Sky went back to her sewing, albeit with her smile reduced.

Gwyn had rung ahead to check that Bon was around in person to pay. She wanted to thank him to his face, she'd said. Peter, the upholsterer, who took the call relayed it to Bon with a wry smile and said, 'And if you believe that bollocks, Bon, you were born yesterday.'

'She'll have sniffed your divorce like vampires sniff blood,' said Mildred. 'I'd get Willy to make you a crucifix if I were you.'

Gwyn Tankersley was attractive, wealthy, self-assured and she gloried in the fact that men found her qualities alluring. When she set her sights on acquiring something – or someone – she had a high success rate. She would have been in like Flynn with Bon van der Meer had it not been for the fact he was married, but now he wasn't and she was conveniently single at present. She knew what buttons to press to make men work. They were simple machines, she'd always thought, although she did like a challenge, as those were all the sweeter for the win.

She didn't have to affect her admiration of Bon's craftmanship skills, though. The desk, a present for herself, was absolutely stunning and, though indulgently expensive, was worth every penny of what she was about to pay him. One of a kind, a future heirloom. She could only imagine what the hands that made it were also capable of.

Bon took out a drawer and turned it upside down so she could see that there had been no skimping where materials had been concerned, no corners cut in artistry. He demonstrated the four lockable drawers, how smooth the mechanism was. And he showed her how to access the secret compartment in the knee hole. She let him show her, all the while wondering what his skin might smell like in bed.

'It comes in three parts, they lock together when they are positioned correctly. No one would be able to pick it up otherwise, it's a solid, heavy piece. I can have it delivered tomorrow morning. I hope your floorboards are strong.'

'I can't thank you enough,' she said, licking her lip ever so slightly, just a small poke out of tongue. Her flirting skills were so refined they kicked into automatic responses, tailored to the subject.

'Bon, I'm having a dinner party next Tuesday night. Just a few close friends; they're all top company. I've hired one of the finalists from *Masterchef* to do the food, it'll be excellent. Do join us. It'll be great PR for you too, especially when they see the man behind the desk I fully intend to show off.

If you are free, it would be wonderful, and I'm sure advantageous, for you to indulge in conversation about what you do here. I'd certainly be fascinated to hear all about it.'

Over Gwyn's shoulder, Bon saw Tony 'Toy' Cropper giving him a cheeky thumbs up. He wasn't a schmoozer, but Gwyn Tankersley was very well connected and if the restorers could get some extra traffic, then maybe it would be worth doing for them.

'Then I'll accept,' replied Bon.

She let out a long breath, as if she'd been holding it in expectation of a positive answer.

'Drinks at six, dinner at seven, dress code is black tie. Don't drive, that's an order. Right, let me pay you for this gorgeous thing.'

Bon led her to his office. He noted that Gwyn's eyes had still not registered Sky, she was not even of the slightest significance. But the look in Sky's eyes when the transaction was complete and Gwyn's parting shot to him was, 'See you on Tuesday at six,' was quite the opposite.

Chapter 32

Miraculously, Ingrid hadn't broken any bones, but her heart rate was up and her oxygen levels were low so they were keeping their eyes on her and the consultant would reassess things in the morning. Amanda texted Bradley to let him know as she'd tried to ring but he hadn't picked up. That was nothing new, but she thought he'd be more interactive, with their mum being poorly.

Someone came to ask questions about Ingrid's living arrangements and she and Amanda went into the lounge area so they could talk in private. As Amanda was filling her in on how her mother lived alone, but with family support, it just didn't seem enough any more. And it was all very well having cameras in the house, but if you didn't man them twenty-four-seven, this kind of thing could – and did – happen. And yes, a pendant around her neck that set off an alarm if she fell had been discussed, but Ingrid refused to wear one and she definitely wouldn't have a key box put outside the house for the alerted call-centre personnel to access her property. Amanda told her that the family were going to act quickly now and move her into more suitable housing.

Ingrid had nodded off when Amanda got back to her but the other women in the bay were awake. The one by the window was shouting for help. 'Nurse, nurse, I need the toilet and I need it NOW.' She saw Amanda glance over. 'What are you gawping at, you lanky arse,' she shouted. 'Get me a nurse.'

The lady in the next bed from her was just lying on her back, her eyes fixed upwards and Amanda wondered what, if anything, was going on behind them. The woman opposite was trying continually to get out of bed and squealing in a high-pitched voice that she needed to go home. A nurse was sitting beside her, calmly telling her she couldn't, replacing her matchstick-thin legs onto the mattress every time they strayed over the side. Her gown had ridden up, revealing a big dressing between her legs and pants halfway down her thigh. *Pull the bloody curtain around her and give her some dignity,* Amanda wanted to scream. The same game played out for the next two hours without cessation: legs working over the edge, legs replaced. 'Please let me go home', her voice high enough to crack glass.

Dear God, get us out of here as soon as possible, mouthed Amanda upwards. Her brain was ringing like an over-struck bell. She wished she could gather her mother up and take her out of this nightmare of degradation. She didn't want her being here a minute longer than she had to be.

★

'You came back,' said Molly, as Erin walked into the teashop for the second of her grief clubs. 'I hoped you would.'

'Yes, I found it ... helped.' It wasn't a lie. Carona had thrown a blanket-thick dark shadow over her life and one session was hardly enough to lift it away entirely but it had shifted position, allowed her to see there was some light outside it, ready to break in.

Alex wasn't there at first and then he arrived as they were about to start. To her surprise, Erin realised how glad she was to see him. Too glad for a mere second meeting.

'Sorry, sorry, I'm late,' he apologised, breezing in. 'I was held up at work, the traffic further hindered me.' He spotted Erin and waved over and her mouth curved into a smile by way of response. He threw himself down on the chair next to her and jogged her arm, nearly knocking her slice of chocolate cake out of her hand.

'God, I'm so sorry,' he said. 'I'm a walking disaster today.'

'Go and get yourself a nice calming cup of tea from Mr Singh, Alex, we can wait for you,' said Molly, chuckling. She dragged two open hands down slowly through the air. 'Let yourself breathe and relax.'

Just being in this wonderful teashop would make that happen. Erin had felt better for merely walking in through the door. She should have come weeks ago.

Jesse opened up a lot more that evening, but the fact that he would never get his answers weighed heavily on him. Had he been a good enough son? Could he have done more to make his father love him? And would he be forever stuck in this state of grieving?

'Oh, we are so hard on ourselves when someone dies,' said Molly. She had such a beautiful voice, thought Erin, like honey. She'd be great at hypnosis. Or telling bedtime stories to small children.

'Grief takes a long time to process, Jesse. Too often we kick against it, swim against the tide, and that's exhausting. Sometimes we need to accept it is a current too strong for us and we should let it toss us around until it tires of us. It does eventually, but it won't be rushed and some people feel stronger currents than others. It's not uniform.'

'My boss at work . . . he said that three months is enough, I shouldn't need any more time to get over it.'

'Well, he's a knob, then,' said Erin. She slapped her hand over her mouth. 'Sorry, Father Paul.'

'I'm inclined to agree,' said Father Paul. 'And I think when your boss is hit with a torrent of grief himself, he might be changing his opinion on that.'

'Do you have any children, Jesse?' asked Molly.

'A little boy. He's eight.'

'Make sure he feels your love so he is in no doubt. That's one thing you can do to help yourself, take your father's mistake and mould it into something positive for your son. Maybe your father struggled to tell you what his feelings were for you, maybe he intended to but time ran out, or maybe he couldn't. Our generation . . . the men . . . often weren't very good at emotion. Maybe him saving up his money and giving it to you was him saying he loved you in the only way he felt able.'

Jesse considered that. 'I hadn't thought about it that way.'

'I'm not saying it is, because we don't know, but then again maybe it's exactly right and it would be a good truth to believe. When we can't find closure, we often have to make it ourselves, pat the problem into a shape that we can control, that will settle quietly within rather than it being a wild whirling thing that keeps changing and won't rest inside us.'

Jesse, for the first time, gave something that resembled a smile – not much of one, but it was definitely a presence on his lips.

Father Paul said that he had made an appointment to see his bishop. He was going to be honest with him and tell him his story. It didn't sit right with him, keeping it a secret any longer. But he was frightened, he said, because he knew he should have avoided Rowena.

'I have to say in my own defence, she made me a better priest, more human, more understanding of people. When I was a younger man, I was definitely on my high horse, vain, holier-than-thou if you like. I thought because I wore the uniform, I was somehow *superior*. I've wondered recently if God decided to humble me. It worked, if that was his plan.'

'Maybe God did send her to you,' said Molly. 'Maybe she made you stronger, not weaker, Paul.'

'I'll let you know what the bishop says.' Father Paul nodded with a soft smile. 'I'm a bit too old to retrain as an electrician if I'm thrown out of the Church.'

Erin had nothing to say today, she was happy absorbing the healing energy the group emitted. Alex said similar. He could feel a definite lifting of his mood. What had helped was him stumbling across an advert for a charity that supported teenagers who were floundering. He knew that Julian would approve of the large donation he'd given them; there was no doubt in his mind about it.

At the end of the session, Erin was very aware that she was hanging back, waiting for Alex to finish talking to Molly, hoping he'd ask if she wanted to call in at the pub again. He did, and she tried to make it look as if she was deliberating over it.

★

Bradley and Kerry arrived at the hospital just as the catering staff were collecting the dinner trays. Amanda had tried to wake her mum to eat something but she wasn't interested. Amanda didn't blame her. She wouldn't have fed the square of grey fish in its watery sauce to a stray, starving dog. Her mother hated green beans at the best of times and the chips had been cold and limp when they'd landed. The shrieking woman had a curtain around her but it wasn't fully closed and she was on a commode, filling the air with a stench, poor old soul.

Bradley was staring down at the untouched dinner plate and holding his nose.

'I couldn't eat that even without *that* going on across there,' he said, none too quietly.

'Well, it's hospital food. It's always bad, in't it?' said his wife.

What would you know? thought Amanda. *You with your private healthcare.*

Then she remembered what it was that Kerry had said that had awoken her at stupid o'clock that morning. It was a question she'd slip into the conversation when chance permitted.

'I couldn't put up with this for long,' said Bradley, as the shrieking woman began crying out for 'Shirley' to come and help her.

Amanda had clocked up over six hours and she needed a break.

'Now you're here, I'm going for a coffee,' she said.

'We'll come with you,' said Bradley.

Amanda bit down on saying, 'Don't you want to stay here with Mum?' They had things to discuss. That might as well be done now, while the metaphorical iron was hot.

*

'What have the doctors said then?' asked Bradley, sitting down with a hot chocolate and a muffin. He'd bought the drinks. Amanda was surprised half a dozen moths didn't fly out of his wallet when he opened it up.

'That they'll look at her again in the morning. The good thing is that she hasn't broken anything, but she's slept constantly. It must have been a real shock to her system. Those bloody stairs—' Amanda groaned. 'I told you there would be an accident sooner or later and it turned out to be sooner. She needs one-storey accommodation and she needs it now, Bradley, you must see that. There was some-one from social care around earlier on who agrees it's the right option.' Small white lie. 'We could have a downstairs toilet built of course, but by the time we've applied for planning permission and got it, and then found a builder, we're still looking at months. We could put a single bed in the lounge, but she wouldn't use a commode, she'd just go upstairs to the bathroom, so there would be absolutely no point in doing that.

'I can't find her bank statements to see how much money she has. I think the best plan is to use her savings to buy a bungalow immediately, and put the house on the market. Even that will take weeks, though. Maybe we can arrange a respite home until completion. I've been looking on Rightmove while I was sitting in the ward, and there's a one-bedroomed bungalow just come up in Dodley Bottom for a hundred and twenty thousand. We could make them an offer. It's nice enough to move straight into and it's easily still walkable for her to get to the coffee shop she likes.'

She saw the glance shared between Kerry and Bradley. It was a flick of their eyes to each other but noticeable all the same, and she wondered what it meant.

Then Kerry said, 'Don't you think she might be better off living with you, Amanda?'

Amanda waggled her head, sure she must have misheard. 'I beg your pardon, Kerry?'

Amanda's affronted tone punctured Kerry's rare moment of bravery.

'I just ... we've been talking ...'

'What Kerry means,' Bradley took over, one slow word after another, 'is can't you move in with Mother for a while?'

Amanda could feel her temper rising.

'If you've *been talking*, as Kerry says, then you'll realise how stupid a suggestion that is. Even if I did move in, she would be alone all day when I went out to work and she would go up the stairs. Why don't you two move in with her? Kerry's given up her job. She could be Mum's carer.'

An equally senseless idea, but she just wanted to see his reaction.

'Don't be silly, Amanda, we have our own house.'

'Am I going mad?' said Amanda with a hard note of laughter. 'I thought I had my own house as well. I'm sure I have. I vaguely remember a roof and a garage. Oh, and what was that Kerry said: that you're having to pay for your private healthcare now, so how come? Aren't you working at Beestock's any more?'

Kerry gave a nervous jerk and Bradley cast her a quick side-eye of annoyance.

'No,' he said, through lips as pursed as his giant pearlies would allow. 'If you must know, we have bought a business.'

'Microsoft?'

The sarcasm was lost on him. 'A sandwich shop, actually. Well, two. Big Baps. Both thriving and profitable, in very busy areas. They run themselves, with the present staff.'

'What? You and Kerry aren't even working in them?' asked Amanda, her brows raised in faux surprise.

'We are both taking a break from industry. Kerry and I have been working solidly for twenty-five years each. That's fifty years between us.'

Those extra maths lessons I gave you didn't go amiss then, thought Amanda. She was furious.

'And when did all this come about?'

'Not long. Six weeks.'

'Three months,' said Kerry at the same time. Amanda was inclined to believe her more because she was as thick as Bradley was wily.

'So, basically, you've been sat on your backside while I've been running around like a blue-arsed fly after Mum is what you're telling me?'

'Absolutely not. We've been busier than we ever were.'

'How could you afford to pack in your job and buy a business?' And there was also the swanky house renovations, the cars, not to mention the blinding white choppers.

'Well ... Father, of course, if you must know.'

'He left you that much?'

'It was a considerable sum. He had property and the shop.'

The way Bradley was spending, Arnold must have left him Necker Island as well. Something didn't add up though; the timeline was all to cock.

'But he's only just died, hasn't he?'

'We got a loan,' rushed Kerry, trying to be helpful but from the look Bradley gave her, she wasn't being.

He expanded on what she said but he wasn't happy about it. 'We took out a loan and Father's money will repay it. We knew it was coming, since he'd been ill for a while.'

'Nice,' was Amanda's only comment. Arnold wasn't exactly parent of the year, but there was a large ick factor in Bradley being so impatient for his inheritance that he'd engineered a way to spend it before his father had even kicked the bucket.

'Not that it is any of your business,' Bradley said, clearly irate at being pressured to explain himself.

He was right of course, it wasn't any of her business. The matter of their mum, however, was very much her business.

'Well, just so we are clear, I'm not moving in because that is stupid and will solve nothing, and she can't move in with me because, as you may remember, my garage is on the ground floor and my living quarters are above it, so that would be an extra flight of stairs to contend with. And even if someone were able to miraculously magic up a lift in my house, Mum would be nowhere near any friends or the coffee shop and she'd be lonely when I was at work. But you have a downstairs bedroom and bathroom, don't you, Bradley?'

'It's our guest room. For friends,' he said.

You have friends? she wanted to throw at him.

'It is a daughter's job to look after her mother,' said Bradley then, in that slow, imperious way of his that got right up her conk.

If Amanda hadn't been in a hospital café she could have grabbed Bradley's big ears and shaken him until his brain turned to mush, which wouldn't have taken that long.

'Is that so? And which seventeeth-century book of bollocks did you pluck that from?' She said it, but she knew he was just spouting their mother's words.

'We've got Kerry's mother to look after.'

'Kerry's got four sisters. And it's *your* job, Bradley, to look after *your* mother as much as it is mine.' He was like a sodding eel, trying to wriggle out of his responsibilities and she wasn't having it any longer.

'Well, you can't expect me to wash her and dress her, can you?'

'There are carers for that sort of thing. You could, if you truly thought anything about her, use some of Arnold's money to hire a private carer. After all, it was her money that helped to set him up in that business you've just benefitted from.' *My own father's money, actually. Intended for me, not that nonce.*

'No,' said Bradley, chewing on his lip, radiating annoyance.

'Or . . . how about this.' Why hadn't she thought of this as a solution before? It was perfect. 'Mum could give up her house and not bother buying another place. She could move into Sunnybank Manor.'

It was almost funny watching Bradley's reaction to that. Sunnybank Manor was a luxury hybrid of old people's home and sheltered accommodation that cost a bomb to live in. The mere idea of his mother paying hundreds of pounds per week for the privilege of residing there almost caused her brother to spontaneously combust.

'Absolutely not. My mother is not going into a home.'

He meant, of course, that she was not going to spend his upcoming inheritance on herself, even if it was – for now – her own money.

'Where are the deeds for the house, by the way, do you know? I couldn't find them.'

'I have the box full of Mother's financial affairs.'

'You do? Since when?'

'Mother asked me to help her with them some time ago. I expect she didn't want you to know she wasn't coping.'

Another rabbit punch. Another Bradley – one, Amanda – nil score. Their mother had turned to son before daughter, as always. Amanda sighed resignedly. Okay then, if that's the way it was, let him do something useful for a change, seeing as all he had to do with his time presently was play at being Alan bloody Sugar. Anyway her head was bursting and she just wanted to concentrate on getting her mum well, first and foremost.

'I'll see you both back upstairs. I presume you're staying for some time with her?' said Amanda, getting up.

'I can't see the point, if she's asleep. We shouldn't disturb her, let her get some rest,' Bradley answered.

'That's what she needs most,' added Kerry, with a sagacious nod.

Thank you, Dr Kildare, Amanda stopped herself from replying.

As she was going up to the ward, she pondered over what Bradley had been hunting around for in her mum's house if he already had the box of financial stuff. Did he know about the existence of the tin of gold but not where it was kept? If that was the case, she allowed herself a wry smile at a rare Amanda – one, Bradley – nil score.

Chapter 33

Mel pulled up in the car park of the pub and wondered if Postman Pat was here yet. Would he be driving that very nice black Merc or the red Jag? Or was that his mountain bike chained up? She checked her watch; she was bang on time. She decided to go in and wait. She pushed open the door and thought, why the hell had she agreed to this? She'd done her best to appear presentable, even if this cold sore was big enough to grow crops on and still repelled all attempts to cover it up. Her jeans felt slack on her waist thanks to the cheating bastard husband diet and she'd resisted wearing black because she thought a pop of colour might lend her some confidence. She'd plumped for a pine green shirt, the one that made her hair look extra bright.

She approached the bar, waiting her turn behind a tall man with thick, greying hair that fell across his forehead on one side like the original Superman's, and a slim woman with shoulder-length dark hair and pretty eyes who was probably years older than she looked; an attractive couple. He was carrying a briefcase and was all togged up in a suit, whereas she had sand-coloured cropped chinos on and trendy loafers.

'Bottle of Peroni Red, please,' Mel ordered when it was her turn.

'Not here for the quiz, are you? Because there isn't one this week,' said the barmaid, popping the top off it and pouring it into a glass.

'No, I'm not,' she replied. Good job really, seeing as her brain was so scrambled at the moment she couldn't even remember her maiden name, never mind who was the President of the United States in 1954.

She heard the outer door squeak open and shut and turned to see Pat had just come in, but not in a postman uniform. Blimey, he even dressed like Liam Gallagher. In fact he looked more like Liam Gallagher than Liam Gallagher's reflection did. He raised his hand in a gesture of acknowledgement. She mirrored it automatically, though unsure what the correct protocol was for greeting the husband of the woman your own husband was banging.

'I'll get these,' he said, taking a wallet out of his back jeans pocket.

'No, it's fine.'

'Bottle of Peroni Red, please,' he ordered. Bloody hell, they were lager twins, Mel thought. They had so much in common.

He handed a twenty note over to the barmaid before Mel had the chance to get her money out. 'For both,' he said. She didn't protest because she couldn't be bothered fighting about anything else. She'd get the next ones, if they were here for that long.

As they made their way to a table, a younger man turned and did a double-take at Pat, and Mel thought it must happen all the time to him.

She caught his scent as she followed him, he'd put after-shave on but she couldn't place it. It was an odd one: earthy, smoky, vanilla, not usually a combo her nose would agree with but she liked it; it was off the wall like he was.

They sat down in a corner by the window. A waitress came out carrying two plates of food and headed past them.

'Do you want anything to eat?' asked Pat.

'It's not a date,' snapped Mel.

'No, I know but ... I ... didn't ... know if you were ... expecting to.'

'Absolutely not.' Scampi and chips would not go well with the conversation they were about to have. *You don't have to answer him in that tone though*, said an inner reprimanding voice.

'Sorry, I didn't mean to snap.' He'd be thinking that's why her husband left, horrible old cow barking at people.

''S'fine.'

They sat in silence for a long minute, sipping at their drinks. Where was the entry point to this tangled mess, she thought.

'I don't know how to start,' he said, echoing her unspoken words. 'Thank you for coming.'

'I wasn't going to. Friends said I should.' *Friends* was pushing it; women she'd met once. Women she'd like to see more of.

He sipped again, she sipped again. It was going to be a very long night if they only said a couple of sentences every five minutes. She dived in.

'Let's begin at the beginning then, shall we? What happened at your end?'

Pat put his glass down slowly before speaking.

'I came in from work on the Monday, found a note on

the kitchen table saying she needed some space and not to look for her, she'd be in touch when she were ready. I went upstairs and saw how much stuff she'd taken out of her wardrobe. I knew it had something to do with that school reunion, she went proper odd after she'd been there. I tried messaging, ringing but she wouldn't answer her phone. More or less what happened last time, really.'

Mel gave a small gasp. 'She's done it before?'

'Yep, couple of years ago. We hadn't been getting on so well, she upped and left, someone she worked with. It all blew out pretty quickly and she came back and we tried to get over it.'

'What does she do?'

'She's a manager of a Tosca coffee shop. I rang them when I couldn't get hold of her but apparently she'd not been in for a whole week. God knows what they thought of her own husband ringing up and not knowing that, they were very blunt with me on the phone. Yet till then she'd been coming home normally as if she'd been working. So I can only presume she was with . . . your husband all the time instead.'

'How did you find out who she'd run off with?'

'My brother knows someone who knows someone who was at the reunion and he did a bit of digging for me. I knew she was with a fella; I knew all that stuff about wanting space was bollocks. When I found out who she copped off with at the party, I looked up his business and got the registered address. I figured she was deffo with him. Apparently they were at it in the school toilets.'

Mel covered her ears. She didn't want to think about Steve doing that, but a picture was now staining her brain of them both passionate and panting and having a long, earth-shattering simultaneous orgasm next to a urinal.

'Sorry, TMI. I thought it might help you.'

She would never get that AI image scrubbed. 'How on earth did you think that would help?'

'In case you were imagining a Hallmark film. Which it definitely ain't.'

Clumsily put, but she understood what he meant, even if she wouldn't have thanked him for it.

'The girls' toilets, in case you were wondering. Not the boys'.'

'I really wasn't wondering.' At least it took the urinal out of the frame.

They sipped at their drinks and then Mel said, 'I didn't even know he'd left me on the Wednesday. I thought he was working away overnight.'

'She'd been gone two days then.'

'He didn't take any stuff with him. Why?' One of the many questions frying her brain.

'Dunno. Maybe he just decided on the spur of the moment that . . . today was the day. Maybe he was dragging his heels and she gave him the now or never ultimatum.'

That sounded plausible.

'Have you heard from . . . her since?'

Pat rubbed his chin and Mel noticed his long fingers, proper guitar-playing hands. Young Jason Jepson had big hands for a kid his size and had been as pleased as punch when she'd told him that he had a great advantage, being gifted those.

'I got a text from her saying that she couldn't wait to see me, *lover*. Then a follow-up saying to ignore the last text, which had been sent in error. She hadn't sent it in error at all, she was just poking the bear. You see, she's all about the drama is Chlo, that much I've learned over the years. She'd like nothing better than to see me and your fella fighting over her, which is basically what happened last time. I didn't feel good about lamping the area manager of Tosca coffee in the car park and denting his Maserati.'

It sounded like a euphemism and Mel made an involuntary snort and tried to cover it up as a cough. It wasn't funny, none of this was funny. But sometimes it was, as Frank Carson used to say, the way you tell 'em.

'I could have lost my job if he'd pressed charges. He didn't, he just wanted it to go away. So I was really angry at myself this time, reacting . . . and I let you have it and you di'n't deserve it. It's not me, despite what you might think. I won't be dancing when she pulls the strings this time. I felt really bad about just turning up at yours like that and I wouldn't have hit him if I'd seen him.'

'What would you have done then?' asked Mel.

'Honestly? I'd have looked him in the eye and told him he was welcome to her,' said Pat.

★

'For a moment there I thought that was Liam Gallagher,' said Alex, quietly, in case he was overheard.

'Wrong side of the Pennines,' replied Erin. The man sitting in the corner of the pub, alongside the woman with the lovely red hair, looked more Liam than Liam did these days.

'How did you find out about Molly's club?' asked Alex. He'd been back to the bar and bought two packets of crisps, torn open the bags for them to share.

'My ex-husband has a repair shop across from the tearoom and so I'd heard about it in passing. As Carona had died very suddenly, he suggested that maybe I would find some group therapy there advantageous; but me being me, I thought I could handle it by myself.'

If she'd told Bon the whole truth six months ago, he'd have frogmarched her to Molly's, she was sure of it. 'What about you?'

'From a solicitor friend. She lost her partner very young in tragic circumstances and she couldn't move on. Molly really helped her. She's married now. To someone, ironically that she met in the group, a fireman. Tell me about your ex-husband.'

'I left him for Carona; he forgave me even though I couldn't forgive myself.'

'Would you go back to him, given the chance?'

'No. We were a mistake. One of my better mistakes, I have to say.'

Alex nudged the cheese and onion crisps closer to her.

'Have some, they're very good for the soul. They leave chicken soup behind in the starting blocks.'

She smiled and reached for one.

'He told me last week that, before I left him, he had been on the cusp of ending our marriage, because he wasn't in love with me any more. I can't tell you how good that made me feel.'

Alex stared at her, trying to work out if she was being sarcastic.

'I mean it,' she clarified. 'He's the last person on earth I would want to hurt and I thought I'd mashed him, but I really hadn't.'

'Has he found someone else?'

'Not yet, but I hope he does.'

'What about you, do you think you'd like to meet someone else, Erin?'

'I can't even think about it, Alex,' she said. 'It frightened me with Carona how much someone could change in such a short time.'

'Do people change? Or do they just present their best face at the beginning and that's what you try to keep seeing as the veneer wears off? Not everyone is different from their initial shine, of course. Did your ex-husband change in the same way?'

Erin shook her head. 'No, he was a constant.'

'There you go, then.'

'Cupid really is a twat, isn't he?'

Alex smiled. 'Sometimes. Not always.'

'I've had an offer on the flat, and so I'm going house-hunting, which will be exciting.'

'I'll come with you if you like.' He held up his hands to indicate that he hadn't meant to imply she might need a man onboard. 'I'm sure you are more than capable of choosing somewhere, but if you need some company I'm more than willing to be dragged around by you.' He added cheekily, 'Unless you'd rather take your perfect ex-husband, of course.'

Erin hooted. 'If you feel you are so bored that you'd want to come, then give me your number.'

Yes, Bon would have gone with her, she knew that, but she needed to stop relying on him so much for support – emotional or otherwise. She didn't want to take up the space in his life some other woman could have. Some very lucky woman.

★

'How long have you been married to … *her*,' asked Mel. She couldn't say the name without conjuring up the scent on

Steve's shirt. The innocent scent she had laughed at before she'd shoved it in the washing machine. The scent that had probably been transferred to him when they were up close and personal against a girls' toilet cubicle wall. *Eat your heart out, Mills and Boon.*

'Fifteen years,' said Pat.

'Any kids?'

'I've got a daughter from an earlier relationship. They never took to each other. My daughter put up with her for my sake, but Chloe's always been jealous of any other female on the scene, including my mam. You?'

'I couldn't have kids. I'd have loved one. I've been with Steve for thirty-one years. It's our thirtieth wedding anniversary in June.'

'Wow. And has he ever . . . done it before?'

'Nope. Not even a glance in another female's direction, this is why I can't get my head around it all. I think he's ashamed. He came home the day after you first turned up and just threw things in a suitcase but he wouldn't talk, just totally shut me out. That says to me that he can't face what he's done, so that shame will be what brings him home, I'm sure of it.'

Pat wrinkled up his nose. 'And would you want him back?'

Mel opened up her mouth to say that of course she would, because she'd never considered anything other, but the words wouldn't come out for some reason.

'Look, it's your life. We don't know each other but all I'm saying is that it's going to be hard either way. I know that because I've done it. I never threw it back in her face after she'd had her . . . fling, because you can't do that, the wound doesn't have a chance to heal if you keep opening it up. It

might not heal anyway; mine didn't. I thought I was at fault
and that's why she'd gone and I was so intent on trying to
fix us that I ignored how I was feeling. She just carried on
as if nothing had happened; it was easy for her, and I tried, I
did, but I never quite bossed it. You can't rewind the clock,
you can't go back to how it was before because they'll never
be the same person again and so you have to learn to live
with the change, the new them.'

Mel hadn't considered that it would not be the same Steve
in her life if he did come back. She only knew that she
couldn't survive it if they ended. She couldn't throw thirty
years away and start again by herself. She kept having flash
visions of herself in a tiny, dull maisonette, lonely, no one
to go on holiday with, watching *Britain's Got Talent* on her
own on Saturday nights with a sad fart microwave meal for
one on a lap-tray. It couldn't happen that way; she wouldn't
let it. And so her whole concentration was screwed onto the
sticking place of him walking through the door and saying,
'I'm home', and what lay beyond that, she hadn't considered.

'What's he like?' asked Pat, breaking into her sad reverie.
'In a nutshell.'

'He works hard, he likes his job and he's good at it, he's
handy around the house. He likes footy, cars, he's a home
bird. He's got a good sense of humour.' She paused, feeling
emotion rise inside her. They used to laugh a lot together,
less so maybe as they'd got older, but everyone got grumpier
with age, didn't they? Although she didn't think she had.
She took a breath and scraped around for something else
to say because he didn't sound very dynamic. 'We like a
holiday abroad. We rub along. We like to eat out . . . well,
it's more me that likes to do that because it gives me a break
from cooking.'

'I do most of the cooking at ours,' said Pat. 'I have the dinner ready for when she gets in. She hates cooking.'

Mel dropped a note of sardonic laughter. 'Steve can't cook for toffee. Sounds like they'll be living on Super Noodles if he can find a recipe for them.'

The thought of it brought her a smug smidgeon of short-lived glee. She wondered how quickly he'd tire of that setup and if the lure of her Sunday roasts would entice him back. He liked his home-cooked meals best of all, did Steve.

'Were you happy? Were there signs that he wasn't?'

'Yes, we were — and no, there weren't,' she answered, slightly affronted. 'We'd got into a routine like any other couple. I suppose you could say it was a bit boring but he never said he wasn't happy: if anything, it was me who made the effort to change things round and keep it fresh, you know. He just wanted to put his feet up when he came home; I would drag him to the cinema or out for dinner and he enjoyed it in the end . . . I think.' *If an 'it was all right that' was anything to go by.*

'Sex?'

Her mouth formed an O of shock. How dare he ask that?

'We were fine,' her tone defensive.

'Chlo likes sex. It didn't put her off having it with me while she must have been seeing your other half. I bet he wouldn't be happy to hear that.'

'Me and Steve . . . ' Mel blurted out, without meaning to and then didn't know if she should finish the sentence. *Oh, what the hell.* They both needed to be aware of all the facts if they were going to try and help each other get through this mess. 'We haven't . . . you know . . . since the school reunion. He was tired the first weekend and the weekend after, he . . . couldn't.' *Guilt*, it had to be. And that was good.

He was a decent man with a conscience. He had far more of one than Chloe – whatever her married name was – seemed to possess from the sounds of it.

'What's your surname?' she asked.

'Gallagher,' Pat replied.

'You're joking.'

'Yeah, I am, it's Bannerman. But if you're asking that so you can go and look her up, she's taken everything down or turned it to private.'

That was exactly why she was asking.

'There's some photos of her on Google if you search,' Pat went on.

'And what's she like?' asked Mel.

'Confident, good-looking, great figure, ambitious, self-obsessed, selfish. She likes the best things, always designer, stuff to show off with; she's like a plate on a stick that has to keep spinning, constantly looking for the next thrill and then she gets bored with it really quickly. We've got a nice house, just around the corner which is why I'm going to have another Peroni in a minute and you don't have to think that I'm drinking and driving.'

'I'll get them,' insisted Mel, jumping up.

There was a queue at the bar so she went to the loo first and looked up Chloe Bannerman on Google images. She had to scroll through a few pages. Then up popped a waist-length shot of a woman in a suit, slender and attractive, shoulder-length dark-brown hair, juicy mouth, big smile, sexy as Nigella, Steve's favourite. It was definitely her because underneath was the wording, 'Manager Chloe Bannerman, Tosca Coffee, Wakefield.' As Mel dried her hands, she caught sight of herself in the mirror above the sink with her pale, drawn face and that cold sore sitting on her lip as if it had taken up permanent residence, and thought, *would Steve really leave that to come back to this?*

★

'So you'll ring me then if you go and view any houses?' Alex looked to Erin for confirmation. 'I've bought a few properties in my time, and do know the right questions to ask.'

'I promise,' Erin drew a cross on her heart.

'I might even be able to fix you up with a mates' rates property solicitor.'

'Now you're talking.'

'I'll see you next week then at Molly's ... or maybe before.' Alex smiled at her and she smiled back. He made the slightest movement forward that intimated he might have been about to kiss her on the cheek, but it didn't happen and she felt a flick of disappointment that it hadn't. She admonished herself for that as she got into her car because she'd met the guy twice, and yet she could feel that familiar stirring that just didn't happen when you were merely friends with someone.

★

'So are we just expected to sit and wait until they decide to call the shots?' asked Mel, standing beside her car. She didn't want to talk any more, she just wanted to get home, in case Steve turned up which was not highly likely but still a possibility. 'Is my marriage over? I don't know what to do.' She made a growl of frustration. 'He didn't even want to go to that sodding reunion. I pushed him, I said he'd enjoy it. Ha. Never a truer word.'

She wasn't sure if this meeting had done her good or not. Before she'd sat down with Postman Pat, she just presumed that Steve would recover from this temporary madness of his eventually and normal service would be resumed. Pat had given her too much to think about. She could see what he meant, though, that her life was going to be impacted by Steve coming back as much as it would by him leaving her permanently.

'He'll be in touch,' Pat promised her. 'They're having a honeymoon period, it's exciting and naughty at the moment, but then real life comes knocking. He'll have money things to sort out, he'll need more of his stuff before you decide to shove it on a bonfire.'

'He won't have considered that,' said Mel with a gasp. 'I'm not that sort of person.'

'As you've discovered, we never really know anyone inside out. If you do want him back, sit tight, don't phone, don't text because you'll get into his head more that way, which sounds nuts, but it's true. Or you can take the control into your hands and pack up his stuff and throw him out.'

'I just want him home,' said Mel.

'I'm done this time,' said Pat. 'At least I think I am.'

Chapter 34

'Well, that's a waste of a tenner,' thought Amanda, as she paid over her money to Scopesearch, put in her mother's property details and up came the information: No neighbourly disputes, it wasn't built over a coal mine, it wasn't mortgaged, any Radon potential was below three per cent, last sold this year for three hundred and fifty thousand pounds. Total rubbish. They'd got it mixed up with next door which had indeed been sold recently and that was a considerably smaller property. Her mother had been overjoyed when those neighbours had gone, because they were always having barbecues or burning rubbish in their incinerator. Her mum's house was worth five hundred thousand at least. Still, she supposed, it gave her a *very* rough guide by comparison. She rang Baker's estate agents to meet her at the house the day after tomorrow, to take the next step.

★

Sky had endured yet another broken night of sleep. Wilton's friend had stayed over, and they'd had the TV up really loud watching sport of some sort. Since she'd threatened to report him to the authorities, he'd been going out of the way to make things extra difficult for her. He'd put one of his greasy black hairs in her bottle of milk; she was almost sick when she found it as she was pouring some over her cereal. She hadn't a clue what his endgame was. It could only be, she decided, that he had such a sad little life that this was how he got his kicks, with some revenge thrown in for standing up to him. They'd fallen asleep on the sofa it seemed, although one of them had been to the toilet in the middle of the night and rapped loudly on her door as they passed it, waking her up just as she'd managed to nod off.

As she stole past the doorway to the lounge on her way out to work, she heard them muttering, chuckling *sotto voce.*

'Sky,' called Wilton in a rough morning voice. 'Come and meet Bri. He's thinking about moving in.'

And Bri waved from the couch and said, 'Pleased to meet you, love. I don't suppose you've got any aspirin, have you?'

She didn't answer. She was already stressed as she closed the front door behind her and it wasn't even half-past eight. She attempted to start up her car and panicked because there was just a click and nothing else. She tried it again and it sparked into life, as if it was only joking with her the first time, as if it had the same sick sense of humour that Wilton Dearne had. But it was a signifier that something needed looking at and it was going to cost money that she didn't have.

As she was driving, she thought that if this was what her life was going to be until the end, what really was the point of it all?

★

Mel had caught her lip as she was washing her face getting ready for work and the cold sore started bleeding and wouldn't stop. She was in the bathroom trying, unsuccessfully, to stick on a square of loo paper when she heard the front door.

She froze, listened hard: someone was moving about downstairs, then she heard Steve's voice call out her name. He was home. She tried to be cool, calm and collected, which was hard with pins and needles of anxiety taking over every limb and a lip bleeding and throbbing as if it had its own heart.

When she got into the lounge, Steve was standing there with his hands on his hips, and no intention of making eye contact.

'Do you want to sit down and talk?' he said.

She wanted to sit down and cry actually, cry from confusion because he wasn't posed in any *happy to be home, I've missed you* stance.

She couldn't trust herself not to say the wrong thing, she felt surrounded by eggshells that might break if she breathed out of turn. This was Steve, her husband of twenty-nine years and ten months and yet she didn't recognise that look on his face, an expression she'd not seen there before, because he'd never not been able to meet her eyes. Not even when he'd had to confess he'd let the budgie escape.

She waited for him to begin, feeling her whole self shaking inside her skin.

He didn't sit down, he shifted from foot to foot with nervous energy before he opened his mouth.

'Look, none of this was meant.'

He let that sink in, not that there was much to sink in.

'I still love you as well, Mel.'

As well?

'You've known her for two minutes, Steve.'

'We knew each other at school. We really liked each other.'

'You kept her quiet.'

'Did you tell me about everyone you fancied? Anyway, I didn't expect what happened to happen.'

She fought against saying, *'What, banging her against a bog door?'*

'. . . But it did,' he continued, 'and I'm not giving her up.'

Mel's breath caught in her throat.

'I'm as confused as you are, if it helps.'

It totally didn't. And she doubted very much that he was confused as she was. She could feel tears making their way into her eyes and she willed them back because if one of them fell, he'd see that as emotional blackmail and use it as an excuse to leave.

He carried on. 'I know it's unfair on you. Just let me have some space.'

Space.

'Obviously this can't go on as it is for ever,' he said.

Eventually, without emotion, she said — because he appeared to be waiting for an answer to a question he hadn't asked — 'You want me to wait for you to sort your head out, is that what you're saying?'

You want to put me on ice so you can do what you want and leave me hanging?

'I'm so sorry about all this.'

So that was a yes then.

'What makes this . . . Chloe' — *tart, bitch, whore* — 'woman so special that you've done this to me?' asked Mel.

'I don't want to say, it'll sound as if I'm rubbing it in.'

He might as well have punched her in the solar plexus.

'You froze the joint bank account.'

'I know, I'm sorry about that as well. At least if I froze it, you'd know that I wouldn't be able to take money out either.'

A small smile appeared on his lips, as if he expected a brownie point for that consideration; instead, it threw a match on the dry tinder of her fast-diminishing patience.

'Weren't you frightened that I'd burn your suits or set up a stall on the street selling everything in the garage for fifty pee?'

The look on his face those words brought was priceless. Maybe it was time he saw she could act out of character too. She would bet he hadn't considered it could be a possibility. Good old faithful Mel. Well, she'd put that worm in his head. Why should she have to do all the second-guessing?

'I'm really sorry, Mel.'

Her eyes narrowed. 'But not sorry enough to come home.'

A slow shake of his head.

'I think you should go, Steve.'

'I will. I'm trusting you not to do anything stupid with my things though, Mel. That would be criminal damage.'

'FUCK OFF,' she shouted, her volume button turned up to the max. She didn't normally swear at all but these days the only words running through her head began with an F, C, B or W. Never mind her not recognising him, she didn't recognise herself. He'd turned her into Shaun Ryder.

He fucked off as commanded. She stood at the window and watched him get into his van and pull away, then she collapsed into the armchair as if someone had reached inside her and ripped out her bones. She could feel the tears racing up to her ducts again and she stamped down hard on them. No, she would not cry because that was being weak and she needed to be strong because being a wet lettuce had done her no good so far. Then she did something ridiculously impulsive. She rang Pat and he said he'd come round after his shift.

★

Sky saw Angel Sutton enter the shop before Angel saw her, thanks to her coat sleeve getting snagged up on the door handle and giving Sky some valuable seconds to act. She slipped away unseen into Bon's office. She thought it was empty and apologised when she found him there.

'I'm avoiding someone,' she explained.

'Oh, the Sutton woman,' he said. 'Is she looking for you?'

'I don't think so, but I'd still rather not talk to her.'

Bon looked out of the glass window. 'She's heading down to the bottom. She's got a big bag with her. Heavy, by the look of it.'

'Is it okay if I stay here until she's gone?'

'Of course. I'll go and keep watch.'

Bon moved out of his office. He was worried about Sky. She was awfully pale, to the point of looking ill. When she walked in that morning, he wanted to wrap his arms around her and press some warmth into her, some comfort. He wished he knew if there was anything worryingly wrong with her health; he wished he could help her. He wished he could love her.

He sauntered down the shop to eavesdrop. Angel Sutton was talking to Jock. He'd better go down in case they needed a translator. Jock had a very thick accent and often had to repeat what he said to be understood. It spoke volumes that a South African had to translate Scots into English for people; they'd laughed about that a few times.

Angel was in full flow, explaining what she wanted from him.

'. . . Anyway, here they are. My grandfather is Archie Sutton, I know you'll have heard of him. These are the very first tools he used when he started working so they're precious to him. They've been in his garage for years and I'd like all the rust removed and the wood oiled or whatever you do and then mounted in a case for him.'

Jock looked at them: an array of old tools with weathered handles in three black drawstring bags. If they were as precious as they were supposed to be, they'd have been kept in a better state than this, was his initial thought.

'I can restore the tools, but you'll need my pal who is over there for the case. He's no' here today.'

Angel reached into her bag: Prada, with flashy gold letters on the side, and pulled out a sheet of paper.

'This is what I want, if I can leave it with you for him, then. The tools mounted and behind glass and a brass plaque on the frame. I've drawn a detailed illustration. It doesn't matter what it costs, I just want it done before September the first. You will take care, won't you? You can throw away the bags they're in. I think there was some old wives' tale idea years ago that if you kept them wrapped in silk it would stop the rust, which obviously hasn't happened in this case; hence the "old wives' tale" label.'

Jock hadn't heard that load of old piffle before, but he didn't say as much.

'Do you want a deposit? Do you have a machine?' She took a gold bank card from the purse in her hand.

'No, you're okay,' said Jock. Bon could tell from his face that he was probably thinking what a stupid idea for a present.

'Can you ring me when it's ready? How long will it take?'

'I don't know. But it'll certainly be ready in plenty o' time for September. I'll need tae take your number.'

'I've written it down on the illustration. Is Sky around today?'

'I have nae seen her,' said Jock, feigning innocence.

'Day off,' said Bon.

'Do you have a telephone number for her?'

'I'm afraid ... we don't give out personal numbers,' said Bon.

Angel made a thoughtful, *hmm* sound.

'I really need to get a message to her. I wonder if you'd pass it on.'

'I can get you some paper if you want to write it down,' Bon offered.

'Or you could just say to her when you see her that we've had a reporter sniffing around. It's coming up to twenty years. She'll know what that means.'

Bon didn't give her the benefit of looking bemused. 'Yes of course, I'll pass that on.'

'She'll understand. Thank you.' Angel smiled and headed towards the exit.

'Twenty years? What's that supposed to mean?' Bon said to Jock.

'It'll be that fuckin' prowler story,' answered Jock, shaking his head. 'Climbs oot the cundie every few years.'

'You wouldn't think it was still newsworthy after all this time, would you?'

'They're still talking about Jack the Ripper, Bon,' Tony Cropper called over.

'That's because they never solved the mystery,' said Mildred, walking over to join in. 'And it's the same with the Prowler. Did he or didn't he have an accomplice who remained at large? If there was a second man, it's no one they had on their list; they were all checked out and there was no evidence to link any of them to the crimes except Craven himself.' Her voice dropped in volume. 'Of course they saw Edek as the most likely, because he lived in a fairly remote place and his alibi was always that he was with his very frail wife and his young daughter at home. His was the least viable to substantiate. I remember hearing some idiot insinuate Edek was angry at the world for his wife being so poorly and as such, he wanted to hurt "normal" women.'

'It's not outside the realms of possibility, Mildred. Look at Sutcliffe. Anyone who knew him would never have believed he was capable of what he was.'

'And therein lies the problem, Tony, because there was a very clear precedent of someone caring and family-orientated having such a hidden side,' said Mildred. 'Anyway, I refuse to believe it. But they will keep dredging it up, hoping someone will come forward with new evidence until the truth is finally uncovered. And until poor Edek is cleared, Sky will never be rid of that awful shadow hanging over her.'

Bon opened the door to his office and then closed it again. Sky was fast asleep on the couch in there, her eyelids fluttering as if she were dreaming. He let himself, just for a moment, imagine he were lying next to her, studying her beautiful face before threading his hand in her hair and kissing her awake.

★

She was still sleeping when Astrid came in for her wage. She always picked it up on Thursdays and then called into the Pot of Gold antiques centre across the square to see Kev's old dealer friends and have a cuppa and a natter with them. Spring Hill Square had quickly become a community that looked after its own. Bon counted his blessings that he'd found it when he had. His was the biggest unit of them all and he hadn't been looking for anything of that size. Then he'd gone into the Pot of Gold and seen all the various dealers who rented space from the owner, Lewis Harley, and it had made him think bigger: about a repair shop emporium of various specialists. They had joined him as if drawn to him by invisible forces, concluding with Sky, who fitted exactly the compact space outside his office which none of the others could have utilised.

'Astrid, I have the cash on me but not the actual printed wage slip. Can I give that to you next week?'

'Of course,' replied Astrid.

'Sky's asleep in my office,' he explained, taking the wallet out of his pocket. 'I don't want to wake her. I'm wondering if she's not well, and when she wakes up, I think I'll ask her to call it a day and go home.'

Astrid humphed. 'I think that is the worst thing you can suggest, Mr van der Meer.'

'Oh, what do you mean?'

Astrid shook her hand as if to wave away her own spoken words.

'I shouldn't have said anything. It's not my place.'

'Oh come on, Astrid,' said Bon, 'you have to tell me now. I'm worried about her, if I'm honest.'

Astrid blew her breath out of her cheeks. He'd convinced her that perhaps she should, in this case, share a confidence because maybe Bon could help.

'Okay, she has a landlord who is a creep. And she wants to leave but obviously she is tied to a tenancy agreement and has *fünf* '– she held up her splayed hand – 'months to go. But he is going into her room and she has to sleep with a chair rammed against the door. Can you imagine? I said to her, I have a room she can rent. It would be ideal for both of us but he won't give her the bond back if she leaves early. He is making life very difficult. One night . . .' She trailed off, not sure if this was too much, then decided that she was in for a penny so might as well be in for a pound: '. . . Yes, one night, I came to do my shift and I was very late and I found her asleep on Peter's sofa. It is so bad for her, that was better than going home.'

Bon listened intently. 'Is that true?' he asked.

'It's true.'

'And you have a place she can stay?'

'I do.'

'Do you have a spare hour, Astrid? I'll pay you double.'

'I do,' said Astrid, feeling a wash of relief that she'd done the right thing.

Chapter 35

Amanda drove over to her mum's house to check everything was okay, and to pick up another nightie and clean underwear from her drawers upstairs. Then, while she was in the bedroom, she moved the unit away from the corner, peeled the carpet back and put the large rusty tin back in the hole. It was her mother's property and she hadn't really any right to take it, she'd decided. She felt better when it was restored to its rightful place.

Bradley and Kerry were sitting with Ingrid when Amanda got to the hospital. Ingrid was sitting up; such a different scenario to yesterday and Amanda was beyond relieved. She glanced at Amanda and smiled, which set Amanda's alarm bells ringing immediately. She couldn't remember the last time her mother had greeted her with a smile so wide.

'Amanda, good news. The doctor said that they're thinking about letting her out tomorrow. Didn't they, Mother, say they were letting you out tomorrow?' Bradley patted his mum's hand while he was talking to her as if she were three.

'Yes. I'm going home, thank god because this place is full

of people I can't stand,' said Ingrid. 'And she's the worst of them.' She jabbed her finger in the direction of the woman by the window, who was fast asleep.

Bradley chortled.

'Oh Ingrid, you can't say that,' said Kerry.

'It'll be nice to be back home. I'll call in and see Edie next door and make sure she's all right. She's had her foot off, you know. Or it might be two, I can't remember.'

Eh? thought Amanda. Ingrid hadn't lived next to Edie for forty years.

'She's got a house in Spain, she's always asking me to go. I've said no so many times I can't count.'

'Have you? You should go,' said Kerry in her best dopey voice.

'They've got too many animals over there, parrots, cats. I can't do with animals. And stairs, loads of stairs. She can't get up them because she's got no feet.'

'Kerry, can you go and get a nurse,' said Amanda.

'What's the matter?' asked Bradley, feathers ruffled that Amanda was ordering his wife around.

'Because neither of you have noticed, have you, that Mum is talking absolute bollocks.'

★

Sky had been in a deep dreamless sleep, deep as Loch Ness. It had caught up with her, having had such a poor night's sleep before. It took Bon a few gentle shakes of her arm to bring her back to the surface. She sat bolt upright, disorientated, embarrassed.

'Oh god, Bon, I'm so sorry,' she said, jumping to her feet so quickly she staggered backwards.

Astrid was standing behind Bon, smiling at her, an unsure sort of smile that went in and out on her lips.

'Sky, I hope you don't mind but I have opened me big gob and said probably more than I should have. I told Mr van der Meer about the creepy man in your house.'

'Okay,' said Sky. It wasn't that big a secret, but it wasn't as if he could do anything about it.

'Sky, Astrid tells me that she has a room you could move into,' said Bon.

'Yes, but I can't expect Astrid to keep it open until my tenancy agreement is up and that's months—'

He cut her off. 'I want you to show me where you live. You're going to be moving out in the next hour, if that's what you want.'

'I . . . I can't do that because—'

'Do you want to leave that house?'

'Well . . . yes, I—'

'That's all I needed to hear, the *yes*,' said Bon.

★

To be fair to the nurses, Ingrid was talking very convincingly about Edie with one foot who kept a menagerie in Spain, but Amanda was totally disgusted with her brother for not spotting the rubbish her mum was coming out with. After further investigation they found she had a water infection which was causing the confusion.

'How was I supposed to know there was no one called Edie living next door?' Bradley seethed at her. 'She might have meant the new neighbours.'

'The young pharmacist couple with all feet intact, as you'd know if you actually conversed with Mum. You swan

in twice a week, Bradley, stay an hour with her if that, you
never take her out—'

'I've got my own life,' Bradley bit back.

'That is your eighty-year-old mother in there, Bradley.
And she thinks the sun shines out of your arse. Now I'm
warning you, on Saturday morning the estate agent is going
round to take photos of Mum's house and it's going up on
the market. And that is final.'

'You can't do that,' said Bradley, his mouth puckering
like a cat's backside.

'Watch me,' she replied and turned to go. She needed a
coffee. Strong.

'I've got power of attorney,' Bradley shouted at her back.

Amanda braked. She turned on her heel.

'You what?'

'Mother gave me power of attorney in case she lost her
faculties. Financial and health. It's all legal. If anything happens to me, it'll be Kerry; that's what she wanted so don't
blame me, it wasn't my doing.'

Amanda was seething. 'Oh, I'll bet it wasn't your doing.
And when did you pull that little trick?'

'It wasn't a trick, Mother asked me to get a solicitor to
come to the house to do it all, and he was assured that she
was of sound mind.'

Amanda laughed, not caring that the sound filled the
hospital corridor.

'Please tell me you don't mean your mate Johnny Wilson?
The one that got struck off?'

'He was reinstated,' said Bradley, breathing so heavily he
was rasping. 'What happens is that I don't step in unless I
have to. Mother remains in sole charge of things until then.'

Amanda opened up her mouth to say the words crowded

in there, but she would have been thrown out of the hospital for the volume and the language. She needed to get away from her brother before she did something she'd regret. No wonder she was drowned in her own menopausal sweat by the time she got to the café on the floor below, and no HRT patch on earth had the power to stop such a tsunami.

Chapter 36

Sky grew ever more tense as Bon's van approached the house, with the three of them sitting together in the front, Sky in the middle. She was cross with herself. She didn't blame Astrid for trying to help her, it was her own fault for opening her mouth in the Tuesday club and it was now going to cause bother. Bon was driving silently and she could see by his expression that he was gearing up for a confrontation. She didn't want him to get into trouble; Wilton would have no compunction about ringing the police on him.

Bon pulled up sharply beside the house. It looked decent from the outside, in a row of other decent houses, but that's because Katy and Jordan and Sky had looked after it, made sure the small front garden was neat, paid for a window cleaner and Katy's sunny yellow curtains were still hung up. Sky got out of the van with her key ready in her hand. She knew Wilton was in because his own van, a much smaller affair than Bon's Mercedes Sprinter, was parked on the road. Bon noticed the state of it inside when they passed it, like a skip on wheels.

Sky put the key in the lock and turned it. The smell hit

them immediately when the door was open: acrid, cigarette smoke. Breathing the air in these days was the equivalent of smoking oneself. Bon gently pushed Sky out of the way and walked in first.

Wilton waddled out of the lounge, hoisting up his customary tracksuit bottoms that were always halfway down his backside. He looked from Astrid to Bon, then to Sky.

'What's going on?' he asked.

'Astrid, if you could kindly help Sky pack up her things,' said Bon calmly, sweetly even. 'There are plenty of boxes in the van. I'll be with you in a matter of minutes, ladies.' He then addressed Wilton. 'Mr Dearne, I believe. I'd like a few words with you.'

He stepped towards Wilton, forcing him back into the lounge and when they were clear of the door, Bon shut it.

Astrid's mouth formed an excited *Ooo*.

'I'll bring the boxes in, you start to pack,' she said to Sky.

Sky didn't bother folding up her clothes, but put them in her case as quickly as she could. Her books, laptop, clean towels, fabrics and sewing machine went in boxes. She would leave the bedding and pillows because however much she washed them, she'd remember that Wilton's body had been on them.

Astrid pressed an ear to the lounge door as she passed by. She heard Wilton swearing at Bon, but there was no heated response from Bon, whatever he was saying was barely audible. She hoped he was coming out on top because it didn't sound like it, even if the flabby landlord would be no match for Bon physically. He was strong as an ox because Astrid had seen him pick up and carry things in the shop, even though he wasn't built anything like her Kevin. He'd needed a huge coffin, Bon and Willy had made it for him together; solid oak, for a solid oak of a man.

Astrid carried the boxes out as Sky filled them. There wasn't much for a young woman's life, she thought. No furniture, other than a pretty writing desk and chair.

Finally the lounge door opened and a puce-faced Wilton scuttled down the hallway past Sky's room to the one that used to be Jordan's. He slammed the door behind him, making his mood clear, then emerged again with a handful of twenty-pound notes.

'Here,' he said, slapping them down onto Bon's waiting palm. 'Now get the fuck out of my house.'

'We'll stay to count it,' said Bon, not in the least cowed by the landlord's tenor. 'Then you can have your key.' He handed them to Sky.

'There should be five months rent there, Sky, and your bond. You check it while we move the rest of your things.'

Sky sat on the bed and counted it. She was six pounds in credit but she wouldn't refund him. She couldn't believe Bon had got it for her.

She came out of the room just as Bon was taking the last box to the van. He was just as delicious from the back as from the front: long legs, strong shoulders, tapering to a perfect waist. She took a final long look at the place she'd been so happy in until those recent weeks. She could see Katy in the lounge scoffing a Pot Noodle, telling her she'd met this great bloke called Ozzy but she hadn't a chance with him. And she could visualise Jordan, cooking his speciality pesto pasta in the kitchen for her after her op. She and Jordan and Katy, their vitality and warmth pressed into the air like a watermark, she'd try and remember this house like that. She couldn't wait to text Katy and tell her what had just happened.

She placed the key on the table and closed the front door. Wilton Dearne was already consigned to the past.

★

Mel tried to ring Postman Pat yet again to tell him not to come round but he wasn't answering. What the hell was she thinking of, ringing him? She left a voicemail to say she was fine now. She hadn't gone to work, she'd rung in sick and her boss Heather was great about it; she said she'd actually suspected Mel had come back too soon after she'd been struck down with that virus and obviously hadn't been ready to return. The branch was closed for staff training to-morrow, so she told Mel to rest up and come back Monday. Mel would have felt awful for lying had she had any room for it in her head.

Pat had obviously been home to change out of his uni-form because the man who swaggered up the drive at three o'clock with Oasis shoulders was in jeans and a navy peacoat. Mel was overcome with guilt, dragging him up here just because she'd had a major meltdown after Steve had left.

She opened the door before he'd had a chance even to knock.

'Y'a'right?' he asked.

'Er . . . yeah . . . yeah. I've been trying to ring you all day to say I was okay now.'

'Had me phone switched off. You don't look all right.' He strode past her and took a seat in her lounge, sat down legs apart, hands on his thighs, a manly, confident pose. His eyes zoned in on her mouth. 'Did he hit you?'

'Wha . . . oh no, it's . . . I keep catching my lip and it's swelled up. I've had a cold sore.'

'I know, I saw it,' he said. It had obviously stuck in his mind then, which was embarrassing. It was a bit of a focal point, to be fair. It felt bigger than her head.

'Sorry I couldn't talk earlier. Mad busy. What happened then?'

'Can I get you a cup of something while we talk?'

'A coffee'd be great, thanks.' He followed her into the kitchen. 'Nice house,' he said, his eyes doing a quick rove around.

'Yes,' she replied. It was supposed to be her forever home. *Their* forever home. That future didn't seem so certain any more.

He sat down at the kitchen table. She put the kettle on and reached into the cupboard. She pulled out a box of asparagus Cup a Soups and took one out. Then realised her mistake and put it back in the box.

'You don't know what you're doing, do you?' said Pat.

'No,' she said, her voice wobbling. She'd gone through every emotion there was since first thing that morning. The anger was better but it had dissipated and now she was two nice words away from collapsing into a pathetic soggy, confused mess.

'Sit down,' he said. 'I'll make them.'

★

They carried the boxes into Astrid's beautiful home. It was flooded with pale pastels, and light poured in through the large windows, entirely different from the dreary, dark place Sky had left. She hadn't noticed the drabness so much when her friends had been there, though; they'd brought the sunshine inside with them. And the bonus with Astrid's house was that it was within walking distance of Spring Hill, too; it was perfect on every level.

'I need to go back to work,' said Sky. 'My car's there.'

'I'll take you,' said Bon.

'Und meanwhile I will get your bed ready,' said Astrid, 'and just give the place an extra little dust.'

She couldn't have found any dust in that house with a microscope, thought Sky.

'I am so chuffed,' beamed Astrid. And she was. She didn't have to vet prospective tenants for weirdness, instead she would have the lovely Sky for company.

'I haven't even asked you how much rent this place is,' said Sky.

'I haven't even thought how much to ask for it,' said Astrid with a titter. 'We will sort it out between us.'

'I can't thank you enough, Astrid,' said Sky, still bewildered by the madness of the day so far.

'And I can't thank you enough for my Kevin bear,' said Astrid. She'd been so touched by that, the favour repaid was a pleasure to give.

Sky got into the van with Bon.

'Thank you,' she said, when they set off.

'You should have told me before,' said Bon. 'I'd have helped you. Any of us would.'

'I didn't have anywhere to go, it was only recently that I heard about Astrid's room. Not that I could have afforded it anyway, not unless Wilton had given me a refund and my bond back. What did you say to him?'

Bon allowed himself the smallest of wry smiles. 'Never you mind.'

'Oh. Okay.' Though Sky wished she could have been a

fly on the wall, not that her admiration could have super-seded what it already was for him. She knew that Wilton was probably a typical bully who could only stand up to weaker people, and Bon was very strong. She thought of how he'd lifted up the box of books that she'd barely been able to drag to the door. He was perfect. And next week the man she was in love with was going to dinner with Gwyn Tankersley who had bought the desk, a woman his own age, polished and glamorous and assured, like Erin van der Meer. He wouldn't have accepted if he didn't like her. *Like* her.

'When your *friend or foe* left earlier, she told me to pass a message on to you. She said that a reporter had been sniffing around. Something about it being twenty years. Does that make sense to you?'

Sky nodded, but didn't say anything. She turned her face to the window. Bon must also know what Angel meant. It would never go away; the rumours, the accusations had followed her father far beyond the grave. It haunted her that he would not lie at rest while they persisted. And there was nothing she could do but let them swirl, because she'd learned that protesting was just talking into the wind and always would be, unless there was proof against them.

★

'Have you heard from . . . your wife?' asked Mel, as Pat put milk into the coffees. She still couldn't say her name because it would make her even more real than she was already. She had a freeze-frame moment then of how odd this was: another man standing in her kitchen making her a coffee. It should be Steve standing there doing that, but it was a postman who was taller and ganglier with a Mancunian accent that made John Cooper Clarke sound like he was playing at it.

'Nope,' said Pat. 'I will when she starts to get bored – and the chances of that are high, trust me.'

'I just can't believe this is happening,' said Mel. 'It's like when Covid first started up and you know it's all real but half of you is thinking you're living in a sci-fi movie.'

'Maybe I was just more guarded than I thought I was and that's why I'm managing it,' said Pat. 'I don't mind telling you the first time it happened, I was in a right state. And then she came back and didn't want to talk about it because she just wanted to forget it and move on, but *I* needed to unravel it all and get it sorted in my head, and I never got the chance. So when he comes back, then you make sure that you have the conversations you need to have for *you* to move forward, because he owes you that.'

'You think he will?' she asked. 'Come back, I mean.'

'I can't guarantee it, but I'd guess so. And I can't tell you if that's because the guilt will gnaw at him too much, or he realises he prefers you to her, or if the shine wears off for her and she dumps him so he's got nowhere else to go. One of us is going to be plan B, is what I'm saying.'

Mel rubbed her forehead as if it were a genie's lamp and could give her a wish.

'But they might decide they want to be together,' she said.

'Yeah, they might,' Pat lifted up his shoulders and dropped them. 'I doubt it, but they might. How would you be for money if he wanted a divorce?'

She hadn't wanted to start thinking about that happening, but she supposed she might have to.

'Okay, probably. I wouldn't want to fight over the microwave. This house is bought and paid for. We've got savings, pensions. I could just about afford to buy him out of the house ...' She wouldn't want that, though; this was *their* house. Steve had put his mark on every room: the walls he'd knocked down, the kitchen he'd put in, the wet room he'd built, the fireplace he'd made. She hiccupped a sob and then apologised.

'You don't have to be sorry; I'm sorry it's my wife that's helped put you in this spot. For the record I think your husband will feel like he's been hit by a train. She's quite a force is Chlo, she enjoys having sexual power; he wouldn't have stood a chance. She'll make him feel like a million dollars, but if she drops him, it'll be from a great height.' He tore off some kitchen roll and handed it to Mel; she pushed her face into it and mopped up the few escapee tears.

'Would you be okay, financial-wise?' she asked, pulling herself together.

Pat brought the coffees to the table and sat down. 'Yeah. We've got a couple of properties we rent out. Good pensions. The idea was to retire early and do what we enjoy. In her case it would have been lying out in the sun all day, in mine it would have been to see a load of bands.'

'Steve hates live gigs. He could never understand why I'd want to be crushed in a mosh pit when I could watch things on the telly,' said Mel.

'You're kidding?' Pat shook his head incredulously. 'Has he never heard of atmosphere?'

'No. And even when I dragged him to see the Happy Mondays he didn't *get it* and it was amazing.'

'Now you're talking my language. Madchester days. And they were mad an' all. Glory days of music. An' I was dressing like this before Oasis hit the scene, just let me make that point before anyone finks I'm some sort of pound-shop Liam Gallagher.'

Whoops, thought Mel. She'd called him that in the friendship group at the diner.

'I was once nearly in a band,' she said. 'But the drummer got pregnant and . . . life happened. I joined a bank instead, just one letter difference but a world apart. My mum and dad were happy though.'

'It's not about what makes them happy though, is it? You can't live anyone else's life for 'em, you can only choose your own dreams. My daugh'er wanted to go travelling. I wanted her to stay home and be safe but I had to wave her off and keep me gob shut, let her do her thing and she did and now she's married and pregnant. I wanted to be a roadie when I was younger, travelling with bands, putting up their equipment, just hanging with them, you know. Me mam said "is there any money in it for you?" and me dad said, "just let him do what he has to do" and I did it and I loved it.'

'You were a roadie?'

'Yeah, went all over the world. Then when I'd had enough, I settled down. Still love my bands, though.' He smiled. He had a great smile, thought Mel.

'What did you play?' he asked her.

'Guitar,' replied Mel. 'Still do. I teach it. An old pal of mine got in touch recently, wanted to know if I'd like to resurrect my ambition and be in the band we never actually got around to setting up.'

He laughed. Like everyone else. Like Steve.

'Well, it's a no-brainer, innit? You got to do it,' he said, shocking her. 'If it's still in there, you've got to let it out to breathe.'

'I said no. Steve said I was way too old.'

'Sod that, ring 'em up and tell 'em you've changed your mind. Nuts to what anyone else thinks.'

'I'm fifty-three.'

'Mick Jagger's a hundred and five and still touring.'

Mel laughed at that.

'You're too old when you're dead, Mel. Until then everything's a possibility.'

'Are you sure you aren't Confucius reincarnated? You're very wise.'

'University of life, I've got a load of Ph.Ds from it,' said Pat to that and brought the cup to his lips.

'Thank you,' Mel said. 'I'm sorry I rang you, I shouldn't have. I panicked.'

'No problem, really. I'd have still come if I'd got your message to say don't come, just to check on yer. Been where you are and it's shit.' He glanced at his watch. 'Listen, I've got to go in a minute. Sorry, it was just a quick call round; I'm taking my daugh'er to look at cars. Her husband hasn't a clue what questions to ask. We'll talk again, yeah? We'll both get *frough* this, one way or another, all right?'

Mel nodded. Pat took his cup over to the sink, swilled it and put it upside down on the draining board.

She saw him out while wishing he'd stayed for another.

Chapter 37

Ingrid had been on intravenous antibiotics for a couple of days to help shift the infection in her system. Amanda sat at the side of her mother's bed, hurting that this woman whom she loved, whom she worried about and had cared for and watched out for didn't love her anything near as much as she did the offspring of a vile old pervert. She knew that Bradley must have cajoled their mother into allowing him to have the power of attorney over her affairs, but also that she would have been willingly cajoled. She didn't entirely blame her mother, who should be able to trust her children, and she only hoped that Bradley did look out for their mother's best interests because if she smelt as much as a whiff of misappropriation, she would not only challenge it but have Bradley's balls in a meat grinder. Maybe she was overreacting, she decided. He might be a selfish twat but that was no real reason to suspect the *very* worst of him. She'd always presumed that Bradley got his self-centredness from his father, but he was just as likely to have inherited it from his mother.

Ingrid's eyes fluttered open and focused in on her daughter.

'Hi, Mum.'

'Oh, hello,' said Ingrid. 'Have you been here long?'

'A couple of hours.'

'Have you been at work?'

'Not today, it's Saturday.'

'Bradley's just left.'

She went with it, knowing he hadn't been near since he'd dropped his power of attorney bomb on her on Thursday. 'Has he?'

'He's been here all night.' Ingrid smiled. 'He loves his old mum.'

'So do I, Mum. I love you too,' Amanda said softly, putting her hand on top of Ingrid's.

'I know you do, but . . . ' Her voice trailed off.

'But what, Mum?'

Ingrid sighed. 'Her dad.'

'Whose dad?' asked Amanda.

Ingrid closed her eyes. 'Amanda's dad. I always told her I loved him, but . . . I never did. I only married him because I was pregnant. He loved me though, and I felt guilty. I was his forever lady, that's what he used to say.'

'That's lovely though, isn't it?' said Amanda, feeling her throat clog up because she knew that whatever was coming next wasn't going to be lovely.

'I just felt trapped. When he died it was like I was free.'

Amanda had no idea who Ingrid thought she was talking to but she had to know more, even if she didn't want to. She spoke softly, so as not to break the spell.

She dared the question she must ask. 'Is that why you didn't love Amanda?'

'Aw, I shouldn't have been like I was with her, I always felt bad. I wanted to, she was a lovely little thing and I know she loves me, she's ever so good to me . . . but . . . '

Ingrid fell silent. The 'but' was such a small word but its weight was significant; a key to a door that Amanda did not want to open. But she had to.

She swallowed. 'But?'

Ingrid sighed, then leaned forward as if to impart a confidence. 'If the truth be told, I couldn't stand her being inside me, I just wanted her out.'

Jesus. As mixed up as her mum was, Amanda knew this was true.

'I didn't want children. Bradley was another accident, but I felt different with him, from the moment I knew I was carrying him. And when he was born I just felt this . . . tidal wave of happiness. A little boy, my little boy.'

Amanda dashed the tears from her eyes away with her hands. She willed herself to stay in control, until all the questions sitting inside her were answered.

'Did you know that Arnold wasn't very nice to Amanda?'

Ingrid opened her eyes and gave a hard huff of laughter. 'He only smacked her bum when she was naughty. He would ask me, you know. He'd say she was giving him cheek and I'd say well, you're the man of the house, you sort it.'

Amanda could still feel the heat of the indignity, of that wiry little man with the pincer-like grip grabbing her arm, forcing her over his knee, yanking down her knickers, the smart of his slaps. She'd never known that Ingrid had not so much stopped him as encouraged it.

'She spoilt it. Arnold left me because he couldn't stand her. It scared him being near children again after what she was saying about him, he didn't even want to be with his own son because of her. We were all right. I liked his company, but he said it was her or me. I thought about putting her in a home at one point. Do you remember me saying that to you? You said, you can't do that, Ingrid, what'll folk say? So I had no choice, did I? I gave him some money to buy the shop, you know, the money that her dad had left for her. I thought that was only fair after what she'd done to him. And he did well with that shop, never missed paying me maintenance for Bradley.'

Amanda felt sick.

'But you didn't give him Fred's box under the carpet? Were you saving that for Amanda?'

Please, please, mum, say yes.

'Oh, is that where it is. I couldn't remember where I'd put it. Oh I am glad you've found it.' Ingrid was overjoyed as she looked into her daughter's eyes but saw someone else. 'I've been saving it all these years for Bradley for when I'm gone. I wish I could be around to see his face. You will tell him where to find it, won't you? Promise me.'

'Yes, I promise,' said Amanda, sad, defeated, broken. 'I will.'

Chapter 38

Mel's phone rang just before twelve and Joss's name was on the screen.

'Long shot, but are you free this aft? Look at the freaky hot weather, not to be wasted. Dad's decided to have a barbecue and I've been out and bought far too much food for it. Please come. You don't need to bring as much as a sausage.' She didn't wait for the answer. 'Good. I'll pick you up at one.'

Mel laughed. 'I'd forgotten how bossy you used to be.'

'Hopefully in a good way. You haven't said no.'

Oh what the hell, thought Mel. It beat sitting in by herself trying not to mope. She was always happiest on Saturdays and this might restore some of the joy of the day for her.

'I'll be ready and waiting.'

She'd take a bottle though. They always had a stock of wine in, Steve liked a glass in the evening.

The thought of him usually brought with it a sharp smart as if someone had twanged an elastic band against her skin, but today she thought, *bastard*. No, she wouldn't sit in the freezer waiting for him to make up his mind which one of them he wanted. She'd put on some make-up, a summer frock, some strappy sandals and she'd party. And on the drive over to Joss's house, she'd do what Pat said she should and tell her she was joining her bloody band after all.

★

'It's nice, I like it,' said Alex, turning around in the master bedroom of the showhouse. Erin had done some investigating on the new estate Bon had told her about. There were only three left and one was in a choice position on a corner plot. It had a bigger garden than the others and a sunroom. The fourth bedroom was downstairs and would make a perfect home office. She could have gone to view it by herself but she rang Alex anyway to see if he was free and he said he absolutely was. So here they were.

It was the first time she had seen him out of his suit and she'd wondered what he would look like in casual gear. He had an ace bum for jeans, great taste in footwear and the plain, blue T-shirt he sported showed off a surprisingly toned physique.

She was too much a creature of impulse, but everything about the house was saying it was the right fit.

'I'm going to reserve it,' she said.

'If you want it, you should have it,' said Alex. 'Let's find the salesperson and strike while your iron is sizzling.'

They found her, she took details, Erin formally reserved 1, Renaissance Place — even the street name was screaming she should buy it. She'd already started to pack up her things in the flat because the buyer was pushing for a speedy sale and she was happy to oblige. She'd probably have to rent somewhere before her new house was ready for her but that was fine; the sooner she could leave the apartment, the better.

This was a grand day. A new beginning secured, with sunshine and good company, because Alex really was good company. Very good company, and he liked hers too, she could tell. They smiled a lot at each other and she wasn't ready to say goodbye to him after the paperwork was completed.

'There's a pub down the road that does great food if you'd like to help me celebrate my new purchase,' she said when they left the onsite office. 'It's on me. Call it a surveyor's fee.'

'Ah . . .' his expression changed into one of polite regret. 'I can't, I'm afraid. I'm going out to dinner tonight.'

She forced out a look that she hoped covered her disappointment adequately. 'Absolutely no problem. I thought if you were at a loose end . . . er then . . . but . . .' She was stuttering and was glad when he cut her off.

'Someone on the circuit. Asked me out of the blue yesterday and I found myself saying *why not*. Put my toe back in the waters of dating.'

That made it totally clear what sort of 'dinner' he was going to.

'Well, you be sure to have a lovely time.'

She doubted Meryl Streep would be checking her out as acting competition.

'Nervous, actually.'

'That's natural.'

'She's nice though. Quite a character.'

She. Erin imagined someone formidable who looked shit-hot in a barrister's wig, who was assured and intelligent and articulate because she would be if she was 'on the circuit'. She wouldn't be a mess who misread signs.

'Great.'

'Anyway,' Alex bent, kissed her cheek. 'Congratulations on your purchase. And I'll see you Wednesday for more revelations from Father Paul. Wonder how it went with the bishop.'

'Well, I hope. Enjoy tonight.'

He turned from her and she let her smile fall because it suddenly felt too heavy to hold up. That's why he wasn't nervous around *her*, because he saw her as a friend, and only that. She didn't want another male friend. She didn't want another female lover. What she did need though was a man to put his arms around her and a cache of female friends, who understood what it was like to be a woman with all their insecurities and fears and faults, to confide in about how she felt.

She got into the car, stupidly tearful, feeling like an idiot, the imprint of Alex's lips still on her skin.

★

Joss's family's house was even bigger than Mel remembered it and even more beautiful.

'Come and meet everyone,' said Joss, pulling her by the hand into a small throng of people. Her mum and dad were much aged, their dark hair now white, their kind faces still instantly recognisable but lined with the paintbrush of time.

'I remember that lovely red hair,' said Joss's father, embracing her.

'Do you still like meringues?' asked her mother. 'I'll never forget making meringues for Joss's birthday party and you disappearing under the table with the plate of them.' She hooted.

'Oh god, did I?' said Mel, horrified. A memory winkled

out of a burial place in her head of her doing exactly that meringue-scoffing thing. Memories didn't die, then; they were just waiting to jump out at you when their graves were poked.

'I was rather chuffed. I thought I'd made a pig's ear of them and no one would want them. It was the first time I'd attempted them.'

'I'm making a pig's ear of these burgers, look, I've burned that one,' said her father.

'I'll have it,' said Mel, 'I'm a speciality in pig's ear disposals.'

'Nope, you're having one of my better ones,' insisted her father.

'Dad, we'll be back, I just want to show Mel something.'

Joss led the way to the barn. There were people inside, Mel could see them through the windows and one of them was sitting behind a drum kit.

'She's here,' announced Joss when they walked in.

'Melinda McVie, as I live and breathe,' shouted the woman behind the drum kit with the same pixie haircut she had at school. Sue Fletcher came dancing over, arms extended, the designated drummer of the band that never was.

'Oh my goodness,' said Mel, walking into the hug from her old friend, inhaling her perfume. *Paris*. Maybe a retro choice but it still smelt great.

'Let me look at you,' said Sue, pushing her out to arms' length.

'Oh don't, I'm a wreck,' said Mel.

'You look great to me,' said Sue. She turned to Joss. 'She's on board then?' Back to Mel. 'You on board? You're doing this with us? Fuck me, you are, you so are.'

'And this rock chick … can you remember her?' asked

Joss, standing with her arm around another woman whom Mel kind of recognised. 'Miss East hated her nearly as much as you.'

'No way – Titch?' exclaimed Mel, laughing, as it came to her who she was. 'What the hell happened, Gina? I mean I know I'm only five three, but I used to look down onto the top of your head.'

'I'm five ten now. Late growth spurt,' Gina laughed and gave her a hug.

'We've got a guitar all tuned up and ready for you. No pressure,' said Joss. 'But if we don't have something to eat first, my dad's been slaving for nothing.'

Sue linked Mel's arm. 'Come on. We've got thirty-six years to catch up on, we can spare another five minutes for a burger.'

*

Amanda walked into Ray's diner because she didn't really know what else to do with herself. She'd spent most of the afternoon crying, and not really sure what was upsetting her most because there were too many contenders for first place. The infection in her mum's body was making her confused, but Amanda knew that what she'd heard from her had been the truth: intact, unadulterated, undramatised. Ingrid hadn't loved Fred and she hadn't wanted their daughter. She'd blamed her for wrecking her second marriage and then punished her by spending the money her dad had left for her. She'd made her pay all the way through her life, exacting duties from her so she could keep the loving, undemanding side of herself for her son. That's what it felt like.

Amanda took a seat in the corner, a sole table for one. The

diner was busy; she didn't want to claim Ray's attention, she just wanted to be there. It felt like a happy place for her, ever more so since Ray had taken it over. His energy, his enthusiasm, his warmth flooded through it.

He spotted her; he waved and mouthed at her to give him a couple of minutes. It took longer than that, but it was good that he was run off his feet. She'd ordered – and paid for – a coffee by the time he was free.

'Well, isn't this a nice surprise. Look at this place.' He threw his arms wide. 'I'm a hit.'

She smiled. 'Of course you are.'

'You want something to eat?'

'No, I've not long ago had my lunch,' she lied. 'I was just passing and I thought I'd call in.' Another lie.

Jean the waitress called his name.

'Go, you're needed,' said Amanda. He wanted to give her more time, that was clear, but he was in demand.

'I'll get to you later. Don't rush off,' he commanded.

'I won't.'

On the next table a woman was sitting opposite her two children. They all had ice-cream sundaes in tall glasses and were poking long spoons into them to get to the good stuff at the bottom. Behind them a couple, her age, were having one of Ray's mixed platters of Texan food. He was telling her to try something, popping it between her lips; she was chewing and making a face of approval. A teenage boy, gauche and thin, yet to grow properly into his limbs was sitting with a girl, both of them eating burgers. Maybe their first date. How long ago her teenage years seemed. And yet she could remember them so clearly. Seth Mason had never quite faded, he'd been preserved as perfect in her memory with his shy smile that made her heart flutter, and his ocean-blue eyes. What might have been, if fate hadn't been such a bastard.

She could have lived anywhere in the world, followed any path, but she'd never found the confidence to move away so she'd stayed around, been a dutiful second-best child, taken second-best jobs, gone out with second-best men because that's all she thought life had to offer her.

The door to the diner opened and in came a woman, round about her age and linking her arm was an old lady who looked as if she'd just come from the hairdresser's because her hair was salon-perfect.

'Come on, Mam,' said the younger woman. She took the table next to Amanda's. She helped her mum get comfortable and then started to read out the menu to her.

'It's a bit warm for chips, Jane,' the old lady said. 'I think I'd like one of those ice creams that those kiddies have got if you don't mind.'

'Mam, it's your birthday, you can have what you like. And we're having a glass of wine as well, so don't argue.'

'I'm not arguing, love. You're a good lass,' said the old lady and gave her daughter the sort of look that Amanda had never seen for herself but always wanted.

It was too much. She felt crushed by the very atmosphere she had come here to be healed by.

She put her cup back in the saucer and hurried out of the door before anyone could stop her.

★

'So have you got a name for yourselves?' asked Mel, sitting with the guitar, just strumming the odd chord, playing with the strings.

'Have *we* got a name for ourselves,' corrected Joss.

'We tried but we haven't got anywhere. Based on our collective experiences in life, how about The Disasters,' said Sue.

'We need something edgy, like The Slits,' suggested Joss.

'The Tits?' tried Gina.

'Something that reflects how we are now,' said Joss.

'The Floppy Tits then.'

'The Menopausals.'

'The Sweaty Heads.'

'Brain Fog?'

'Miss East's Rejects.'

'The Resilient Fuckers.'

Ideas came flooding in, a couple of possibles, most of them very funny and totally unusable.

'Let's play something, anything,' said Joss. 'Let's just make a starting point. We don't have to plan a world tour yet. How about "Wind of Change", can there be anything more appropriate? Also I'm word perfect and I can do all the whistling. C Major, first chord F, I do believe. Mel, if you don't mind.'

Mel strummed the first F chord, changed it to D minor. They were born.

Chapter 39

Mel came in from work on the Monday with a carrier bag of presents and cards. She pushed open the door and saw the mail on the mat. She wondered if Steve's card would be posted or hand-delivered? She sifted through them: a card from her Auntie Celia on the Isle of Wight, a card from someone she used to work with – they hadn't seen each other for twenty years, but they never missed birthdays or Christmas. A new bank card, an appeal from a charity, a flyer advertising gardening services, a fucking funeral plan leaflet – nothing else. Her sister's always arrived a week late, which used to make Steve cross because he was Mr Punctual with everything. If he had intended to send something, she would have had it by now.

She'd spent all day in a state of anticipation, imagining what sort of card it would be, what he'd say in it, because it didn't cross her mind it wouldn't be here, despite their circumstances. He'd never missed, not in thirty-one years. And now he had.

With a heart weighted with sadness, she put the flowers her boss Heather had given her at work into a vase and set them on the dining room table. They'd all bought her bubble bath, a book, a cake – for two people – and a carton of cream and a bottle of pink champagne. Young Stella, the graduate trainee had bought her a 'Sex Kit for a Sex Kitten' which had some handcuffs, chocolate sauce and 'tingle gel', whatever that was, and a bottom spanker with the word SLUT cut out, presumably to leave a raised imprint on a lucky buttock. She said it was just a jokey present really but everyone had laughed and said they'd be watching for how carefully Mel sat down over the next week. Mel had laughed along with them and said thank you and then had a little sad moment in the toilets.

She opened up a bottle of red and raised a glass to herself in the mirror.

'Happy Birthday, Melinda English,' she said and wondered if she would ever go back to being Melinda McVie. She'd liked that name. Melinda McVie had been full of burning ambitions and dreams and hopes before life threw a damp cloth over them all, snuffing them out.

There was a rap on the back door and her heart made a giant leap in her chest. But she knew it wasn't Steve from the shape in the frosted glass panel. It was too tall, just different, unfamiliar.

She opened it up to find Pat there.

'Hiya,' he said. 'I've got news. Can I come in?'

She stood aside and he walked into the kitchen and saw the flowers and the cards.

'Oh, is it your birthday?'

'Yep,' she said. 'Fifty-four today.'

'You don't look it.'

'I feel a hundred and four. How old are you?'

'I'll be fifty-two on Christmas Day. Chloe's fifty-one on Halloween.'

That brought a wry smile. She loved his accent, though she hadn't given it much thought when she'd first heard it. It was both rough and smooth on the ear at the same time.

'Want a glass of wine?'

'Er, yeah, okay,' he said. 'I'll have one with you.' He picked up the sex kit present.

'One of the girls bought it for me,' she said. 'I doubt it'll be getting used. And I'm not sure I dare put it in the charity bag.'

She poured him a glass and set it before him on the table.

'You all right? You look better than you did. That's gone, hasn't it?' He tapped his lip and pointed at hers.

'Finally. I thought it was going to be my new live-in partner,' said Mel.

'Nice weekend, weren't it?'

'It was great. I ended up at a barbecue and I joined a band.'

Pat grinned. 'The one with your school mates. Mint. What you called?'

'We haven't decided on a name. It all got out of hand.'

'I'll come and see you when you're on stage. First gig. I'll be there in the mosh pit.'

'You might be the only one there,' said Mel.

They both sipped their wine.

'I had a text,' he said. 'From Chlo. She said, *"What's the state of play with us if I come back?"*'

Mel's whole body stopped, like a clock with a buggered mechanism.

'I didn't reply, in case you're wondering. She'll know I read it, but I sent nothing back. Sometimes you say more when you say nothing at all, as some wise person once said.'

'Ronan Keating?'

He tutted. 'Winston Churchill.'

It was news she'd been waiting for, that the cracks were showing, but she felt strangely flat.

'I was going to order a pizza for my birthday,' she said. 'Would you care to join me?'

'Er, yeah, that sounds good,' he said. *He's probably being kind because it's my birthday*, she thought, but she'd take the sympathy offer anyway, because she didn't want to be alone.

★

When Amanda went up to the hospital that evening, she found that Ingrid had been moved into an individual room because she had developed shingles. Her immune system was low and the virus had taken advantage of her guard being down. She slept peacefully for the first four hours Amanda was there. She texted Bradley to tell him the latest development because she thought he should know and she was all about the duty. He texted back that he wasn't sure he could get up there tonight as he had really bad toothache.

★

'That was a fantastic pizza,' said Pat. 'The best one I've had in ages.'

Mel filled up their glasses. She was a bit tiddly, but what the hell. Alexa was pumping out some tunes and if the only people she could have a birthday party with were her and a postman who smelt really nice then so be it. *Oud Wood* by Tom Ford, he told her. One of those marmite fragrances people either loved or hated, but he really liked it, and so did she.

'How about finishing off with some cake?' said Mel.

'Yeah, I like cake,' replied Pat.

Mel got two bowls out of the cupboard and cut her mini cake in half, covered both portions in cream.

'Do you want me to sing happy birthday to you?' said Pat. 'I will warn you, I don't actually bear any resemblance to the Gallaghers when I'm banging out a tune.'

'No, but we should make a wish,' said Mel.

'Well, I wish that you get what you deserve,' said Pat. 'Cos I think you're a lovely woman. Really pretty as well. Especially now that thing's gone on your lip.'

Mel hooted. 'That's probably the nicest thing anyone has said to me in ages. And I wish the same for you. Because I think you're really—'

Mel never finished off that sentence because Pat leaned across and kissed her on the mouth. Then he pulled away.

'Sorry. That was supposed to be a kiss on your cheek but you turned and—'

They were kissing again and neither would ever remember who instigated it, but his hand was entangled in her hair and hers was gripping his shoulder. And to the lyrics of the Soup Dragons singing about loving someone and holding someone, they were heading up the stairs, crashing into Mel's bedroom, onto the bed.

She had never had sex with anyone but Steve before. This felt wicked, really naughty, she should stop before it got too far, although it was already that because her shirt was off. Pat was kissing her neck and her blood had turned to Krug and was fizzing through her veins. Where his hands went, his lips followed and he was in no rush about it either. Steve never did anything like this, he wasn't one for long warm-up acts before the main event. She couldn't open her legs wide enough.

If someone had told her about fifty-somethings having sex like this when she was a teenager she'd have vomited up her space dust.

Steve said it put him off when she made a noise, but she freed all the vowels she had at full volume now.

She wanted to rip her own knickers off.

'No, keep them on until you can't stand it any longer,' Pat said, grazing his stubble against her inner thigh.

My sweet lord, she cried, and not in a George Harrison way.

It wasn't so much an orgasm as a tidal wave.

'Right, let's have them off now,' said Pat.

★

Amanda was about to leave when her mother stirred.

'Is that you, Amanda?' she said.

'Yes, Mum, it's me.'

'You're not going, are you?'

'No, not if you don't want me to.'

Amanda sat back down, next to the mum she had cared about and watched over and loved consistently. But then love didn't need two-way traffic to subsist and this was the only sort of love she knew, the pattern replicated over and over in her life. She took hold of her mother's hand, the one that wasn't dancing about in the air, pointing. 'Who's that in the corner?' Ingrid asked her.

'Who do you think it is, Mum?'

'I don't know.' Ingrid stared hard and then her face registered recognition. She chuckled lightly. 'All right, I'm coming soon. Just let me have a little rest first.'

She sighed and closed her eyes. And they never opened for Amanda again.

★

Mel and Pat were staring at each other by the light of the bedside lamp, their breath slowing to normal. She didn't really know what to say because she was on alien territory here. Did this make her a tart? She had just bonked someone else's husband – three times, though she'd had two extra bonus orgasms on top of that. He'd said 'Happy Birthday' when she came the last time and she'd laughed and said it was much better than cake.

It had been odd feeling the weight of another man on her, a longer, heavier weight. And she couldn't remember the last time she'd felt as if she had been made love to, rather than just 'done it' because it was the Saturday night custom, the itch scratched. Pat had been tender and intuitive; he'd given more than he'd taken from her and he hadn't just rolled over after each time but held her and kissed her and told her how soft her skin was and how mad her hair was. She fought against batting back the compliments, because it was a bit late in the day to be bashful when she'd been riding him like Frankie Dettori, too far gone to worry about her bits jiggling and bouncing all over the shop. Rather than the sight putting him off, he'd been fully invested, if the noises he was making were anything to go by. He'd made her feel sexy and liberated and feminine and *wanted*. He'd been a thousand-volt jolt to her near-dead spirits and other bodily parts.

'Don't take this the wrong way, but I'm going to have to go home,' said Pat, reaching over, stroking her cheek with a gentle thumb. 'I'd stay if I didn't have such an early start. I'm up at three. It would have been nice to fall to sleep and wake up with you.'

'I get it, you really don't have to apologise.'

'I think we both needed that. I wasn't using you.'

'I was using you.'

He smiled. His cocky edginess hadn't been her idea of fanciable when they'd first met but since getting to know him, that had changed because he really was a dish – inside and out. She hoped he wouldn't come to regret it and she hoped her memories of this night wouldn't be soured by regret either, because the cold light of day could be a bastard. Also, if she'd known what one-night stands were all about, she'd have had a few more before she settled down.

He levered himself out of bed, put on his clothes and she slipped on her towelling robe.

'I'll try and go out discreetly so the neighbours don't see,' he said.

'I don't care,' she replied. She'd bang a drum if there were one handy.

At the door, he turned to her, took her face in his hands.

'I really do hope you get what you deserve, Mel. I meant that. You are a beau'iful woman, a proper prize, so you don't sell yourself short. Take your time to work out what *your* feelings are and don't be rushed over it, neither.'

He kissed her on the lips, soft, caring, sweet.

And then left her, his Oud Wood fragrance lingering in the air and on her skin.

Chapter 40

Lancashire Bugle, Tuesday 30 April

'THERE WERE TWO PENNINE PROWLERS – I KNOW BECAUSE I SURVIVED THEM.'

It is thirty years since Gillian Smith, 62, was walking home from her job as a barmaid in Skelshill Lancashire when she was accosted by a man who asked to escort her home as 'there are nutters about at this time of night'.

That was Wayne Craven, dubbed the Pennine Prowler, who was caught twenty years ago this week, after Smith recognised his voice in a Yorkshire pub. Craven had taken his new wife out to celebrate her birthday and Smith overheard him talking while she and her mother were eating. Shaking, she rang the police from the toilets. DNA samples taken from the Prowler's later attacks matched Craven, who surprisingly had never been registered on the police database and so had evaded detection.

'I don't remember much about that night because of the damage to my head, but I would never forget his voice or that I was attacked by two men. The other was much bigger but I never saw his face and he never spoke. I have wondered if that's because he had an obvious accent.'

The second man remained at large and though there was a strong suspect in Edek Urbaniak, a Polish-born toy repairer, who died in 2018, Gillian Smith failed to pick him out of a police line-up.

'They didn't really believe me when I told them there were two,' she said. 'They might have if the DNA samples taken from me hadn't been lost by the forensic officer. Then Craven got sick and told the priest there was a second man, at least for some of the attacks, but he wouldn't give him up. He toyed with the police for five full months and when he was ready to say the name, he died before he could. Is that second prowler still out there? Who is he? Because someone knows who he is. How can I truly rest until I know too?'

Chapter 41

There was a woman, around mid-thirties, smartly dressed, already waiting for Sky when she got into work. She was standing there, looking at the bears, turning them over in her hands and admiring the craftmanship.

'Hi,' she said, her accent unmistakeably from Lancashire. 'These are lovely. You never get too old to own a teddy bear, do you?'

'That's what I'm counting on,' Sky replied, getting out the bear she was working on from the drawer under her bench. 'Please take your time, I'm not a high-pressure salesperson.'

'Did you make them all?'

'Every one,' said Sky.

'Ah, so I presume then you're Sky, are you – as in *Sky* Bears?'

'That's me,' said Sky, sniffing a sale, which would be good.

'Sky . . . Urbaniak.'

A cloud drifted across the face of the sunny interchange.

'Yes,' she answered cautiously. She'd used the name Urban since her father died. If anyone mentioned her old name, it aroused her suspicions instantly.

'Is there somewhere we can talk?' said the woman.

Sky was on her guard now. 'What about?'

'I'm Diana Nelson, I'm a freelance reporter and I'm on your side. You met Wayne Craven, didn't you? He was friends with your family, wasn't he? You need to get hold of a copy of today's *Lancashire Bugle*, because you'll find out they've stitched up your father and I can counterbalance that if you'll give me your story. I'm going to write a piece anyway, so you'd have nothing to lose in giving me your side of things.'

'I have nothing to say,' said Sky. 'People tried that line on my father and they twisted everything. You're partly the reason why he—'

'Oy,' said Woodentop, striding down the shop towards them. 'You all right, Sky?'

Bon cut off the call he was on in his office and threw open the door after hearing raised voices.

'What's going on?'

Diana Nelson was holding up her hands. 'I just want to talk to this young lady.'

'I don't think that young lady wants to talk to you though, does she?' said Woodentop.

'You should leave,' said Bon.

Nelson wasn't shifting.

'With respect—'

'You had no respect for my father,' said Sky. 'My dad had nothing to do with any of it.'

'Know that for a fact, do you?' threw back Nelson. The smiley veneer had slid fast off her face.

'Yes, I do.'

'He didn't have great alibis though, a poorly wife and a kid.'

'Get out,' said Sky, grinding out the words through gritted teeth. She wanted to throw something at this woman but the bear in her hand wouldn't have made much impact.

Bon moved in front of Sky, blocking Nelson's view of her.

'Sky, don't say anything else,' he whispered to her. 'Go in my office, out of the way. Go on. Give her nothing.'

'Oh come on, don't be stupid,' Nelson appealed to Sky's back as she disappeared into Bon's office. 'You're missing a great opportunity to put the record straight. You owe it to your father. We can pay you two thousand pounds.'

'Enough now,' said Bon to her.

'There's a TV programme in the making about it. I'm just saying if she talks to me she can drive the narrative and—'

'I think you should fuck off, love,' said Woodentop and if Bon hadn't held an arm out to stop his advance, he'd have physically thrown the reporter out and that would have spelt trouble for him.

Diana Nelson shook her head from side to side. 'She'll regret this,' she said.

'No, she won't,' said Bon, herding her towards the exit.

'Okay, I'm going, I'm going.' Nelson arrived at the door, still holding her hands aloft as if she expected if she didn't she'd get shot in the back.

'Bloody bastards,' said Woodentop when she was out of the way. 'And here we are again with it all. Poor Eddie. They won't let him lie in peace. I wish I could solve the bloody mystery for them. It's haunted me for all these years an' all.'

'Because you were Eddie's friend?' asked Bon.

'I was. But it's not that, Bon. It was my lad who lost the

DNA samples that might have caught Craven and the other one sooner.'

Sky was sitting on the sofa in the office, shaking, her arms protectively across her chest, trying to still her racing heart. She didn't want to have an attack now, not in front of Bon. She didn't want him to know about her health problems. Sympathy for her was not what she wanted to see in his eyes.

'I'll make you a drink,' he said.

'Thank you, but I'm fine.'

He sat down on the chair by his desk and waited for her to talk. He could almost hear her thoughts flapping like frightened birds in her head.

'Do you know what she was on about?' she said eventually.

'Yes, *bokkie*, I do.'

'I wish they'd leave us alone. He was the gentlest man you could ever meet. Wayne Craven loved my dad because he was the only person in his life who never let him down. That's why he smiled when the police read out that list of suspects' names to him on his deathbed, people they thought Wayne had reason to protect. He wasn't signalling he was "the one", he was just remembering his friend. The policeman who read out the list always said it was obvious to him why Wayne reacted to Dad's name, he told me that off the record. But others preferred to believe it was a pointer and worth further investigation. The gossip machine went into overdrive when the police started bringing people in for questioning, and they took my dad in more times than anyone else: a huge, powerful man when they were looking for a huge, powerful man who "didn't talk because he might have given himself away with an obvious accent". They painted my dad into that description, but they still couldn't pin anything on him because it wasn't him. Even when Wayne died and the policeman retired and did a story in the newspapers, they twisted what he said about being there at Wayne's side reading out the list of names. They printed that he'd nodded – *nodded* – when he'd mentioned Dad's name. He contacted me to apologise and said he'd talk to the paper. They ran a tiny retraction that no one saw.

'My dad even wrote to Wayne in prison to try and persuade him to give up the other person; we managed to keep that out of the press because they'd only have made out as if it was some sort of sick game, some hiding in plain sight ploy.'

Her voice failed her. Bon wanted to put his arms around her so much and hold her.

Instead he said, 'Do you want to go home?'

But she didn't. She wanted to be here with her friends, because here she felt safe among this crew who might not have known the absolute truth, but they sure as hell knew the lies.

Chapter 42

Bon drove to Gwyn Tankersley's house, despite her command not to. She was very disappointed in him.

'It's fine, one glass of wine is enough.'

She had been hoping to ply him with wine, soften him. That's why she had told him to be there before everyone else arrived, except he arrived after them. Ah well, she'd have to work extra hard, then.

He brought a bottle of Kanonkop pinotage and a DeMorgenzon chenin blanc with him, both South African, she noted – nice touch. And while she didn't know either wine well, she trusted Bon to have brought something decent, chosen thoughtfully.

'Come in and meet my guests, everyone is here,' she said. 'And they've all seen my beautiful new desk and want to meet the man who made it.'

She took his hand and led him through to her grand salon. Bon could tell instantly they weren't his sort of crowd, but he wasn't doing this primarily for pleasure. Gwyn threw names at him that he was unlikely to remember unless reminded, except for one – Richard

Sutton: only son of the pike in the pond that was Archibald Sutton. The apple hadn't fallen far from the entitled and grandiose tree, that thought money bought class and respect when it merely bought toadies. His wife, Bon presumed, was sitting next to him. Their daughter, whom Sky avoided when she came into the shop, was very much in her mould.

'We were just talking about your gaff,' Sutton said. Bon was surprised to hear a broad Yorkshire accent rather than the polished, affected one he'd thought would have come out of his mouth. But yet it was overly loud and proud, the sort of accent that spoke of inverse snobbery. 'I'll have to go up and take a look.'

'You're very welcome to,' said Bon.

'We'd like to buy the whole Spring Hill venture but the Irishman isn't playing. You should have a word.'

How rich we are, Bon heard. He knew that Shaun McCarthy wouldn't sell Spring Hill Square to them for any price. And Bon wouldn't be having any words to try and convince him otherwise.

'As it's my birthday, no shop talk,' Gwyn admonished Sutton, wagging a finger at him.

'I didn't realise it was your birthday,' Bon said.

'Because I didn't tell you, I didn't want to put you under any obligation. You brought wine,' said Gwyn. 'Which is more than this lot did.'

The crowd of six laughed and made jokey protests about never bringing wine. Gwyn's soirées must have been a regular occurrence, Bon thought, to which she invited a lot of impolite people.

A young woman appeared at the door in chef's whites and checked trousers.

'Dinner is going to be served at any moment, if you'd like to take your seats,' she said.

'I never asked you if you had any intolerances,' said Gwyn to him as they filtered through to the dining room.

Only to evenings like this, thought Bon.

★

When Amanda arrived at the diner for the meeting, Ray was just filling the pots of coffee. He said hello with a concerned expression.

'Where did you go on Saturday?' he said. 'One minute you were there, the next you were gone.'

'I'm sorry,' said Amanda. 'I've just got a lot on my plate at the moment. My mum's in hospital, my brother's a dick . . . family stuff.'

'Wanna talk about it? Offload?' he offered.

She smiled at his consideration but no, she didn't want to burden him with tales of skullduggery and hidden treasure chests, stone-cold mothers and sons with teeth like a seaside donkey's. He was best kept out of her world for his own sanity.

'Thank you, but I need a break from my life.'

He nodded. 'Okay, well I can help you with that. Tomorrow night, be hungry and come here at nine o'clock. I'm going to cook for you.'

'You don't have to do—'

'I want to.' He looked at her with his beautiful blue eyes, unblinking, waiting to exact a promise that she'd be there.

'Okay, I'll be hungry and here for nine.'

'Good. Now I'll go and get the *biscuits*. You say biscuits here, don't you, and not cookies?'

'Well, I'd say they're cookies you serve up, not biscuits. And please, don't convert your language, stay Texan. *Biscuits* doesn't sound right at all coming from you.'

'Ah, but we have biscuits. They're nothing like yours. Pie, however, is universal. At least we have that in common.'

He was so very sweet. Amanda wondered what his mouth would taste like on hers, what his arms would feel like around her, whether his hands would move fast or slow undoing the buttons of her shirt. She gave her head a rattle in case she had suddenly grown a transparent brain case and he could see what was going on in it. That flaming HRT was working a bit too well on some parts of her body.

The door opened and a new woman arrived: casually dressed, but expensive casual, about the same age as herself, glossy brown hair that fell in waves just past her shoulder. One of those women who looked as good without make-up as with it, Amanda would guess. She had that unsure look that made Amanda presume she wasn't here for a dinner booking but for the group.

'Welcome,' she said. 'You here for the six o'clock meeting?'

'I am, yes.'

'Just go down there to your right, it's the door next to the loos. Have a coffee, take a seat. With any luck the others will be along shortly. Or we'll be having a tête-à-tête.'

Erin smiled; even a tête-à-tête would be good. Anything to take her away from the turmoil in her own head at the moment.

★

Salmon Three Ways was followed by Lamb Wellington, not Bon's favourite meat, though it was cooked to perfection if one liked lamb so pink it could be resuscitated by a good vet. The accompanying vegetables were exquisite, though; shame the company wasn't.

Bon had the misfortune to be sitting opposite Sutton junior, who chewed with his mouth open and talked while eating, as if he were above table etiquette, as if money bought you that privilege.

'Had any undesirables up at your place, then, *Bon*?' Sutton asked him, putting a scathing emphasis on his name. 'The press, I mean. I know you've got Urbaniak's daughter working there.'

'There was someone, yes, earlier today,' Bon answered him.

'What's this?' said Gwyn.

'Twentieth anniversary of the Pennine Prowler's arrest,' said Sutton, waggling scary fingers. 'It's resurrected the sodding thing yet again. My mother's gone all jittery, worse than bloody usual. She doesn't want the fuckers upsetting my father and spoiling his seventieth birthday celebrations. Big party planned, costing us an arm and a leg.'

'Why would it do that?' asked the silver-haired woman on the end, who was called Koo.

'Dad gave Craven casual work occasionally which – can you believe it? – put him in the frame of being his accomplice. The police really were scraping the barrel by then. So there's a lesson: never be kind, because it can spectacularly backfire.'

Koo's mouth formed a long 'O' of shock before she said, 'I never knew that. How ridiculous.'

'The clever money was always on a Polish man called

Urbaniak. Huge he was, like a grizzly. Ironically, he made teddy bears.'

'Are you making this up as you go along, Richard?' asked Koo's husband, Jerome, with a chortle.

'It's got a Netflix series written all over it,' said Koo, lifting a spear of asparagus to her lips and biting down.

'It was definitely him if it was anyone. The police know it but they couldn't pin it on him. Urbaniak looked after the little runt at school and they stayed friends right until the end. Craven loved him like a brother.'

'He does sound guilty,' said Koo, and Bon was only glad she wasn't a high court judge.

'What happened to him?' asked Dunny, whom Gwyn had introduced as being 'at the very top of the commodities ladder', whatever that meant.

'Which one? Craven served five years and then snuffed it. Urbaniak turned to drink, and died a sad old alcoholic.'

'Sounds like a guilty conscience to me,' put in Dunny's wife, Andrea, who was sloshed. 'Trying to block things out with alcohol.'

Bon wished he could block this lot out with alcohol.

'Who knows?' said Sutton. 'But what I *would* like to know is who sent that fucking reporter up to my parents' house today. I hope it wasn't teddy-bear man's daughter trying to deflect, or I'll be paying her a visit.'

Bon felt his patience crumbling, but he was very good at staying calm, even when he was at his most enraged.

'I was there when a reporter came this morning to talk to Sky, who wouldn't give her the time of day. The only place the woman was sent was out of my shop.'

'That only makes them keener,' said Gwyn.

'Dad's got early onset dementia, poor bastard, and this

party means a lot to the family, because it might be the last he has where he knows who we are. So if anything, or anyone, gets in the way of it, they'll have me to deal with and it won't be pretty,' said Sutton, spitting gravy as he threatened.

Bon sighed inwardly and tried not to look at his watch.

Chapter 43

Erin and Sky both did a double-take when they saw each other and both had a moment of unease, but it quickly passed. Sky was only glad she hadn't confessed that she was in love with Bon when she was at the first meeting because it would have been bad enough when Astrid turned up the week after, but if Erin had got to know that would have been excruciating. She wondered if she knew already; women were intuitive about such things.

Erin also thought she recognised the red-haired woman from somewhere, but couldn't place her.

'Can I just say that if anyone had any further thoughts about how we might be able to improve things in the workspace for women who are going through life changes, perimenopause, menopause, postmenopause, it would be great to hear them,' said Amanda, when they were all settled. She did need to complete this report for Linus at some point.

'And can I just say something before we go there,' said Sky, because it had been on her mind since that reporter had ambushed her this morning, and she wanted to blow it apart, before it blew her apart. 'I'm not really called Sky Urban; my real name is Sky Urbaniak, and you might hear my surname mentioned in the press over the next week or so because it's the twentieth anniversary of the Pennine Prowler being caught and some people thought my dad was his accomplice.'

It was better not to pussyfoot around things, she thought, and to dive straight in. 'It's rubbish. I'll be brief but I would rather you knew.'

She filled them all in on the history, the real history, the story she would have given the reporter today if she could have trusted her. How her dad and Wayne Craven might have been friends once but their lives took different paths as they got older. Her dad wanted nothing more than to settle down with a wife and run a shop, have a family. Wayne was a chancer, a thrill-seeker, chaotic, but her father always felt his deprived, abusive upbringing had had an impact on the man he became. Her father's compassion, coupled with their close childhood friendship, had provided grist to the rumour mill and fuelled the accusations that had followed. Her father had been naïve at first, had trusted that the truth would come out, but it didn't and instead, his business had gone down the pan. Then his wife died and he gave up.

She looked around the room, having told them, and everyone's eyes were on her. 'I'm sorry if all that was a bit heavy,' she said then, immediately regretting her impulse to open up to them. What was she thinking of? That reporter had stirred everything up, made her lose her grip.

Amanda laid her hand over Sky's and gave it a squeeze.

'That's why we have this space, Sky,' she said. 'Exactly for this sort of thing.'

'I didn't want to take over the meeting,' said Sky, feeling

as if she had because she'd shocked them all into silence, even Astrid. No one knew what to say for the best afterwards. Except Erin, who decided that, possibly, she had something that would transfer the heat away from her.

'Maybe I should take this moment to introduce myself,' she said. 'My name is Erin Flaxton; some of you will know me as Erin van der Meer. My story is that I left my husband for someone else and had the worst two and a half years of my life. She died in horrible circumstances and I joined a grief counselling group and I've found myself falling for a man there who I thought was interested in me and he isn't. I'm a total mess. So that's me in a nutshell.'

Again that pin-drop silence, then Mel said, 'Well, you're going to fit in perfectly with us lot, then.'

Astrid served up coffees and distributed snacks. Ray had laid on his famous blueberry pie today and it was turning out to be a comfort-food pie-eating sort of meeting.

'I would love to have my own business,' said Astrid, when Erin had told them about her graphic design firm. 'I am feeling very . . .' – she tried to put it into words that made sense – '. . . very . . . as if I have energies that I don't know where to put.'

'What sort of business?' asked Erin. 'In my case I was passionate about art and design and so that was my starting point, but then I really got into the business side of things, which I hadn't expected.'

'You'll laugh if I tell you what ticks my boxes,' said Astrid, cutting into her pie with a cake fork.

'We might, but tell us anyway,' Amanda nudged her playfully.

'Okay then . . . crackers,' said Astrid.

No one laughed, which surprised her.

'The type you pull,' she clarified, in case they thought she meant crackers one put cheese on.

'I work a couple of days a week in a factory that makes them; I have done for some years now,' she went on. 'I love it. I love making them, I love working with the people. I sometimes go into the office and do the wages and sometimes I have been out on the road with my boss to meet clients. I love everything about it and I have ideas buzzing around all the time about what else we could do.' Astrid smiled sadly. 'But, it has gone up for sale.'

'Will the new owners keep you on?' asked Sky, who knew that Astrid had this job but not that she liked it quite as much as she clearly did.

'Maybe, maybe not. But it won't be the same.' They wouldn't call her off constructing to help with the accounts or liaise with suppliers like the Pandoros did. And if Manbag bought it, he'd be closing it down and setting up in Tring.

'Why don't you take it over, then?' said Erin.

Astrid gave her a look that said she was barmy, *verrückt*.

'Could you afford the finances?' asked Amanda.

All eyes were on Astrid.

'Er, yes ... yes I could, I'm sure. But ...' And she laughed, because it was laughable. '... I couldn't run it.'

'Sounds to me as if you're involved in quite a lot of aspects of the business already, though,' said Erin.

'Well, yes, I cover all of what is needed to be done ...' Astrid's voice tailed off as she realised that what she was saying was absolutely the truth. But still ... Her in charge? *Come on.*

'I think you need to have a word with yourself, Astrid,'

said Sky. 'What would Kev do if you told him you were thinking about buying the cracker firm? Would he laugh?'

Astrid imagined him standing in front of her, shaking his head.

'*Are you nuts?*' he'd say. '*Stop fannying about doubting yourself and wasting time.*'

'What you don't know, you can learn,' said Erin. 'But it appears to me that you'd be starting off at a more advantageous point than many do.'

Astrid nodded. 'I'll think about it,' she said, her calm, quiet tone giving away nothing of her whirling, giddy thoughts. She just couldn't imagine such a thing . . . but also she wanted to – very much.

'How's the landlord situation, Sky?' asked Amanda.

'Solved,' she said. At least she had some good news to bring to the table. She got a round of 'Hurrah!'s for that.

'I have a new tenant,' Astrid beamed over at her. 'And it is working out very well.'

'What happened? Did you get your money back?' Amanda thought the situation Sky had previously described sounded pretty hopeless on that front.

'Plus six pounds,' said Sky with a smile.

'I opened me big gob, that's vhat happened.' Astrid tutted. 'I told my boss at the repair shop that Sky was in the power-grip of an evil landlord. He threw boxes in the back of his van and then loaded up Sky and me and we drove over to the house,' said Astrid with relish. 'There was no messing with him, he was like a superhero.'

'Well, he sounds a bit of all right,' said Mel. 'Is he married?'

Sky didn't dare to look over at Erin for fear of giving anything away, but Erin answered anyway.

'Not any more, but he was – to me. We split up a long time ago but we've stayed good friends. And he is every bit a knight in shining armour.'

Although she did think that in this, he had gone some-what further for Sky than he would have done for anyone else: the way he seemed to have gone storming in was a clue. He wasn't someone who acted on immediate impulses usu-ally. That was very interesting. And also she thought that, had she herself not been here at the meeting, Sky might have gushed a little more about his rescue mission.

'I've never managed to stay friendly with an ex,' said Amanda, shuddering inwardly. She wouldn't have wanted to keep any of them around.

'Ditto,' Erin agreed with her, 'except for him.'

'Crikey, have you seen the time?' said Mel, noticing her watch. It was nine o'clock. What had they talked about for three hours? Three hours with barely a thought of Steve. She hadn't thought it was possible.

Erin pulled up Sky by the door as she was leaving with Astrid, who walked on ahead to give them a moment.

'Sky, I hope you didn't feel I was being deceptive when-ever we met. It was Bon's idea not to say anything to *anyone* about us divorcing, not until it was all done. Not that he thought we would have any change of heart after the decree nisi, but he likes to keep his business private. It felt very odd going into the shop and people addressing me still as Mrs van der Meer, which I suppose I was legally but—'

'Honestly, it's fine. I understand,' Sky said. It was Bon all over really, wanting things to be straight.

'He put me in a bit of a spot with it to be honest. I was glad when we could tell the truth. Don't think ill of me – or him, for that matter.' Erin smiled, hoping to convey her sincerity. 'He thought it was our business, no one else's, that we had to acclimatise to it without having to explain it away. It was easier for him, of course, because he wasn't in another relationship and it caused problems in mine. But then, when things started going wrong, I found a sort of protection in staying married to Bon because ... I ... we ...' She stammered. It was horribly complicated, she wasn't even sure she understood the psychology behind it herself. 'I'm not explaining it well, Sky, but ... Bon is the best person I know. I told him about that woman who was in the shop the day I bought the bear. I didn't like the vibe of her and I wanted Bon to watch your back. I happen to know he's very fond of you. He wouldn't have stormed in and sorted out a landlord for just anyone, you know.'

Erin wanted Sky to catch the hint. She couldn't tell if she had from her expression, though. She was as deep as Bon and that didn't make for easy matchmaking.

Mel helped Amanda collect the mugs and plates after everyone had gone. There were no cookies left today and Ray had baked extra for them. Plus there was pie, which had been totally devoured.

'I really do have to get some ideas for my boss about the sodding menopause,' said Amanda, being reminded of it by the telltale prickling in her scalp of an imminent sweating episode. The HRT patches hadn't totally cured them but they were more spaced out now, and not as severe when they did occur. And being able to string a sentence together alone made every penny she was paying for them worth it. She did wish someone at the clinic had told her how to take the patch glue off her bum, though, before she'd looked it up on the net after scrubbing herself raw with a body brush. It should have been standard information: baby oil and a cotton wool pad.

'I'll ask at work, I promise,' replied Mel. 'We have too many stories to share about other things, don't we? How's your mum, by the way? You didn't say much about her and I wondered what you weren't telling us.'

'I wasn't hiding anything, there really isn't much to tell,' Amanda answered. 'She's just lying there, letting an antiobiotic drip fight various infections in her body. I think they're playing Whac-A-Mole with them.' She would be heading up to the hospital after this to see how things were at first hand, but she could spare another five minutes to talk to Mel. She sat down. 'I needed tonight. I look forward to this Tuesday get-together so much; it's better than I'd hoped it would be when I thought of setting it up, you know, just sitting in a room of women sharing our lives makes you feel that you aren't alone wading through shit. Nobody's comparing what's happening, no one feels that their rubbish is worth more or less than anyone else's.'

'Yep, we've got a fair bit going on between us,' said Mel, sitting down also. 'Unrequited love, cheating husbands, career crossroads, serial killers . . . didn't see that one coming; did you?'

'Poor Sky, though at least she's away from that creepy landlord.'

'Might have to call in to the repair shop and put a face to the name of this Bon bloke. I wonder if he's any good at mending broken marriages. I suppose they must get things in there they just have to admit defeat with. Or is there hope for even the most battered of things?'

'Mel, I didn't want to ask and put you on the spot because

I'm sure you'd have told us if you wanted to,' said Amanda, 'but do I detect a bit of an upturn with you since last week? Anything you wish to report?'

Mel hadn't said anything in their meeting other than that she was doing okay, keeping positive. She wasn't sure how her big news would go down. She hadn't quite got it square in her own head yet. But also the blood was whooshing in her veins just at the memory of it.

'I . . . ' she began and then shut up. Dare she say? *Oh bugger it, why not.*

'I shagged the postman.'

That really wasn't what Amanda had been expecting her to say.

★

Richard Sutton reached for the bottle to replenish his wine. Bon noticed how he filled up his own glass but didn't think to offer his wife any. He was very observant of people's behaviour; their manners helped to build up a picture of them and he had Sutton's portrait finished in fine oils after that one single self-absorbed action. He stole a glance at his watch to check the hour and wondered when would be a respectable time to leave. He didn't like any of these people, each full of their own hype and pretensions, worshipping at the altar of cold, hard cash. Gwyn was the best of them, but Bon was under no illusions why he was here and it wasn't primarily for networking purposes, that had just been the lure to reel him in. He wasn't interested, and he was careful to show his boundaries were clearly marked.

'Oh, do leave the car and have a drink.' Gwyn wrapped herself around his arm, putting her head against his shoulder.

'Thank you, but I never drink more than one glass of wine on a weeknight, I have too many early starts at work.'

'Then I should invite you again at a weekend,' she whispered, her breath tickling his neck.

'You're all invited to my father's birthday party so save the date: thirteenth of September. Everyone who is anyone is coming,' announced Sutton, his voice on the wrong side of slurred. He lifted the cigar out from the long, slim box he'd put on the table when he first came into the room, bit the head off it and spat it into his hand. A sophisticated man would not have done that: Bon knew as much because he was what Sutton wasn't.

'He's always been so on the ball up here but not these days.' Sutton tapped his temple. 'It's more for my mother than him, really; she wants some happy memories to take forward before the rot totally sets in. What do you buy the man who has everything for his birthday, though? My daughter's apparently having something made for him at your shop, Bon . . . ' He stalled as if listening to himself as a third party. 'What sort of name is that anyway – *Bon*? What's it short for? Bonzo? Bonkers?' He guffawed at his own wit.

'I was named after my grandfather Boniface, but only given the shortened version of it,' Bon answered him.

'Lucky for you,' said Mr 'top of the commodities ladder' Dunny with a barely disguised snigger, and Bon thought that anyone sharing his name with a *kakhuis* had no grounds for scoffing.

'It's a fabulous name, it suits you,' said Gwyn, still coiled around him.

'Anyway, as I was saying,' Sutton continued, now puffing on his cigar, 'is there anything else you do up there that would be suitable for a seventy-year-old? Maybe one of your desks. How much are they, anyway?'

'If you have to ask, you can't afford one,' said Gwyn, finally releasing Bon to pour herself a glass of his chenin blanc.

'I can afford *anything* he's got up there, don't you worry about that,' said Sutton.

'Maybe, but I have a waiting list for desks.'

'How much to jump the queue?'

'That's not how I work.'

'That's how everyone works, for the right price. Anyway, that's a shit idea. He can't write his own name any more, what would he need with a fucking desk? Don't be overcharging my daughter because you know we've got plenty.' He jabbed his cigar in Bon's direction.

Bon wasn't intimidated by the Suttons of this world, who were all flab and bluster. They were the ones intimidated by class, finesse, or honour, because they had no idea how to acquire those things that couldn't be bought.

Gwyn stood up, stretching like a contented cat.

'Can I get anyone a cognac? A scotch?'

Bon took his cue. He got up.

'I will leave you to enjoy your digestifs. It has been a pleasure to meet you all.' He swung his head from one side of the table to the other. There was a cry from the women for him not to go so early. Jerome was asleep at the end of the table, his face resting onto the pillow of his chin.

'I'll be in touch, Boniface,' Sutton said, drunk and under the impression he had something to get in touch with Bon about. Bon headed out with Gwyn pressing him also to stay, even for just a little longer. He smiled politely and said he was sorry but he couldn't.

'It's very attractive when a man is so resolute in his

decisions,' she said at the huge front door. 'I absolutely applaud your professionalism. And I'm sorry we are all plastered, Bon. When you get to know us properly you'll realise we can just be ourselves when we're together, warts and all. It's not all hot air that comes out of Richard's mouth, he was just willy-waving tonight. Do come again and you'll see that.'

Bon bent to kiss Gwyn's cheek without committing himself to an answer. He felt her twisting, hoping to find his mouth but he straightened in time to avoid it.

'Enjoy the rest of your birthday evening, and thank you for your hospitality.'

'You have future customers in that room,' said Gwyn, thumbing behind her. 'I'll make sure of it.'

He opened the door.

'Stay tonight,' she tried again, one last whispered attempt to show him her hand. 'No strings.'

'Good night, Gwyn.'

His rebuff was as gallant a one as it was possible to give. Gwyn would roll around on her sheets later replaying his refusal to take advantage of her inebriation. It would only make him more attractive in her eyes.

Chapter 44

'*And?*'

Amanda was waiting patiently for details because Mel couldn't just leave that big revelation hanging in mid-air with nothing to follow it.

Mel dropped her head into her hands.

'Oh, Amanda, what have I done? I'm as bad as Steve.'

'I doubt it, but I will need to hear more just to make sure about that.'

Mel lifted her head to find Amanda grinning. For a brief moment there, she'd thought she might not have been joking.

'This is why I didn't say anything, because so much has happened this week. I met him . . . Postman Pat; we went for a drink last Wednesday, to talk. He said that his wife had done this sort of thing before. He was nice, actually. Then the day after, Steve came round to tell me that he had absolutely no control over what he was doing and could I please put myself in the freezer until he works it out.'

Amanda's eyebrows nearly shot off the top of her head.

'He said that?'

'More or less.'

'Did you tell him that he couldn't have his cake and eat it?'

'I told him to do one. And then I rang Pat and he came round.'

'And this is when it happened?' Amanda was on the edge of her seat.

'No, he made me a cup of coffee and told me I should join a rock band. A friend of mine is setting one up: long story but we were going to do it as teenagers, but stuff happened . . . and it's a now or never thing. Steve thought I was way too old, Pat, however, said I should go for it.'

Amanda wondered if she should admit that she quite liked the sound of this postman, but she didn't have time because Mel launched into the next part of the story.

'It was my birthday yesterday. I was feeling a bit sorry for myself. Pat came round to tell me his wife had been in touch, and I asked him if he wanted to share a pizza. He was probably feeling sorry for me when he said yes, but we had a drink and a chat and the next thing we're stumbling up the stairs and into bed. I could have stopped it, but I didn't.'

Amanda put her hand over her mouth to stifle the giggle that was threatening to escape.

'And . . . how was it?'

Mel also put her hand over her own mouth to stifle the giggle that was threatening to escape.

'It was fantastic. I felt . . . injected with joy.'

'And . . . how was his syringe?'

Mel hooted. 'It hit spots I never knew I had. Do you know, Amanda, I'd got bored with sex, always the same formula, I did it out of habit and only ever on a Saturday night. But this . . .' She blew a full mouthful of air out and fanned her face. 'I've been like bloody Tigger all day. I shouldn't be, should I, because I've been unfaithful. I've lost my moral high ground. But it wasn't just the sex, it was how he made me feel. As if he really ... *enjoyed* me.' Yes, that was the word, she'd been searching for it when she'd been analysing it, replaying it.

It was clear to Amanda that Postman Pat had given Mel an intensive course in being valued; it was oozing out of her pores. People really did have an effect on each other that was like magic sometimes; a little water went a long way on a parched throat.

'So where does that leave you?' Amanda asked. 'Is he coming round for a repeat performance anytime soon?'

Mel chuckled at the notion. 'I doubt it. It was a one night only event, but that's okay. I get the feeling his wife will be coming home with her tail between her legs soon enough' — how could she give him up. He was kind, considerate, funny and flipping fabulous in bed — 'and if she does, I should expect Steve to follow suit.'

The intonation in her voice was that of a firework on its way down after being spent.

'And do you want him back?'

'Honestly? I have no idea,' said Mel.

Chapter 45

'I hear on the grapevine,' said Iris the next morning, leaning across the table as she rolled up a cracker, 'that Manbag, the miserable one in the Columbo coat, has put in an offer for the factory, but it's well short of the asking price.'

'Where did you hear that?' asked young Venus.

'Annie told me,' said Iris.

Venus tutted. 'I thought you'd been on a secret spy mission.'

'I don't need to. They're going to tell me, aren't they? I'm their most trusted employee.'

Then she and Venus both exchanged glances as Astrid got up and marched over to Annie's office, shutting the door behind her.

'What's got into her?' said Iris, in a low voice. 'She's been ruminating all morning, I could hear her cogs grinding. Summat serious going on in that German head of hers.'

In the Crackers Yard office, Astrid took a deep breath and began.

'Please don't laugh, Annie, Joe, but I want to ask you something.'

They both stared at her, and nodded for her to begin, wondering what on earth she had to say that was causing such an agitated expression on her face.

'I want to buy the factory,' Astrid said, waiting for their laughter to begin. Despite the encouragement she'd had from the women at the friendship club about this being a real possibility, the thought of herself in Annie's seat was still bonkers. But, as with last night, there was no laughter.

'Can you teach me what to do, how you run it? Can I do this? Am I being stupid?' Astrid was clearly emotional.

'No, of course you aren't being stupid,' said Annie. 'And of course you could run this company. Look at everything you cover for us: production, sales, accounts, customer service. If I thought you'd been in the slightest bit interested we'd have had this conversation before, Astrid. We would love to pass it into your hands.' Annie was getting equally emotional. The ideal scenario was that their beloved factory went to someone who could offer continuity, for their customers and their loyal work force.

'This is the best news we could hear,' said Joe. He stood up, opened up his arms and squashed Astrid in his tightest embrace. 'My dear lady.' He was almost crying, but then Joe wore his heart on his Italian sleeve and could cry at the bins being collected.

Astrid walked into the productivity room and addressed her workmates.

'Okay, I have an announcement. I'd like you to meet your new boss,' she said. 'Me.'

And they didn't laugh either.

★

That evening, Erin settled down to watch a box set and tried not to look at the clock. They'd be starting the grief counselling meeting now. They wouldn't be waiting for her because she'd emailed Molly to say she wouldn't be there, she'd made the excuse that it wasn't for her at this time, but really it was because she couldn't face Alex. She'd made things irrevocably awkward between them, asking him to lunch, misreading his attentions, her emotional compass clearly far off course, the magnet pointing nowhere near north. She could die of embarrassment just thinking about herself standing outside the housing estate office, trying to stutter and stammer her way back to the footing they'd had before she'd opened her big mouth – and failing.

Would Alex ask where she was? Would he wonder at the reason why she hadn't turned up? Maybe he wouldn't turn up himself, because he was on a second or even third date with the colleague he'd had dinner with on Saturday.

The 'Tuesday club' at the diner would give her what she needed more than Molly's group: women who understood women, any barriers of age, background or creed obliterated by friendship, with no added complications of attraction to someone else in the group getting in the way. It was all she needed for now, until her ship steadied and stopped forcing itself towards stormy waters before she had rebuilt, recalibrated; no change in heartbeat, no ensuing disappointment, just acceptance.

★

Amanda had to reapply her eyeliner three times from scratch because she was making such a cock of it. She was nervous, though she had no real reason to be. Ray was making her dinner because he was grateful to her for spreading the word about his diner, this was *not* a 'date'. He wouldn't try and roger her on the serving counter; at best she'd go home with a take-away box full of whatever she hadn't cleared from her plate.

She had been on the brink of cancelling, because it didn't seem right having a meal out when her mum was in hospital. She'd been to see her after work to find her still sleeping peacefully and a slight improvement in her infection levels, so she'd taken that as a sign to have a full night off for herself, with good company and food. So here she was, trying to decide what to wear that said, *I've made the effort for you but not too much that you think I've misread your invitation to mean something it isn't.*

Her phone must have realised that she was going to be in close proximity with a man because twice in the last twenty-four hours she'd had junk emails for tackling vaginal dryness, which could potentially give her something else to worry about. She hadn't a clue if she was dry down there; it might have closed up like her second earring hole for all she knew. Anyway, she wouldn't be finding out if she was the female equivalent of the Kalahari tonight so no need to add that stress onto the pile.

She decided on black jeans which made her legs look extra-long and slim, and her favourite boho top that was patterned enough so that if she dropped any food on it, it would be disguised by all the swirls. She twisted her dark-brown hair up into a bun. There were no twinkles of grey showing yet. Her mother hadn't gone grey until she was seventy so she'd obviously inherited those genes from her; probably the only ones. Bradley got the rest: the blue-eyed gene, the short height gene, the gene that made one think the world revolved around oneself. He still hadn't come back to her about where their mum was going to live when she came out of hospital but she couldn't face talking to him at the moment. She needed some distance from him; she knew the more she pushed, the more he'd push back. It would be better that he formulated a plan by himself, then he could crow about what a clever boy he was to her.

She applied a slick of lipstick, a new one that promised not to transfer onto your teeth when you smiled. She had her father's lips, full and generous, and his brown eyes with an unusual gold ring around the pupil. And she had his heart too, one that loved a woman who didn't love them back.

'You'll do,' she said to her reflection and then took the wine out of the fridge, picked up the box of salt water taffy she'd bought to give Ray a taste of home, and set off for the diner.

*

Two more newspapers had run a story about the Pennine Prowler on the anniversary of his arrest, his deathbed 'statement' being the focal point. People loved to be amateur detectives; they were the villagers of yore brandishing their torches and journeying en masse to burn the beast in the big castle, except nowadays their weapons were keyboards. Diana Nelson's piece was the worst of them all, and as if in revenge for Sky's non-compliance, she had been particularly vicious in her implications that the local known as the Teddy Bear Man turned to alcohol to chase away his demons. Sky knew it was no good threatening to sue the newspaper; one had replied to her in the past that if she could prove the information they'd printed was false, then she should go right ahead.

'Do not let them get to you,' said Astrid, tapping the lid of her laptop. 'Turn it off.'

'How can they get away in spreading so much made-up crap? How would—'

She cut off her words; this attack had come without warning. She could feel her heart struggling to find its rhythm. Astrid saw the panic in her face.

'Sky! Sky, what's up?'

'I need my spray.'

'Where is it?' Astrid looked around. 'What does it look like?'

'White ... canister. It's in my bag.' She bent over, in obvious distress.

Astrid scurried around; she'd seen Sky's bag somewhere. On the back of a chair, she thought. She rushed into the kitchen and found it where she'd imagined it to be. She unzipped it, took out the canister, popped off the top and handed it to her friend. Sky held it near her mouth, gathered a breath, pressed the dose under her tongue, then let it take effect.

Astrid watched in shocked concern while trying to remain calm, because she thought that was what Sky might need her to be, rather than flapping and fussing.

'Sky, what is it, darling?'

'It's my heart,' said Sky. Once upon a time, she'd thought it couldn't get any more damaged than it already was, and she'd been wrong.

★

The diner was empty when she arrived there but Ray was in a fluster.

'Come in and please be seated,' he said, dropping a bow before showing her to a table which had been set for two and with a lit candle in the middle.

'This looks lovely,' Amanda said.

'I had walk-in customers who stayed late, I haven't had time to change . . .'

'It doesn't matter,' she replied.

'You look great.'

'Thank you,' she said after a reticent pause, because it had taken her a few years to learn how to accept a compliment instead of batting them all away. She hadn't had many growing up, she couldn't remember her mother ever saying to her, *You look nice*, only ever *Doesn't he look sweet?* Bradley had been about as sweet as diabetes growing up, and he still was.

She sat down, he poured her a glass of wine.

'How's your mom doing?'

'A teeny bit better,' she said, pinching her finger and thumb together to illustrate how much.

'That's good news. You hungry? It's all ready.' He disappeared into the kitchen to fetch their starters.

'Smoked brown sugar and honey ribs,' he announced, putting them on the table along with another plate. 'Maybe I didn't think this through, they're kinda messy.'

They smelt wonderful.

'I love mess. And garlic bread.'

'Excuse me, young lady, this is Texas toast.'

'Sorry, and what exactly is that then?'

'Well . . . it's . . . sort of . . . garlic bread.' He grinned, she laughed, picked up a rib. When was the last time a man had made her dinner? She couldn't remember. Had anyone ever? She had a vague recollection of someone serving her up tinned ravioli and Micro Chips with Viennetta to follow.

As if he was reading her thoughts, Ray said, 'I was thinking earlier, I can't remember anyone ever cooking a romantic meal for me.'

Is that what this is – romantic? She tried not to let herself get carried away by that one single word.

'Weren't you married?' she asked.

'Yeah, but if you blinked you'd have missed it.'

'I'll cook you a meal next time,' Amanda said, leaving out the adjective.

'You cook?'

'That's what I always wanted to do when I was young, be a pastry chef – a *pâtissière*. I wanted to work in restaurants all over the world creating magic with meringues.'

'And why didn't you?'

'Ah . . . long story. I got a "proper job" instead. I can retire next year. I can give up the daily commute. Or I can carry on until I'm sixty-seven and have a fuller pension pot.'

Sixty-seven sounded an awful long way off when she was considering what she should do.

The ribs were delicious, but thank goodness she was wearing a heavily patterned shirt.

'So, if you did retire, what would you do with your days?' asked Ray, making an equally messy job of eating, so she had no reason to feel alone.

'I've been thinking that I'd like to open up a tea room with wonderful cakes in it. Sort of like this place used to be. I could be the new Bettina Boot of Barnsley and die on the job at ninety cutting up a blueberry pie.'

Ray's blue eyes widened in horror. 'You'd sell blueberry pie? You'd be my rival?'

'Okay, I'd leave the pie off the menu as a courtesy to you.'

'Why don't you come and work for me? I'd love to have cake-to-go. You have that over here, right?'

'Yes, of course,' said Amanda, tutting. 'We had it way before you lot.' She didn't take his suggestion seriously. *As if.*

'Can I just say, you have the most beautiful eyes,' said Ray. He knew from her reaction that she probably wasn't used to getting compliments, even though those big brown, gold-flecked eyes of hers should have commanded them every day. He didn't want to embarrass her. 'As you were,' he said and picked up another rib.

★

Sky told Astrid that few people knew about her heart condition. When anyone had seen her using her spray at work, she'd explained it away as a touch of asthma. She coped adequately; she didn't want sympathy, there was no reason for anyone else to be party to such information.

'It's hereditary, a sort of angina,' she said. 'My mum should never have had a child, it was too much strain on her and she became much worse after having me, but she always said it was a risk she wanted to take. I suppose I'm lucky that the risk of my ever getting pregnant was taken away when I had to have a hysterectomy. I really wasn't designed to be a mum.'

Astrid had had no idea that her friend had been through all this. So much to deal with, so young. And she still had too much to deal with now. She couldn't bring herself to ask about what the future might hold for her, but Sky addressed it anyway.

'They're making medical advances all the time on

conditions like mine, at least that's what they tell me. But if I keep well and calm, watch what I eat and drink, no bungee jumping, I can give myself the best chance of having a "largely normal life".' She drew the quotation marks in the air with her fingers.

It was a good job they'd got her out of that house, away from that *kotzbrocken*, thought Astrid. And what a vile chunk of vomit he was.

'No more looking at news for a while,' said Astrid sternly. 'It's my house rule. You are not to, or I will terminate our tenancy agreement. Okay?'

'Then if it's a rule, I have to abide by it,' returned Sky with a soft smile.

'Good. Now I will go and put the kettle on.'

★

Ray's main course was chilli, made the Texan way with no beans; the beef was tender, swaddled in a thick sauce that had been spiked with fresh green chillies. Ray served it with rolls of corn tortillas and sour cream to counteract the heat. He'd made rice too, a concession for foreign heathens because that wasn't the way they did it back home, he informed her.

Amanda coughed with her first mouthful.

'Gets you at the back of the throat, doesn't it?' he said.

'It's certainly shocked my tonsils awake,' said Amanda.

Ray chewed, swallowed, then put down his fork.

'Thank you for what you did for me, Amanda.'

She flapped her hand, waving his words away. 'You said that already too many times. I hardly did anything. I can't take credit that isn't mine.'

'I think you did. That article in the *Yorkshire Standard* brought me a lot of interest. And the interviewer told me that there was a long waiting list to be featured but that any friend of yours was automatically a big friend of hers, and she bumped me up to the top because of you. And whatever you said to make the pensioners flood in, boy – they fill up the place most mornings. Then they buy pies to take home. I was serious, I need a proper "to-go" service. So I'm going to leave that there with you.'

'I told one of my mum's neighbours about you, Ray, that's all I did. She's exactly what you need if you wanted to spread the word. I've always said you should never underestimate the power of the geriatric PR machine.'

'Whoever it was, she is good. You need to tell her about the to-go service when you set it up here.' He winked and Amanda felt something deep inside her pop like a balloon full of warm air. She allowed herself for a moment to imagine what it would be like working alongside Ray, here, seeing him on a daily basis. She'd be constantly sighing like a Disney princess in the orbit of her Prince Perfect. Ridiculous notion really. As ridiculous as Mel joining a rock band in her fifties, or Astrid buying a cracker factory in her forties and yet she was ready to encourage them to follow their dreams.

'Weed whacker,' said Ray then, looping back to the game of cultural oneupmanship they'd started earlier. 'That's a much better name for it than *strimmer*. It whacks the weeds. I think we win that one.'

'Slip roads. We slip into the flow of traffic. What on earth does on-grid and off-grid really mean?'

'We gave you Halloween.'

'Don't be ridiculous, Ray. We celebrated that before

America was even founded. We used to bob for apples and tell ghost stories before the Romans landed. Admittedly you may have been responsible for bringing trick-or-treating over here. I'll give you that.'

'A jumper is someone who jumps, it's a ridiculous name for a sweater,' said Ray, not to be outdone.

'Sweaters are people who sweat,' Amanda came back at him, wrinkling up her nose.

'Okay, proms then.'

'Some schools had leavers' dances, even if they weren't called proms.'

'Did you have one at your school?'

'No.'

She'd snapped the answer without meaning to.

'We should have had one but it was cancelled,' she went on, aware that he was looking at her for clarification because he could sense the shift in atmosphere, the drop in temperature – slight, but unmistakable.

'Why?'

'A boy in our year died.'

Ray stopped eating.

'Did you know him?'

'We used to catch the same bus to school. His name was Seth Mason and he was sixteen. He was our year's "It" boy, I thought he was gorgeous but I knew he wouldn't be interested in me, I was just Miss Skinny Ordinary back then.'

Ray was listening intently. She didn't want to bring down the mood and shouldn't have started this story, but he was waiting for her to continue.

'Then he started to talk to me when we were on the bus. And when the dance was announced, he asked if I'd go with him. I thought he was joking. I mean – *me*.'

She'd wanted to float home but also she never believed it would happen. She thought he'd let her down at the last minute. Her mum wouldn't buy her a dress that she'd wear just the once, so she'd bought it herself from her wages washing up at the local Italian; it was darkest blue velvet. She never wore it; she'd ripped it up and buried it at the bottom of the bin.

Seth was captain of the rugby team and two days before the dance, when he'd led his team out onto the pitch, he'd winked at her and her heart swelled to fifteen times its normal size. She remembered worrying, *I hope he doesn't get a black eye.* But then again, it wouldn't have made any difference.

She knew that other girls were thinking it, *did he just wink at Brundell?* She'd never been envied before. She envied herself. She wondered if he'd kiss her at the end of the evening.

'He was playing rugby. I was watching because it was a big inter-school competition. He went charging up the pitch, he clashed, he fell down ... and he never got up again.'

The medic wandered on, no one thought it was serious at first; she could see it now, the memory was as horribly clear as if it had just been repainted, the reverberations of the scene had followed her down the years.

'That's why we never had our end of year dance.'

'Jeez, that's ... bad,' said Ray.

Those beautiful blue eyes, forever closed. She looked up and saw Ray Morning's blue eyes and it was as if the past had bobbed forward to say hello.

Until now, she'd never met anyone who made her feel quite like she had in the orbit of Seth Mason: it was as though the sun followed him. But here she was with Ray Morning and it felt like a grown-up version of the same.

As if in slow motion she saw his hand reach across the table to take hers . . . and then her phone went off in her bag and it was Bradley's name on the screen when she looked.

Chapter 46

Amanda bolted into the hospital and up the stairs because the lifts usually took ages to arrive. She crashed down the corridor and rang the bell for admittance to the ward. She had to ring again, her impatience burning a hole inside her.

Bradley and Kerry were sitting in the private room where their mother was put after her shingles diagnosis. Ingrid was lying peacefully, her mouth fallen open, but she wasn't asleep, there was a telling difference in her waxy pallor, the essence of her missing.

Amanda leaned over the side of the bed and held her, the little girl inside her letting out, *Mummy, mummy, I love you.* A last kiss, her skin was already cold.

'What happened?' she asked Bradley.

'She died,' said Kerry, sorrowfully dabbing her eyes with some tissues grabbed from a nearby box.

Amanda could have lamped her.

'When?'

'We hadn't been here long. She was sleeping, then she let out this long ragged breath and Kerry had the foresight to go and fetch a doctor. She slipped away, just like that. We had to go and get a coffee and something to eat ... for the shock. And we rang you from the cafeteria.'

Amanda slumped down onto the chair beside the bed. *This* was too big to take in, she hadn't expected it. Ingrid was getting better, they said, the infection was clearing. Another change to acclimatise to. She couldn't cry, her tears were frozen behind her eyes.

'Her heart just stopped. It couldn't have been more peaceful. I was holding her hand,' said Bradley.

'She'd have liked that,' replied Amanda. No better way for her to go. 'What happens now?'

'They've given me a booklet. As next of kin, I—'

'Sorry, what?' Amanda's head snapped up.

'Amanda, don't let's argue now. Mother named me as next of kin. You know she was like that, the son should be next of kin.'

'It's not the time nor the place to argue,' added Kerry in that silly squeak of hers.

Amanda's eyes burned in her direction and Kerry took her cue.

'I'll let you talk,' she said and scurried out.

'I might as well tell you, Mother wanted one of those no fuss cremations,' said Bradley, when the door was shut.

'What?'

'She said—'

'For god's sake, Bradley, do we have to talk about this now? She's only just gone.'

'I don't want you inviting all and sundry to something that isn't going to happen.'

Her mother was dead, they were talking about funerals. It didn't seem real. Her brain couldn't absorb the reality. It was too much all at once.

Bradley was still chuntering on. 'She was adamant about it, made me promise.'

Amanda switched her attention to what he was telling her. Not even he could believe the tripe coming out of his mouth.

'You know as well as I do she wouldn't have agreed to that.' Her mother had said more than once that she was quite excited about her funeral, as if she would be able to attend it herself and enjoy the fuss. The same way she would be looking forward to seeing Bradley open that big tin box sitting under the bedroom carpet.

'Well, she *did* agree to it. I mean . . . suggest it. She'd seen an advert on the televis-ion.' He pronounced it *telly-viz-ion*, exactly the same way his money-grabbing creepy-arse father had; he'd absorbed all his pretensions and added to them. 'More and more people are seeing the sense in not throwing all that money on a fire these days. Literally.'

'A cost-cutting exercise, eh? Wouldn't want to eat into the capital, would we, Bradley?' Amanda snarled. If looks could kill, Bradley would have been toast at that moment.

He stood, pulled his trousers up and over his gut.

'I think emotions are bound to be running high, so Kerry and I will go home and I'll be in touch.'

'I want to see the will,' said Amanda. 'I want to see where these wishes of hers are stated.'

'In good time. I think we both need to grieve first.'

He really should have been a comedian.

She stayed for another half an hour just sitting in the calm, imagining what her life would have been like had she not felt so obliged to stay close to a woman who blamed her for so much that was wrong with her own. And the irony that, as the daughter 'whose job it was to look after her mother' she would be denied the all-important duty of giving her the send-off she had wanted.

Her phone beeped in her bag and when she lifted it out it was Ray. They'd swapped numbers before she left; he had wanted to drive her here, and she'd said no because she didn't want his world venn-diagramming with this world of hers, she wanted to keep it pure and away from infection.

Are you all right? Come back here x

said the text.

She replied that she was, but was going home. The evening was over, its earlier magic drowned by a sweet-and-sour motherlode of past memories and a present she needed to try and get her head around. She wouldn't have been surprised to find out that their mum had hung on, refusing to bow out until Bradley made an appearance, because she loved him that much. She was capable of that strength of feeling – but only for her son and not her daughter. And now she was gone for ever, leaving Amanda with more questions than she had ever answered. Amanda wished she could fast-forward to next Tuesday and unpack all this with the women in Ray's back room. It couldn't come fast enough.

Chapter 47

Mel had just finished giving young Jason Jepson an extra lesson on Saturday because he had an exam coming up. She had no worries about him passing, though. He didn't want a cheese toastie because he was meeting a girl for a Nandos. *Ah,* she thought, *young love.* She remembered well that giddiness of someone being on your mind so much you should have charged them rent. She remembered it because it was recent history. Pat had been on her mind too much, and her thoughts kept returning to their evening together as if they were boomerangs. She was wise enough to realise that her ego was as damaged as her heart and she'd found a worthy bandage for it in his attentions. But was it just that? She'd enjoyed talking to him; she'd joined the still-nameless band because of his encouragement, they'd laughed together, he'd made her feel valued and listened to. Maybe in time she'd see it was merely gratitude she felt, but then gratitude didn't tend to set off small bombs in one's nether regions.

She'd stopped checking her phone to see if she'd missed any calls from Steve, she'd just got on with her days. There was more and more time between thoughts of him, and what he might be doing with Chloe who smelt of Chloe. If anything, her thoughts were too occupied with those five orgasms in one night; they'd taken top spot in her own personal Guinness book of records and she felt ever so smug about that.

She hadn't changed her sheets since then, even though they were due a wash. She'd lain in bed where Pat's scent was still present if she pressed her face hard into the pillow and inhaled and relived what they'd done. God, his tongue, no wonder she'd screamed. Steve was crap at oral. He couldn't find the sweet spot with a satnav and a Sherpa. More often than not she'd had to commit the cardinal female sin and fake a climax when he was down there, under duress. So it was partly her fault when he repeated what he thought worked. She wouldn't do it again – not after being with a man who made her feel as if it had been his pleasure to give her every one of those five orgasms. That's one thing at least she'd take forward with her from all this,

'An injection of joy' had been an off-the-cuff remark to Amanda, but it summed it up completely. She'd be okay either way. If Steve didn't come back, she'd work through it because she'd have to. But, if he did come back, as Pat thought he might, she had to make sure that she wasn't so keen to forgive him that she ignored what her feelings were about it. He owed her whatever it took to get things straight in her head and that wouldn't happen overnight. Either way, she had a journey ahead of her and it wasn't going to be easy.

Today, though, she felt all right; in fact she was looking forward to bingeing on a new Netflix box set that the girls were talking about at work. It was a bit of a dark subject matter for an afternoon's viewing, but who was here to tell her she should be watching it at night? Having the TV all to herself was great, no one to keep switching over mid-film to check how the cricket/snooker/football was doing.

She'd lost weight with all the trauma, and it felt good to be wearing a pair of chinos she hadn't been able to fit into since Clinton was president. She fancied a bag of popcorn to go with her dark drama so she slipped on her Crocs and pootled down to the corner shop. When she returned, she put her key in the door to find it was already unlocked. She must have forgotten to lock it on her way out. That was the trouble with doing things on automatic pilot; more often, she fretted that she hadn't done them, even if she always had – well, apart from this one rogue occasion. How many times had they gone out and she'd had to ask Steve to drive back to check that she'd turned her hot brush off. It used to drive him insane. Anyway, he wasn't here to moan at her.

But when she walked into the lounge, she found that actually, he was.

★

Amanda took the milk, bread and Saturday newspaper out of her shopping bag. She felt numb, dry; there had been no great outpourings of grief since her mum died on Wednesday. She felt as if she were walking around, waiting for an avalanche rumbling far above her to descend. She'd heard that bereaved people entered a kind of limbo until the funeral, but there would be no funeral if Bradley had his way and so where would be the relief, the prick in the balloon that would release the tension and give her the starting point to heal?

She'd been to see Dolly Shepherd, her mum's next-door neighbour, and the crew at the coffee shop that her mum used to frequent to deliver the news on Thursday morning. No one knew really what to say because the normal dictionary did not serve the bereaved; there were no words that brought comfort, only silly bloody platitudes about time being a great healer, except it wasn't. There were welts inside her that had been there for decades that would never heal.

'You'll feel better after the funeral,' said Dolly.

'I don't think there will be a funeral, Dolly. Apparently my mum's wishes were that she didn't have a service.'

And Dolly spoke for her too when she said, 'Eh? That's not right.'

Because it was wrong, so very wrong and there was nothing she could do about it since Bradley had sent her a photo of the part of the will that said Ingrid didn't want a funeral. She'd even rung a solicitor to find out if she could contest this idiotic stipulation which she knew her mother must have been coerced into. He explained that the funeral wishes were not legally binding but the executor was in charge of the decision-making and Bradley was sole executor – because he'd photographed that part of the will for her too.

Amanda sent a text to Bradley, because if she rang she just might lose her temper and say something she shouldn't. She volunteered to pay for the funeral herself. He replied not long after that he'd consider her request, as if she were a charity on the scrounge for a raffle prize.

She made herself a cup of tea and prepared to lose herself in the newspaper, divert her thoughts away from what was happening around her. Shit seemed to come in great big clods, it was never evenly spaced out to give one time to breathe between assaults. Luck never came like that: it came in a five-pound lottery win and then nothing for weeks, but crap . . . barrowfuls of it, *this way please, just dump it right here on my head.* Bradley was enjoying being in charge because he was an ineffectual little twerp who always lost whenever they confronted one another. Now, he held all the cards, all the power and he was loving lording it over her for a change. God knows where Kerry got her specs from to see him as Leonides, king of Sparta, over the breakfast table in their glossy white kitchen with his ridiculous racehorse teeth.

She read, but none of the news was uplifting: stabbings; peaceful protests that turned violent; some holier-than-thou MP caught on the fiddle; a scandal in the making of old people being ripped off by unscrupulous equity release and home reversion companies that seduced them into selling the houses they lived in but for way below the market value. They arranged the quickest of sales with misleading small print in the contracts. Some pensioners, led to believe they would be in situ for life, had been evicted and it was all legal and above board.

She turned the page, but there was something about the ripped-off pensioners that made the piece stick in her head long after she'd finished the whole paper, where it sat and fermented.

Chapter 48

Steve was sitting stiffly on the edge of the sofa, large as life, his suitcase beside him and some carrier bags full of more clothes. He looked like a *tableau vivant*, one for which an artist would have had a whole gamut of titles to choose from: *The Prodigal; The Homecoming; The Reject; Cheating Wanker with Tail Between Legs*.

It was obvious this wasn't just a flying visit for fresh underwear, but the big homecoming moment was not how Mel had imagined it being over the weeks. She didn't dive on him crying with relief; she didn't throw her arms around his neck in gratitude that he had picked her above Chloe-scented Chloe. Actually, she felt as if someone had jabbed her with a stun gun and suspended her ability to emote.

'I've come back,' said Steve, jutting out his chin.

'So I gather,' she said.

'Do you want to talk?'

'I've wanted to talk since you left,' Mel replied. Now *he* wanted to, it would happen.

'Well, sit down then,' he said. His tone was a bit off, but that was because he was out of step, on the defensive, his guard up against any unexpected reactions on her part, she guessed. They hadn't been in this situation before, so they'd have to feel their way out of the maze they'd found themselves in. She wondered if Pat was having the self-same conversation with *Chlo*.

Mel sat down on the armchair and waited, and considering he had requested they talk, Steve hadn't said a word. The silence was sucking all the oxygen out of the room. If she hadn't punctured it herself, their lungs might have imploded.

One word that hung in the air like the single note of a funeral knell.

'Why?'

He must have rehearsed in his head what his spiel was going to be, she thought, but still he took his time to deliver his answer.

'I don't know. Opportunity, maybe; boredom, the feeling that life was passing me by. I haven't analysed it. It was a mistake and I'm sorry. I'm really sorry, Mel. Can you forgive me?'

He stood up and held out his arms like Christ the Redeemer in Rio. She stood up and moved into them and those extended arms closed around her.

'I've missed you,' he said.

She looked into herself to work out what she was feeling and she wasn't sure if she'd gone over to him just then because she wanted to, or because she didn't want to leave him standing there like a lemon.

Over her shoulder he could see her cards standing up on the display cabinet.

'I'm sorry I missed your birthday. I'll make it up to you.'

He released her and walked over to them, picking them

up one by one and reading them. Then he saw the sex kit tin and opened it up.

'Who bought you this?'

'One of the girls at work.'

He lifted up the spanky paddle to see what the lettering spelled, then replaced it, closed the lid, his nose wrinkled with distaste.

'So ... do you want to pick up where we left off?' he asked.

'Do you?' she threw the question back at him, because she honestly didn't know. They'd been with each other for thirty years. They had a forever house together, joint savings, pensions. And yet she didn't know.

'Of course I do or I wouldn't be here, would I?'

'Who finished with who?' Mel asked.

A pause. A very telling pause, before he said, 'I finished it, if you must know. I wanted to come home.'

'I don't know how to go forward,' Mel said.

'We'll just have to go through the motions and eventually we'll get back in the groove of it,' he said.

'We can try,' she replied, wondering why she wasn't feeling the swell of jubilation she should be feeling, only a soupçon of smugness that she'd *won* him back, because he'd picked her over Chloe, her lure was the stronger. And yet also a strange smack of disappointment that she wouldn't be able to sit and watch her box set and scoff the giant bag of sweet and salty popcorn.

★

Something was bugging Amanda about that newspaper article featuring the duped pensioners. She was probably being really stupid but her intuition wouldn't allow her to let it go. She got out her laptop and pulled up the Scopesearch report she'd paid for. She was allowed three searches for her tenner. Her mother lived at 3, Winter Place. The people who held the perpetual barbecues lived at number 5. She requested a search of that property, to read that it had been sold, in January, for four hundred and ten thousand. Amanda went cold. The properties couldn't have been mixed up, but why was it saying that her family's home had also been sold in January this year, and for less than the smaller one next door. She went onto Zoopla to find exactly the same price information. Number 3, Winter Place had been sold four months ago, and it had been sold for far less than its market value.

Her mind was sparking like a Catherine wheel, making connections between facts: Bradley sending her choice parts of the will; the power of attorney; her mother naming him as next of kin; the his and hers brand-new Audis on his drive and his Miele appliances; sandwich shops and Turkish cosmetic surgery that he said had come to him from a loan and his father's money; his absolute refusal to entertain the mere idea of selling their mum's house so she could have a bungalow.

Because he'd already sold it?

He was a total arse but he wouldn't. He *wouldn't*.

Her hands were shaking as she reached for her phone to confront him and find out. She was about to press the connect symbol but stopped herself, because did she really think he'd confess on the spot? She needed to take a breath. She needed to keep biting her lip so she could get her own way with giving her mum the send-off she'd been looking forward to. And then, if he'd done what she thought he had, she'd have his knackers in a blender.

★

How did you put a broken marriage back together? Mel wondered if they had a department for that in the repair shop where Sky worked. Small pieces carefully glued back into place so the cracks didn't show, like a smashed favourite flower vase. But even if they were more or less invisible, you *knew* they were still there and it wouldn't hold water any more. It wasn't the same vase, it had to be seen as a different one, isn't that what Pat had told her, and that it would never be the same again? There was no rewind button to take it back to the moment before it was trashed.

They'd ordered a Chinese for two and were eating it at the table with a bottle of wine. She was sitting in the chair where she'd had only a mouthful of birthday cake before Pat had leaned over and kissed her. She gave her head a rattle to shoo the memory away because it wasn't helpful when she was supposed to be on the first step of the rebuilding-their-marriage path. This 'going through the motions of living again as husband and wife in the hope of picking things up where they left off' might have been easy for Steve, she thought, but *he* hadn't been the one who'd been crushed by a steamroller and somehow had to reconstitute himself from the pancake of questions and anguish and shattered bits of heart and ego he had become.

Mel couldn't just pretend that all that was required to fix the hole he'd blown in their relationship was a quick piece of netting over the top, because the hole would still be there unless she packed it with the answers she needed to hear from him. How did it all come about? When did they decide to run off together? What had he told Chloe about her? Did they go out to restaurants together? Did they hold hands? What was the sex like? Pat had said he owed her those answers. He owed her some of his own discomfort if it helped to assuage her own.

She forced herself to swallow the boiled rice that was just rolling around in her mouth, unenjoyed, before she dropped the first of her many questions.

'Why did you come back?'

'I told you, because I missed home.'

'Home – or me?'

He tutted. 'Both.'

And she thought, why didn't he say, *I missed you, of course. I wanted you, not her.* He was making it sound as if she was just part of a list of comforts: 55-inch TV, wet room, Sunday roasts, big armchair, Mel.

She picked up a crispy wonton and listened to the thoughts in her own head, trying to connect with her feelings.

Why isn't he on the floor, on his knees, begging for your forgiveness, Mel? Why isn't he telling you he loves you and is going to do everything in his power to make you forget this ever happened?

That's what she would have done, had she been him. She wouldn't have pulled out a takeaway menu from the drawer and said, 'Let's have a banquet for two.'

'Why di—'

He cut her off impatiently. 'Let's not do this post-mortem thing, Mel, please. I'm here, aren't I? So we don't need to talk about it. Whatever has happened, has happened.'

'But I need to talk to make sense of it,' she said. 'You lived it, you know what happened but it's all a big blur to me. You owe me.'

'Then there's no point in us even trying to go forward, is there?' he snapped back.

Her throat felt constricted. She was chasing him away

again as soon as he'd got here. She shut up and drowned the next question cued up in her throat with a large glug of wine. She'd have to just stumble through this landscape, blind and uninformed and heal alone, with the aid of any stray sticking plasters she came across. And how long would that take?

She bit down on her wonton, feeling as lost and panicky as she had when she couldn't get hold of him the night he'd left her, as if she were standing on a rug that might be pulled from under her at any time. How could she live like that?

As they were clearing up the plates, he turned from the dishwasher and said, 'You hear about these mid-life crises but you never think it'll happen to you. I just wish . . . ' He waved his next words away, but she had to know what he wished: that he hadn't been such a prick? That she'd forgive him? She pressed, needing to hear it, needing to see his knee bending before her, even a little, to show he was putting her feelings above his own.

'Okay then, I just wish you hadn't forced me to go to that school reunion when I'd said I didn't want to.'

She couldn't speak. She might have *encouraged* him to go to it, but she hadn't bundled him through the door of a building where he'd bang his old girlfriend in the bogs before the night was over. Her face must have said what her mouth couldn't, because he scowled at her.

'Don't look at me like that, Mel. It can't have been all my fault. There must have been something wrong with us for my head to be turned. What I'm trying to say is that maybe we both need to work at it, right? Let me go find something for us to watch on the telly.'

As Mel was putting a tab in the dishwasher she felt the heat of anger begin to cauterise her sensitive nerve endings. She let herself recognise it, that she had a right to it, as Pat had told her she had because her feelings were valid. Steve couldn't stick a spoon in her life and stir her all up and then expect her to stop swirling the moment he walked in through the door. How dare he be the only one to dictate the terms of their reconciliation. She'd always considered she had a happy marriage, but having a few weeks outside it had been an eye-opener. It wasn't just him who had a new shape: so did she, and it was bigger than the one she'd been pre-his school reunion. She'd joined a rock band, she'd found friends, she'd had her heart tickled by a postman who had made her feel worthy of being desired. She had expanded beyond the rigid box of her relationship with Steve and it wasn't going to be easy for her to fit back into it either.

Steve announced he was tired just after ten. Mel imagined that he wanted to get to bed and wake up to their familiar normal. Except the old normal had gone for them both. Could they find a new normal? They'd have to for this to work.

He brushed his teeth with the toothbrush that was sitting in the glass by the sink, still waiting for him like a faithful hound because he'd forgotten to take it with him. He climbed into bed, she slipped in beside him and thought how odd it felt that he was there again, as if nothing had happened. Except it had.

''Night,' he said. 'Tomorrow's a new day, right?'

'Yep,' she said, knowing he meant that today is the carpet that everything will be swept under.

'Do you want me to give you a kiss?'

'If you like.'

She felt him shuffle towards her in the dark and then suddenly stop dead. She heard him sniffing. Then he said:

'Is that bloody aftershave I can smell?'

Chapter 49

Oh shit, thought Mel listening to Steve snuffling around on the pillows, on the sheets like a pig hunting for truffles. Could a man-dog smell another man-dog's presence, using some deep primal perception? She could still smell Pat's strong Tom Ford scent but her olfactory senses were pretty highly tuned. Maybe if she'd not been put on the spot she might have been able to think of a believable excuse, but she couldn't for the life of her drum one up at a moment's notice.

Steve scrambled out of bed and flicked on the big light. The fact that Mel hadn't said, 'Don't be silly, what are you talking about?' was telling, in fact her silence was screaming the answer.

'Who's been in this bed? *Our* bed?' he asked, each word enunciated, squeezing the juice out of every letter. 'Is it a man? Have you had someone in here? Who? WHO?'

There was a freeze-frame moment, she was at an important crossroads. Saying she'd gone mad in Boots and had sprayed loads of testers on herself, or was using a new fabric conditioner that smelt like an aftershave would have sounded like the lies they were. But, telling him the truth was an extreme measure. Then again, if he wanted answers, she should give him answers, seeing as here he was, Mr 'Don't ask me any questions' flinging questions at her like Jeremy bleeding Paxman. How come it was okay for him to do that and not her?

'Well, to be fair, you'd left me for someone else and that made me single.'

Which was not saying, *No one, Steve. I've had no one in here.* His mouth dropped open.

'You've slept with someone else – is that what you're saying?'

Oh my god, the look on his face poked her anger muscle so hard it started to bleed. The nerve of him. Maybe he deserved to feel some of what she'd been through.

'There wasn't a lot of sleeping going on, to be fair,' she replied.

'Whaaa ... Who was it?'

'I don't want to talk about it,' Mel replied, as cockily as she could. 'I thought you said that whatever's happened has happened. Tomorrow's a new day, right?'

'Don't you throw my own words back at me.'

He was turning redder by the nanosecond. She shouldn't enjoy the sight, but she couldn't help herself.

'Who was it?' he asked again.

'No one you know, so there's not much point in telling you.'

'You had sex. In our bed. How many times?'

'I can't remember. I stopped counting after five.'

Steve pushed his hand into his hair and started pacing about. It looked as if his brain was torturing him. Yep, she could recognise that. *Horrible, isn't it, Steve?*

'I can't believe you had sex with someone else!' Each word punched out and occupying a space of its own.

More pacing. A thought hit him hard, by the expression on his face.

'That sex tin thing. You used that, didn't you?'

She couldn't resist. 'Yes, we did actually. I was walking around for days with the word SLUT in raised lettering on my arse.'

His face registered disgust.

'How could you, Mel?'

'You didn't want me. You'd left me,' she matched him in volume.

'Not for *ever*.'

'And I knew that exactly how?'

'Well, you should have known that, for god's sake. It was a stupid blip, a mistake and I said I'm sorry.'

'Well, what I did wasn't a mistake, it was fantastic and I'm not sorry in the slightest.'

Steve's head pulled back into his neck. 'I beg your pardon, what?'

'I'm not sorry – and I don't want you back.' Mel heard the words come out of her mouth and she saw them written in the air as surely if they were encased in a speech balloon. She said them a moment before she realised they were true.

'Eh?'

'No, I really don't. Thirty-one years together and I wasn't even worth a Dear John note. You had absolutely no thought for how upset and worried I'd be when I found out you'd upped and left. What did you think I'd be like, Steve?'

'I said I'm sorry and I am—'

'Oh well, that's okay then.' Mel huffed. 'Not really, of course. You either can't or won't understand what I went through and now you can't or won't try to do anything to make me feel okay again because *you* don't want to talk about things. You smashed up the trust, but it looks as if you expect me to be the only one that puts the work in to rebuild it. Well, I won't. Why should I? Especially when I know that she dumped you and that's the reason why you've come back.'

It was a guess, a bluff and he fell for it.

'It was not. We both decided.'

She knew it was a lie. Chloe had chewed him up and spat him out and he'd gone home to Plan B. Mel saw in front of her months of suffering, sifting through whatever he said for the real truths, worrying when he went out of the front door if he'd be back, wondering how much Chloe was on his mind. Wondering if she'd click her fingers and he'd go running.

'But you had sex with someone else, Mel. Doesn't that even it up?'

He was looking for anything to shift the blame. He wasn't strong enough to accept it, to carry it on his shoulders. Not even at this important time which should have been the peak period of penitence.

'I think we're done, Steve.' She was calm and in control, more so than she thought she could be, at least on the surface.

He stood there as if waiting for her face to crack and announce it was a joke. When a long enough time passed, he picked up his pants from the floor, stuffed his legs into them and his joggers, pulled his top on.

'I'll sleep at my mother's,' he said. 'I'll see you tomorrow.'

She didn't try to stop him. She traced the sound of him taking the stairs, going outside, opening the garage and driving out.

She felt numb but she knew that would change and loads

of emotions would come flying at her and probably over-whelm her. She got out of bed and went down for a cup of tea because she was wide awake, adrenaline coursing through her body like Usain Bolt around a track. She won-dered if Chloe was now back at home telling all the same lies to Pat, lies that he just might choose to believe.

Chapter 50

Bradley rang Amanda first thing on the Sunday morning.

'Kerry and I have been talking and we have decided that we must adhere to mother's wishes,' he said. 'There will be no funeral.'

Amanda wasn't sure if it was his callousness, or that Kerry should have any opinion on it before herself, or the stupid, slow way he spoke that was angering her more. She knew he wouldn't budge; he was having his little moment of power, but if she screamed at him he'd use that to manipulate her: *I was open to reason but, alas . . .* and she wouldn't give him the satisfaction.

'Which undertaker's is she at?' asked Amanda, doing everything she could to keep her temper on a leash. 'I'd like to at least go and sit with her.'

'Of course,' he said, as if granting her a favour. 'She's with Mr Hyde.'

How appropriate.

'Thank you,' she forced herself to say. She had nothing to thank him for but she wouldn't rip into him yet. Not before she was fully armed.

'Contrary to what you may believe, Amanda, Mother *was* of sound mind when she wrote her will.'

Lying arse. 'I'm sure she was.'

'I am going to email you the full copy. I didn't want you to be upset at what she had left you. I did point out that it wasn't very fair to leave you so much less than me. I said it would cause trouble.'

I'll bet you did.

She willed herself to stay calm.

'It was her money to do with as she wished, Bradley.'

'I might not agree with it but I intend to follow it to the letter, for her.'

'That's very honourable of you.' She hoped she'd kept the sarcasm out of her voice, but she wouldn't have put her life savings on it.

'I wasn't sure if you were aware, Amanda, but Mother sold the house earlier this year to one of those home reversion companies. I had no idea that's where she was getting the money from to loan to us for our business.'

He could have shoved a pound of butter in his mouth and it wouldn't have melted.

'No, I didn't know. They give far less than the market value. She probably threw away over a hundred grand. How very stupid of her.' *How very stupid of you.*

'I'd have stopped her if only I'd known. Not that it matters now of course.'

She wanted to shake him by the neck until both sets of those horrendous teeth had fallen out of their gummy holdings.

'No, it doesn't matter now.'

'Is there anything you'd like from the house? Any souvenirs?'

There wasn't. And unless it was something of no monetary value, she wasn't likely to get it anyway. She didn't want her mother's wedding ring, as a daughter might ask for, because it was the ring pervy Arnold gave her. And she didn't want to hear Bradley tell her that he'd already given that to Kerry. No, there was nothing in that house she wanted other than distance from anything connected with it.

'No, thank you.'

'The company have given us three weeks to clear the house before they take full possession,' said Bradley and Amanda wondered if he meant by that, that she was the one expected to order skips, empty cupboards, ferry clothes to charity shops. He had about as much chance of that happening as Barbara Broccoli ringing him up and asking him to be the new James Bond. She left a silence instead of replying to him, which eventually he filled with words covered in his best crawling Bradley honey.

'Just one thing before I go: did Mother say anything about an old tin to you? She mentioned it a couple of months ago. It has my father's Timex watch in it and a few old letters he'd written her. Just sentimental things, of neither use nor interest to anyone but me. She'd forgotten where she'd put it, but wanted me to have it.'

So it *was* the tin he was hunting for when she'd seen him snooping around the house. He'd taken her measured responses at face value; concluded from them that his sister had believed everything he said and would be reasonable, compliant, honourable. What a despicable, odious, fatheaded plank.

Amanda pretended to ruminate.

'Erm . . . hmm . . . No idea about that. Do you want me

to have a look for you when I go up to Mum's? I need to pick some clothes for her to wear.'

'Oh, don't worry,' said Bradley. 'I've had to change the locks anyway, I lost the front door key and was forced to take precautions. Kerry picked something for her.'

Amanda stuck her nails in her palm to stop her reacting. He really was a piece of crap.

'Okay, goodbye then. Talk later.'

Then she pressed disconnect before she either broke down or pulled up Google to find a hitman who specalised in slow, painful deaths.

*

Mel slept better than she thought she would. She got up, went for a newspaper and sat at the dining table trying to read it and not let her thoughts ping off to what was going on in Steve's head this morning. What was going on in her head was more important, said an inward voice that strangely had a Mancunian male accent.

She pulled a notebook out of the drawer and made two columns on a page, one headed: REASONS TO SAVE, the other: REASONS TO END.

It was easier to save their relationship, especially in their mid-fifties. They were looking forward to a retirement together and that was on the near horizon if they wanted it to be. Company: Someone to go out with and stay in with. Everything she wrote down, she noticed immediately, was a reason for not being alone, not for staying with Steve.

Reasons to end: not as many, but it was telling how they outweighed everything on the other list. He hadn't cheated because he had a rush of mid-life hormones, some sort of 'male menopause' that forced his hand, he'd chosen to do it. Another: the lack of respect he'd shown to her and their marriage vows. She would always be waiting for the mended vase to leak. She didn't need any more reasons.

She used to scoff at people who said *love wasn't always enough*, because what else was more important? Well, she'd just had a hard lesson in that, because love was worthless without trust and respect.

She was under no illusions, she'd hurt for a long time, but she'd heal. And sleeping with Pat wasn't the reason she was thinking like this. This wasn't a Hallmark film where the postman turned up and lived happily ever after with her; she probably wouldn't ever see him again unless he had to cover for his mate's round and had a parcel for her. But he'd had his part to play in why she felt like this. If she hadn't met him, she might not have realised she deserved better.

Steve turned up at three with a sponged-off gravy stain down his top because he wouldn't have come round before his mother's big Sunday roast. His brother would have been there as well as his parents and no doubt her name would have been chewed over as much as the beef.

It wouldn't have crossed his mind that she really wouldn't want him. He'd presume that by now, she'd had her hissy fit of temper, said her piece and got it out of her system.

She told him that there was no way back for them. When he walked out on her to go to another woman, he'd taken her trust and love and respect with him, on a single and not a return ticket.

'I can't believe you are going to throw away thirty years of marriage for a stupid fling,' he said. And she replied:

'I didn't, Steve. You did.'

Chapter 51

As Amanda poured out her heart to the women of the Tuesday club, she was wondering how she could only have known them for such a short time. This was her safe place and these were her safe people and if she'd had to describe them to anyone, she would have used the word 'friends' without even thinking about it.

She told them the lot, her spot-on suspicions about Bradley and the house sale and how Kerry had chosen the clothes her mother was lying in. She told them about the will that clearly stated Bradley was the sole executor unless he didn't want to be, and then his wife Kerry would take over the duty. Her mother had left her thirty thousand pounds, a respectable figure that might make her unlikely to try and sue for more. She had no doubt it would be difficult because Ingrid would have signed anything Bradley told her to. Going by the date on the new will, his dodgy solicitor pal must have endorsed her as being of sound mind in a face-to-face assessment at a time when Ingrid was showing definite signs of mental weakness, not that there was any medical report to support that. Had it all been fair and

above board, Bradley having been left more than Amanda
was something she would have had to swallow, but she'd
never know what might have been, because her mum had
been duped by her own flesh and blood, a son she trusted
and idolised – and she couldn't swallow that, at least not
without choking.

'You could always try and contest it, after all the years
you've spent looking after her,' suggested Erin.

'She might end up spending more in legal fees than she
inherits,' Mel said to that.

'He's going to have to pay a lot of tax on that money. Isn't
there a rule that if you've handed over a lot of cash but die
within seven years, the taxman comes sniffing? He won't
escape them.' Erin was certain of it.

That brought a modicum of comfort, but not enough to
offset the heartless, grasping duplicity of her brother.

'I can't believe he'd do this,' said Amanda. She'd vented
and she'd sobbed tonight and she was full circle back to
spitting like a cobra again. He'd not only robbed his own
mother but cheated her out of a decent send-off. That's what
stuck most in Amanda's craw.

'What about a memorial service?' Sky suggested. 'He
can't stop you having one of those, can he? Then all your
mum's friends can come and pay their respects.'

Amanda gasped in surprise. She hadn't thought of that.
She could have kissed Sky. In fact she did; she grabbed her
lovely face and laid a smacker on her cheek.

'Oh Sky, that is a wonderful idea.'

'Might be worth asking if Mr Hyde would take your
mum up to the crem in a hearse rather than one of their
vans,' said Mel. 'He's a nice man, kind, he looked after my
mum and my dad.'

'Can I say what a bastard your brother is, though?' said Astrid, crunching down on a cookie as if she were sinking her teeth into Bradley's head.

Amanda's mouth spread into a slow smile. 'I've got a plan where he's concerned, but let me keep my powder dry for a while until it's in place. It's the one thing keeping me going at present. Now, someone, please tell us some good news.'

'I've got some.' Mel stuck up her hand. 'Steve came home at the weekend and I told him we were done. Totally finished. Didn't want him back.'

The others were clearly confused, if their expressions were anything to go by.

'No, honestly, it really is good news,' said Mel. She'd give them the short version of what happened for now, minus Steve sniffing the pillows like an off-his-tits bloodhound. 'I'm okay. I know I've got a hard road ahead of me, but I would have had anyway. At least letting him go won't turn me as barmy as him staying and trying to stuff everything under the carpet. I'd have just been looking at the big mound and trying to ignore it, avoid it, and I couldn't have.'

'Oh, Mel,' said Amanda.

'I might have been able to if I hadn't shagged the postman, but I did, and—'

'Whoa, whoa, rewind that cassette,' Erin yelled over. Astrid almost spat out her mouthful of coffee.

Mel realised she'd only told Amanda that choice detail after everyone else had gone the previous week, so filled them in.

'I know in Steve's eyes I'm as bad; I've lost the moral high ground.'

'But he threw you away!' Astrid was outraged on Mel's behalf.

'According to him it was a mere temporary dumping,' said Mel to that, which was greeted with a round of gasps, 'What the actual . . . 's and a 'bellend'.

'Did you really think he'd come back, Mel?' asked Erin.

'No, I didn't. I was trying to keep my hope alive but in my head, Chloe was this sort of Cleopatra and why would he have left that to come back to me? My heart was hanging on but my brain was saying, *Mel, as if.* Pat told me to concentrate on *my* feelings, what *I* was going through. I've been doing a lot of that over the past days. When Steve told me that he couldn't help what was happening to him and could I please wait so he could make up his mind . . . I think at that point I realised he had no respect for me at all. When he turned up on Saturday and I found myself going through the motions, getting a takeaway, sitting watching TV, going to bed with him, it didn't feel right at all. The best way I can describe it is that it felt like I'd buried a dead dog and the next minute it had turned up on my doorstep, and so I'd put its food out and pulled its bed out of the bin and all the while I'm thinking that something is very wrong here.'

'And the postman?' asked Sky, the question to which they all wanted to know the answer.

Mel smiled, because she always did now when she thought of him.

'I haven't heard anything more from him and I doubt I will. Maybe he let her back in. Some people just cross your path for a little while, don't they, like a small temporary gift, not meant to be kept. And his gift to me was that he made me realise I deserve, at the very least, respect in a relationship, and to be valued, and to be able to trust. And foreplay, I should have loads of that.'

She laughed at the round of applause that erupted.

'You'll be okay, Mel. You can do all the emotions in front of us all when you need to.' Astrid leaned over, squeezed her shoulder.

'I can help you with any divorce paperwork,' Erin said to her and that reminded her: 'Talking of which ...' She reached into her bag and pulled out a folder. 'I have something for you, Amanda. I've asked around and I've emailed just about everyone I know, and they've asked around and I've collected a load of suggestions that women of our age might find beneficial in the workplace. Some are taking the piss, obviously, but ninety per cent of what's been written makes good sense.'

That triggered reminders for the others. Sky had made notes to bring for Amanda; Mel had been asking around, too; and Astrid had a few suggestions for women who might be feeling anxious and scared about their advancing age and concerned that the clock was ticking, so maybe now they needed the encouragement to realise some unfulfilled ambitions. 'Maybe not as drastic as buying a cracker factory, but then again ... if the *kappe* fits.'

Was it any wonder that Amanda broke down then, a mixture of sad and happy tears and all sorts in between?

Chapter 52

- *Advice about vitamins and minerals that isn't sponsored by the suppliers of them. We need an unbiased sort of 'What Menopause' guide.*
- *Best exercises for people with arthritic knees.*
- *Gyms in the workplace with a personal trainer for women.*
- *Learning how to meditate and whatever the chuff mindfulness is? Heard it's supposed to be good.*
- *Bringing HR in so if we need time off for various symptoms they don't think we're wagging off.*
- *A room if we have a sweat fit with some towels and anti p and stuff.*
- *Catnap room.*
- *Free samples from companies – Tena Ladys, leak-proof pants.*
- *A visiting expert coming in every so often to give advice about nutrition.*
- *Stress balls that we can draw a face on of someone who really isn't helping.*
- *Loan of fans if we need one by the desk.*

- *Flexible hours so we can make up time if we need to.*
- *Some memory aid lessons. How can we help ourselves?*
- *As a boss, it would help if I knew what my team was going through so I can be sympathetic and 'on it'.*
- *Sleep assistance. Does stuff like lavender oil on the pillows work?*
- *How can I treat depression. I feel overloaded. I'm worrying constantly about everything and I never used to.*
- *How to increase my metabolism. I'm putting weight on round my middle and I'm eating less than ever.*
- *HRT advice. Does it work? How much does it cost if the doctor won't give it to me.*
- *Permission to knee anyone who makes inappropriate comments about it to me in the balls . . .*

Chapter 53

'This is pretty amazing, Amanda,' said Linus, thumbing through the many-page report she'd brought to his desk last Friday for him to read over the weekend. It exceeded his expectations, for not only was there lots of feedback on what women went through in the workplace during the menopausal time of their lives, written sensitively and without womansplaining, but there were some incredibly practical and infinitely doable suggestions that could be implemented almost immediately, and probably should have been a long time ago.

Amanda had left in some of the more frivolous ideas to amuse him and also to illustrate the frustration that had triggered them.

'Permission to knee anyone who makes inappropriate comments about it to me in the balls,' read Linus trying, unsuccessfully, not to chuckle.

Amanda had wanted to do exactly that to Philip this morning when she'd told him where and why she was going. He'd made some throwaway remark, meant to be overheard, to Chris his bum-licky junior about discussing women's bladders being more important than the month-end figures.

She could have made a retort, but Mother Nature would pay him back for her one day when she targeted his prostate.

Linus was still leafing through the sheets, so much to go at.

'How can I thank you for all this?' He could already see the trade mags queueing up to interview him about the initiatives he would introduce to Mon Enfant, and the ripple effect that would result.

'Trust me, Linus, the whole process of getting this info together has been a joy.' Her Tuesday club had come from it, and the friendships formed there that were keeping her presently afloat. She didn't know what state she'd be in if it weren't for those women. She'd probably be in prison for fratricide.

She was sitting in front of him mopping her brow because she was having a hot flash, as if her body had decided to showcase some of the embarrassing crap many women had to put up with at this point in their lives. Maybe if it hadn't, though, he might not have just gone the extra mile after his next words.

'There must be something I can do for you to say a proper thanks. This is going to be big, you know. Everyone is going to want to jump on.'

She wouldn't have asked, she shouldn't have asked, but oh, sod it.

'There's a whisper around the company that there might be some redundancies . . . '

Linus pressed his fingers together, bopped his lips with them, gave his head a little cock to one side.

'Possibly,' he said, not committing himself.

Here goes. 'If there are, I'd like to volunteer myself.'

'No. I want to keep you around,' said Linus, because he did. He wanted more Amandas and fewer Philips.

'I'd like a change, Linus. I'd like to live out some of my own unfulfilled ambitions. I can access my pension pot at fifty-five, but some extra money would come in handy before then.'

He didn't give her a repeat no, but his eye activity said he was thinking about it.

'Okay then, if I were to . . . influence that, could I count on your support before you went, to put a structure in place, be an . . . in-house menopause consultant, and help me to help the colleagues here and more women in the future?'

'Does it come with a company Bentley?' asked Amanda, eyes twinkling.

'Don't push it,' he replied, twinkling back. Then he held out his hand.

'I can't possibly guarantee it, of course,' he said, as they shook. But they both knew that it was as good as in the bag.

*

Angel Sutton walked into the repair shop too late for Sky to get out of the way. She was with the same woman she'd turned up with the first time, when Erin van der Meer had managed to shoo them off.

'Have you been okay, Sky?' asked Angel, making a bee-line for her, her friend Helen trailing behind. 'I've thought about you so many times recently, with all the newspaper coverage and the awful comments online about your father. I hope you didn't read any, you would have been so upset. So don't go looking for them.'

'I don't take any notice of scurrilous gossip,' replied Sky, aware of the friend looking her up and down as she was rearranging a shelf of bears after selling another ten to the woman in Harrogate.

'Anyway, I thought I'd say hello while we—'

Bon bobbed out of his office.

'Sky, there's a phone call for you.'

'Excuse me,' said Sky, grateful that whoever was ringing had timed it perfectly.

Bon closed the door behind Sky as she went over to the office phone but it was still on the cradle.

'I lied,' he said. 'I saw *friend or foe* and improvised.'

Sky smiled. Could she love him any more than she already did? He cared for her, she knew, but after Erin had said that he wouldn't have gone rushing in to rescue just anyone when he'd driven over to where she'd been living, she wondered if that meant he felt something deeper. She would love to have known what Bon had said that had done the trick and made Wilton Dearne give her the rent back. Her imagination had run wild on it: Bon telling Wilton that he would do anything, *anything* for his future wife was her favourite mini-fantasy.

She'd almost publicised her feelings the previous week when Gwyn Tankersley came in to see Bon on the pretext of picking up some of the repair shop business cards to hand out to her friends. Sky had eavesdropped on the conversation that had taken place between them: Ms Tankersley had said that she wished he hadn't gone so early when he came to hers for dinner and next time he must be the last to leave and not the first. Bon had been polite but that was all, he clearly wasn't interested in Ms Tankersley. Sky hadn't realised she was leaking her relief until Mildred broke into her thoughts and said, 'What are you grinning at?'

And Sky had drummed up something that was a bad attempt at a lie because she'd been put on the spot to explain herself.

The office phone really did ring then and Bon picked it up and took a message for Woodentop.

'He's in trouble,' said Bon to Sky, when the short call

ended. 'He must have his phone on silent. Let me just go and tell him.'

He brushed her arm with his sleeve as he passed her and her skin exploded into tingles. If only he knew what she felt about him and then maybe it would bring out what he felt about her. But what if it was nothing? Was it better to keep the hope alive or take the risk of dashing it?

As Bon approached Jock's unit, he could hear the not-quite-pleasant exchange between Jock and Sutton's daughter.

'As I said, they're no' here.'

'But as *I* said, I need them back.'

'Can I help?' Bon butted in because Jock might have been great at his craft, but his customer service skills could have done with some serious repair.

'The tools I brought in to be cleaned and mounted, I want to cancel the job. I don't mind paying for any work done, I know you're inconvenienced but I've to take them back,' Angel replied to him.

'And as I'm trying tae tell her, I have nae got them. I was too busy, so I subcontracted the job.'

'To whom?' asked Angel, getting even more annoyed.

'A subcontractor.' Jock matched her snotty tone.

'Can you *please* get hold of them and ask them to bring the tools to you immediately?'

'I can try,' replied Jock.

'We don't want them restored. Apparently, it was a silly idea.' Angel was obviously put out by whoever had told her that.

'He's on holiday this week, though,' said Jock.

'Oh for god's sake,' Angel huffed, rolled her eyes: 'Well, just . . . just ring me when they're here and I'll pick them up. If he's already cleaned them, then he's already cleaned them and there's nothing I can do about it. Okay? You still have my number?'

'Aye,' said Jock.

'I am so fucking cross,' Bon heard Angel say to her friend as they turned to go. 'Granny blew a fuse with me. She says she wants them dumped because they remind her of when he wasn't as he is now, which you think would actually be a reason to keep them. So what do I get him instead? I haven't a fucking clue. I might not even fucking bother getting anything.'

'Where's Willy?' Bon asked Jock.

'He's behind yer,' said Jock, as they saw Willy with a sandwich bag coming in through the door that Angel Sutton had just left by.

'Your son's been on the line, he's been trying to ring you,' Bon shouted across to him.

'Has he? Oh, chuff.' Willy threw his sandwich down on his desk and took his phone out of his jeans' back pocket. 'Eight missed calls,' he said aloud, looking first to Bon, then Jock. His son had news he was trying desperately to deliver, then.

Willy rang him; Bon and Jock waited nearby.

'Sorry, Mick,' Willy began and then listened, his face giving nothing away. 'Okay, well ... You're sure ...? You are.' He sighed, a long outward breath. 'Bye then. Thanks for letting me know.'

Willy disconnected the call, the small shake of his head giving them a clue as to what was coming.

'We always knew it was a long shot. Too long, as it happens. It's just rust, boys,' he said to them both. 'Just sodding rust.'

Chapter 54

After work, before the Tuesday meeting, Amanda went to sit with her mum at Hyde's funeral parlour. She was comforted by the fact that they told her she was dressed in a black beaded suit and black shoes with bows on the front. It was what her mum liked to wear when she wanted to look smart, so that was one thing Amanda had no need to get irate about.

Mr Hyde's assistant had told her they were taking her mum up to the crematorium on Friday morning. Amanda had asked if they could take her up in a proper hearse and she'd pay for it. She'd tried and failed not to break down when she explained why, and apologised for putting him in a bit of a difficult position by asking. The assistant said he'd have a word with Mr Hyde and come back to her as soon as he could.

She didn't request to see her mum, she'd already kissed her goodbye, but she just wanted to sit in the room with her closed coffin. She put her arms around it, placed her cheek against the wood. The moment was indicative of their whole relationship: a daughter wanting to be close to a mother but there always being something in the way of it.

'I did love you, Mum, all my life, even though you drove me bonkers for most of it. I wish you could have loved me. I just want to say that I'm letting you go with my forgiveness that you couldn't manage it. I wouldn't want you not to lie at peace.'

Ingrid had backed the wrong horse. But even now, if she were to miraculously wake up and find out what her beloved son had done, she'd have merely said, 'Well, the money would have been his anyway in the end, so what does it matter how he got it?' It wasn't worth Amanda having another sleepless night over.

When she came out, Mr Hyde himself met her at the door and said that they could do as she requested, as long as she was happy to bear the additional cost. The driver would be leaving at eight-thirty and if she wanted to be here and follow them up, there could be no objections.

As she was transferring him the money for the hearse, she asked Mr Hyde if Bradley had been up to visit, and was told that he said he wouldn't be coming up. Apparently there was a note on the file that his sister would be collecting the ashes. And would she like to take her mother's rings now, or should they send them to her brother?

★

When Erin got home from work she found a letter on her doormat, her address written in what looked like an elderly person's spiky handwriting. She opened it up to find another envelope inside and a piece of paper wrapped around it. A note, from Molly at the grief club. It said that if ever she wished to return at a later date, not to hesitate to ring her, and to take good care. And that enclosed was a letter which Alex in the group had asked her to forward, because she would not have compromised Erin's privacy by giving him her address.

It was a blue envelope with her name written on the front in large, slanted lettering.

She opened it: there was a mobile phone number on the top right.

Dear Erin

How stupidly remiss of me not to store your phone number or know how to get in touch with you, so I'm resigned to Molly post which I hope is quicker than a pigeon.

I'll be brief. I told you the last time we met that I was going on a dinner date with a very nice person — and she was. But ... she wasn't you and I spent all evening wishing she were. And I was building up to telling you that at the next Wednesday meeting, but you didn't come and the dip that brought to my spirits was quite telling. VERY telling.

Please ring me if you think that we might meet again, but not as friends, I have enough of those bastards. We can inch along at our own pace like the battered midlifers we are. I promise to hold your heart in cushioned hands, but I would like very much to see you, and say all this to you in person.

Alex

She didn't tell them about the letter when she went to the diner for their Tuesday meet-up. She needed to think about it clearly, with no interfering radio waves. She let the others talk: Amanda about her mother and the non-funeral and her tosser brother; Astrid about her new business venture; Mel about the band. They'd finally found a name: The Change and they had a gig lined up already – and as it was for charity, Mel said, it didn't matter too much if they were totally shit. Erin made the coffees and commented on other people's business, but kept her own locked up inside her for now.

★

Erin wasn't the only one who hadn't totally bared her soul that evening. Mel had only shared the good news about the band. It all started to feel a bit real now they had a name, which wasn't that groundbreaking, but it seemed to fit them, in more ways than one.

She knew they had a deal not to compare what they were going through, nor hold back from saying what was bothering them, but still, she didn't feel right laying it on her new friends how she was doing at present, not with all the rubbish that Amanda was having to cope with. She knew that she'd brought the name 'Steve' to the coffee table too much. Or 'Sieve' as it said on the money-clip; she never did get round to sending it back.

She hadn't seen or heard from him since she'd told him they were totally over. There wouldn't have been any point in him sending massive bouquets of flowers and lying prostrate on their path in the hope of forgiveness, but he didn't try anyway. He'd be getting looked after at his mum and dad's and they'd be saying all the things to him he needed to hear. She didn't really blame them, families should be loyal to their own. Her mum and dad would have been the same with her if they'd still been here and she really wished they were.

Steve must have been back when she was at work today

because some of his things had gone from the house. She'd had a little hiccupy sob about it, but she knew it was just a ghost feeling, her body so used to being stung it was merely trying to act on a familiar response. She'd had plenty of weak moments recently but every time she did, she forced herself to think of Steve with his trousers round his ankles bonking Chloe in the school toilets. The image helped to reinforce that she deserved better.

It also helped that when Steve was picking up his collection of expensive trainers and other detritus, she was in the solicitor's in town in her lunch hour, because she'd taken control and started the painful business of pulling apart thirty years' worth of strands. Every strand separated was one nearer to the end of her hurting, to finding her equilibrium; she had to think of it in bite-sized pieces.

She finally changed her sheets when she got home from the diner; that act had been way overdue. She took in a long, last noseful of faded Oud Wood before she stuffed them in the machine. A bittersweet goodbye.

Chapter 55

'I said I'd take you out to dinner when I sold my house,' Erin said to Bon.

'Firenze, though; too much,' said Bon. It was the 'in' place around here: wonderful location, superb food, fabulous décor, eye-watering prices; an oasis of the real Italy in a corner of South Yorkshire.

'Not too much. And I can easily afford it,' she replied to that.

'You've completed, already?' he asked.

'Not quite, but nearly. I'm slightly worried, Bon. They've knocked those houses up at a rate of knots. They're probably held together by string.'

Bon laughed. They chose their food; their drinks and starters arrived and he waited for her to tell him why he was really here.

'How's things?' she asked.

'Good, nothing to report. And you?'

'Yes, I'm good too.'

She chewed a prawn, swallowed, then sighed.

'I've met someone,' she said and he knew this was why

they were here. Because it wasn't straightforward, he guessed.

'Am I allowed to ask who he ... she is?'

'A barrister, Alex.' Then she clarified, because she realised that 'Alex' could be either male or female: 'A man.'

'Okay,' said Bon. 'And?'

'I met him at the grief club.'

'Ah, I see.'

Erin heard the note of concern in his voice, imagined his thoughts.

'He's not trying to plug up the space of someone who's gone. He's a lot more together than I am. Who isn't?' She dropped a hard laugh, Bon gave her a reprimanding look, then lifted his glass of wine and Erin thought how classy he made even such a simple action look. Bon van der Meer was a stick of rock with 'gentleman' written all the way through him.

'The elevator-pitch version: we were getting on really well. I misread the signs. I didn't go back to Molly's club because I was already too far in and I just couldn't face him, and then I got this forwarded to me a couple of days ago.' She pulled the letter out of her bag and handed it over. Bon reached into his jacket pocket for his glasses, black heavy-framed; they couldn't have suited his face more if they'd been designed around it. As he read, she watched his eyes follow Alex's words, left to right, top to bottom.

'What do you think I should do, Bon?'

Bon folded up the letter and handed it back.

'You know what you want to do, Erin, you don't need me to tell you. But if you feel you need to hear it, then all right: there are no guarantees in anything, but you shouldn't let fear hold you back from taking your chance, because we only have one life and it shouldn't be full of regrets.'

'I did need to hear that from you,' said Erin. 'And I also want to take those words you've just given to me as a gift and give them back to you.'

'Stop,' he said, turning his head from her. 'I will never take advantage of a young woman who, if she has any feeling for me at all, sees me as a father figure.'

'If anyone sees you as a father figure they need therapy,' Erin said to that. 'And if you were, you'd be a FILF.'

'Stop.'

'I'll stop if you start seeing Sky as a fully grown woman who knows her own mind and not some fragile wisp of a girl. I've got to know her so well over the past weeks. I might not be able to sort out my own love life, but I can spot two people who are perfect for each other.'

'Eat your prawns.'

What a revelation it would be to see yourself through the eyes of others, said someone somewhere. For a man imbued with such wisdom, Erin thought, Bon van der Meer, in this, was borderline obtuse.

She reached over the table and put her fingers on his arm.

'One last word on it, then I promise to leave it: there are no guarantees but don't let fear hold you back either, my darling friend,' she said.

Chapter 56

When Amanda turned up at Hyde's funeral parlour on Friday morning with the floral arrangement she'd picked up the night before, it was to find Erin, Mel, Astrid and Sky there waiting in the car park for her, bunches of flowers in their hands. She could have cried with gratitude at their consideration if she'd any tears left inside her. She'd cried them all during the night and now she needed to be composed, focused, strong.

Mr Hyde opened up the back of the hearse and put her spray of cream roses, gold-tongued lilies and gysophila on the top of the coffin with her card among them: *For Mum, from your always loving Amanda*. Then he placed the others around, with their cards: *Rest in Peace; For Ingrid, beloved mother of Amanda; Mein aufrichtiges Beileid; May He grant you eternal rest*. Bradley hadn't even ordered some flowers from the money he'd screwed out of his mother. Amanda hadn't thought she could be any more disgusted than she was with him, but she'd been wrong.

They'd all taken the morning off work to be with her, a show of solidarity and friendship that they hoped would help Amanda on this hard day, made harder for too many reasons to count.

Their cars all followed the hearse as it drove at a respectful speed through town, up the hill, into the grounds of the crematorium, a small cortège, but a cortège all the same. Amanda blew a kiss as the hearse drove around the side of the building and she felt a stab of anger that it wasn't pulling in at the front with a line of people waiting to file into the chapel and pay their respects.

The others met up in a small café just around the corner from the church. The service would start at ten. Amanda didn't join them, she was going to pick up Dolly Shepherd and two of her mum's friends from the coffee shop that her mum liked to frequent. She parked up early outside the house she had grown up in and just sat, remembering. But there wasn't much she wanted to remember really other than the wall at the side where she and her dad would sit when they had anything to talk about, although she couldn't for the life of her dredge up what they did talk about. But he was always calm, he never shouted, he never hit her. He had loved her and she missed that love when he'd gone because she didn't feel it again in that house. It was that wall she'd gone to when she'd seen Seth die and sobbed and asked her dad to take care of him for her. If only she'd been Bradley, she'd have been able to recall it all so differently: as a house full of affection and indulgence.

She pulled herself together and called for Dolly and the other two ladies. They were in their best black, head to foot, a sign of respect for their friend. Amanda knew that their mother would have wanted nothing less than the traditional gravitas on her big day.

In the church, she wondered if Bradley would have heard

about the service from a third party, because she hadn't invited him, but walking in, a quick glance at all the back of the heads yielded no sighting of his big bald patch. He wasn't there, but plenty were which Ingrid would have been proud of.

Amanda delivered the eulogy to a mum who was a good cook, kept an immaculate house, who enjoyed her friends and trotting down to meet them for coffee and who'd had a healthy and long life, give or take a couple of minor blips. Dolly had given her some nice anecdotes to include. They sang her favourite hymn, 'How Great Thou Art' and to-gether they recited the Lord's prayer. And though the coffin was not there for the vicar to say his final words over, it didn't matter; he sent Ingrid Ann Worsnip on her way, in absentia, to meet her maker, who would forgive her sins and grant her eternal peace. *Amen*.

There was tea and coffee, sandwiches and cakes laid on in a room at the back of the church made available for services. A lucky and convenient arrangement, as the vicar's wife did the catering and was the daughter of one of Ingrid's coffee crew. They had connections everywhere, that lot.

It had gone well; Ingrid's friends needed that final full stop, they wanted to say goodbye to her formally. Mainly because they knew her real thoughts on what she would have wanted, not the ones written in her new will.

There was a valuable exchange of information at the wake. Amanda learned, for instance, that Arnold Worsnip had died with a fair amount of creditors chasing their share of his estate. Poor Bradley hadn't been expecting that, then. *Shame*. It appeared that the stories Arnold encouraged of his purported wealth had been greatly exaggerated.

Dolly was still confused about the whole 'lack of a proper'

funeral, though, and wasted no time in pinning Amanda to a pillar to get her answers.

'When you said Ingrid wasn't having one, I thought, that's not right. She was looking forward to it,' Dolly said, sweeping up some more ham and mustard sandwiches. She liked the funerals here best as the buffet was always very acceptable. 'Where is Bradley, anyway? I haven't seen him and I wanted to offer my condolences. I'll have to watch out for him up at the house. I did try ringing but all I get is a dead line.'

He'd changed his number, obviously. *Wonder why.*

'Well, about Bradley . . .' Amanda bent her head in preparation for taking Dolly into her confidence. 'This is strictly between us of course . . . ' There was no better surefire way of making sure that Dolly spread news as far and as wide as possible than by telling her to keep it to herself, because a secret's only value to Dolly was the sharing of it. Dolly Shepherd made Hedda Hopper look like a Trappist monk. Amanda asked her if she wouldn't mind doing a favour for her. And then, by way of a reward, she told her *everything*.

Chapter 57

The following Tuesday, just before the close of business, Bon looked through the glass window of his office at the beautiful sight of Sky Urbaniak sewing and he cursed a god that had brought her into life so long after him.

He wasn't stupid, he could tell from how Sky was in his presence what her feelings for him were. She wasn't a girl, she was a woman, Erin had said. She was softening him with her confounded persistence, making him believe that he should let Sky in, look after her, take it slowly like the barrister wanted to do with her: 'hold her heart in cushioned hands', love her — let her love him. What if the opportunity arose like a gift — would he let it pass him by?

He was musing on this when Jock and Woodentop crashed into his office, scattering his thoughts. They stood before him, Jock with a grin on his face the size of a crescent moon. In all the years they had worked together, he had barely seen Jock as much as crack a smile before. It signified, ironically, that they'd brought some serious news.

★

Amanda was in her car, just about to drive home after work when her mum's doorbell alert went off, signifying motion. The phone company would have needed a month's notice before they cut off the line so that's why the wi-fi was still working. What an added bonus to be able to witness what she hoped was about to happen then and not just imagine it. *Thank you, God.*

She turned on the ignition so the sound would play via bluetooth through the speakers. Then she enlarged the view on her mobile screen to see Bradley about to stick his key in the lock and Dolly from next door toddling fast up the path, shouting his name.

'I've been trying to ring you,' she said, none too patiently.

'Sorry, I changed my number, I was getting loads of funny calls,' he replied. *Lying tosser,* thought Amanda.

'Anyway, I've been watching out for you coming here. I've got a message to give you. From your mum.'

Dolly had remembered. 'Oh, Mrs Shepherd, I love you with all my heart,' said Amanda aloud.

'Now, let me think and get it right,' said Dolly, tapping her lip. 'Your mum said that when she passed I've to tell Bradley it's in the bedroom, in the corner, under the carpet behind the unit. She said, *he'll know what you mean.*'

'Right, thank you, Mrs Shepherd,' said Bradley, who was suddenly on double-speed. He couldn't get the key in the door fast enough. 'I'll have to hurry. I need the toilet really badly,' he added by way of explanation.

'Oh, another thing before you go,' Dolly said. 'I never liked you that much before, but after what you've done, Bradley Worsnip . . . I'm just glad everyone knows now what a piece of work you are.'

Then she turned on her heel and marched back down the path, triumphant. Job done for her old friend.

★

The door was closed but Sky could hear Willy Woodentop's voice full of animation, as were his hands. Whatever story he was recounting had Bon enthralled, she could see him through the glass, rapt. Jock's voice now, guttural and excited. She saw Bon glance up as if feeling the heat of her gaze upon him and she hurriedly dropped her eyes. Then Willy and Jock came out and as they passed she saw they were grinning and that was weird because Jock's default expression was that of a bull who had spotted a waving red cape in the near distance.

Something was going on, she couldn't work out what. Bon came out of his office then and beckoned her in.

'Sky, darling, can you come here for a moment.'

Darling, although it wasn't said the way she wished it were. If only, because she needed just the slightest encouragement he felt the same and she would tell him what was in her heart. Then she'd know for sure what she meant to him. And if she got it wrong, then her heart really couldn't be more broken than it was. The most broken thing in this repair shop.

He told her to sit down on the sofa, he pulled up a chair so he was sitting opposite and he took her left hand between his two.

'Sky, I have something to tell you . . .'

Her bones began to tremble, she could feel them under her skin. She didn't know what he was going to tell her but whatever it was, it was something big.

★

Bradley hadn't yet discovered the cameras so Amanda watched in glee as he made a beeline for the stairs, stumbling up them in his haste to reach the top, huffing and panting like Ivor the Engine on forty a day. She switched view to the bedroom, because of course he'd gone in there.

Dear Dolly had delivered the message more or less verbatim. *If you wanted to get some revenge for what he's done to your friend – his own mother – trust me, this is the way,* Amanda had told her. She pressed the record button so she could show Dolly the footage later; she owed her that.

She watched Bradley scoop all the ornaments off the corner unit and dump them on the bed and the floor, not caring if he chipped any. Ingrid had collected them for years; they weren't worth anything to anyone but her, so the treasures she'd dusted and displayed were destined for a black bin liner and their own final resting place: the landfill site. She saw him wheeze as he pulled the unit away from its corner position, then he folded down onto his knees. He peeled back the carpet and she heard his delighted little yelp.

'Whee hee, come to daddy.'

He tugged at the tin impatiently, trying to free it from where it had been lodged under a broken floorboard. The sight of his arse-crack moving in and out, like something on a builder's porn film, was something Amanda wished she could scrub from her eyes but the pensioners at the coffee shop were going to love it. She was glad she'd put the tin back now, it was the right thing to do. Amanda had promised her mother she'd make sure her beloved Bradley got it, and she was about to deliver on that promise.

The floorboard gave, he wiggled the tin back and forth,

and it was finally out, in his hands. He shook it, felt the gratifying weight of it, then he prised off the lid with his non-existent fingernails.

She heard his 'What the fuck?' as he lifted out the house brick. Then she pressed the microphone icon on the phone so he could listen to her laughter bounce around the bedroom at the loudest volume the speakers were capable of.

★

'This is top secret,' said Bon. 'At least for now, but I have to tell you because you out of everyone should know, and everyone else will know soon enough.'

Her hand felt so delicate between his own. He could feel it fluttering like a small bird.

'Sky . . . the police have found someone they think might be the second Pennine Prowler.'

She didn't answer immediately because his statement brought up too many questions and it was impossible to know what to ask first.

'They've arrested Archie Sutton,' said Bon.

'Archie Sutton?' Sky couldn't absorb it. 'What . . . How . . . how . . . I don't understand. Why now, after all this time?'

'Well, as you know, he was a suspect briefly in the original enquiry, because he was a big man, like your dad, and he gave Wayne Craven work when few others would. But he was dismissed early on in the investigation, because he had what seemed to be solid alibis. Plus he was a successful businessman, he didn't fit the profile that the experts had come up with. There was no evidence against him.

'And you know Willy's son was the scene of crime officer who lost the vital samples? I think he always hoped that one day he would make up for that mistake. Then Sutton's grand-daughter brought in those tools to be cleaned. Jock thought the rust looked suspect, like dried blood. It was a ridiculous long shot of course, but then so was the fluke of one of the victims being in a random pub and recognising Wayne Craven's voice. Many criminals have been caught by stranger coincidences. So Willy bagged them straight up and took the tools to his son. He works in a crime laboratory now.'

'Oh my god,' said Sky. 'And it was—'

'No, it wasn't,' Bon jumped in. 'It was just rust, only rust. That part was a wild goose chase.'

Then Sky really didn't understand.

Bon squeezed her hand. He wasn't trying to spin out the story, but he wanted her to know how it had unfolded.

'You mustn't tell a soul, Sky, not until the current inves-tigation is concluded, because Willy's son shouldn't even have told Willy, and he'll be in serious trouble if this gets out . . . It wasn't the tools,' he went on to explain. 'It was the bags they were stored in. Three large, black drawstring bags, apparently. Willy's son noticed when he unwrapped them that the bags had two holes in them, oddly neat holes, oval and deliberately cut, the same width apart on each bag. They looked to him like eyeholes, and then he realised they could have been used as hoods.

'Fabric can hold all sorts of evidence, it seems: fibres, hairs, traces of bodily fluids, DNA. I don't know what he found exactly – Willy says he was very clear that he couldn't reveal those sorts of details – but it was enough to lead to Sutton's arrest.'

'Ugh,' said Sky, trying to process all this. 'If that's true, about the hoods, whyever would anyone want to keep such a thing?'

Bon shrugged. 'Who knows? Trophies, perhaps. Or to remind him of having got away with it ... Speaking of which,' he said carefully, 'before you get too many hopes up, you know there's a long way to go on this still. He's only just been arrested, not yet charged, and we know he has dementia, so that will affect his capacity to answer questions, let alone stand trial.'

Sky's face fell. 'You mean it might all come to nothing?' she said. 'And I'll be right back to square one?' She didn't think she could handle this up-and-down switchback of conflicting emotions.

'Not quite,' said Bon. 'There's something else. Sutton's wife. She broke down when he was arrested, cracked completely. Said that his alibis were false, and that she'd feared this day would come, ever since he'd asked her to lie for him that he'd been with her when he wasn't. She even said she *knew* his early onset dementia was a punishment for what he did to those women. Clearly the strain of it all unravelling finally was too much for her.

'We don't know what sort of tale he told her about his guilt or innocence, or what he did to persuade her to keep silent for all these years. I'd guess she wanted to preserve and protect her family unit.'

Bon didn't tell her his own theory because Sky had enough to deal with regarding the facts, plus it was just that — a theory. Jock and Willy said it held water though: that a god-fearing pillar of the church community such as Mrs Sutton would have afforded him the chance to save his soul and she'd have covered for him, lied for him for the greater good of this life they had built together. His stopping then, while he had the golden opportunity to remain in the shadows, would account for why Craven acted alone for the later attacks. And though Archie Sutton might have counted his blessings and slept like a baby, Mrs Sutton would have always weighing on her mind that one day their sins would be found out and the knock on the door would come.

'When they came for Sutton, his wife was hosting a charity lunch in the garden. Plenty of people heard and saw far more than they should, and took it home with them. The news didn't stay contained for even five minutes.'

The gossip machine. Sky knew only too well how that worked. But this time, *please God,* it had cranked up and was running for the right person, rather than against the wrong one.

There was a lot to take in, and suddenly, Sky felt light-headed, her breath coming shallow, fast, in line with the thoughts zipping around her head. She felt the warning sharp pin-prick of pain in her chest. She tore her hand away from Bon's and scrabbled in the pocket of her work apron for her spray. Bon saw it and knew what it was, and he knew what it was used for.

It was a rogue twinge, she was fine. She was more than fine.

Bon was asking her, 'Are you all right, Sky? Oh, my darling.'

The concern in his voice, the way he was looking at her. The way he was holding her arms. The way he said 'darling' this time. There was no doubting any of it.

'I love you, Bon,' she said. She couldn't have held the words back with an army.

★

Erin pressed in the number. This was the sixth time in the day she had attempted to ring but chickened out on the last digit and flicked away the phone screen. But this time, she completed it, let the dialling tone kick in.

'Alex Forrester.' His name, his voice.

'Alex, it's me. Erin.'

'Hello, you.' She could feel the smile warm his words.

'I got your letter.' She was trembling like a sodding teenager.

'And what did you think?'

'You should have been a doctor with that handwriting.'

He laughed, a big sincere boom.

'What about the content? Did that pass muster?'

'Well, it made me ring you.'

A beat.

'And?' A change of tone, uncertain.

'I think yes, I'd like to see you again too.'

★

Sky was in disbelief that she'd said it. She could have attempted to pull the words back, explained that she'd said them in misplaced gratitude but she didn't, she let them whirl in the air and do what they must.

Bon knew there was no other way to interpret what she had said, not when accompanied by that look in her eyes, her beautiful sky-blue eyes.

He took her face gently between his strong hands. His brain was commanding his voicebox to say all manner of sensible things and it was refusing.

'Bon, please don't even attempt to tell me how I'm feeling, because I know. I don't want to waste any more time. I want to spend all my future days with you, because you are everything to me.'

'Oh, sweetheart.'

He didn't want to fight it any more. His own words came to him, the ones he'd said to Erin, the ones she'd gifted back to him: *there are no guarantees in anything, but you shouldn't let fear hold you back from taking your chance because we only have one life and it shouldn't be full of regrets.*

'I will make you happy. My darling Sky.'

There were questions filling his head, but they would all wait, this moment was all that mattered. His lips were on hers, his arms around her and it was everything and more than they both thought it would be.

'Aye, aye,' said Jock, craning his neck. 'Guess what's happening in the office.'

'Is it what I think it is?' asked Tony, taking a break from unscuffing the Tiny Tears doll's cheek.

'Aye,' said Jock. 'Aye'

Mildred let loose a long breath. 'About bloody time,' she said.

Chapter 58

Yorkshire Standard

MAN ARRESTED AS SECOND PENNINE PROWLER AFTER TWENTY YEARS LIVING IN PLAIN SIGHT

A 69-year-old retired businessman has been arrested after new forensic evidence was revealed linking him to the murders committed by the Pennine Prowler who was active in the mid 1990s to early 2000s. A 73-year-old woman has also been arrested on suspicion of perverting the course of justice. Police believed there was a second prowler after victim Gillian Smith reported she was attacked by two men, but the second man remained at large as Wayne Craven, who died in 2009, refused to identify him.

One theory is that Craven kept silent in exchange for his wife being looked after financially, although she subsequently died less than four months after he did. The only known connection to date between the suspect and Wayne Craven is that Craven was at one time employed by him on a casual basis. We can only hope fuller details will come to light in due course.

What is clear is that for the family of Edek Urbaniak, who was believed for many years to have been the prime suspect, a man who was tried in the court of public opinion and found guilty, there may be peace at last. But the victims of the second Prowler, however, may still be denied justice, as the man arrested is reportedly in poor health and may not be capable of standing trial.

Chapter 59

One month later

'I have no idea what state I'd be in if it wasn't for this club,' said Mel, as they wrapped up another Tuesday. It was always too soon, however much they overran on their allotted time. 'It gives me a place to just talk through things, put my head in order. Would I have stayed with Steve if I hadn't met you lot?'

'To be fair,' said Sky, claiming another of Ray's cookies, 'I think you've got the postman to give all the credit to for that.'

'Do you ever hear from him, Mel?' asked Amanda.

'Naw,' replied Mel. 'I wish I'd bump into him. I deleted his number on my phone, which was the right thing to do because I've been tempted too many times to ... see how he was.' She didn't know if he and Chloe had got back to-gether. She presumed so, seeing as he'd never got in touch either. But wherever he was and whoever he was with, she hoped he was happy.

'Is Steve still at his mother's?'

'For now, yes. Did I tell you that I saw her in Sainsbury's and she walked past me as if I was invisible. Everything will be my fault. She'd blame me for the Falklands War if she could. I don't think she ever forgave me for having a faulty womb and not giving her grandchildren. Damaged goods.'

'Oh, Mel,' Sky gasped. 'Then you're well shot of the lot of them.'

'I'm packing up my things. Steve's going to buy me out. He asked if I wanted the house but I don't, so he's having it.'

'I hope he's being fair,' said Amanda.

'Very, actually. We've managed to save ourselves a few bob with the solicitor and work out an amicable split. He did ask me at the weekend if I still wanted to go through with it.'

'Oh my god, Mel,' said Sky, open-mouthed. 'And you said . . . ?'

'Do you really have to ask?' Mel tutted. She'd been as open-mouthed as Sky when he'd said it. But she was no one's plan B.

'I want to start again, I'm only fifty-four, it's the new fifty-three.' She laughed and they laughed with her. 'I'm going to have a music room in my next place.'

'We're coming to your first gig, you know,' said Amanda.

'That would be good, because I'm worried no one's going to turn up to watch a whole load of menopausal women banging out rock music, even if it is for a good cause.'

'I am going to distribute the flyers everywhere,' said Astrid, picking up some from the batch that Mel had brought with her. 'May I also say, you look very hot on them.'

'I don't look too shoddy, do I?' said Mel with a grin. 'Thank the god of photoshop.'

'I can't see much *change* between this and that,' replied

Astrid, flicking her finger from the flyer to Mel in person. 'See what I did there.'

Astrid could easily imagine Mel on stage. She oozed confidence these days, flicking her red hair over her shoulder like a supermodel. She didn't look like the same person now as the one she'd been when they'd first met. Astrid wasn't the only one either who wished she'd bump into the postman again and be injected with his joy syringe. They were still laughing about the lie she'd told her husband about having SLUT in raised lettering on her bum. She deserved better. They all deserved the best.

'Have you heard any more about your dad, Sky?' Mel asked her.

'No, it's all under wraps now, a big police investigation is going on.' She'd had a visit from a retired policeman who'd wanted to tell her to her face that he had never believed her father was involved, but was always convinced that Sutton was the man they were looking for. He'd been waiting for it to come out for fifteen years. And he hadn't been alone in his suspicions.

'What about the press? Have they been in touch yet?' Amanda bet they had, sniffing around what was going to be a huge story.

'Oh yes. I've been told not to talk yet, but trust me, I will be making sure that every rotten story about my dad over the years is overwritten with the truth.'

She smiled and her friends smiled back at her. No one mentioned it for fear of embarrassing her but Sky had colour in her cheeks, they were flush with life and happiness. This wonderful knight of hers had done a magnificent repair job on her. Probably his best to date.

'I'm presuming Angel Sutton hasn't been back in the shop

this past month?' asked Erin.

'Funnily enough, no.'

'Same time next week then, ladies?' Amanda enquired of them.

'Same time next week,' Mel stuck up her thumb.

'Definitely,' Erin nodded.

'Of course,' said Astrid, as if it could be in any doubt.

'Wouldn't miss it for the world,' replied Sky.

Erin caught up with Sky outside.

'I know I've said it before but I really couldn't be happier for you and Bon,' she said. She'd always listened to Bon's advice and, for once, he had listened to her and he'd been right to.

'Thank you,' said Sky awkwardly, because she still felt odd talking to Bon's ex-wife about them, even though Erin had been genuinely delighted for them from the off. Sky had told her before she'd said anything to the others as a matter of courtesy. Erin had shrieked and hugged her but it didn't make it any less weird. 'It's a bit of a funny situation, isn't it?'

'Life is a funny situation, Sky, it's messy and complicated but sometimes things turn out just as they should,' said Erin. 'I moved on a long time ago from Bon. And I'm in the right place now. Well, so far, so good. And I am no longer using the name Mrs van der Meer anywhere, by the way. I've changed everything officially, so if Bon pops the question you'll be the only one on the scene.'

Sky chuckled, at the same time dismissing it with, 'He won't.'

'Oh, he will,' said Erin. There was nothing surer. And she would be the first to congratulate them.

The diner had emptied when Amanda took the last of

the coffee pots through. They'd all drunk far too much of it, none of them would sleep tonight.

'I would love to sit in with you sometime,' said Ray. 'What do you all find to laugh about so much?'

'Oh, just life,' said Amanda, because laughter took the sting out of hurty knees and hurty hearts – and hurty brothers. Bradley had been in touch with her twice in the past month, via his dodgy solicitor mate, Johnny. The first letter accused her of stealing from him because the tin had been promised to him by their mother and he was going to sue her. And Amanda had wished him luck because she knew he had the tin, she'd got a video of him finding it under the floorboard. *Goodbye.* The contents, however, were a different matter; no one had asked her to hand over those. And goodness me, the price gold fetched these days. Her dad really had been able to look after her in the end.

The second letter stated that Bradley and his wife were severing all contact with her forthwith and demanded she give him their mother's ashes. They were already in the sea in Blackpool, where Ingrid and Arnold had honeymooned, Amanda thought she'd have liked that. Luckily, she had kept the emptied urn, not really knowing what to do with it. She'd filled it up with ashes from her woodburning stove and threw in some chicken bones for good measure before dropping the consignment off on Bradley's doorstep. She wished she had a camera trained on him for when he took that lid off. The Tuesday club had split their sides when she'd told them this. It nearly topped the brick in the biscuit tin, but not quite.

'How have you been?' asked Ray tenderly in his gorgeous southern drawl. 'I've kind of left you alone, I knew you had a lot going on.'

'I'm okay,' she said. 'Really.' She still had some things going on because she had a solicitor of her own looking at her mother's financial situation. It would be too costly to pursue too far really but she knew that it would send Bradley's bowels into spasm when a solicitor's letter from her side popped through his letter box, asking for further information.

According to Dolly, who had turned into the bastard child of Agatha Christie and Arthur Scargill because she'd become obsessed by what Bradley had done and was determined to see him suitably punished, he wasn't having too good a time of things. People from the coffee shop had picketed outside both Big Baps shops with placards saying various things on the theme of Bradley being a thief who cheated his own mother out of her house and savings to buy the shops and their Mr-and-Mrs matching teeth. And that the poor old lady had died from the stress, because there was always someone who liked to add a bit extra to make a story extra spicy. Some of the staff had walked out because they didn't want to work for someone like that, and Bradley and Kerry had been forced to roll up their sleeves and make the sandwiches themselves. Except they had no customers to serve either, because people didn't want to buy their snap from mother-abusers and they often had a lot of paint and eggs to clear up from their windows in the mornings.

Dolly had also heard that both Bradley's and Kerry's teeth were giving them a lot of gyp. It appeared that the cheap Turkish dentist had sold them turkeys.

'When are you coming to work for me, then?' said Ray.

'I'll be made redundant in the next couple of months, then I'm going to weigh up my options,' she replied.

'Am I one of those options?' he asked.

If only he meant it in a different way from making cakes for him, she thought. Ray Morning — he was so well-named, Texan rays of bright morning sun brought to Barnsley. He made her smile every time she saw him, he turned on a warm light inside her heart.

'Of course,' she replied. 'I've been thinking about it a lot.'

'I've been thinking about you a lot,' he said.

That came from left field and she wasn't sure what he meant.

'Have you? Why?'

'You see . . .' He edged a little closer, forcing her to take a step back. 'I give you free dessert whenever you want, I give you a room to hold your club in, I make cookies for you and bring in coffee, I cooked you dinner, I massaged your neck when you said you were in pain. I gave you my phone number in case you needed me and . . . I don't know how many more hints I have to give you before you get the message. I really thought that English women did nuance.'

Her back was against the counter, she couldn't go any further.

His eyes were locked onto hers, gorgeous blue eyes that weren't saying to her that what he most wanted from her was to make some buns for his customers to take away.

'May I . . . ?' he asked, edging closer still.

Was he really asking what she thought he was asking?

It turns out that he was.

Chapter 60

Six weeks later

There was a capacity crowd in Pogley Working Men's Club to see The Change. And the audience knew what they were about because the lead singer, Joss had told them: that they were a group of old birds doing what they should have done thirty-plus years ago, but better late than never, eh? And that the band name was on point because they'd all gone through big changes in their lives but were here, still standing, still rocking. So grab your chances, she said, make your changes while you can because we only get one crack at this life lark. And if we sweat on stage, at least we can blame the lights, and the drummer has to jiggle a lot to ease her sciatica.

Yes, the crowd loved it because it was real and it was honest and it was actually very good.

They covered a Mock Turtles hit and it was while they were singing into their mikes about how big and strong they'd grown and were standing on their own that Mel noticed him at the front in a mad swirly paisley shirt when the lights did a circle over the audience. Standing in the 'mosh pit' just as he said he would be when she did her first gig. It threw her and she momentarily lost her concentration, thought she'd hallucinated him, but he was still there when they broke after the first half for the raffle draw and for a young lad called Jason Jepson to have a guest spot.

'All right,' Postman Pat said when Mel hopped off stage without any accompanying noises of pain, because her knee was having a lot of good days at the moment. She shook the heat out of her red hair and wished she could shake it out of the leather trousers.

'That were proper good, that.' He had such a great accent.

She was full of beans anyway but the adrenaline that came with performing wasn't wholly responsible for the width of her smile.

'It's great to see you again, Pat. How are you?'

'Good, good. What about you?'

'I'm good, what about you?' She'd just asked that, he'd shaken her up like a snow globe. 'Sorry, I—'

'You look *really* good.'

'Well, you can see for yourself how big and strong I've grown,' she semi-trilled because she was a bit stuck for what to say and nervous enough to make a fool of herself.

'Don't know about big, you look pretty trim to me.'

She'd lost two stone since their first meeting on the front step. Her dodgy knee had been much better for it too.

'It's called the divorce diet.'

'Divorce? You didn't get back together again?' He hadn't been expecting that, from the way he asked.

'For about three hours,' she said. She didn't say it might have been for slightly longer if she'd changed her sheets. Someone nudged past her and sent her into Pat, close enough to smell the cologne that had lodged on her pillows and in her brain because it triggered off a rush of serotonin.

'I thought it was nailed on that you'd ... I'd have ... If I'd known,' he stuttered and she filled in the gaps for herself.

'So you ... didn't ... you ... either?' she stuttered back.

He made a face, shook his head. 'Not a chance. Not even for five minutes. Couldn't.'

'Right.' She wondered if it had anything to do with her.

'Listen, I'm going to have to go because I've got an early start—'

'Of course,' she said, talking over him. 'I know you have and it's totally fine. Thank you for coming at all, I—'

'Shut up, will you, and let me get a word in. I've got some tickets to see a band in Manchester Arena. I thought you might want to come *wiv* me. Be a shame for 'em to go to waste.'

She was fifty-four years old and her brain had just yelled 'Yippee'.

'Great. Who?'

'Whoever you want to go and see.'

'When?' She tried not to let the smile gush out and drown him.

'Whenever you're free. I thought we could make a night of it. Have some dinner. Maybe get a hotel, couple of rooms.'

'Or just one room with twin beds ... be cheaper,' she said.

'Yeah. Although I don't mind sharing a big bed.'

'Neither do I really.' She grinned like a teenager. He grinned back.

'Great then. I'll be in touch. I kept your number.'

He leaned forward, kissed her on the cheek and her knees crumbled in a way that had nothing to do with wear and tear.

Chapter 61

Six months later

'Well, there they are, Mr and Mrs van der Meer,' said Erin, as she watched Sky and Bon about to climb into the silver Rolls en route for their wedding reception in Ray's diner. Sky could have picked anywhere, but she wanted just two things on her big day: to be married in the church where she had said her last goodbye to her father, because she would feel him close to her then, and a reception at Ray's diner, because that was a happy place for her. It was the happy place for them all, because there they had each found friendships and through them, the strength and courage to take the paths that had led them to today.

'How gorgeous does she look?' said Erin looking over at the newlyweds. Sky looked beautiful, glowing, well, loved. And Bon, handsome, happy. Happier than she had ever seen him before.

'Don't you feel the littlest bit odd about it?' Mel asked Erin.

'Nope,' said Erin. 'Not at all.' Her dearest old friend and one of her dearest new ones, a perfect match in her eyes. 'He will absolutely cherish her.' She had no doubt about that. But she felt pretty cherished herself, she wasn't missing out on her fair share of that.

'I bet you'll miss her, Astrid,' said Mel, having to look a long way up because Astrid had her big heels on, sky-blue silk to match her long silk frock. Sky had asked her to be a bridesmaid, to make her wish come true.

'Very much. But I have Venus, one of my employees from work moving in with me soon as a tenant. It will either be the biggest mistake of my life or the best fun.'

'I think you know which one it's going to be.' Mel thought Astrid's fond smile was a good indication.

'I still can't believe I am a managing director,' said Astrid. 'I have a parking space with the sign over it. Me.'

Astrid had slipped into the role as if she had been born to it. 'The Queen of Crackers', the local newspaper had called her in an article. Venus had said the title was right on more than one level. Iris had told her not to be so bloody cheeky.

'It must be true then, Astrid Kirschbaum-Clegg. You have to use the double-barrel if you're an MD.'

'Mel, can I make the observation that you've started to absorb the Mancunian accent?' Amanda gave her a nudge.

'I have absolutely no idea how that could have come about,' Mel replied, giving her words the full Liam treatment.

'Do you have any raised lettering on your backside you wish to disclose?'

'As if I'd tell you lot,' Mel grinned.

At least these days when she put clean sheets on the bed, it wasn't too long before they smelt of Oud Wood again. Who would have thought postmen were so hot in the sack.

'How's the baby?' asked Astrid.

'He's gorgeous,' said Mel with a doting sigh. Pat's daughter now had the most beautiful little boy and it was magic to be able to spend time with him. Pat's family were as warm and welcoming as Steve's weren't.

'You two must be the coolest grandparents on the planet,' Amanda said with a chuckle. 'I vaguely remember mine on my dad's side and they never looked like you two dudes.'

Mel laughed. 'I'll take that.' She sometimes teased Pat about being a grandad and he shut her up in the most wonderful of ways.

'Can't wait to see the wedding cake, Amanda,' said Astrid.

'Oh, it's pretty spec if I say so myself.' Amanda had put everything and more into it. Just as a one-off for a friend, though in exactly seven weeks her new business would be opening up at the diner: 'Ray-to-Go', cakes by Amanda to take away. Ray was a great boss, and she got all sorts of bonuses that his other staff didn't get.

Linus had been as good as his word and made her redundancy happen with a generous walk-away package. He'd even put on a small party for her in the boardroom and name-checked her whenever he had to talk about his initiative to help women in the workplace. The company had bought her a beautiful gold bracelet as a parting gift, something she wouldn't be trading in. She took a solo trip to Venice after she'd finished at Mon Enfant, paid for by her mother's rings and two chunky necklaces which didn't even make a dent in her daddy's cache of gold.

Dolly was a regular up at the diner these days and often brought with her a couple of new friends to introduce to the place, and the latest gossip. The two Big Baps sandwich shops were up for sale, for a pittance apparently because they had no customer base left.

The four friends walked towards the waiting taxi. Another change to get used to: Sky becoming Mrs van der Meer. Hard to think that when they first met, Amanda had been resigned to always being second best and now she got nosebleeds from the height of the pedestal she'd been put on. Sky had been hiding in a long, dark shadow and in love with a man she never imagined would want her – and yet here she was today, a bride bathed in bright, happy sunshine. Astrid: lonely, unfulfilled, grieving, now counting her many blessings with a circle of close friends to call on anytime. Erin: damaged and fearful, had her confidence back, her faith in love restored. And Mel, broken and desperately lost, these days as resplendent as her red hair, thanks to all the fun she was having and those regular 'injections of joy'.

Life, as they'd found, came with no route map, no instruction book or guide rope and they'd learned that the best navigational tools they could have were friends who looked out for each other, who were there when the sun shone and the rain fell. And they couldn't have been luckier in finding the best of them in the back room of a diner every Tuesday night.

As Bon van der Meer had put it to Erin, there were no guarantees in anything, but you shouldn't let fear hold you back from taking your chance, because we only have one life and it shouldn't be full of regrets.

Every one of the five was determined they were going to make up for lost time, to savour the years that followed, adjust to the changes that would inevitably come, never settle for less when they could have more. And they'd be there for each other, to make sure they did exactly that.

Acknowledgements

Writing the thank yous for my books is always a pleasure. I'm indebted to the kind people who help me get my facts right and fashion my words into something that I'm proud of. My books are my children and I love them all, and none of them go out into the world unless they're ready.

Thank you to my fabulous publishing team: SJ Virtue, Matt, Maddie, Rich, Dom, Heather, Louise, Sarah, Odiri, my editor Clare who is the best in the blimming business. And Ian 'God' Chapman who takes me to the Ivy so I know I'm still in the job when he does that, and Suzanne Baboneau who said one rainy October many moons ago 'I want to make an offer on this book' and my career was born. I'm still in their nest, the fledgling grown to an albatross.

Thanks to my agent, the amazing Lizzy Kremer who is everything and more than an agent should be. Someone there in the sun and the rain, someone always in your corner, someone formidable – and kind. And the crew behind her, especially Maddalena Cavaciuti who is a rising star in this industry in her own right.

Thanks to my copyeditor Sally Partington who still has some hair left – she hasn't quite pulled it all out yet. I love working with you, Sal, if you're reading this. It's my favourite part of the whole process, apart from getting paid.

Thank you to everyone at ED PR who are a joyous, efficient machine to work with. Thank you Emma, Annabelle (miss you!) and Katie and Katey.

Thank you to the blogging community who support me with their wonderful reviews and advertising and bandying me around on social media and magazines. Thank you for your devotion and selfless work, all for the love of reading. Especially when you do it for us romance and humour writers. And super-especially for those of us up north.

The hospital scenes may be coloured by my less than ideal experience when my mum was at the end of her life, but I nonetheless remain indebted to the care she, and my father, both had from good doctors and nurses over many years. When the NHS is good – it's very good. It is a jewel in the crown of our nation and we must do everything we can to improve it, to pump money into it – and to save it.

Thank you for the expertise of solicitor Gareth Williams and my pal Michael Lawless at GHW Solicitors LLP in Ramsbottom. They gave me far more information than I needed to use in the end but I feel equipped enough now to set myself up as a legal bod. I could even help the lady who came up to me at an event after I announced my book was in part about wills, and she said, 'We're okay now, but when my mother died, me and my sister didn't talk for twenty-four years over a tablecloth'.

Thank you to my writer friends – no one understands this job like people swimming in the same pool because it's the bloody weirdest job if you sit down and think about it. No wonder most of us are nuts: Phillipa Ashley, Trisha Ashley, Cathy Bramley, Jane Costello, Lucy Diamond, Jane Fallon, Katie Fforde, Veronica Henry, Catherine Jones, Bernie Kennedy, Jill Mansell, Carole Matthews, AJ Pearce, Lynda Stacey, Jo Thomas. I'll have forgotten someone – forgive me if I have, we are legion. A special thank you and big hug to Debbie Johnson who is the wisest, kindest best friend sort of person on the planet. We try to keep each other sane in this crazy world, I'm not sure we quite manage it.

And my unwriterly pals who are my old stalwarts, the best of women – and men: Traz, Cath, Kath, Rae, Maggie, Al, Sus, Pam, Karen, Helen, Nigel. I love you all. And Happy 60th Birthday, my dear Amanda B.

Thank you to the people in my home town of Barnsley and my home (God's own) county of Yorkshire who have lifted me up on their shoulders and given me this wonderful career. You cannot buy the wealth of support and PR they give me. It's 'right up t'fish' (if you know, you know).

To my family, sadly smaller this year, my wonderful Other Half, Pete, who is the best present buyer on the planet, the most considerate man and the steadiest rock on the sea front. And my boys, Tez and George, who aren't boys but men really, but tucked up in their mother's heart, they'll always be my babies.

Thank you to Rosie Fiore for helping me with some South African wordage.

And thank you to my readers, all over the world, for enjoying my books (if you did), for buying them and borrowing them from libraries and lending them to your pals to introduce them to a new author they might like. Keep reading books by women who slave over a hot keyboard for you, especially books in our genre. Books that are written to cheer and keep hope burning that life can throw up some great surprises; books about the extraordinary things that happen within the parameters of ordinary life; books that make this world a little bit more bearable and bright. No one says to Mick Jagger or AC/DC 'Oh so you're a rock musician? You don't write rubbish songs about love do you?' and yet they'll say it about writers. Nothing silly or trivial about our crafted, polished, pieces of art that millions of people all over the world enjoy. Our books change lives and educate, they help with stress, they give comfort – and pure, unadulterated entertainment. They are not lesser books. And if you love one of our novels, please write us a nice review on Amazon because it does something magical to algorithms. It's the best karma and increases your chances of winning the lottery by over a thousand per cent. Even if you don't buy a ticket.

A final thank you to my sadly late friend Dave Myers, who I met after I was sent a video of him, taken by darling Laura Kemp, telling me how much he loved my books – he and his wife Lili used to listen to them together on audio, every single one of them. I was his favourite author (me and Lee Child). He was as lovely, friendly, kind and gorgeous in the flesh as he was on the screen, both he and Si 'Kingy' King. I will miss his texts telling me which of my lines cracked him up the most, but I am glad I had him in my life for a few years, and will always think of him with a smile. And he would have been delighted, I'm told, that at his funeral I met Roy Wood. 'He'd have loved that he brought you together, even that way' said one of his friends. Yep, the opportunity to tell Dr Wood himself, 'I'm not a crank but it was me who sent you that book named after *I Wish It Could be Christmas Every Day*.' I could hear Dave sniggering in my head about me feeling a tit for introducing myself like that because only cranks say 'I'm not a crank'. My point is, if my books are good enough for a famous, respected, much-adored Hairy Biker who was loud and proud about saying he loved them, then that's all the seal of approval I need. Sod the snobs.

Thank you, everyone, for enjoying our books. Thank you for enjoying mine.

#RespectRomFic

Change

Let's face it: change is scary. We know where we are with a comfort zone. And we know that stepping outside it is a gamble. But, like pension investments, there are different degrees of gambling. We might not step outside our comfort zone if there is evidence of hungry sharks but – as the saying goes – ships are not built to stay in harbours. Who knows what joys and delights we might be missing out on by staying put inside a prison of our own making, because a comfort zone *is* a prison, albeit one with cushions of your choice.

Once upon a time, I was stuck. I did think that if this was all my life was going to be, it was going to be a very miserable existence. In a way it was helpful that I was desperate for things to change – and they did, because I took a couple of risks, I put myself out there. I didn't want to become an eighty-year-old who had never really gone for what she wanted most in the world: to see my name on the front cover of a book. I consider myself a bit of a poster girl for what you can achieve if you put your mind to things. I've always thought that we are all like Mary Poppins's bag: none of us knows what is inside us until we reach in and

forage and then pull something out. I know this because
every time I start to write a book, I have no idea where
I am going with it. I might have a basic concept of a storyline, but I just start at the beginning, put one word down
in front of another and, at some point in the next months
or so, I find I have somehow achieved a novel of ninety
thousand words. And every time I marvel that it was sitting
inside of me all the time and I never knew. One word in
front of another, one foot in front of another. It's a cliché
but a journey of a thousand miles is just the culmination
of many small steps and it starts with a mere one of them.

If we want something, we have to go for it. I've learnt
that sitting on my bum and waiting for things to land in
my lap isn't likely to be the way to achieve them. For me,
in the early days, having aspirations of becoming a novelist
was like wanting to be an astronaut. People like me – from
oop north, from working-class backgrounds, who spoke
with short vowels, with no connections in publishing,
with no creative-writing degree or any endorsements from
discerning people who could spot a good writer – did not
become novelists. The agent I approached had hundreds
of submissions per month and maybe took on a handful of
writers per year. The odds were well stacked against me.
But I wanted it enough to at least die trying. And here I
am having completed my twenty-second novel. It might
have taken me a long circuitous route and many years,
but I made it. I have changed my life totally and I'm so
glad I did because it was painful being where I was – on
the wrong track. And some of those people who want to
become astronauts, became them. Every head of Classics
in a university started off with their first Latin lesson: *amo,
amas, amat*. We are all capable of great things, of change

and growth. But we must be prepared to feel the cold a little – it's to be expected when one sets sail out of that snug familiar harbour for uncharted waters.

The fear of the unknown can be torturous. Leaving an unhappy marriage, for instance. There are many strands to untangle, but every one untangled is one closer to the goal. Change is not easy, but it's worth the struggle. It is in our nature to go forwards, to progress; some say that staying still is actually going backwards. Being afraid of what could go wrong if we try to change things holds us back from what might go fabulously right.

We get things wrong in life and we learn from that, we refine. Getting things wrong is a step on the path to getting things right. So many people are content in jobs they never imagined themselves to be in when they were younger. I learned this when I was a speaker at an event for a group of loss adjusters. 'Who wants to be a loss adjuster when they're at school?' one told me when we were having a chat. She'd landed up in her chosen career because she'd got her law degree, but being the solicitor she'd imagined was her ultimate career destination didn't cut the mustard for her in practice. Learning what we *don't* want is a step towards the place where we should be.

Sometimes changes are thrust upon us and we can rail against them, bang our heads against the closed door, even if it is a futile exercise, or we can adjust and take an alternative path. That's easier on the head – less concussion. Be brave and make the changes you need to make.

Enjoyed this book? Discover more from your favourite author...

©2024 David Charles Photography

For news, appearance dates and information about Milly Johnson's other books, visit her at
www.millyjohnson.co.uk

booksandthecity.co.uk
the home of female fiction

NEWS & EVENTS | BOOKS | FEATURES | COMPETITIONS

Follow us online to be the first to hear from
your favourite authors

booksandthecity.co.uk @TeamBATC

Join our mailing list for the latest news, events and
exclusive competitions

Sign up at
booksandthecity.co.uk